SOUNDING LIKE SHAKESPEARE

A Study of Prosody in Four Japanese Translations of
A Midsummer Night's Dream

DANIEL GALLIMORE

Kwansei Gakuin University Press

SOUNDING LIKE SHAKESPEARE
A Study of Prosody in Four Japanese Translations of
A Midsummer Night's Dream

Copyright © 2012 by Daniel Gallimore

All rights reserved

No part of this book may be reproduced in any form or by
any means without permission in writing from the author

Kwansei Gakuin University Press
1-1-155 Uegahara, Nishinomiya, Hyogo, 662–0891, Japan
ISBN: 978–4–86283–103–3

CONTENTS

Preface   3

ONE   TRANSLATING THE *DREAM*
~ LANGUAGE, CULTURE AND HISTORY   5

    Shakespeare in Japan   5
    Natsu no yo no yume   11
    Four translators – four translations   18
    Comparison and evaluation   26

TWO   STRESS AND ACCENT   35

    Modernism and the Meiji reformers   35
    Colloquialisation in poetry and prose   41
    Reading prosody   43
    Odashima and poetic drama   47
    Setting the pace: the first six lines of the play   49
    Rhythm foregrounded: Puck's 'every turn'   55
    The long and the short of it: punctuation and sentence structure   59

THREE   SYLLABIC METER   65

    Syllabics and free verse (1): detachment and engagement   65
    Syllabics and free verse (2): 'riding the horse'   71
    Ignoring pitch accent: Titania's lament   77
    Back to basics: an analysis of the syllabic structure of Act 1, Scene 1 (Fukuda)   83
    Riding the horse: the lovers' fight   98
    The rhythms of prose: Bottom's dream   102
    The limitations of stylistic mixing: Quince's Prologue   107

FOUR   RHYME AND WORDPLAY   111

    Rhyme and wordplay: properties and possibilities   111
    The sonnet in Japanese and in translation   115
    Share light and serious   121
    Rhyming verse: Helena's lament   128
    Trees and spirits: translating the pun   135
    Jumbled sounds: alliteration 'cooked' and 'uncooked'   142
    Baying hounds: musicality in Act 4, Scene 1   150

FIVE	SPEAKING SHAKESPEARE IN JAPANESE	157
	Height and depth: the Shakespeare recitals of Arai Yoshio	157
	'Neither noisy nor declamatory': Fukuda's Subaru	167
	'Power up': Odashima Yūshi and Shakespeare Theatre	171
	Film or opera? Ninagawa's 'Dream'	173
	Where accent matters: Shimodate Kasumi and Shakespeare in dialect	176
	EPILOGUE	187
	Glossary	197
	Works Cited	199

Japanese names and transliteration
Throughout this monograph, names of Japanese people are given in the Japanese order, with the family name first. Except for the analyses in Chapters Two and Three, dipthongs and double vowels are denoted with macrons.

Cover illustrations
Left: 'I am that merry wanderer of the night', illustration from *Midsummer Nights Dream* by William Shakespeare, 1908 (colour litho) by Arthur Rackham (1867-1939) (after); The Stapleton Collection / The Bridgeman Art Library; English / out of copyright

Right: Katsuchika Hokusai (1760-1849), detail of a bestiary drawing showing a *kappa*

PREFACE

This monograph was originally written as a doctoral thesis at the University of Oxford. During the process of research and writing from 1997 to 2001, I became especially indebted to my three supervisors: Dr Ann Pasternak Slater (English), formerly Fellow of St Anne's College, Dr Brian Powell (Japanese), formerly Fellow of Keble College, and Dr Phillip Harries (Japanese), Fellow of The Queen's College.

My initial motivation for writing the thesis was to amalgamate my two academic specialisms of English literature and Japanese studies within a field of research – the study of Shakespeare's reception in Japan – that had become influential in the 1990s. Although general academic interest in the subject may have lessened since then, I believe that the focus of my thesis on the physical thrust of language in intercultural communication remains relevant. In that sense, my thesis is a reflection of mainstream historicist research into how the historical voice and voices of Shakespeare still affect people today.

Over the four years of study, I became indebted for the advice and support of numerous individuals, among whom I would particularly like to mention the following: the late Anzai Tetsuo, Arai Yoshio, Ashizu Kaori, Jon Brokering, Deguchi Norio, Bjarke Frellesvig, Paul Harvey, Hayashi Misa, Joy Hendry, Theo Hermans, Higuchi Masahiro, the late Hirai Masao, Thelma Holt, Alex Huang, Ishihara Kōsai, Kawachi Yoshiko, Kawai Shōichirō, the late Dennis Keene, Kobayashi Kaori, Matsuoka Kazuko, Peter Milward, Minami Ryūta, Niki Hisae, Ninagawa Yukio, Odashima Yūshi, David Rycroft, Shimodate Kasumi, Suematsu Michiko, Suzuki Masae, the late Takahashi Yasunari, Takamatsu Yūichi, Takiguchi Susumu, and Michael Watson.

I am also grateful to Linacre College and the Oriental Institute, Oxford, for financial support towards the three research visits I made to Japan, to Oxford Brookes University (where I worked from 2000 to 2003), and to Japan Women's University (where I worked from 2003 to 2011) for enabling me to develop my research through classroom teaching and publication.

An adapted version in Japanese of Chapter 3 was published in 2005 in the Japan Women University's Faculty of Humanities Journal. Likewise, I am grateful to Dennis Kennedy and Yong Li Lan for publishing a reduced version of Chapter 5 in *Shakespeare in Asia* (Cambridge University Press, 2010) and to Tom Bishop for publishing a version of Chapter 2 in *The Shakespearean International Yearbook 2006* (Ashgate, 2006).

Finally, I would like to express my deep gratitude to the staff of the Kwansei Gakuin University Press for enabling the publication of this volume, and to Ōyama Misako who supported me throughout its research and writing.

CHAPTER ONE TRANSLATING THE *DREAM* ~LANGUAGE, CULTURE AND HISTORY

SHAKESPEARE IN JAPAN

The meeting of the Fifth World Shakespeare Congress in Tokyo in August 1991 is regarded as a watershed in the study of Shakespeare's reception in Japan.[1] Not was only was this the first such Congress to be held outside the Anglophone world (and the first in Asia), but it coincided with the longest 'boom' in Shakespeare production in Japanese theatrical history. Shakespeare's plays and poetry had been read, studied and performed in Japan for over a hundred years, but the Congress gave occasion for Japanese and non-Japanese scholars to reflect on what Shakespeare might mean in a culture that had been largely isolated from Western culture until the late 19th century.

The Shakespeare 'boom' coincided with Japan's bubble economy of the late 1980s and early 1990s. Opportunities for performing and seeing Shakespeare had already increased during the period of high economic growth of the 1960s and 1970s, and Shakespeare was inherently a vehicle for the policies of internationalisation which Japan's leaders promoted in the 1980s. In a collection of reviews from this period, Ōzasa Yoshio groups his reviews for the year 1990-1 under the heading 'Shakespeare boom', in contrast to years marking a high point in *kabuki* drama (1991) or the death of Emperor Hirohito in 1989 (Ōzasa 1992). Thus, Ōzasa's reviews from 'the year of Shakespeare' may reveal some of the factors that account for Shakespeare's enduring popularity in Japan. In fact, only one of them is of a Shakespeare production. The rest are mainly of Japanese drama, suggesting that Shakespeare's influence has been wider than the narrow field of Shakespeare production. The qualities that Ōzasa observes in these productions are traditionally Shakespearean qualities: the assimilative, integrative, and humanist (ibid., 318). My monograph also explores Shakespeare's influence on modern Japanese culture, but at the more fundamental level of literary translation, arguing that

---

[1] The conference was hosted by the Shakespeare Society of Japan under its president, Takahashi Yasunari (1932-2002), professor at the University of Tokyo and one of the leading exponents of the internationalization of Shakespeare in Japan.

Shakespeare's language both shapes and is contained by Japanese poetics during a period of radical linguistic change.[2]

Since the study of Shakespeare in Japan has inevitably been associated with the learning of English in Japan, it is hardly surprising that most of Shakespeare's leading translators and interpreters in Japan have been professional academics. Academic reflection on Shakespeare in Japan dates back to the Meiji era (1868-1912) to the writings of Tsubouchi Shōyō (1859-1935). Tsubouchi was neither the first to study nor the first to translate Shakespeare but he was by far the most prolific. Essays by Tsubouchi from the Meiji era comparing Shakespeare with the traditional drama include his 'Preface to a commentary on *Macbeth*' (1892) (Tsubouchi 1977a, 161-69) and 'Chikamatsu as compared with Shakespeare and Ibsen' (1909) (Matsumoto 1960, 207-39). The history of Shakespeare's reception in Japan can be said to begin with an adaptation by Tsubouchi of *Julius Caesar* in 1884.[3]

Tsubouchi's ambition was the modernisation of his native drama, and he makes frequent comparisons with that tradition in his writings on Shakespeare. His approach is therefore more representative of the specialism of Shakespeare in Japan than purely Shakespeare-centred scholarship, and in the process he introduced many of the critical issues that still concern scholars and translators. The most important of these has been that of how Japanese people should view Shakespeare: as a classic, contemporary, or (in Tsubouchi's case) something of both. Tsubouchi was a Meiji nationalist with a characteristic belief in national literatures and in the necessity of creating a modern Japanese literature that could compete with Western models.[4]

While for Tsubouchi this nationalism found expression in the field of comparative literature, Toyoda Minoru's historical survey of the first sixty years of Shakespeare in Japan, written in English and published by the leading academic publisher Iwanami in

---

[2] The written and colloquial forms were gradually amalgamated between the 1880s and 1920s, with Tokyo dialect serving as the standard. Further reforms followed the war, notably the simplification of the writing system.

[3] Kawato (2004) offers numerous examples of Shakespeare's appropriation prior to Tsubouchi. The importance of Tsubouchi's adaptation was that it was relatively literal and accurate, was the first to address the problem of adapting Shakespeare to traditional Japanese narrative techniques, and was clearly meant to refer to the political movements of the time, in particular the attempted assassination of the liberal leader Itagaki Taisuke in 1882. Yet it was not until the 1900s that an academic approach to Shakespeare became established; Meiji Shakespeare adaptations are generally known for their experimentalism, or at least free appropriation to Japanese names and genres.

[4] Tsubouchi's nationalism is implicit in works such as *Shōsetsu shinzui* (1885) (Twine 1981) which lamented the poor state of the Japanese novel in comparison with the novels being introduced from Europe and the United States at that time. In Jansen's description, Tsubouchi 'announced the arrival of a new age of culture which would match that of Periclean Athens, but stressed that this had become possible through arms and war. [Tsubouchi] wrote that war made a nation out of a people, and cited European authors and examples to buttress his argument of the critical importance of war in a nation's history.' (Jansen 1982, 75)

1940, went yet further by extending support for Japanese imperialism.[5] This support is confined to a few words in the preface but is nonetheless bound to Toyoda's historical sense of 'the high tide of the national spirit' (Toyoda 1940, 77).[6] This latter phrase was lifted from the preface to Asano Hyokyō and Tozawa Koya's joint translation of *Hamlet*, published in 1905, where they were alluding to the Japanese victory that year against Czarist Russia. Toyoda adds that 'the Japanese are proud as a nation but in the long run they have never failed to appreciate everything truly great and good' and hopes that his book will 'by the story it tells, reflect credit on Japan as well' (161).

The three major historical studies to appear between 1940 and 1991 give a more subdued version of events.[7] Kawatake Toshio's thorough documentation of the reception of *Hamlet* in Japan (Kawatake 1972) hints that Meiji fascination with this power play may have had more to do with feelings of national and personal insecurity in the face of rapid modernisation than appreciation as a work of art.[8] Moriya Sasaburō's portraits of seventeen leading Shakespeareans (Moriya 1986) reveals the wide influence of Shakespeare on modern Japanese literature.[9] This is also an approach adopted by Mizutani Noriko (Mizutani 2003). The essays edited by Anzai Tetsuo (Anzai 1989) present the most formal historical analysis.[10] Starting with the four periods outlined in his own introduction, a generational and theoretical dialectic is maintained throughout.

Anzai was among the first to develop a decisively conceptual framework, perhaps because of his experience as a stage director. His study was published to mark a hundred years of Shakespeare's reception in Japan and although it begins in the 1880s its focus

---

[5] Toyoda Minoru (1885-1972) studied Shakespeare under John Lawrence, a graduate of London and Oxford universities and professor of English literature at Tokyo University from 1906 to 1916. His book was the first substantial history of Shakespeare in Japan (in either English or Japanese) and was written while he was professor at Kyushu University. The book was first published in *Transactions of the Japan Society of London*, Vol. XXXVI, before being published in Tokyo by Iwanami.

[6] 'I am inexpressibly grateful for the peace and tranquillity in which I have been able to finish my task, for that peace and tranquillity have been dearly won for us at home at the cost of peril and hardship to our brethren at the front in the midst of the China Affair' (ibid.). The China Affair to which Toyoda refers began in 1937 with fighting in northern China between Japanese Imperial forces stationed in the Japanese colony of Manchuria and Chinese nationalist forces led by Chiang Kai Shek. Japanese forces had made a successful push into the rest of China, the eastern part of which was rapidly absorbed into the Greater East Asia Co-Prosperity Sphere.

[7] As is evident, there are no major historical studies from the first three decades of this period. Shakespeareans of the 1950s and 1960s, such as Fukuda Tsuneari, were more concerned with universalizing than historicizing Shakespeare, and in technical issues of translation and performance.

[8] See also Takahashi (1995).

[9] Writers discussed include such well-known names as Mori Ōgai, Natsume Sōseki, Shimazaki Tōson, Shiga Naoya, Akutagawa Ryūnosuke and Dazai Osamu.

[10] Anzai Tetsuo (1933-2008) was a scholar and translator of Shakespeare, later emeritus professor at Sofia University in Tokyo. He also acted and directed Shakespeare for the theatre group he founded, Gekidan En.

is on the contemporary, offering solutions to the issues raised by the previous twenty years of activity (for example, the significance of the new translations by Odashima Yūshi). Both Anzai (Anzai 1989a, 3-15) and Kadono (1989) argue that the resourceful, contemporary Odashima style rode on the wave of a rapid popularisation of Shakespeare during the 1970s.

By contrast, the essays that appeared in *Shakespeare Translation and Shakespeare Worldwide* between 1975 and 1995 adopted the linguistic approach of the translator, being concerned with original factors behind specific linguistic problems (Donner 1975).[11] *Shakespeare Translation* was founded following a report by its editor Ōyama Toshikazu to the Investigative Committee on Shakespeare Translation at the First World Shakespeare Congress in Vancouver (1971) in which 'he drew attention to the impact Shakespeare criticism, including its modern developments and turbulences, is bound to have on Shakespeare translation' (Habicht 1977, xi). The 1970s was itself a period of some uncertainty for Shakespeare translation in Japan as the Tsubouchi translations had been gradually abandoned during the 1960s and – until Odashima – no clear successor had been found. Yet although these two international journals were both edited by Japanese scholars, the contributions raised more questions than answers with regard to the translation of Shakespeare into Japanese.

The most detailed map of the terrain is to be found in Niki Hisae's study of *Shakespeare Translation in Japanese Culture* (1984), where she gives examples of how the translations have been contained by the forces of history, language and culture. That an overarching synthesis should be beyond her remit is no doubt a problem typical of a study more analytical than theoretical. Niki insists that translation is not always possible, so that that the translator is left guessing at what the source text means and then finding an equivalent that can be no more than plausible.

Since the 1980s, Japanese scholarship has been increasingly informed by the insights of New Historicism and Cultural Materialism, for example Yoshiwara Yukari's essay on 'Money and sexuality in *Measure for Measure*' (Yoshiwara 1998) and Kobayashi Kaori's cultural history of *The Taming of the Shrew* (Kobayashi 2008). These approaches are intended to promote a dialogue between the age of Shakespeare and the Japanese present, based on a theoretical framework and detailed historical research, and can be said to have various implications for the study of 'Shakespeare in Japan'. One may be that Japanese Shakespeareans have become more fully aware of their own historical context, a tendency that may or may not coincide with the school of cultural nationalism known as *Nihonjinron*, the notions of the uniqueness of Japanese identity that became prevalent in the 1970s.[12] In the more sober economic climate of the Heisei era (since 1989),

---

[11] *Shakespeare Translation* was edited by the Shakespeare scholar and translator Ōyama Toshikazu (1918-84) up to his death. The name of the journal was then changed to *Shakespeare Worldwide* and edited by Kawachi Yoshiko. The journals, which were published by Yushōdō in Tokyo, included articles about translation into most of the major non-English languages.

[12] There is a thin line to be trod between cultural chauvinism and specific styles of Shakespeare ↗

a postcolonial impulse becomes evident, as intellectuals have distanced themselves from the naïve nationalism implicit in pre-war Shakespeareans such as Tsubouchi to realise that it can no more be said that Japan has 'conquered Shakespeare' than that Shakespeare has conquered the world (Gallimore 2010b).

The twenty years that have passed since the World Shakespeare Congress in Tokyo have produced a rich crop of new publications and productions, of which it is striking how many are conducted within an ongoing dialogue with Japan's own theatrical traditions, in particular *kabuki* and *nō*. Among these, the best known are the Shakespeare productions of Ninagawa Yukio (b. 1935), many of which have been performed in modern Japanese translation to audiences in London and other locations outside Japan, and even if Ninagawa has sometimes been criticised for commercialism,[13] there has been no shortage of smaller, less commercial companies, such as Ku'Nauka and Ryūtopia, offering their own more 'authentic' versions. Of course, economic growth has also enabled Japanese enthusiasts to see Shakespeare performed in English in London and at Stratford-on-Avon. One of the boldest steps in the direction of authenticity has been the Tokyo Globe opened in 1988 as a quasi-authentic replica of Shakespeare's original Globe Theatre, nine years before Sam Wanamaker's Globe was opened in 1997 on London's South Bank (Suematsu 2009). The Tokyo Globe was temporarily closed in 2002 for financial reasons, but for over a decade served as an unprecedented centre for Shakespeare performance in Japan, including visiting productions by the Royal Shakespeare Company and experimental stagings such as Takahashi Yasunari's *kyōgen* adaptation of *The Merry Wives of Windsor*, which was first performed for an audience of academics at the World Shakespeare Congress.

If the focus of academic study during the 1970s was on translation, then it has to be admitted that the focus of most of the studies to have appeared since 1991 has been on performance. By the 1990s there was already a well-established set of translations by Odashima Yūshi that were popular in the theatre, while one of the perceived advantages of Shakespeare production in Japanese was a freedom from the authority of Shakespeare's original texts, a tendency to treat the translated version as an actor's prompt.[14] Moreover, scholars such as Fujita Minoru and Leonard Pronko, who edited

---

↘ performance in Japan, but as I have argued elsewhere (Gallimore 2009a, 119), 'Shakespeare in Japan is a resourceful creature, adapting to the culture by using a variety of styles and rhetorical devices.'

[13] The label of commercialism has a slightly different meaning in its Japanese context because, with little state sponsorship of the arts, it is impossible for the large theatres where Ninagawa nowadays works (such as Bunkamura Theatre Cocoon in downtown Tokyo and the Sai no Kuni Saitama Arts Theatre just outside Tokyo) to be anything but commercial. Such theatres contrast with small semi-professional companies such as Studio Life who can afford only to stage limited runs in small theatres. What critics such as Kishi Tetsuo (e.g. Kishi 1998) have noted is a tendency for superficial impositions of Japanese genres on Shakespeare that are of limited theatrical value.

[14] Matsuoka (1993 and 2011) makes a similar point, while cautioning that a greater awareness of Shakespeare's texts can also give them a greater awareness of his subtexts as well.

a collection of papers arising from the Congress, were looking for 'a total theatre', or common theatrical vocabulary with the potential to unite 'east and west', that could not be achieved through language alone (Fujita and Pronko 1996). The recent success of Ninagawa's *kabuki*-style *Twelfth Night* in both Tokyo (2005 and 2007) and London (2009) is indicative of what has been achieved so far in this field.

Other such publications to have followed include *Shakespeare and the Japanese Stage* (Sasayama et al. 1998), which includes a generic comparison by Sasayama Takashi entitled 'Tragedy and emotion: Shakespeare and Chikamatsu' (Sasayama 1998) that recalls Tsubouchi's original study of 1909, *Shakespeare in Japan* (Anzai et al. 1999), and *Performing Shakespeare in Japan* (Minami et al. 2001). These are edited volumes including contributions from specialists outside Shakespeare studies, and thus explore the rich tradition of Shakespeare's appropriation within Japanese culture. A thorough historical survey is offered by Graham Bradshaw and Kishi Tetsuo (Bradshaw and Kishi 2005), which despite its brevity offers a complete and insightful overview of how Shakespeare's works have been translated, adapted, staged, filmed and otherwise appropriated from Tsubouchi onwards (Gallimore 2007).

In the new century, the scope has widened even further through the efforts of international Shakespeare scholars such as Dennis Kennedy (Kennedy and Li Lan 2010) and Alex Huang (Ross and Huang 2009), who have edited volumes locating Japanese Shakespeare within a broader Asian context, notably against the long history of Shakespeare's reception in China. This is important in redressing the balance against a certain tendency to idealise phenomena such as 'Ninagawa Shakespeare' as possessing a vitality and creativity that is perceived to be lacking in the British theatre,[15] and so support a postcolonial approach that treats Shakespeare as neither defining nor defined by Japanese culture but rather in a dynamic, intertextual relationship, the one with the other. Two examples may suffice. Tsutsumi Harue's play *Kanadehon Hamuretto* (1993) dramatised the difficult, but ultimately liberating encounter between *kabuki* actors in Meiji Japan and Shakespeare's tragedy, with Tsubouchi's academic solutions being portrayed as almost equally problematic. In March 2009, a joint Japanese and Korean production of an adaptation of *Othello* by Miyagi Satoshi, and co-directed by Lee Hyun Taek, succeeded in bringing out the underlying tensions of the original.

This monograph, therefore, is one in a series of recent studies of Shakespeare in Japan, but differs from most of them in its focus on translation. On the one hand, it returns to basic questions posed by Niki and others in the 1970s about how Shakespeare's texts are translated into Japanese, while on the other its analyses of the poetics of Japanese Shakespeare translation seek ultimately to locate the translations within the culturalist, postcolonial discourse of the present. This is to argue that much of the discursive power of Shakespeare's representation in modern and contemporary Japan originates in the apparently trivial linguistic details of the dominant translations

---

[15] This point of view is probably derived more from a respect for traditional Japanese drama and contemporary pop culture than for their freedom with Shakespeare's texts.

(such as those discussed in this monograph), that the translations are no more than processes in an incomplete and ongoing process of interpretation that goes back to Shakespeare's own, unstable texts, and that the relationship between Japanese poetics and the source texts is also dynamic and incomplete.

NATSU NO YO NO YUME

Arguably the second-most popular Shakespeare play in Japan

A Midsummer Night's Dream (rendered either literally as *Manatsu no yo no yume* or more commonly nowadays as *Natsu no yo no yume*, 'a summer night's dream') is a dominant play within the matrix of culture, history and language that encompasses Shakespeare translation in Japan. It was not the first of the plays (or even comedies) to be translated into Japanese, and even after Tsubouchi finally translated it in 1915 was not produced on the Japanese stage until 1923. It was definitely among the second generation of Shakespeare plays to be popularised in Japan.[16] According to Toyoda, the play was translated by Kawashima Keizō in 1887 but the translation was never published (and the manuscript lost). A translation by Shima Kasui of the narrative version in the Lambs' *Tales from Shakespeare* (1810) was published in 1899. Although the story, therefore, may have been generally known among Japanese scholars by the time of Tsubouchi's translation, at least nine other plays (including *The Merchant of Venice*, *The Tempest* and *Twelfth Night*) had already been translated and staged by Tsubouchi and others (Minami 1998, 258-67). Of these, *Hamlet*, *Julius Caesar*, *King Lear*, *Macbeth*, *The Merchant of Venice*, *Othello* and *Timon of Athens* would comprise the first generation of plays to have been staged frequently enough in translation or adaptation to have become widely known.

The first generation was represented above all by *Hamlet* and can be said to culminate in 1911 with the first complete, unabridged production of the play in Japanese translation, in fact the first of any of the plays. Like *Hamlet*, the first period had been marked by a spirit of searching: for inner truths and comparative viewpoints and for ways of translating and staging Shakespeare appropriate to Japanese practice. For all the production's shortcomings, the 1911 *Hamlet* showed that Shakespeare in Japan was eminently possible, although it is questionable as to whether this production was a theatrical achievement or a self-serving failure that provided Tsubouchi with the

---

[16] Sasaki (1990) lists translations (and reeditions) up to 1989 which put *A Midsummer Night's Dream* (48) sixth after *Hamlet* (91), *Romeo and Juliet* (70), *Macbeth* (61), *Othello* (56) and *The Merchant of Venice* (51). Yet according to Ishihara, *A Midsummer Night's Dream* was staged 94 times in translation and adaptation between 1988 and 1997 coming second only to *Hamlet* (98) during the Shakespeare 'boom' (Ishihara 1998, 7-12).

experience he needed to embark on his translation of the Complete Works.[17]

Although Tsubouchi went on to translate the remaining thirty-six plays (and revise most of his new translations),[18] only twelve were ever staged in full during his lifetime: *Julius Caesar* (1913), *Romeo and Juliet* (1914), *Macbeth* (1916), *Othello* (1917), *King Lear* (1918), *The Merchant of Venice* (1921), *A Midsummer Night's Dream* (1923), *The Merry Wives of Windsor* (1926), *Coriolanus* (1926), *Twelfth Night* (1928), *The Taming of the Shrew* (1929) and *Much Ado About Nothing* (1929).[19] *Hamlet* remained a perennial favourite but it was not until Fukuda's 1955 production that the play was again to be the subject of experimentation. His version fulfilled the promise of the 1911 *Hamlet* by assimilating contemporary British theatrical technique with Fukuda's reading of early post-war Japan (Anzai 1999, 6-7). This second period was a period of retrenchment rather than development, since half the plays listed above had been performed in adaptation prior to 1911.

A Midsummer Night's Dream became established under Tsubouchi in a way which was never seriously challenged until Peter Brook's production for the Royal Shakespeare Company that visited Tokyo in May 1973. New productions have sometimes happened to precede events of national significance. The first such – in English by a group of expatriate amateurs – took place in May 1912, two months before the death of the Meiji Emperor on July 30th. The first Japanese production, in Tsubouchi's translation and directed by his adopted son Shikō, took place a month before the Great Kantō Earthquake of 1st September, 1923. The next production was staged in July 1928 to commemorate the publication of the first edition of Tsubouchi's translation of the Complete Works,[20] and there were two more pre-war productions of the Tsubouchi translation, both in 1934, a year before his own death.

---

[17] Brian Powell concludes that nothing like it 'had ever been seen before' but 'the range of reform, viewed in the context of theatre history, may have kept the audiences at some distance from the play.' (Powell 1998, 52) The production was for the Bungei Kyōkai (Literary Arts Association), founded by Tsubouchi in 1906 and disbanded in 1913 which with the Jiyū Gekijō (1909-19) was one of the two groups to pioneer modern realist theatre (i.e. *shingeki*) in Japan. The 1911 *Hamlet* was followed soon after by a much more highly rated production of Ibsen's *Doll's House*.

[18] Tsubouchi revised his translation of *A Midsummer Night's Dream* for publication by Chūō Kōron in 1934, but since the focus of this monograph is on the comparison of the four translators rather than Tsubouchi's stylistic development, the analysis that follows is of the initial translation made in 1915. Tsubouchi's revisions are generally slight, although indicative of Tsubouchi's awareness of how current colloquial usage was changing during the Taishō and early Shōwa eras. See Gallimore (2011) for a stylistic comparison of Tsubouchi's initial 1909 translation of *Hamlet* with his 1933 revision.

[19] These are listed in chronological order of first production.

[20] This was an innovative production, using the revolving stage of the Imperial Theatre and the original musical accompaniment by Mendelssohn, and directed by the three leading figures in modern Japanese drama at that time, Osanai Kaoru, Hijikata Yoshi and Aoyama Sugisaku. The production aroused considerable critical interest, was broadcast on Japanese radio, and thus established the play as one that could be revived (Gallimore 2006).

In the introduction to his original translation (Tsubouchi 1977, 174), Tsubouchi identified three issues that are of critical relevance to his role as translator: one is the supposition that the play may have been written to celebrate an aristocratic marriage;[21] the second the blatant discrepancy between the title and Theseus' reference to 'the rite of May' in Act 4, Scene 1;[22] and the third is the resemblance of Puck to the *kappa* sprites of Japanese folklore (185).[23] All three issues are stock concerns of editorial introductions then and now but in Tsubouchi's essay they are united by a concern with authenticity that embraces his translating style; they may even be seen to justify his decision to render the speech of the mechanicals in rural dialect when they are actually townsfolk (187).[24] From the beginning, *A Midsummer Night's Dream* was regarded as a play whose extraordinary themes and narrative allowed for liberties in translation; it was itself a figuration of the hidden and mysterious.

Two other pre-war productions of some note were musical adaptations, the first in 1933 by the Shōchiku Girls' Revue Company and the second in 1940 by the

---

[21] Tsubouchi predates the research by Peter Alexander (*Shakespeare's Life and Art*, 1939) which argued that the likeliest occasion was the marriage of Elizabeth Carey and Thomas, son of Henry, Lord Berkeley, in February 1596 (Brooks 1979, lv-lvii). He does not side with any of the other possibilities except to cite the 1590 Sidney-Essex marriage as one of them. Tsubouchi is more interested in the likelihood that the play was written for a special occasion and that that occasion was a marriage.

[22] 4.1.132. Tsubouchi (177) translates Dr. Johnson's query of 1765: 'I know not why Shakespear calls this play a Midsummer-Night's Dream, when he so carefully informs us that it happened on the night preceding May day.' (Raleigh 1925, 171). For the Japanese translator, there is the added complication that specificity in seasonal references is a defining feature of traditional Japanese poetry. It would be impossible for a *haiku* poet, for example, to get away with such a liberal confusion of spring and summer, which is not to argue that it would not be unappreciated by Japanese audiences already used to the fantasy elements of the play.

[23] *Kappa* are diminutive, childlike water nymphs, green in colour and more malevolent than Shakespeare's fairies; they lure lone travellers to their deaths in desolate ponds and bogs. Tsubouchi refers to the ethnologist Yanagita Kunio (1875-1962) whose writings introduced all aspects of Japanese folklore to the modern world. In 1927 Akutagawa Ryūnosuke (1892-1927) published his novella *Kappa* (Akutagawa 1970), in which a patient in a mental hospital tells of how he has been lured to a strange land by a *kappa* where – like Jonathan Swift's Gulliver – he encounters an unknown people, and is classified insane when he recounts these experiences on returning to the human world. Like Swift's work, the novel satirises various kinds of human censorship and oppression. *Kappa* would seem to occupy the same psychological territory as *A Midsummer Night's Dream* although the play as a whole opened up imagined worlds unfamiliar to a Japanese readership. Akutagawa himself was interested in Shakespeare from his high school days and read English literature at Tokyo Imperial University under John Lawrence (Moriya 1986, 148-54); it is likely that he would have known the story at least of *A Midsummer Night's Dream*. His son Hiroshi (1920-81) became one of the leading Shakespearean actors of his generation.

[24] English editions obviously do not refer to *kappa* but they do seek to explain Puck and the other fairies in terms of Elizabethan folklore (e.g. Brooks 1979, lx-lxi).

better known Takarazuka Revue Company.[25] The latter was to be the last Shakespeare production until 1946 when Hijikata Yoshi's production of the play reestablished Shakespeare on the Japanese stage after Japan's defeat in the Asia-Pacific War.[26] Both this and the 1928 production would have been directed in the realist *shingeki* style (of which Hijikata was a pioneer) but the two all-girl productions initiated a tradition of stylising the fantasy elements of the play that continues to the present.[27] As for *shingeki*, the playwright and director Fukuda Tsuneari (1912-94) launched his new group Kumo (Cloud) with a production of his own translation of the play in March 1962; the Tsubouchi translation was last used professionally in 1968. Fukuda had modernised the language, although it was not until Peter Brook in May 1973 that the possibility was realised of a Japanese *Dream* which combined fantasy with modernism.[28] For Brook's fusion of styles was a little of 'the shock of the new' for Japanese Shakespeare watchers (Kino 1996, 142-44).

In 1975 *A Midsummer Night's Dream* became one of the first of the plays to be performed in the new translation by Odashima Yūshi (b. 1930), which has been in continuous use ever since. It was precisely the combination of Odashima's contemporary, actor-friendly language with innovative production techniques that helped to make it the second-most frequently performed play after *Hamlet*. For a brief period it seemed as if it had been harnessed to its own good fortunes: the play was produced professionally a

---

[25] In both cases the casts consisted exclusively of teenage girls. Since Takarazuka was founded in 1913, it has performed a number of Shakespeare adaptations and remains commercially successful. Its style combines professional glitz with high moral standards and has been compared with other native traditions such as *nō* and *kyōgen* as representing a distinctively Japanese style.

[26] Hijikata Yoshi (1898-1959) founded the Tsukiji Shōgekijō (Tsukiji Little Theatre) in Tokyo in the wake of the Great Kantō Earthquake of 1923. Although it was primarily a centre of *shingeki* activity, one of its first productions was of Tsubouchi's modern translation of *Julius Caesar* in 1925 (also directed by Hijikata).

[27] Mainstream Shakespeare production in Japan through to the 1970s tended to be realist and textual with little reference to the performance-centred styles of traditional Japanese drama, although it is significant that innovations were often made following direct contact with the Western theatre (e.g. Fukuda's experience of seeing Richard Burton play Hamlet at the Old Vic Theatre in 1953). In addition, there has always been a fringe of stylised adaptations, such as the Takarazuka revues and a *bunraku* adaptation of *Hamlet* by Ōnishi Toshio in 1956, and in fact it was only with the rise of first *shimpa* in the 1900s and then *shingeki* in the 1910s that realist Shakespeare became the norm.

[28] Brook's framing of the stage with three white walls became the most memorable example of how a modernist representation of space could permit the representation of fantasy, with fairies being suspended from the ceiling on trapezes. For young directors such as Ninagawa the production authorised a three-dimensional approach to Shakespeare: an active involvement of audience similar to that which had been developed in the underground theatre since the 1960s (Gallimore 1999, 328-31). Ninagawa himself started to direct Shakespeare soon after and although he has never used trapezes he does favour three-dimensional sets with steps and platforms and often has objects falling from the ceiling. Brook's treatise on drama *The Empty Space* (1968) was soon after translated by Takahashi Yasunari and Kishi Tetsuo (1971).

record five times in 1990 (having been staged once in 1988 and twice in 1989).

The ambivalent position of this play in relation to the history of Shakespeare in Japan corresponds with recent critical consensus about this late early comedy. Hackett's assertion that the play 'actively explores the intersections of comedy and tragedy' (Hackett 1997, 45) is typical of a view that recognises the role of the imagination in averting a potentially tragic situation. *A Midsummer Night's Dream* is closer in this sense to the late romances, such as *The Tempest* (1611), than it is to early social comedies such as *The Comedy of Errors* (1592), where Doctor Pinch's performance as an exorcist is essentially comic. Romantic criticism and dramatic interpretation had been divided between those who appreciated the play's 'magic', which usually meant the coordination of poetry and rhetoric to elements of fantasy (Foakes 1984), and those like the Romantic critic William Hazlitt who deplored the betrayal of dramatic realities. In 1817, he dismissed a contemporary production as follows (Price 1983, 61):

> The *Midsummer Night's Dream*, when acted, is converted from a delightful fiction into a dull pantomime. All that is finest in the play is lost in the representation. The spectacle was grand: but the spirit was evaporated, the genius was fled. – Poetry and the stage do not agree well together ... That which was merely an airy shape, a dream, a passing thought, immediately becomes an unmanageable reality.

For her part, Hackett surmounts the problem of credibility by admitting the ambiguity of genre; once the play becomes a play about life and death, then the imagination can be appreciated for what it is, a faculty rich with cultural and historical resonances.

The imagination creates worlds of possibilities that according to Peter Milward, who has taught Shakespeare at Sophia University in Tokyo since the 1950s, are well understood by Japanese audiences (Milward 1999, 233-34):

> if I am asked which [comedy] most strikes a chord of sympathy in the feelings of the Japanese, I would say, without any hesitation, *A Midsummer Night's Dream*. This is due, I would explain, not to its main theme of contrasting fancy and love, not to its subsidiary theme of a comic tragedy of love in the play-within-the-play, but to its pervading atmosphere of fantasy. In other words, of the three plots with which the play is interwoven, the main plot of the Athenian lovers, the sub-plots of the Athenian artisans and the fairies, it is the third which claims precedence in the eyes of Japanese audiences – as perhaps of most English audiences, too. In our rational minds, like Theseus, we may no more believe in fairies than in the fantasies of 'the lunatic, the lover and the poet' (5.1); but in our hearts and inmost feelings we are deeply influenced by them, or by beings similar to them – whether we call them angels or devils, gods or demons. And I find the Japanese, lacking as they do the rationalistic formation of Western nations, more disposed – at least, the women among them, who are the majority of my students – to be influenced by such belief.

Despite Milward's final reservation, it seems that male critics and directors are equally enthralled by the elements of fantasy, and at the same time keen to understand their actual relevance. Kawai (1997) marvels at the play's various triplicities. Deguchi Norio's 1990 production built a fantasy world out of memories of his own childhood.[29] Ninagawa's 1994 production fantasised about the ties between past, present and future.[30] This enjoyment of fantasy may reflect an urge to escape from social constraints as well as a consciousness of becoming an object of fantasy; it may reflect wider social frustrations as well as personal ones, such as the difficulties still faced by young Japanese women in combining a career with marriage.

The language of A Midsummer Night's Dream

Together with *The Merchant of Venice* and *Romeo and Juliet*, two plays also completed in about 1596, the language of *A Midsummer Night's Dream* comes during a transition from Shakespeare's early conventionalised style, where the tendency is toward formal rhetoric, to his later, less opaque style, rich with 'figures which condense experience' (Ewbank 1986, 60) – the language of *Othello* (1604) and *The Winter's Tale* (1610). Ewbank describes this shift as 'a progressive marriage of verbal and structural rhetoric' (ibid., 58) and so the extent to which this marriage occurs over the course of a single play can only depend on the extent to which the language is itself tested.

Language in Shakespeare is frequently tested by speech acts that threaten the linguistic order of the social hierarchy, with the actual danger of a speech act depending on its relation to that hierarchy. Hermia's protestations to Theseus in the first act of *A Midsummer Night's Dream* (e.g. 1.1.58-64) are in this sense the most dangerous in the play, although Demetrius' plea for forgiveness in Act 4 (4.1.159-75) and some of the talk of the mechanicals (e.g. 3.1.9-12) is also tainted with fear of offending the hierarchy. Yet, *A Midsummer Night's Dream* is not a play in which authority is challenged or subverted to any significant extent and so not one in which linguistic resources are persistently stretched in either defence or aggression.[31] Blake notes the scarcity of questions, adding that 'the play creates a dream-like atmosphere to which scenes of verbal ingenuity would be inappropriate' (Blake 1989, 129).

---

[29] Deguchi (b. 1940) transformed the wood outside Athens into a typical primary school of forty years ago with Puck appearing as a schoolboy with a satchel on his back. In 1994 he developed the idea by running three different concepts of the play one after another: a school version, a masque version and a version set in a bar. The production was by the Shakespeare Theatre company founded by Deguchi in 1975 initially to stage Odashima's translations of the Complete Works (completed in 1985).

[30] Ninagawa's simplest device was to use sand to connect the ancient world of Theseus' Athens represented by a traditional Japanese rock garden with illuminated columns of sand descending from the ceiling in the imagined world of the wood outside Athens (Gallimore 2009).

[31] Puck and indeed Oberon and the other fairies act to subvert the human order but not through linguistic exchange. Bottom's language remains unchanged by his encounter with Titania.

The unity of language and dramatic structure which Ewbank describes is often characterised in the later plays by a use of deixis and metatheatrical allusions that dramatise the characters' performances within their own dramatic worlds.[32] This sense of the play as world is absent from *A Midsummer Night's Dream*, where the mechanicals' play in Act 5 goes no further than comic irony, and there are no explicit recognitions on either side. As in Act 1, the tone is set by Theseus; his speech on 'the lunatic, the lover, and the poet' (5.1.2-22) serves to abstract the lived experience of his subjects over the previous three acts and so keeps the dream going until the end.

Dramatically, the dream is sustained by the efficient segregation of the court from fairyland; poetically, it depends on the predominance of lyric as a means of expression. Rhetoric is the expected means of character development and dramatic narrative in Shakespearean drama, but *A Midsummer Night's Dream* is rich with lyrical moments that do not seem to have any direct relevance to the plot. Even Titania's lament at the disruptions to the natural world caused by her quarrel with Oberon (2.1.81-117) would seem metaphorical rather than factual, since there is no evidence anywhere else in the play – either in the wood or in Athens – of such things occurring as Titania describes them.[33] The speech is rhetorical in technique but its actual purpose is a lyrical expression of feeling since it does not move Oberon in any way other than to confirm his desire for reunion with Titania on his own terms.

This subordination of rhetoric is fundamental to all lyric poetry but of particular relevance to translations in the Japanese tradition. The language of *A Midsummer Night's Dream* in Japanese is probably closest to the language of *shingeki*, that is to say to contemporary, colloquial Japanese. Shakespeare, although not exactly a modern Japanese playwright, has always been at the fringes of that movement as an ideological and dramaturgic influence, and the influence has been reciprocated, Fukuda and Kinoshita Junji (1914-2005) being the two best known *shingeki* playwrights also to have translated Shakespeare. Especially in its early period, *shingeki* was dialectical in style and ideologically committed; although my thesis does not make a stylistic comparison with *shingeki* drama, the basic difference in motivation is relevant to the cultural context and may explain why *A Midsummer Night's Dream* is still regarded in Japan as a fantasy detached from reality and realism.[34]

---

[32] For example, Prospero in *The Tempest* (4.1.156-57): 'We are such stuff / As dreams are made on; and our little life / Is rounded with a sleep.' The difference between Oberon and Prospero is that Prospero belongs to the human world. Deixis is common to all of Shakespeare's plays but in later plays the space between theatre and metatheatre is more thoroughly explored.

[33] It never even rains in *A Midsummer Night's Dream*, for all Titania's complaint that 'the moon, the governess of floods, / Pale in her anger, washes all the air, / That rheumatic diseases do abound' (2.1.103-5).

[34] The fundamental difference between *shingeki* and traditional drama was that it originated in a democratic era and could therefore be used as a forum for ideological debate. Left-wing *shingeki* predominated in the 1920s but was later suppressed by the militarists. Directors such as Senda Koreya (1904-94) kept the proletarian spirit alive after 1945 but there were numerous ↗

The further interest of the play's lyricism is that lyric is itself fundamental to Japanese poetics but, as Earl Miner defined it, as 'an expressive form that does not seek to convince or persuade, certainly not with any moral intention' (Miner 1990, 99). Lyricism is also fundamental to traditional Japanese drama, where dramatic tensions may be experienced emotionally through the stylistic elements of text and performance but are seldom developed dialectically. Even narrative is conveyed by a chanter or actor who sits apart from the arena of dialogue and action. There is no straightforward correspondence with Shakespearean lyric and rhetoric. The Japanese translator who forces a rigid equivalent of Shakespearean lyric with the seven-five syllabic metre of Japanese tradition risks ignoring the rhetorical dimension of the source. Conversely, the translator who makes no reference to poetic tradition risks denying the audience the sense that Shakespeare originally wrote poetic drama. Departures from tradition are all the more exciting (and credible) for being departures from the conventions to which the translator adheres.

FOUR TRANSLATORS – FOUR TRANSLATIONS

The decision to concentrate on only four translations of *A Midsummer Night's Dream* and ignore the other ten or so by other translators is intended to give the monograph historical continuity.[35] The play is a dominant one within Shakespeare

---

↘ Shakespeare directors who were to the right of Senda's political views.

[35] The other published translations are Hokiyama (1927), Satō (1929), Doi (1940), Hasegawa (1947), Nogami (1951), Nakano and Mikami (joint, 1953), Mikami (1954), Hirai (1964), Ōyama Toshiko (1970), Takahashi (1981) (as listed in Sasaki 1990, 522-29), and Tanaka (1993) (Sasaki 1995, 202-3). The only ones to have been staged are Mikami (1972) and Takahashi (1992 and 1993, both times directed by the Swedish director Peter Stormare). Mikami Isao (1907-97) was a Shakespeare scholar who translated thirteen of the plays of which he is best known for his 1937 collaboration with Senda Koreya (1904-94), the pioneer of Brechtian theatre in Japan, on *The Merry Wives of Windsor*. The only translations to have been published five or more times are Mikami and Hirai. Hirai Masao (1911-2005) was one of the leading scholars of English literature of his generation. Hirai's translations of Milton's *Paradise Lost* and Swift's *Gulliver's Travels* are regarded as standard versions, and he was the first to translate the Collected Poems of T.S. Eliot. Ōyama Toshiko was the wife of Ōyama Toshikazu and herself a distinguished scholar and translator. Her English publication *Shakespeare's World of Words* (1975) includes one chapter on the rhetoric of *A Midsummer Night's Dream*. All the translations up to Mikami are translations that were largely eclipsed by Tsubouchi's, which continued to be the translation of directorial choice into the 1960s. Doi Kōchi (1886-1979) studied with Toyoda Minoru at the Imperial University under John Lawrence; his study of flowers in Shakespeare (1929-30) was one of the first original pieces of Shakespeare scholarship by a Japanese scholar, predating Caroline Spurgeon's work on Shakespeare's imagery (1935). These additional translations are so-called 'academic' translations, intended for the purpose of reading, but it should be noted that even the translations by Tsubouchi and Fukuda ↗

in Japan and so too are the four translations dominant in their respective periods. Following an initial period when the play was known only through the source and the Lambs' *Tales of Shakespeare*, the period of dominance by each translation can be outlined as follows.

(1) 1884-1916 : pre-Tsubouchi
(2) 1916-57 : Tsubouchi
(3) 1957-75 : Fukuda
(4) 1975-97 : Odashima
(5) since 1997 : Matsuoka

The dominance of Tsubouchi and Odashima is easiest to establish. Although at least six translations by other translators were published between 1916 and 1957 not one of them was ever produced on stage and – unlike Tsubouchi – not one of them ever went into a second edition. Odashima has met with rather more competition, but his version is still by far the best known in contemporary Japan. Fukuda's translation was produced only three times between 1957 and 1975 and on each occasion, as on subsequent occasions (1985, 1988 and 1991), under his own direction.[36] He is included because of his formative influence as a scholar, director and translator of Shakespeare (Namba 1989), an influence from which Odashima undoubtedly benefited.[37] Matsuoka is included as the only woman among the four, bringing a contemporary feminist sensibility to her ambition to translate the Complete Works, of which she has so far completed twenty-four.[38]

The other reason for choosing these four translators is that they each have their own distinctive translating styles, which are soon enough apparent in comparison and are summarised below. The differences arise from the need to find subjective and yet contemporary solutions to common challenges; the fundamental challenge is simply to make Shakespeare entertaining and accessible to Japanese audiences in their own language. Subordinate challenges would include relevance to contemporary Japanese

---

↘ have been produced on only a handful of occasions, and that it was only with the Shakespeare 'boom' beginning in the 1970s that the play came to be performed with anything like regularity.

[36] This production was co-directed by the British actor and director Terence Knapp, who had been working in the Japanese theatre since the 1970s. Since Fukuda's death, his translations have been quite regularly performed, in particular his *Hamlet* translation by the Shiki theatre company.

[37] Odashima first studied Shakespeare in the Tsubouchi translations but began to teach Shakespeare at the time that Fukuda's star was waxing. It seems that Fukuda's rather literary style had begun to date by the 1970s (Rycroft 1999, 195); what Odashima would have learnt from Fukuda was a belief in the power of Shakespeare's meanings to infiltrate Japanese culture and, above all, pace.

[38] Matsuoka has now translated some twenty of the plays. Although Odashima remains the translator of choice for many amateur and professional groups, Matsuoka replaced Odashima as Ninagawa's translator at the Sai no Kuni Saitama Arts Theatre in 1997 in his plan to produce the Complete Works, and her translations have also been used by Ryūtopia and Studio Life.

concerns and Japanese theatre reform.

Tsubouchi Shōyō (1859-1935)

Tsubouchi wanted to bring Shakespeare to as wide an audience as possible. His criticism is informed both by the latest in Western scholarship and an awareness of parallels and divergences from Japanese tradition; he wanted to give Japanese audiences a Shakespeare that was authentic and yet accessible. What Tsubouchi meant by authenticity was a match of semantic precision – not just of individual words but of whole phrases and metaphors – with the authority of scholarly interpretation. Authenticity did not preclude formal or stylistic licence, and indeed Tsubouchi's translations are far from literalist in either form or syntax.

His translation of *A Midsummer Night's Dream* comes in the fifth of the five periods of his translating career: by far the most substantial of the periods, in which he translated thirty of the plays and revised his translations of the other seven. Yet the previous stages not only encompassed a longer period of time than the final one of twenty years but are also landmarks in the development of what was to become his dominant style of translating Shakespeare. They are usually summarised as follows (e.g. Moriya 1986, 37-38): 1. *jōruri* adaptations of *Julius Caesar* (1885) and *Hamlet* (1886); 2. literalist translations of *Macbeth* (1892-4) and *Hamlet* (1897); 3. two experimental stage translations for the Bungei Kyōkai of *The Merchant of Venice* (1907) and *Hamlet* (1908); 4. mixed literary and colloquial translations of *Hamlet*, *Julius Caesar*, *King Lear*, *Othello* and *Romeo and Juliet* (1910-14).

Tsubouchi's discovery was not that the language of Shakespeare was necessarily unlike Japanese *bungo* (literary language) but that they were sufficiently similar in rhetorical impact to risk obfuscating each other; a Japanese Shakespeare that was merely another version of *kabuki* risked trivialising those meanings that were comprehensible to Japanese people but at the same time unfamiliar. Following the fourth stage, he came to realise that contemporary language was the most appropriate idiom for translating Shakespeare but that it had to be ornamented with archaisms and other literary touches if the warmth and the rhythms which he experienced so deeply in the original texts were to be preserved. Tsubouchi writes that (1978, 256; Gallimore 2010a, 51)

> If you translate in literary language, with all its distinct associations, then it becomes difficult to understand, sounds too Japanese, positively ancient in fact, which is not the case if you translate in contemporary style. I feel that those famous old words which can be difficult even for English people to understand, expressed in complex, sometimes fearfully concise archaisms, richly metaphorical and bound up in old grammar, move me mysteriously and speak directly to my heart, and I believe that in the mouth of a Portia or Cleopatra, a Stephano or Bottom, Macbeth or Lady Macbeth, they are to be heard in the Japan of today. When all is said and done, it is the warmth of the language that matters, its mysterious vitality and

relevance. The natural and contemporary feel of contemporary colloquial language recalls the unchanging naturalness of Shakespeare's works.

A Midsummer Night's Dream has a special place in this enterprise as being the third comedy that Tsubouchi translated after *The Merchant of Venice* and *The Tempest* (1916). Comedy and romance were unknown as specific genres with the *kabuki* tradition with which Tsubouchi was most familiar, which is not to suggest that *kabuki* is lacking in either comedy or romance, and although *The Merchant of Venice* evidently aroused interest in Meiji Japan (Kawachi 1998), the stories of the other two plays must have been considered quite bizarre.[39] Their strangeness no doubt gave Tsubouchi the licence to develop his contemporary style, since he would have needed to make the folklore and classicisms from which that strangeness derives accessible to his readership. Yet it is more significant that the two translations came so soon after his productions of Shakespeare for the Bungei Kyōkai (1907-13). Prospero and Oberon are both directorial characters who exercise a magical influence over events (not unusual in classical Japanese drama) and like *Hamlet* – of which Tsubouchi's translation had been the centrepiece of the Bungei Kyōkai's achievement – *A Midsummer Night's Dream* contains a play within the play; his interest had evidently been roused in the Shakespearean metaphor of stage as world. Tsubouchi was insistent about the Englishness of the play and although he does not give clear reasons for this conviction, an Anglicised representation would also have been welcome during this period of strong Anglo-Japanese relations.[40]

Fukuda Tsuneari (1912-94)

Fukuda Tsuneari is identified as representing the next major phase in Shakespeare translation and production in Japan (Anzai 1989 a): of having initiated the process which made Tsubouchi all but redundant by the late 1960s.[41] Like Tsubouchi, whose main career had been as a professor at Waseda University, Fukuda was a university professor, albeit not one so singlemindedly devoted to Shakespeare, whom he did not translate until his forties.[42] Tsubouchi was privileged, in a sense, as a pioneer whose first task had been simply to read and know the plays of Shakespeare and yet it was due to his efforts that Shakespeare was already well established on the literary curriculum by the 1930s when Fukuda first encountered him. Fukuda's agenda had to be a personal one.

---

[39] In addition to being a playwright and scholar of *kabuki* himself, Tsubouchi used to read a handful of classical *kabuki* plays before translating a Shakespeare play. It goes without saying that he knew *kabuki* before he knew Shakespeare.

[40] Japan was an ally of Britain during the First World War.

[41] Recent uses of Tsubouchi translations have been a *bunraku* adaptation of *The Tempest* in 1992 and a stage production of *King Lear* in January 2000. Tsubouchi's translations are also produced annually by an amateur group in Tokyo called Gekidan Za.

[42] Fukuda taught at Tokyo Women's University and had already translated D.H. Lawrence's last work *Apocalypse* (1931) by the time that he began to translate Shakespeare.

Fukuda saw in Shakespearean drama a humanism with the power to restore spiritual values to a Japan that had been shattered first by totalitarianism and then by war. Disasters such as these provided an obvious incentive for cultural reform; but what Fukuda was searching for in order to implement his reformist incentive was a way of performing Shakespeare that was a slave neither to tradition nor to the foreign. Ironically, he found it in Michael Benthall's production of *Hamlet* at the Old Vic theatre in London, with Richard Burton in the title role, and although it would be quite unjust to suggest that all Japanese productions for the next twenty years were slavish imitations of the style of a single English production, Fukuda had without doubt discovered a Shakespeare with the authority to create values.[43]

The translations that Fukuda completed during the 1950s and 1960s are characterised as 'avoiding rough-hewn everyday language and using frequently archaic or obsolete words to heighten the poetic effect' (Kawachi 1995, 93). He was conscious of the need to tell a story, and although this belief may test his audience he also drew on his experiences as a director and playwright to make his narratives dramatic.[44] According to Kawachi, Fukuda believed (*pace* Robert Frost, who defined poetry as 'that which is lost in translation') that ninety percent of Shakespeare's poetry was lost in Japanese translation and although some readers do find his style poetic, he argued at the same time that loss of poetry could be compensated by the preservation of important dramatic qualities, in particular *sakugekijutsu* ('the technique of constructing a play') and *dorāma no ikkansei* ('dramatic consistency or unity') (Kawachi 1981, 81).

A Midsummer Night's Dream was clearly important to Fukuda in being the first comedy and the sixth of the plays that he produced after *Hamlet* (1955), *Macbeth* (1958), *Othello* (1959), *Julius Caesar* (1961) and *Richard III* (1962). Revived by Fukuda in 1965 and 1973, the production was the first to be done by his new group Kumo, and coincided historically with the launch of Prime Minister Ikeda Hayato's Income-Doubling Plan in 1962. Incomes doubled in only half the ten years expected: more than anything else it was surely the high economic growth lasting through to the oil shock in 1973 and picking up again in the 1980s that facilitated the growth in

---

[43] He later wrote that he already regarded 'the essence of Shakespearean drama as being a kind of temple pageant bringing forth life out of death' but that it was not until meeting Michael Benthall (1919-74) that Fukuda understood what the drama might actually feel like (Fukuda 1961, 200). Fukuda invited the British director to Japan in 1965 to direct a Japanese production of *Romeo and Juliet*. Fukuda's vision of Shakespearean drama as resurrection is similar to Brook's notion of 'holy theatre' and may thus share in those faults which Brook believes Shakespeare had transcended (Brook 1990, 51): 'it is not the fault of the holy that it has become a middle-class weapon to keep children good'; Shakespeare's underlying 'aim continually is holy, metaphysical, yet he never makes the mistake of staying too long on the highest plane' (ibid., 69).

[44] Fukuda's conservatism, in particular his support for the renewal of the United States-Japan Security Treaty (*anpo jōyaku*) in the 1960s, inevitably distanced him from Marxist dramaturgs and from the post-*shingeki* theorists who emerged in the late 1960s, who could not believe in resurrection of any kind.

Shakespeare production during that period.[45] Fukuda should be credited as a visionary whose authoritarian style inspired the younger generation to surpass him. He is the most modernist of the translators, coming between the Meiji generation who had been thoroughly educated in the Chinese and Japanese classics and the generation who came of age in the 1960s, who had the ideological prerogative to create a Japanese Shakespeare.[46] In other words, his style of translating inevitably pales in comparison with Tsubouchi but rapidly became obsolete in the 1970s.

Odashima Yūshi (b. 1930)

Tsubouchi wanted his audiences to know the richness of Shakespeare's plays, Fukuda wanted them to experience their meanings as dramatic realities. Odashima can be similarly said to be concerned with accessibility and the historical background. Fifteen years younger than Fukuda, Odashima was at the fringes of the underground theatre movement (*angura*) that emerged to challenge the grip of mainstream *shingeki*, which began in the 1910s and in which Fukuda was such a prominent figure. Although *angura* was kindled by frustration among the younger actors at the conservatism of the *shingeki* hierarchy in the allotting of parts, it was more fundamentally a conflict about where the modern theatre stood in relation to 'the rationalist West'.

In 1961, the Kennedy administration implemented the renewal of the US-Japan Security Treaty. Ideological opposition to the Treaty, later fuelled by a worldwide student movement, was supported within the underground theatre by a demand for native themes, forms and language (Goodman 1988, 3-32). Although Shakespeare remained the preserve of *shingeki* throughout the 1960s, it was realised that Shakespeare could be appropriated by a more radical theatre – in terms of both performance styles and interpretation – and it was for this theatre that Odashima first translated. Seven of Odashima's translations were produced by different directors between 1968 and 1975, in which year he started his highly productive collaboration with Deguchi

---

[45] Among the major venues for Shakespeare performance in Tokyo to have opened since 1980 are Bunkamura Theatre Cocoon in Shibuya (1989), the Tokyo Metropolitan Art Space in Ikebukuro (1990), the Setagaya Public Theatre in Sangenjaya (1997), and the New National Theatre near Shinjuku (1997).

[46] As Morton (2004) and others have insisted, the definition of either modernity or modernism in Japanese culture is far from straightforward, and somewhat broader than the images of affluence associated with the era of Taishō democracy (1912-26). Literary influences are just as likely to come from Victorian rather than overtly modern European literature, as well as from within Japanese culture itself, and were above all meant to promote new identities and means of self-projection. Japanese modernity thus develops as a phenomenon that is distinct from its American and European counterparts. In the case of a cultural ideologue such as Fukuda, we can see how Shakespeare answers certain questions emerging from within his cultural experience as a Japanese person who came of age during the period of militarism and war rather than providing a definite model of cultural development.

Norio's Shakespeare Theatre. Deguchi eventually directed all thirty-seven of the translations, although Odashima's translation of *A Midsummer Night's Dream* was first directed by British director John David for Tōhō Production in August 1975 (not by Deguchi). Deguchi's style was innovative in its informality and appeal to youth, and the collaboration with a non-Japanese director was also perhaps typical of the new generation. His technique was to use a small and inexperienced cast who would learn their Shakespeare through a routine of short rehearsal times and plenty of improvisation. Sets and costumes were minimal and contemporary.

The obvious difference between Odashima and Fukuda, apart from era, is that Odashima confined himself solely to the role of translator whereas Fukuda usually directed his own translations. Fukuda had an authoritarian style of directing while Odashima was known for his sensitivity to actors' needs and audience response.[47] One can appreciate that Fukuda felt reluctant to be a poet as well as a playwright in translation, also that a translation stripped of Shakespeare's poetry would have by default exposed the framework of logical argumentation that drove Renaissance culture (hence the label 'rationalist').

Odashima's more limited role gave him greater freedom to recover some of the charm which Tsubouchi had so valued. He was not the first translator to use free verse, but, as I aim to show, Odashima combined rhythm, wordplay and other euphonious techniques to achieve a sensuality of effect and of language that was immediately accessible to his youthful audiences.[48] Unlike Fukuda, he left the drama to the actors, and unlike Tsubouchi, there was nothing, as far as Odashima was concerned, especially magical or mysterious about Shakespeare, just a heady draught of poetry, humour and common sense.[49]

Matsuoka Kazuko (b. 1942)

Matsuoka Kazuko lies within the Fukuda tradition if only because she herself worked for two years as an intern at Fukuda's Kumo during the 1960s. Matsuoka has

---

[47] Odashima is renowned as a theatregoer, seeing up to 300 performances a year in various genres and languages, and latterly served as artistic director of the Tokyo Metropolitan Art Space.
[48] Mikami was translating in a free verse format in the 1950s.
[49] There is a strong ludic character to much of Odashima's writings on Shakespeare, e.g. *Dōke no me* (The eyes of the fool, 1990), *Odashima Yūshi no Sheikusupia yūgaku* (How to have fun with Shakespeare, 1991) and *Shi to yūmoa* (Poetry and humour, 1995). Odashima's translations remain popular among a range of amateur and professional groups, although are no longer used by Ninagawa. My own most recent experience of his unique style was an adaptation I saw of his translation of *A Midsummer Night's Dream* at the Ikebukuro Sunshine Theatre in July 2011 by the Shakespeare for Children company (Kodomo no tame no Sheikusupia); I later translated this adaptation for the Asian Shakespeare Intercultural Archive (a-s-i-a-web.org). It was evident that the relative simplicity and harmony of Shakespeare's language leant itself to this kind of interpretation, which used puppets to help narrate the story and to bring out the comic aspects.

never directed, having spent the first part of her career as a professor of English and American literature at the Tokyo Medical and Dental University, but her translating career and approach to translation manifests a belief in the authority of the translator in the present age of specialisation. Whereas Odashima started to translate Shakespeare in his late thirties and was producing four or five new translations a year in addition to fulfilling his teaching commitments at Tokyo University, Matsuoka's first translation was not staged until 1996. Matsuoka combines a knowledge of textual criticism and Shakespeare production in Britain and Japan that is rare among her peers and probably superior to the other three translators at the time when they started translating.[50]

The Tsubouchi, Fukuda and Odashima translations all filled distinct cultural lacunae, but in 1990s Japan, with the Shakespeare 'boom' over and Odashima's translations still accessible, one may reasonably wonder why yet another translation was required. Matsuoka justifies her ambition by claiming that the Japanese language has changed significantly since the 1970s and that a new translation is required to reflect those changes. Although *hyōjungo* (the standard Tokyo dialect) is still dominant and the language of Odashima still the language of many of the older generation, relationships within the social hierarchy – especially between young men and women – have altered and styles of communication shifted accordingly.

It is not just that many young women now use the masculine *watashi* ('I') instead of feminine *atashi*, but that a greater proximity of male and female roles (together with greater awareness of gender difference) has broader implications for the representation of men and women in Shakespeare translation and production in Japan (Matsuoka 1998, 214).[51] Matsuoka has been part of the rising generation which has brought about these changes but also, as a one-time actress and later avid theatregoer, she is keenly aware of the relationships between men and women as a dramatic as well as a linguistic phenomenon. Almost all of Matsuoka's predecessors have begun their translating careers with the great tragedies (usually *Hamlet*) and although her first translation to be staged and published was indeed *Hamlet* (1996), the first plays that she actually translated were *A Midsummer Night's Dream* and *The Comedy of Errors*, in 1993. Her translation of the former was staged and published in 1997. Unlike Odashima, Matsuoka has been deeply involved in the production process, working with Ninagawa on numerous productions at the Saitama Arts Theatre, as well as British directors such as John Caird, to ensure that Shakespeare's lines are properly understood by Japanese actors, and if necessary making adjustments to her translations. One of the themes of her writing on Shakespeare has been the necessity of exploring Shakespeare's subtexts, so that the texts are not summarily subordinated within the director's overall scheme, as has been the

---

[50] Prior to Shakespeare Matsuoka had also translated plays by Caryl Churchill and Tom Stoppard.
[51] Gender is evidently of academic interest as well since in 1999, with an increasing number of female Shakespeare scholars such as Ichikawa Mariko and Kobayashi Kaori becoming known outside Japan. In 2005, Kusunoki Akiko of Tokyo Women's University became the first female president of the Shakespeare Society of Japan.

tendency among Japanese directors, but interpreted with greater linguistic subtlety and awareness of the source texts. This approach may be called postmodern in the sense that it leads to a more diffuse style of production that questions overarching narratives.

Another sign of Matsuoka's postmodernism is her awareness of metatheatre in Shakespeare: that Shakespeare's theatre is not universal but a world in itself, self-reflective. Tsubouchi, Fukuda and Odashima can be said to have created (or recreated) Shakespeare in Japan in the hindsight of their respective generations but in Matsuoka's case it is rather a case of *déjà vu*. Metatheatre is one of the features of the post-*shingeki* movement of the last thirty years (Senda 1997, 1-14), not to mention a feature of *A Midsummer Night's Dream*,[52] and for Matsuoka it becomes a feature of her translating style as well. One of her most striking characteristics, although she is by no means alone in this, is to shift from a plain, contemporary style to a more complex, affective register.

COMPARISON AND EVALUATION

The careers of the four translators are all mirrored by the great social and historical events that have brought Japan from feudalism to capitalist democracy. This movement has swung periodically between Japanese and Western values and so, although they are all four united by an impetus for change, one may conclude that it is Tsubouchi and Odashima who are drawn towards Japanese values (Shakespeare as Japanese) and Fukuda and Matsuoka towards the Western.[53] Tsubouchi and Odashima's translating careers coincide with periods of economic growth and growth in national confidence (the Taishō era and the 1970s); Fukuda and Matsuoka's careers begin in periods of uncertainty and national self-doubt (early post-war and post-'bubble'). This monograph seeks to demonstrate some of the differences and continuities between the four translations through an analysis of their translations of one play. The achievement of the postmodern culture to which Matsuoka belongs has been cultural pluralism, but pluralism can lead easily to ideological confusion, to trends rather than convictions. Comparing translations is one means of appreciating the discursive power of Shakespeare's representation in modern and contemporary Japan.

Comparativism is itself one of the salient characteristics of discourse on modern Japanese literature, created out of an ongoing comparison with Western writers. A naive and sometimes chauvinistic approach has been to make comparisons with the foreign as a means of defining what Japanese literature is not. This approach often refers to a subjectivism typical of much modern Japanese literature; it makes basic points of

---

[52] The play-within-the-play in Act 5 can be said to return the lovers to normality after their extraordinary experiences in the wood and so prepare them for the married life thereafter.

[53] For traditional comparisons of Shakespeare with Japanese culture, see Miyoshi (1983) and Milward (1999).

comparison but is frustrated by the reality that national literatures do not necessarily run in parallel or synchrony with each other. Tsubouchi's comparison of Shakespeare with Chikamatsu (1909), for example, indicates generic and thematic referents but can go no further than cultural and historical differences allow. The following statement is typical of an admission that the two playwrights are bound to the cultures which produced them (Matsumoto 1960, 235):

> Chikamatsu's *jōruri* are essentially musical plays. They are pitched higher than Shakespeare's. This does not mean that *jōruri* are more high-toned than the former. The two simply cannot be compared.

The concept of national literatures is more tenable but is again limited by the reality of plurality among writers even of the same nationality.

A more sophisticated approach admits the extent to which translated literature affects and even constructs the recipient culture, which is the conclusion of Susan Bassnett and others in the field of comparative literature over the last twenty-five years (e.g. Bassnett and Lefevere 1998): comparisons can only be made with some awareness of translation as an historical event, and the reader reads a translation as a historical interaction between the source text and the context in which it is translated.[54] Most historical evaluations (e.g. Maruyama and Katō, 1998) assume without question the influence of translation on modern Japanese culture, and indeed translation of all kinds has played a far greater role in modern Japan than in Anglophone countries.[55]

Japanese translation studies may have been short on theoretical discussion but, as far as Shakespeare is concerned, the work by Niki (1984) and others is informed by the same sense of shifting equivalences outlined above, the realisation that what constitutes equivalence is informed by the translator's historical as well as ideological perspective. When Ōyama wrote of his experience that he never forgot 'to add that sometimes the Japanese translator could *add* something to Shakespeare, that sometimes they could translate Shakespeare one hundred and *ten percent*!' (Ōyama 1975, 36), he was arguing that sometimes the translator can create a particular resonance which makes sense in the context of the translation but which Shakespeare – so distant in time and space – could not have intended. Ōyama's 'ten percent' will be discussed later, but for the time being

---

[54] Bassnett controversially concluded in her 1993 study of comparative literature that 'Comparative literature as a discipline has had its day. Cross-cultural work in women's studies, in post-colonial theory, in cultural studies has changed the face of literary studies generally. We should look upon translation studies as the principal discipline from now on, with comparative literature as a valued but subsidiary subject area.' (Bassnett 1993, 161). Bassnett's argument recognises translation as the sole medium through which it is possible to compare literatures.

[55] The number of prominent writers who have admitted influences by Western writers is significant, from Turgenev on Futabatei Shimei in the 1890s through to Raymond Chandler on Murakami Haruki in the 1990s. Translation historians such as Yanabu Akira commonly refer to Japan as *honyaku kokka* ('a translation nation').

it is valuable as a reassertion of comparativist methodology. The translators are located on a historical continuum that connects basic norms as to what is and is not possible in the translation of Shakespeare. Sometimes, as Ōyama suggests and as in any literary tradition, these norms are challenged and the challenges justified.

The Schleiermacher model

Ōyama's statement indicates another of the assumptions of this thesis: that translation is at once objective interpretation and subjective recreation. The theory was first formulated in full by Friedrich Schleiermacher (1768-1834) in the early 19th century (Schleiermacher 1992, 38):[56]

> every free and higher discourse wants to be perceived in a twofold way: on the one hand, out of the spirit of the language of whose elements it is composed, a language that is bound and defined by that spirit and vividly conceived in the speaker; on the other hand, out of the speaker's emotions, as his own action, which can only be produced and explained by his nature.

The virtue of Schleiermacher's methodology, and the reason why it has been so influential, is that it steers a middle course between literalism and adaptation, which in turn acknowledges the political status of translation as a vehicle for international exchange. From the beginnings of modern Japan the plays of Shakespeare have been understood at the very least to offer insights into their creator.[57] Both agendas risk being compromised by translations that neglect either the source or target language, although it should be mentioned that literalism of word or metaphor has never been held to be a serious shortcoming of Shakespeare translation into Japanese. Loss of sub-text and a tendency to explicate difficult metaphors are more typical problems.

The more serious danger of Schleiermacher's methodology is of it becoming a strict and normative methodology. It might be hypothetically possible to judge a translation against whatever interpretative framework was current at the time of translating along with whatever was known of the translator's ideology, but although the conclusions reached would be of undoubted value they would not necessarily account for the individuality of either translator or translation. They are subverted by such

---

[56] Schleiermacher is also significant to Shakespeare translation in that his theory was based on a systematic analysis of the Romantic methodology inherent in the German translation of Shakespeare by his contemporary August Wilhelm von Schlegel (1767-1845).

[57] Critical interest in the life of Shakespeare and the history of English literature is a theme of Meiji scholarship. The first translation of a major critical work was of Edward Dowden's *Shakespere: A Critical Study of His Mind and Art* (1875), published between 1894 and 1899. The first work by a Japanese scholar to be devoted exclusively to Shakespeare was a biography by Nakamura Yoshio, published in 1901.

variables as the translator's inability or unwillingness to know his own ideology as well, of course, by the inevitable subjectivity of interpretation.

Translators both individually and generally seek ever 'better' translations but improvement is relative to cultural and literary history, not to any absolute norms. Schleiermacher's formula offers a highly valuable methodology to the individual translator, but whether it has any normative application is questionable. The history of literary translation in Japan, especially since the Meiji Era, has been just as much a search for good practice as elsewhere, all the more so as the role of foreign literature has been realised. Yet just because the translators of Shakespeare have been mainly academics working in a narrow range of institutions (mainly in Tokyo) does not mean to say that they have not been informed by individual tastes and preferences, nor driven by their own creative talents. The comparativist Willis Barnstone writes that (Barnstone 1993, 266)

> A translation is a friendship between poets. There is a mystical union between them based on love and art.

The translators discussed in this monograph were each no doubt informed by a nebulous sense of what looked and sounded right, and it was from that point that their relationships with the source texts began, not with some abstractly conceptual model. The Schleiermacher model becomes interesting when it is seen how, and for all kinds of reasons, translators react against it not as a methodology but as a model of perfection. The model strikes a balance between the source and target languages, so long as language is understood as the system in which the translator articulates his creative response. The problem is that the middle ground represented by Schleiermacher is unstable, unbreakable perhaps, but difficult to quantify.

The question of accuracy

The further important question is whether it is possible and, indeed, necessary to assess the accuracy of the four translations. The significance of error in literary translation depends partly on the kind of translation being attempted. A literalist translation creates a context in which mistakes of syntax or vocabulary are judged harshly whereas the agenda of the liberal translation is centred more on pragmatic accuracy (e.g. consistency of tone and thematic development). If it is true that the four translations veer towards the liberal, it is by the second criterion that they should be judged.

Translations which are consistently insensitive to the stylistic nuances of their source texts will still mean something in the target language but give a false impression of whatever was meant and continues to be meant in the source culture. Barnstone asserts that (Barnstone 1993, 123)

> The most grievous error is infidelity to quality. Except in cases of specific cribs and interlinear trots (for which there is academic dispensation), there is only fitting punishment for qualitative felonies: the silence of nonpublication.

That all four translators are indeed sensitive to 'quality' is evident from the fact that the first three have run into several editions, and Matsuoka is already popular both on stage and in print. The recipient culture has recognised these four as being as close to 'the real thing' as they are likely to get. Yet it is worth noting that their credibility as translators has come primarily from their knowledge of Shakespeare rather than their talents as professional writers.[58] Translation has long been close to the heart of literary endeavour in the Western world with contemporary poets such as Tony Harrison and Adrian Mitchell trying their hands at translating classical drama, but in the history of Shakespeare translation in Japan there have been only a handful of translators who have been better known for their other work, of which Kinoshita Junji and the novelist Mori Ōgai (1860-1922) would be the two most prominent. To translate Shakespeare into Japanese is still recognised as a literary achievement, but the narrowness of this particular world does not exclude it from the wider culture. This monograph can afford to be critical of obvious lapses of style.

'Shakespeare in Japanese' is always an achievement, because of the great cultural and linguistic differences that have in some way to be surmounted. It is for these differences that Niki declares of Shakespeare translation in Japan that 'debating questions of literal accuracy is quite fruitless' (Niki 1984, 33). Linguistic literalism is probably more feasible than Niki's claim might suggest, especially as most audiences can tolerate a degree of alienation, but the focus of Niki's concern is those images and themes which if consistently untreated end up obfuscating Shakespeare's meanings.

'To be, or not to be'

Niki illustrates her discussion of the problems encountered by Japanese translators of Shakespeare with the example of Hamlet's soliloquy on suicide and the nature of existence (3.1.55-87) (Niki 1984, 98-111). It seems that not only was Hamlet's question 'To be, or not to be' unfamiliar as a subject of soliloquy for Meiji audiences when Tsubouchi and others first translated it,[59] but that having made the subject plausible, the further problem remained of finding an equivalent for 'to be' that contained the dual

---

[58] Tsubouchi and Fukuda were both respected playwrights in their own right. It is arguable that Tsubouchi's attempts at historical drama in the 1890s clarified his understanding of characterisation and generic differences in preparation for his translation of Shakespeare (Keene 1999, 411-15) and that the humanism of Fukuda's view of Shakespeare is also apparent in his plays (ibid., 484).

[59] The most important of the early translations are the separate translations by Toyama and Yatabe in *Shintaishi shō* (1882), the joint translation by Asano and Tozawa (1905) and Tsubouchi (1909). See Kawatake (1972) and Takahashi (1995).

meanings of physical 'live' and abstract 'exist'; translators felt constrained into making a choice between one of two interpretations, the literal or the existential. Most kept it a straightforward matter of life and death[60] in the hope that such a stark statement would effectively dramatise Hamlet's situation and that the existential subtext would emerge through the imagery of the rest of the speech.[61] Odashima (1972) is the only one to approach Shakespearean ambiguity in the sentence itself: *kono mama de ii no ka, ikenai no ka, sore ga mondai da* (freely back translated, 'Can I carry on like this? Can't I? That's the problem.')

Ōyama Toshikazu takes the problem a step further in realising the potential diversity of the audience's response (Ōyama 1975, 32):[62]

> The translator is well aware of how strange Hamlet's expression sounds, but it is his sincere wish that it will some day – in all its tragic complexity – become a commonplace expression in Japanese, especially among the younger generation who are always susceptible to such innovations.

His own version of the line (1968) tried to capture that strangeness by using one of the more literal equivalents of 'to be', *iru*, which usually refers to nothing more than being as location: *Iru ka, sore tomo iranu ka, sore ga mondai da.*

The significance of this example is not so much the problem of translating a famous speech from Shakespeare but the crucial translator's dilemma that it epitomises: the degree to which a personal interpretation of the target text is permissible and comprehensible to audiences. Literalism is not only a straightforward linguistic transfer of syntax and vocabulary but also refers to the extent to which the translator can explain the source text to his or her audience while all the time sustaining the dramatic illusion. This dilemma underscores the need to recognise the achievements of Japanese translators of Shakespeare as much in terms of their own contexts as the problems they encounter in the source texts.

It is at this stage that the project of Shakespeare into Japanese moves from the theoretical to the technical; there are two basic problems. The first one contains the hidden advantage of relating Japanese translators to Shakespeare's own literary context, and is the problem of rhetoric. Rhetoric has already been discussed in relation to *A Midsummer Night's Dream*, but as the example from *Hamlet* indicated, it is also a literary-historical issue. That soliloquy was absent from the *kabuki* suggests a very different tradition of rhetorical discourse, one of which the literary pioneers of Meiji were only too aware.

Tomasi has chronicled how Meiji Japan was flooded with translations of Western

---

[60] One example is Kume Masao's translation (1916): *Sei* ('life') *ka* ('or') *shi* ('death') *ka ... sore ga* ('that') *mondai* ('problem') *da.* ('is'). This version uses the plain, contemporary style.
[61] For example, the meditation on death and sleep (ll. 60-69).
[62] I have slightly paraphrased the English of Ōyama's statement in order to clarify his meaning.

primers on rhetoric, which while failing to introduce a comprehensive taxonomy of Japanese oral and written styles certainly succeeded in providing 'a solid platform for debate and deeper understanding of the needs of modern Japanese language and literature' (Tomasi 1999, 356). At a time when many in the Realist and Naturalist movements were arguing for a plain literary style that did away with the rhetorical ornamentation of the older tradition,[63] the comparison with Western models and terminology forced the realisation that rhetoric was not necessarily without meaning. As the rhetorician Igarashi Chikara wrote in 1909 (qtd. ibid., 355),

> Writing without affectation means abolition of unnatural ornament and classical conventions, it does not mean that all stylistic devices should be regarded as unnecessary.

Rhetoric can indeed become meaningless when the possibility of rhetorical statements being actively misinterpreted by a rhetorically uneducated underclass is circumscribed, and its only use is to sustain the discourse of a literary élite. Shakespeare was for the Meiji literati a prime exponent of drama that was inherently rhetorical, testing the translators' understanding of the rhetorical relationships between text and reader, actor and audience, and yet one of the arguments of my study is that the translators have needed to look no further than their own literary culture to discover the language of Shakespeare in Japanese; in other words, the rhetoric was already there.

The art of making the language rhetorically effective in the culture from which it comes is largely a matter of craft, but it can be described at least as an awareness of how apparently different scales of Shakespearean rhetoric translate into Japanese forms and language. What, for example, to do with Shakespearean pithiness when Japanese translations inevitably contain more words than the source? The answer is not just to produce fewer words but simply to be pithy by Japanese standards, perhaps by inverting the usual word order. Such pragmatic equivalence is at the heart of Japanese translations of Shakespeare.

Holmes and pragmatic equivalence

The second problem connects rhetoric to the earlier discussion about models of translation. This is the question of the type of translation that each translator chooses.[64] Niki borrows from the translation theorist James S. Holmes[65] when she argues that

---

[63] The two movements, which originated in the reformist movements of the 1880s and affected all the literary genres, can both be regarded as reactions against a cultured, self-conscious objectivism.
[64] 'Type' differs from 'model' in describing an active process of translation (as against a static paradigm).
[65] James S. Holmes (1924-86) was a translator of modern Dutch poetry who developed an influential theory of translating poetry, advocating four strategies that depend roughly on ↗

Japanese translations of Shakespearean blank verse are either 'content-derivative' or 'extraneous' in nature, and it is a description that could well be extended to other stylistic aspects beyond blank verse (Niki 1984, 52).

Content-derivative translations communicate the semantics of the literary forms and other devices employed in the source text but are seldom able to achieve an exact equivalent of form or even structure. Holmes' other name for this type is 'organic', whereby the semantic material is allowed 'to take on its own unique and independent poetic shape as the translation develops' (Holmes 1994, 27). 'Deviant' or extraneous translations make an even more radical departure from the source in that 'the form adopted is in no way implicit in either the form or content of the original' (ibid.). It is reasonable to conclude that Japanese translations veer between the content-derivative and extraneous. Holmes' typology was originally intended for translations of poetry not drama, and although the four translators are quite capable of writing poetry it is not always necessary or even desirable to be consistently poetic.

* * * * *

My study attempts to illustrate the problems discussed in this introduction by examining the prosody of the four translations of *A Midsummer Night's Dream*: how they sound in Japanese and what their prosodies reveal of the interpretive choices made by the translators.[66] Chapter Two is the most specifically linguistic, examining how Shakespeare's prosody meets with the intrinsic prosody of the Japanese language, above all accentuation. Chapter Three discusses the outward prosody of the target texts, with particular attention to the possible correlation between blank verse and syllabic metre; the prosody is extrinsic in so far as it is imposed upon the language rather than originating from within the individual phonemes and can also be applied in that sense to whatever rhythms are applied to the texts in performance. Accentuation can also be extrinsic but is categorised as intrinsic in Chapter Two since most (if not all) of the accent markings are unambiguous. Chapter Four extends the discussion to an examination of the translators' use of rhyme and wordplay, possibly the most fruitful topic of them all. As in this chapter, each of the three chapters is prefaced with a literary-historical introduction to relevant aspects of Japanese poetics.

In Chapter Five, I examine how the translations have been vocally articulated by one individual exponent and four contemporary theatre companies. Although translation began in the Meiji era as a literary activity, where Shakespeare's plays

---

↘ the relationship of the source and target languages: '(a) mimetic, where the original form is retained; (b) analogical, where a culturally corresponding form is used; (c) organic' and (d) deviant or extraneous (Connolly 1998, 174).

[66] The term 'prosody' is used both in its linguistic sense to mean the phonological patterning of a language, and in its literary sense to refer to the formal or informal rhythms and rhymes adopted by the writer.

drama have made their greatest difference to Japanese culture has been in the modern theatre, since it is in the physical space of the theatre that the language and meanings of Shakespeare in translation are physically absorbed and expressed by actors and received as such by Japanese audiences; it is there that the performance and reception of Shakespeare becomes a communal experience. In conclusion, I consider the future of Shakespeare translation in Japan in the light of contemporary translation theory and theatrical practice.

CHAPTER TWO   STRESS AND ACCENT

Prosody (*inritsu*) constitutes the aural dimension of Shakespeare's style and the styles of his Japanese translators.[67] It includes the rhythms and rhymes of both Shakespearean drama and of traditional and modern Japanese poetry and the Japanese language, as well as less formal devices such as wordplay. Japanese translators have their own prosodies, determined as much by personal preference as by the state of the language. Each of these prosodies occurs at a point where Shakespeare's and Japanese prosodies intersect in the translators' minds with the translators' interpretive choices and stylistic preferences. Yet, as Holmes argued, equivalence with the source is 'an unattainable ideal' (Holmes 1994, 10). Even mimetic verse translations must be considered as metapoems rather than equivalents; the lack of symmetry is more apparent in translations from English to Japanese (where the writing systems differ as well as the syntax and lexis).[68] Stylistic influences are undeniable but often elusive in meaning, and only understood in their historical context. Fortunately, there is quite a body of information suggesting reasons as to why the prosody of Shakespeare translations has developed as it has, elucidating its function and meaning in any given context. There is a tradition for translating Shakespeare into Japanese, and prosody is part of that tradition.

MODERNISM AND THE MEIJI REFORMERS

Louis Allen reiterated one of the refrains of modern Japanese literature (e.g. Katō 1997, 256) when he wrote that 'modern Japanese writers – all of them, not just poets –

---

[67] The character *in* by itself can mean 'rhyme', 'elegance', or 'tone'. The character for *ritsu* can mean either 'law' or 'rhythm'; thus, the word *ritsubun* using the same characters has two possible meanings, namely 'legal provisions' and 'poetry'. *Inritsu* is divided into two categories: *in*, 'rhyme', and *ritsuin* (the two characters in reverse order) meaning 'rhythm'. *Inbun* is rhymed or metrical verse and *sanbun* (literally 'scattered letters') is prose.

[68] Holmes argues that a verse translation becomes a new poem in translation, however far removed its form is from the source, although it is now generally accepted that equivalence between any source text and its target, however contingent their linguistic and cultural background, is impossible (Holmes 1994, 23-33).

conceive of themselves as heirs to a universal tradition, not merely to their own' (Allen 1988, 28); in other words, the literary heritage of the outside world, with its multiplex ideological and stylistic practices, belongs as much to Japan as vice-versa. Since 1868, the main barrier to translating Shakespeare's prosody into Japanese has been linguistic rather than historical.

The recognition of a global tradition is of relevance to prosody for two reasons: prosody has always contributed significantly to the identity of the strong poet while globalisation became the enemy of poetic individualism in the 20th century.[69] In the Anglo-American tradition the free verse polemic of Ezra Pound during the first two decades of that century reacted against the oppressive musicality of Victorian prosody in order to advocate a means of expression that was – to begin with at least – wholly individualistic. In early modern Japan, experimenters in both free verse (e.g. Hagiwara Sakutarō) and traditional forms (Kawahigashi Hekigotō) asserted a new identity for Japanese poetry that was regarded by some as a denigration of the literary heritage.[70] Yet what the reformers sought to overcome was an archaic and sentimental image of ancient Japan that was easy prey to exploitation from within and outside; the detachment of the individual poet from the past was the first step towards recreating a tradition laid bare by the Meiji Restoration.

Writing at the end of the Second World War, Erich Auerbach described the relegation of traditionalism to the past in similar terms (Auerbach 1968, 552):

> The strata of societies and their different ways of life have become inextricably mingled. There are no longer even exotic peoples.

Replacing a previous age of mutual incomprehensibility and exoticism, one ironic effect of modernity was a growing recognition of influences and parallels between different cultures; as Auerbach's book illustrated, literary translation was essential to the new consciousness. Yet it would be naïve to assume that this process was without tension. The debates between the Meiji reformers and conservatives and among reformers themselves were heightened by the unanimity of their desire to protect and enhance their national literature; there is a similar tension in the history of Meiji translation.

---

[69] To adapt Harold Bloom's argument, prosody becomes one of the main tools in the poet's rejection of rhythmic influences, leading to the discovery of an authentic personal voice; this argument could be extended to the relationships between major *haiku* poets like Buson (mid 18th century) and Shiki (late 19th century).

[70] Meiji *tanka* poets like Hagiwara and Ishikawa Takuboku retained their belief in traditional qualities such as *yūgen* (the ideal of mystery and depth) but sought to locate those qualities in the present through the use of brilliant imagery, colloquial vocabulary and liberties with the fixed syllabic structure (5-7-5-7-7); this approach was sometimes associated with unconventional lifestyles. Metrical experimentation was considered more scandalous among the *haiku* poets, perhaps because of the greater brevity of the form (5-7-5). It should be noted, however, that there has always been allowance made in both traditions for slight deviations from the fixed forms.

Although translations came to occupy a sizeable proportion of Meiji literature, the range was eclectic and the tastes of readers selective (Keene 1984, Ch. 3 *passim*).[71] There was also a gap between the translators and educated readers, who knew the source texts firsthand, and the wider population, who read only the translations. Except for a few amateur translations, such as the influential *Shintaishi shō* (1882),[72] the prosody of Western poetry was largely imperceptible to a general readership but was more the concern of translators and the literary movements in which they were located. This dichotomy between reading as a passive process and translation as an active one is present from the early days of literary translation but is particularly apparent in the case of prosody, whose origins in the source are more hidden to the target reader than is metaphor.

Not all translators are effective prosodists. They may be unresponsive to the music of prosody and insensitive to the effect of their prosody on readers, which is no doubt why 'many writers have claimed that one must be a poet to translate poetry' (Connolly 1998, 175). Pound in particular objected to the mindless musicality of much Victorian poetry (including translation) (Apter 1984, 142). In Pound's view, the Victorian translators were primarily concerned with quantity (as a kind of mathematical exercise) rather than with accentuation and the rhetorical impact of their prosodies. The greater control of Pound and the free verse prosodists over their metrics allowed for a more responsible musicality.

The same was conversely true of the Meiji reformers. Japanese poetry had always been based on quantity but – especially in the case of *haiku* – the musical potential of both *haiku* and *tanka* had been ignored by poets writing in the fifty or so years leading up to the Meiji Restoration. The forms had never lacked a visual dimension but the experimentation with new modes of expression gave rise to a new awareness of the sounds of language, even to some extent releasing them from conventional frameworks of association. Translators such as Tsubouchi Shōyō worked against a background of heightened metrical awareness but also, as pioneers of Shakespeare translation, their initial encounters with the plays were very much through the prosody.[73] Fussell refers to both Coleridge and I.A. Richards when he argues that 'we read prosody before meaning' (Fussell 1979, 5), and the same was true in a yet more self-conscious way for the Meiji Shakespeareans. There was no equivalent to blank verse in Japanese

---

[71] Hara and Nishinaga (2000) reveal the scope of Japanese literary translations since the Meiji era from both ancient and a wide range of modern languages.

[72] *Shintaishi shō* included translations of verse by Shakespeare, Gray, and the Romantic and Victorian poets. The metre adopted was the conventional seven-five and so the prosodic differences were foregrounded more by the literalism of the translations and the form of the long poem. In his portrait of one of the three compilers, Toyama Masakazu, Moriya notes his strict adherence to Shakespeare's lineation (Moriya 1986, 10-11).

[73] Following the *Julius Caesar* adaptation in 1884, Tsubouchi became interested in the aspect of Shakespeare as a poetic dramatist before becoming embroiled in 'the hidden ideals' debate (*botsuri ronsō*) with Mori Ōgai in 1891.

poetry; an understanding of the structure of blank verse would (as it is now) have been a prerequisite to reading it. The term for blank verse is *kyōjakuon* (literally, 'strong-weak sound') but even this is just a coinage for a non-Japanese form. The one possible equivalent was *chōka*, the 'long' poem that was developed in the 7th and 8th centuries. Although its indeterminate length gave it the potential for a similar rhetorical scope to blank verse, it shared with *tanka* (literally 'short poems'), the seven-five metre based on quantity rather than stress accent.

In 1890, Tsubouchi founded a *rōdoku kai* at the Tokyo Senmon Gakkō (later to become Waseda University), which brought together staff and students to read aloud the plays of Japanese and Western playwrights, including some Shakespeare but mainly historical *kabuki* dramas (Powell 1998, 41). *Rōdoku* means 'recital' rather than 'reading'; the practice of reciting Shakespeare must have made the Japanese participants conscious of the sounds and structures of Shakespeare's verse – especially since opportunities to hear the verse spoken by native speakers were few and far between[74] – and thus of the differences between Shakespearean and *kabuki* prosody as well.

In the English-speaking world, the early period of Shakespeare's reception in Japan coincided with the height of prosody, almost as a discipline in its own right. This interest was typified by George Saintsbury's three-volume *History of English Prosody* (1906-10) but also found its way into editorial introductions to the contemporary editions of Shakespeare, many of which would have been available to Japanese scholars. A 1905 list of editions recommended to Japanese students includes the Cambridge, Eversley, Globe and New Variorum Shakespeares, all of which contain glosses on prosody.[75] An edition popular with Tsubouchi was Deighton's, with his extensive notes (Toyoda 1940, 166). By the time that Tsubouchi came to translate *A Midsummer Night's Dream*, it is likely that he would have read the first of Granville Barker's influential *Prefaces to Shakespeare*, published in 1914. In his introduction to his translation (180), he criticises Granville Barker's Orientalised production of *A Midsummer Night's Dream* (1914) for its departure from what he felt instinctively to be the playwright's original intent. He had seen photographs and a firsthand account of the production for which the first of the *Prefaces* were published as a handbook. Granville Barker himself regarded

---

[74] These would have been limited to university lectures by foreign professors and to amateur productions by foreign residents and occasional touring productions. Tsubouchi's initial exposure to Shakespeare was as a 16-year old pupil at the Aichi Foreign Language School in 1875 where a teacher named Maclaren impressed him with dramatic renditions of Hamlet's 'To be, or not to be' soliloquy. He later studied Shakespeare under James Summers, Professor of English Literature at Kaisei Gakkō from 1877 to 1883, where it is known that Summers required his students to memorise excerpts from *Hamlet* and *Henry VIII*. In May 1891, Tsubouchi saw English productions of *Hamlet* and *The Merchant of Venice* by the visiting Miln Company at the Yokohama Gaiety Theatre (Kobayashi 2006).

[75] The list, reprinted in Toyoda, was compiled by Asano Hyōkyō for his preface to his joint translation of *Hamlet* with Tozawa Koya (Toyoda 1940, 8-10). They were former students at Tokyo University of Lafcadio Hearn.

his task as a director and critic as being the recovery not of Shakespeare's original practices but of his meanings.[76] He did not want his actors to speak like Elizabethans but with the sense that Shakespeare intended, as (for example) the fairies in *A Midsummer Night's Dream*:

> The lilt, no less than the meaning, helps to express them to us as beings other than mortals, treading the air.[77]

Perhaps Tsubouchi was puzzled as to why an English director should want to orientalise what was so clearly 'an English play', but their difference of opinion also suggests a different approach to Shakespeare's subtexts.

Despite their differences, Granville Barker's idea touches on one of the central concerns of Tsubouchi's career, expressed in his first critical work *Shōsetsu shinzui* (1985) (Twine 1981), in which Tsubouchi argued for the reform of Japanese fiction by realistic characterisation, an argument which is relevant to prosody, since one of prosody's main functions in Shakespeare is to distinguish between characters, and the prosody of the *kabuki* dramas from which the plots of many of the novels that he criticised were taken is essentially ornamental. The essay became something of an exercise in comparative criticism as he wrote that 'Western poetry bears more resemblance to the novel than it does to Japanese verse, in that it strives to portray situations from life' (ibid., 7). This statement suggests one significant motivation for his eventual translation of Shakespeare's poetic dramas, and is amplified by this insight into the generic differences (ibid.):

> Where once a mere thirty-one syllables [the fixed quantity of classical poetry] sufficed to reveal the thoughts of our unsophisticated ancestors, today those of modern man cannot possibly be encompassed by so few.

If one were to synthesise the two statements, one might conclude that an appropriate strategy for translating Shakespeare would be to adopt a loosely metrical prose style, which is indeed what Tsubouchi attempted. The two poles that condition the balance of form and content in his style are what he called *jōmi honi* and *chōshi honi*; *honi* is the underlying intent of the writer (or translator), *jōmi* the emotional

---

[76] 'If we are to make Shakespeare our own again we must all be put to a little trouble about it. We must recapture as far as may be his lost meanings; and the sense of a phrase we *can* recapture, though instinctive emotional response to it may be a loss forever. The tunes that he writes to, the whole great art of his music-making, we can master. Actors can train their ears and tongues and can train our ears to it. We talk of lost arts. No art is ever lost while the means to it survive.' (Granville Barker 1993, 16)

[77] Granville Barker's attitude to the verse is that it is a significant component of the drama but no more than that (ibid., 35).

flavour and *chōshi* the rhythm. These poles affect narrative and characterisation but must be coordinated effectively with each other for the two to be distinguished; they can also correspond to tone and pace. Tsubouchi's experiments with metre – in particular his shift from the conventional syllabic of his early translations to his loosely metrical mature style – were largely for his own purposes but cannot be isolated from developments in contemporary Japanese poetics. His style is renowned for its musicality, which is the result of a productive tension between tone and pace (between individual and repeated sounds and the line).

A further reason for mixing poetry and prose was that it represented a closer approximation of the Shakespearean balance of dramatic event and dramatic structure. Earle Ernst (1984) argues that the concept of structure is much weaker in *kabuki* than in Western drama: in *kabuki*, drama occurs moment by moment, as typified by the *mie* (a stylised gesture accompanied by the clapping of wooden blocks occurring at the climactic moment of a scene or dance). According to Ernst, 'The pattern of line reading in *kabuki* is clearly derived from the actor's movement and dependent upon it' (Ernst 1984, 175), which implies that the text plays little role in shaping the dramatic structure. Even in the more literary *ayatsuri jōruri* (doll theatre), 'the vocal pattern ... arises out of a prolongation of the words rather than that of a melodic pattern imposed upon the words' (ibid.). Although some prosodic devices in *jōruri* texts do have a structural function, these plays never attempt even the loose, unclassical structures of Shakespearean drama.[78]

Tsubouchi inevitably refers to the *kabuki* idiom when he uses *shichigo chō* (7-5 syllabic meter) in his translations, and it is that tendency for reference rather than strict imitation of Japanese convention that has characterised the Japanisation (including translation) of Shakespeare. Japanese translations of Shakespeare were more likely to occupy that dramatic space between reality and unreality if they are developed within their own distinctive idiom, which in prosodic terms has generally meant the mixing of poetry and prose.[79] Tsubouchi's greatest influence from Japanese drama was the *jōruri* and *kabuki* playwright Chikamatsu Monzaemon (1653-1724), regarded as the most literary of the classical playwrights; Tsubouchi was not alone in calling him 'the Shakespeare of Japan'.[80] According to Shively, Chikamatsu's richly associative style was derived from his experience of composing *haiku* sequences (*haikai no renga*) (Shively 1953, 13). Yet such experience is by and large lacking among Japanese translators of

---

[78] These are typically wordplays rather than metrical rhythms.

[79] The concept is central to *nō* and *kabuki* aesthetics and refers to a tension between stylised and realistic elements of performance. It could be applied in Shakespeare translation to a tension between patterned and unpatterned language.

[80] Andrew Gerstle develops the comparison, writing that 'If I were to draw out one major theme common to both, it is that of placing individuals in crises which lead to tragic situations in which they must ponder private interests and public responsibility, and eventually act. Both question over and again the meaning of human dignity and the notion of virtue.' (Gerstle 1996, 69-70)

Shakespeare, and the *haiku* is too subtle a form to correspond with the larger, uneven scale of Shakespearean drama.[81] *Haiku* works well as a medium between general and individual circumstance but is insufficient for grander rhetorical modulations. To paraphrase Suzuki Gorō, a *haiku* can evoke context through the specificity of a moment, which may be thought similar in effect to dramatic generalisation in Shakespearean tragedy (Suzuki 1999, 43). Yet it is an isolated, poetic moment rather than one embedded in a narrative structure.

COLLOQUIALISATION IN POETRY AND PROSE

It is significant that the reforming movements which the development of a prosody of translation paralleled devolved mainly on issues of spoken and written communication, although *kabuki* was of course excluded from the debate as being performance-centred. Linguistic contact with the outside world brought inevitable adjustments to the ways in which Japanese people communicated with each other (Tomasi 1999). The *genbun icchi* movement to integrate the colloquial and literary styles (initiated in the 1870s but not fully completed until the post-1945 reforms to the Japanese writing system) gave translators such as Tsubouchi a powerful precedent to translate Shakespeare in a colloquial style and to some extent retell the story of Shakespeare's own stylistic education. For just as the Meiji rhetoricians acquired from Shakespeare something of the meaning of rhetoric as the art of speech, so too was Shakespeare's native language enriched by the classical rhetoric learned at Stratford Grammar School (Joseph 1947, 8-13). As the son of a *samurai*, Tsubouchi himself was a product of a Confucianist education and was wary of excessive colloquialism, although the battle was largely over by the time that he produced his semi-colloquial translation of *Hamlet* in 1911.[82] His experience as a director may also have taught him the value of rhetoric to drama: that a classical style could enhance the rhetorical force of colloquial speech and, conversely, the colloquial could be used to communicate things ancient to a modern audience (Rycroft 1999, 196-97).

The main target of the *genbun icchi* movement was prose; poetry had its own rules and reformers. Yet the invention of a new poetic form, the *shintaishi* or 'new-style

---

[81] Of the four translators discussed in this thesis Tsubouchi and Odashima had experience as poets. Odashima wrote free verse rather than *haiku*; his use of euphony and wordplay is itself reminiscent of Chikamatsu's style. Tsubouchi wrote a considerable number of *haiku* in later life, although he had long had experience of writing in syllabic meter, for example in his initial translation of *Julius Caesar* (1884).

[82] Tsubouchi's education was enriched by his reading of Edo *gesaku* fiction, which was embued with Confucianist values and written mainly in a literary style that had changed little since the Heian era.

poems', with the publication of *Shintaishi shō* in 1882 can be described as an attempt to mix the old with the new in the way that *genbun icchi* intended. The book contained translations of poetry written in English by three junior professors at the Kaisei Gakkō, all of them known to Tsubouchi. These were made in conventional seven-five syllabic; what was innovative about them was 'the use of modern language and the direct and unaffected expression of the poet's feelings' (Keene 1999, 197). In addition to fourteen translations, the collection contained five original *shintaishi*. Yatabe Ryōkichi prefaced his poem 'Sentiments on Visiting the Great Buddha at Kamakura' as follows:

> In general, the peoples of the entire globe, and not only the Western countries, use the language of ordinary speech when they compose poetry. That is why they are all able to express easily and directly what they feel in their hearts. The same was true of Japan in remote antiquity, but poets of recent times use Chinese vocabulary when they compose *kanshi* [poems derived from classical Chinese] and archaisms when they compose *waka* [poems of thirty-one syllables]. They avoid the language of daily life as vulgar. How could this but be a misconception?[83]

With a few exceptions, the attempt was a poetic failure but was undoubtedly significant for the development of Shakespeare translation in reviving the concept of a form which was nearer in scope to Shakespearean verse, the long poem. Moreover with its translations of three Shakespeare soliloquies, *Shintaishi shō* was closely connected with early Shakespeare scholarship in Japan (Toyoda 1940, 92-96)[84] in that it helped to establish both the tradition of the scholar-translator of Shakespeare and Shakespeare's reputation as a modern.

Despite the popularity of *shintaishi* well into the 20th century, the form's retention of traditional metre ultimately proved too great a restraint on poets seeking their *rhythme personnel*, and in the 1920s gave way to the free verse and prose poetry of writers such as Hagiwara Sakutarō (1886-1942). The inspiration came from another translation: by Ueda Bin (1874-1916) of French Symbolist poetry under the title *Kaichō on* ('Sound of the Tide') and published in 1905. The musicality of those poets (both in their originals and in translation) echoed the calls of Meiji reformers for more music and indeed the connections between prosody and personal rhythm became something of an obsession through to the 1920s. 'Rhythmic obsession' has never been a great concern of Shakespeare translators, who are governed by a text other than their own, but the concept of individual styles or voices among writers in non-traditional genres (including in Shakespeare translation) is certainly relevant. In this sense, the strict adherence to syllabic metre was yet another constraint – together with those imposed by the source –

---

[83] Quoted in Keene (199, 196-97) (Yamamiya 1951, 40).
[84] In particular, the so-called 'rival translations' (*kyōyaku*) of Hamlet's fourth soliloquoy by the three translators promoted interest in the character of Hamlet and in that speech in particular, as well as the possibility of writing blank verse in Japanese.

on translators' freedom to recreate Shakespeare in their own image.

The loss of syllabic metre in the new poetry meant the loss of a framework in which musicality could be understood. Musicality risked becoming a meaningless end in itself and was gradually supplanted by visuality (i.e. by the primacy of word pictures as the vehicle of metaphor) from the late Meiji Era onwards (Shiffert and Sawa 1972, 19-20). The visible could be shared by everyone; visuality accommodated democratic urges more easily in that visual images – as communicated for example to the live audience of a Shakespeare production – could be comprehended among large groups of people. Of course, the danger of visuality is that the personal becomes commonplace. The visual style of Fukuda's 1950s productions, in which language was subordinated to a shared theatrical experience, served its purpose in popularising Shakespeare but it was a single vision.[85] The musicality of Odashima's translations two decades later sought a renewed respect for the individual voice.

READING PROSODY

The demonstration of historical parallels between Shakespeare translation and other movements within and outside Japan can easily distort the mechanics of the prosodies involved (the ways of reading them) when in fact the prosodies of both English and Japanese poetry have seldom been far from controversy: 'no two people are going to hear verse in exactly the same way' (Hobsbaum 1996, 13). The basic structures of both blank verse and *shichigo chō* are straightforward enough, and occasional excess or missing syllables are recognised as exceptions that prove the rule. What are harder to ascertain are the rhythmic structures that occur in the line or syllabic group and, in the case of Japanese poetry, the role of pitch accent.[86]

With both blank verse and *shichigo chō*, one should be able to read the rhythms in at least one of three ways. The first of these is the strictly semantic approach which always relates rhythm to content, in particular syntax and lexis. Although there is some phonological support for this approach (for example, relating stress contours to syntactic logic), it depends on a strict integrity of form and content which can not necessarily be proven and is not necessarily to be welcomed. In the dramatic context, a discrepancy between rhythm and line might well indicate a subtext of uncertainty

---

[85] Fukuda's realism as a director and translator, the importance that he gave to narrative structure and reluctance to indulge in poetic effects all contributed to a tightly controlled dramatic image.

[86] The main difference between English and Japanese accentuation is that English is based on stress and Japanese on modulations in pitch; unlike the tones in spoken Chinese, pitch changes seldom determine meaning in Japanese. Among traditional prosodies, blank verse is regarded as the closest approximation to the typical accentual patterns of everyday speech. The relevance of pitch accent to traditional Japanese poetry is more ambiguous due to the predominance of syllabic metre.

or deception. The second way, the non-semantic approach, is prescriptive, referring to historical models and treating line and rhythm as separate entities. This allows for greater musicality on the one hand, the rhythms supporting the line almost (one might say) like the sound of *shamisen* accompanying the actor's voice in a *kabuki* performance. On the other hand it inevitably preempts the possibility of a dramatic integration of rhythm and line. For these reasons, I prefer to adopt the third way, one that is semantic or non-semantic depending on circumstance and based on the two key prosodic features of repetition and periodicity. Although the iambic pentameter is of sufficient length to establish the iamb as a repetitive device, the *shichigo chō* rhythm occurs over a period of usually five lines and repetitivity is established more out of the reader's experience of having read other examples of the metre.[87]

The problem of analysing the nebulous mix of prose and loosely syllabic metre that constitutes the bulk of Shakespeare translation into Japanese is precisely this: that it combines poetic and phonological prosody when both are dogged by uncertainty. The basic unit of Japanese phonology is the pitch accent, for which there are few clear rules. Some authority can be gained from reference to native speakers and to an accent dictionary but accentuation will always be affected by sentence structure, and there also remain considerable dialectal and individual differences between the typical accentual patterns of native speakers.[88]

The final point of reference is the personal, that is to say one's own interpretation. Using these three points of reference, it should be possible within phrases of at least five (preferably seven) syllables and between smaller groups of three or four syllables to relate meaning to accentual patterns and thus by the regular practice of identifying those patterns develop a way of reading the translations' prosody. This way of reading, it should be emphasised, can only be learnt with practice, which is why it is demonstrated at some length in the second half of this chapter and the first part of the next. Moreover, it has little precedent in studies either of Shakespeare translation in Japan or of Japanese poetry, except for a few observations about the rhythmicality of selected translations (e.g. Niki 1984).[89]

One analogy can be made with Japanese prose fiction. 20th century novelists such as Tanizaki and Mishima frequently intersperse non-metrical phrasing with defined syllabic groupings, although the nature of the genre makes these rhythms difficult to

---

[87] The most basic unit of periodicity is the mora which is used in Japanese phonology to distinguish between monosyllables (e.g. *o*) and long (*oo*) and double vowels (*ou*). In syllabic metres periodicity is generally recognised in terms of the space in time occupied by one or more sounds; in accentual metres it is recognised in terms of longer, artificial structures.

[88] The dictionary I have consulted has been *Shin Meikai kokugo jiten*, Tokyo: Sanseidō, 1987.

[89] Niki either refers quite generally to the rhythmicality of a translator's translating style and sometimes gives specific examples (Niki 1984, 54). Her analysis of the latter ignores pitch accent and focuses on other, more literary features that may contribute to sound patterning, e.g. syllabic metre and rhyme. More recently, Kawasaki (2010) has made a study of how the rhythms of spoken Japanese can be organised to correspond with the iambic pentameter.

identify with precision, even though they might be quite evident to the individual reader. As for poetry, discussions of pitch accent are largely absent from writings on the prosody of traditional forms. Modern prosodists (e.g. Matsubayashi 1996) have focussed on quantity, in particular the positioning of natural breaks or caesuras within and between lines, and also the musicality of sound combinations. Both these features can be affected by accentuation since a single pitch accent may affect the rhythmic and musical structure of a given phrase. Yet perhaps aware of the differences of their own accentuation from that of other speakers, the prosodists have limited themselves to strictly literary features.[90] One exception would be Yuyama who drew a sharp distinction between rhythm and stress in English poetry and the musicality and emotional structures specific to Japanese poetics, in particular the accentuation of external and internal syllabic boundaries (Yuyama 1954, 250-432 *passim*). Relevant also is Sakuma, who explored the analogy between pitch accent and music, for example with *fushi* (melody in traditional Japanese chanting) (Sakuma 1968, 65-98). He insists, however, on the difference between accent as an inherent characteristic and intonation as an emotive technique.

Accentuation is learnt in childhood, is usually an instinctive process, one that is taken for granted. So too is stress accent in English phonology; but it becomes a consciously literary device when rendered as metre. Japanese syllabic metre is derived from sentence structure but becomes literary when groups of syllables are separated from each other at fixed intervals. It might be productive, therefore, to look at examples of how pitch accent and syllabic metre interact with each other. Matsubayashi is not exceptional when he insists that '*tanka* and *haiku* have to be read with a smooth accentuation' (Matsubayashi 1996, 27), in other words one that minimises the effect of pitch accents,[91] but this way of reading is somewhat removed from the cut and thrust of a Japanese production of a Shakespeare play where intonation is a basic tool in the actor's interpretation of the lines.[92] Where syllabic metre is absent or redundant, pitch accents may help actors to identify key words and points of emphasis and thus audiences to hear likewise. Accentuation may become an essential means of establishing patterns which can be read semantically or non-semantically.

The *haiku* scholar R.H. Blyth wrote of the Japanese language that 'there is simply ceaseless becoming' (Blyth 1981, 318), which could equally describe the periodic and

---

[90] Accentuation has become standardised to some extent by the acceptance of the Tokyo dialect as the national vernacular in the post-war era (Higurashi 1983), although local dialects are still dynamic and it is dialectal differences more than anything else which make different accents noticeable in daily life (Vance 1987, 107). Dialect is the most obvious means available to Shakespeare translators for registering social differences between groups of characters.

[91] In *kukai* (*haiku* readings) a reader (*yomite*) is appointed to recite poems selected by participants and will read the poems clearly with due regard to syllabic rhythm and accentuation.

[92] Linguists usually treat intonation separately from accent as varying according to speaker, although some intonational patterns are used by all speakers, for example the rising pitch in questions.

repetitive nature of Japanese pitch accentuation, namely its tendency for successive rather than alternate rhythm (Kubozono 1993, 4). A successive rhythm comprises a stretch of unaccented syllables leading to an accented one; alternate rhythms comprise more equal periods of accented and unaccented syllables. Kubozono goes on to argue that alternate rhythm is also present in Japanese, and that successive and alternate rhythms 'are not mutually exclusive, as has traditionally been assumed, but can coexist in a single phonological system as independent rhythmic principles' (ibid.). Moreover, Haraguchi (1991) proposed that the usual positioning of accents in nouns in Tokyo dialect gives it an accentual system that is strikingly similar to stress accentuation in English, although the accentual patterns would still not be consistent enough for the translator to be able to reproduce iambic rhythm.

Successivity helps to determine the accentuation of a given phrase but it can also be considered a poetic device in itself. Indeed, my analysis posits successivity as the major prosodic alternative to *shichigo chō* in making sense of the four translations. The syllabic metre can never be wholly ignored but there is a danger of grafting the prosodies too deeply to tradition as there is more generally of seeing 'Shakespeare in Japan' solely in terms of traditional drama. A reading that denies accent (possibly replacing it with a stylised syllabification) risks returning the texts to the melodramatic *shinpa* style in which they were produced at the beginning of the 20th century.

Although one would always hope to construct a methodology for reading the prosody of these translations, problems of authority and consistency still remain and these problems begin with the translations themselves. When Ōyama Toshikazu remarks that 'even in prose, there is a tendency to follow the [seven-five] rhythm pattern, especially when one's feelings are excited' (Ōyama 1975, 32), he is alerting the reader not only to the presence of seven-five in Japanese translations of Shakespeare but also to two possible pitfalls, first that translators may use seven-five without regard to an overall stylistic strategy and secondly that they may use it to describe their own response to a line or passage rather than as a framework for what they understand the characters concerned to be saying. Seven-five may well be too deeply embedded in the Japanese consciousness for translators to be able to take an objective view in the same way that for many native English speakers iambic rhythm is somehow representative of all poetic rhythm. There is one element, however, that does connect seven-five with accent, which is the phrase. As Backhouse notes, 'within a single phrase, the basic accentual contours of individual words are smoothed into a single contour' (Backhouse 1993, 35). It is rare for a given phrase to contain more than one accent; the phrase will also be the basic unit of the syllabic analyses in Chapter Three.

ODASHIMA AND POETIC DRAMA

It is a challenge for any translator (and translation critic) to stretch their minds beyond their subjective responses and even more so in the matter of rhythm. The poetry translator Jackson Matthews touches on the problem of subjectivity when he argues that (Matthews 1996, 70)

> rhythm is the one feature of a foreign language that we can probably never learn to hear purely; rhythm and the meaning of rhythm lie too deep in us.

The translator's and the critic's solution is to contrast their knowledge of their own prosody with as much material as they can gather on the prosody of the source language and writer they are dealing with.[93] In this sense, the post-war translators have been at a disadvantage to the pre-war ones as prosody declined as a subject in English literary criticism and also in significance to Japanese poetry. One exception – and perhaps one of the causes of this trend – is the influence of T.S. Eliot in the early post-war years.

Odashima's translations were born in an atmosphere of social change and confusion in which patterns of emotionally-charged behaviour came tantalisingly close to the patterning of dramatic rhetoric.[94] Within the Shakespearean canon *A Midsummer Night's Dream* is renowned as a play in which 'strongly patterned language tends to occur in emotional contexts' (Willcock 1954, 16), a factor that would surely have appealed to audiences during this period of social upheaval.[95] The patterned language serves a particular purpose of dramatising and eventually resolving the emotional chaos of the play. In appreciating and to some extent appropriating Shakespeare's rhetoric in translation, Japanese audiences may have found a way out of their own upheavals based on the privilege that is allowed every new translation such as Odashima's, a rereading of the subtexts. The impetus for social change comes from a rereading of the subtexts. An awareness of subtexts opens up a broader range of interpretive possibilities, and is

---

[93] In her essay on translation criticism, Katharina Reiss makes the point that 'The real debate can only be on whether versions in a target language should or should not be considered translations if they serve a particular purpose, especially a purpose *not* addressed by the original.' (Reiss 2000, 90) This monograph aims to show that in adjusting their translations to the prosody of the source text, the translators do indeed seek to address a similar rhetorical purpose, and can be evaluated as such.

[94] See Gallimore (1999, 326-28) for a brief account of the relationship of the underground theatre to political protest during the late 1960s.

[95] This was also a feature observed at the time of the play's first production in Japanese by the Tsukiji Shōgekijō in 1928. The left-wing playwright Kubo Sakae wrote in the company's journal that 'Theseus and Hippolyta, Lysander and Demetrius are no more than mechanical puppets, Hermia and Helena mere toys.' (Sakae 1928)

thus more open to debate than surface meaning. It is also the natural habitat of prosody, whose relationship to the line is far from stable. The greater openness to Shakespeare's subtexts from the late 1960s onwards is indicated by the greater range of productions that emerged on the Japanese stage.

Odashima's prosody, characterised by its emotive euphony and subversive wordplay, has its roots in the early post-war translations of T.S. Eliot and in the Arechi group.[96] Arechi was the first important post-war group of poets, flourishing between 1947 and the early 1950s, and it took its name from Eliot's long poem *The Waste Land* (1922), or *arechi* in Japanese. The Arechi poets insisted on 'the internal nature of poetry, as opposed to its possible uses or misuses' (Keene 1999, 370) and looked for inspiration from younger English poets such as W.H. Auden and Cecil Day Lewis. Eliot's concept of the auditory imagination was significant in Japan as connecting with a strand from a previous generation of Japanese poetry, notably through Ueda Bin's translations of the French Symbolists published in 1905. (Eliot himself was influenced by many of the poets Ueda translated, such as Mallarmé and Verlaine). The Arechi poets looked with horror on the physical and spiritual wasteland of their defeated country and expressed their hopes for salvation in 'the loneliness of sounds' (Kuramochi 1997, 130). Like some of the Arechi poets themselves, the immediate generation of Shakespeareans were more interested in Eliot's ideology than his style. As a student at Tokyo University in the late 1940s, Odashima read both Eliot and the Arechi poets and even wrote some poetry of his own in the Arechi style, but by the time he started translating Shakespeare at the end of the 1960s the debt had become purely stylistic.[97]

Odashima has been influenced by other modern English playwrights as well, including the verse dramatist Christopher Fry, but it was the legacy of Eliot as a poet and critic who also wrote poetic drama that provided the strongest model of how Shakespearean drama might sound poetic in Japanese translation.[98] Eliot's statement of 1936 sets the agenda (Eliot 1936, 994):

> It is fatal for a poet trying to write a play, to hope to make up for defects in the movement of the play by bursts of poetry which do not help the action. But underneath the action, which should be perfectly intelligible, there should be a musical pattern which intensifies our excitement by reinforcing it with a feeling from a deeper and less articulate level. Everybody knows that there are things that can be said in music that cannot be said in speech. And there are things which can be said in poetic drama that cannot be said in either music or in ordinary speech.

---

[96] Although Eliot was known in Japan in the 1930s, the first full translation of his poetry did not appear until 1946.

[97] In an interview with me (20.10.99), he even remarked that 'Shakespeare is good for your health but Eliot makes me sick!'

[98] Other dramatic influences are George Bernard Shaw, Tom Stoppard and Arnold Wesker (Odashima 1995).

The translation into Japanese of such a lyrical play as *A Midsummer Night's Dream* is necessarily about poetic drama. If the four translations are seen to engage, as Raffel believes literary translation should do, 'with the passionately held inner convictions of men and women' (Raffel 1989, 53), then a good part of that engagement is expressed through what happens to the prosody: to the shapes, sounds and rhythms that form the material of dramatic voices. The analysis that follows is intended to demonstrate that engagement, which should also be apparent from the historical relationship of the four prosodies to Japanese tradition.

SETTING THE PACE: THE FIRST SIX LINES OF THE PLAY

The influence of Shakespearean prosody is sought most obviously in lineation but felt most deeply in the rhythms established at the beginning of the play. Thus, a critical comparison of the four translations of the first six lines of the play suggests not only stylistic differences between them but also information as to how the four translations might progress. In the source, the metre is blank verse, and the potential for the metre to be subverted is established in the very first foot. Theseus is speaking to Hippolyta (2.1.1-6):

> Now, fair Hippolyta, our nuptial hour
> Draws on apace; four happy days bring in
> Another moon: but O, methinks, how slow
> This old moon wanes! She lingers my desires,
> Like to a step-dame or a dowager
> Long withering out a young man's revenue.

A strictly iambic reading gives stress to the following monosyllabic words: 'fair', 'hour', 'on', 'days', 'in', 'moon', 'O', 'slow', 'old', 'wanes', 'or', 'out' and 'young'.[99] Three other iambs fall on syllables which though belonging to words of more than one syllable also make sense by themselves: '-pace', '-thinks' and 'step-'. A reading that allows for the occasional replacement of iambic with spondaic or trochaic rhythm might put additional stresses on four more words: 'now', 'draws', 'moon' (l. 4), 'like' and 'long'. This reading raises a skeleton of words that refer, like the passage itself, to the movement of time. The proximity of 'moon' and *O* prefigures its feminisation in line 4 and throughout the play. Another prefiguration is suggested in the proximity of 'old' to 'wanes' against 'out' to 'young'. Subversion of authority is one theme of the play and one that is eventually achieved in the marriage of Hermia to Lysander against her father's wishes. It is echoed here in Theseus' simile: the more that the young man's desires are frustrated ('revenue

---

[99] The first foot of line 5 ('Like to') would probably be read as a trochee rather than an iamb.

withered'), the greater they will grow. Theseus' figure of desire maps the moonlit adventures of the lovers in Act 3. The less iambic reading resists the conventional rhythm, suggesting a dynamic relationship between Theseus and the dominant image of waxing and waning. For example, a heavy stress on 'Now' could support an illusion that Theseus is master not only of Hippolyta and his court but also, dramatically, of time itself. 'Draws' and 'long' might refer to the drawing of swords in his war against the Amazons and so remind Hippolyta of his authority over her.

The openness of the metre to at least two different interpretations – one less assertive but experiential, the other more authoritarian – paves the way to a similar diversity of response in translation. Tsubouchi's version is in prose but quite clearly rhythmical (191).[100] It should be noted of both the Tsubouchi quotation and those that follow how often pitch accents define the breaks made by punctuation and between phrases (e.g. *kekkon no hi wa* and *mou ma mo nai*), whether these are metrical or not.

```
      1       2       1        /           /1        1
Nau, Hiporita dono, washira no kekkon no hi wa mou ma mo nai.
        3  /  /    1        4    2   1  1   2   /    2
Ureshii hi ga yokka tateba, atarashii tsuki ga kuru. Aa, shikashi, kono furui
        3   1    2          2           2             /
tsukime wa, dou yara kakeru no ga noroi you da. Nasanu naka no hahaoya ya
      /           /           /        2            / 2
koushitsu ga, shinabiru made, isan wo wakai mono ni yuzurioshimu you ni,
         /       /    2          /1
machikanete iru kokoro wo jirase oru.
```

This version contains a possible twenty-two pitch accents compared with a possible thirty-eight stress accents in the source, although the fifteen rising tones create a slighter rhythmic modulation. The accents come in the following words (in their semantic equivalents): 'now', 'Hippolyta', 'our', 'already' (negated as 'no longer'), 'not', 'happy', 'elapse', 'new', 'moon', 'come', 'O', 'but', 'old', 'moon', 'how', 'wane', 'slow', 'unrelated' (literally 'unrelated mother' or 'step-dame'), 'young', 'to be stingey', 'heart' and 'to be' (in 'burn'). Ten of these items coincide with the source, with eight of the items referring in some way to time. Unlike the source, where the idea of time is figured outside and beyond the text, the translation does contain just one word that can literally mean 'time'. The word *ma* towards the end of the first sentence refers more to time in its spatial dimension as interval, and it is used here in the phrase *ma mo nai*, meaning 'there's no time left'. The phrase's urgency is matched by its position at the end of a succession of five monosyllabic and two bisyllabic words: *no hi wa mou ma mo nai*, the last four being closely alliterated. The accent in *nai* ('not') at the end of the first sentence relates

---

[100] Throughout this monograph, the quotations from the four translations are cited with the relevant page number only.

primarily to *ma* but, as with the explicit mention of time in the target text, can be said to introduce a negative tone that is only implicit in the source (where negatives are absent). However, the accents on *atarashii* and *furui* ('new' and 'old') support an antithesis that is at least half present in the metric of the source: the stresses on *-no* (in *another*, referring to the new moon) and on *old* fall in the same first iamb of the consecutive second and third lines.

Considered as a whole, Theseus' speech is constructed around the iamb and spondee in line 4: 'This old / moon wanes!' The spondee (which is reinforced by a caesura at the end of the sentence) halts the momentum created by enjambement at the end of each of the first three lines and thus signals Theseus' discontent that his desire cannot be more quickly fulfilled. It is a kind of cadence: a rise in excitement broken by Theseus' mental realisation (*methinks*) that he must wait, and then frustration with the moon deflected onto female figures, the 'step-dame' and 'dowager'. Ten of the twenty-two pitch-accents in the translation are amassed in the second third of the speech and a further five in the second half of the first line. The concentration of accent coincides with Theseus' tension as the harbinger of desire admits the old moon of present reality.

Despite the tendency for Tsubouchi to generate the greatest number of accents, Fukuda's version of the speech in this instance is slightly longer than the Tsubouchi translation (11):

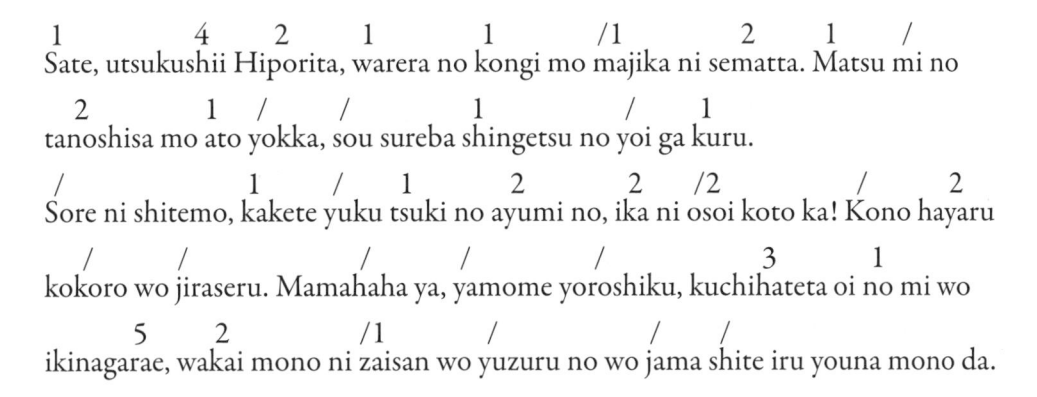

```
       1           4    2    1       1     /1         2        1         /
Sate, utsukushii Hiporita, warera no kongi mo majika ni sematta. Matsu mi no
         2         1   /        /         1         /       1
tanoshisa mo ato yokka, sou sureba shingetsu no yoi ga kuru.
  /                 1    /  1           2      2   /2           2
Sore ni shitemo, kakete yuku tsuki no ayumi no, ika ni osoi koto ka! Kono hayaru
      /          /          /          /       /          3    1
kokoro wo jiraseru. Mamahaha ya, yamome yoroshiku, kuchihateta oi no mi wo
         5    2        /1        /              /    /
ikinagarae, wakai mono ni zaisan wo yuzuru no wo jama shite iru youna mono da.
```

Fukuda's translation contains 141 syllables against Tsubouchi's 133 and twenty-three accents against Tsubouchi's twenty-two. Accent distribution is similar as well, being concentrated in the first half of the speech in both cases, especially in their translations of the central phrase 'how slow this old moon wanes'. With Fukuda, the accents come in the following semantic items: 'now', 'beautiful', 'Hippolyta', 'our', 'wedding', 'close', 'approached', 'wait', 'pleasure', 'after', 'new moon', 'come', 'waning', 'moon', 'pace', 'how', 'slow', 'impetuous', 'heart', 'decayed', 'aged', 'linger', 'young' and 'inheritance'.

A comparison with Tsubouchi shows their mutual acknowledgement of the centrality of time to the passage. Their interpretations start to differ in at least two aspects, which, since they affect pace, may also be considered aspects of rhythm. The first concerns the use of long vowels. Where Fukuda uses seven, Tsubouchi uses twelve, two of which come at the start of sentences and are thus given special prominence: *nau* and *aa*. These open sounds decelerate the speech's pace when it has hardly begun and support an interpretation of Theseus as being dreamy and preoccupied, in love. Fukuda's rendition of the same is *sate* and then *sore ni shite mo*. Both phrases generate pace through their connective function, and contain the fricative *t-* which is heard still more emphatically between the two in *sematta*.

The rapid pace supports an interpretation of Theseus as being in control of his emotions, perhaps about to make a comment (which he does). The other aspect relates to the speech's organisation. Apart from some slight differences of phrasing, Fukuda follows Tsubouchi in his arrangement of phrases and sentences over the first section. In the final sentence, Fukuda opts for an alternative arrangement, keeping the phrase 'She lingers my desires' in place at the beginning by translating it as a whole sentence, whereas Tsubouchi, following Japanese sentence structure, has to hold back his verb *jirase oru* (literally 'irritate') until the end. Tsubouchi's translation is integrated, Fukuda's tense. Fukuda's juxtaposes a short sentence against a longer one so as to produce a tension that is lacking in Tsubouchi but at one with the sense of urgency that has already been generated.[101]

The comparison of Tsubouchi and Fukuda shows how rhythm can be experienced both as pitch accent and as a structural feature. The latter has a further dimension in the use of Japanese syllabic metre in the translations, which will be discussed in the next chapter. From Odashima (8) and Matsuoka (9) we can expect something different:

ODASHIMA

/   3   4   2   /   /   2
Tokorode, utsukushii Hiporita, wareware no konrei no toki mo

/1   2   3   1 /   2
majika ni sematta. Tanoshii hibi wo ato yokka sugoseba

1   /   1   1   1   4   2
shingetsu no yoi to naru. Daga nanto modokashii koto ka,

/   2   2   1   /   /   /   /
kono furui tsuki no kakete iku no ga. Watashi no nozomi wo nakanaka

/   4   /   / 3   2   1
kanaesasete wa kurenu, tsugihaha ya miboujin ga itsumade mo

/   5   /   /   /1   4
ikinagaraete wakamono ni yuzurubeki zaisan wo kuchisaseru you ni.

MATSUOKA

1   4   2   /   /   2
Saa, utsukushii Hiporita, watashitachi no konrei no toki mo

---

[101] It is also striking how the vowels and dipthongs in Tsubouchi (starting with *Nau*) give it an expansive feel that is lacking in Fukuda's more consonant-bound version.

```
  /   3     /      1           1
chikazuita. Shiawasena hibi ga yokka tateba
  1         1  1    2     2       2
shingetsu da. Daga, aa, furui tsuki ga kakeru no ga
  1   /      2          2    /    /      1       2
nanto osoku omoeru koto ka! Tsuki wa watashi no yokubou ni matta wo kakeru.
  /    /   3       2       4
Marude tsugihaha ya miboujin ga nagaikishi
   2   3      /    /1      /
wakai atotsugi ni yuzuru zaisan wo suriherasu you na mono da.
```

Once again, the translations differ from expectations in being longer than the earlier ones, Odashima's having 156 syllables and Matsuoka's 142.[102] The number of accents is also higher, Odashima with twenty-five and Matsuoka with twenty-four (although all four are agreed in giving the clear majority of accents to the first part). In Odashima, the accents fall on the following semantic items: 'now', 'beautiful', 'Hippolyta', 'time', 'near', 'approached', 'enjoyable', 'after', 'exceed', 'new moon', 'become', 'but', 'what', 'irritating', 'thing', 'old', 'moon', 'run', 'cause' satisfaction ('satisfy'), 'mother', 'widow', 'forever', 'live long', 'inheritance' and 'cause to decay'; in Matsuoka, 'well', 'beautiful', 'Hippolyta', 'time', 'approached', 'days', 'elapse', 'new moon', 'but', 'oh', 'old', 'moon', 'wane', 'how', 'be thought', 'thing', 'moon', 'waited', 'suspend', 'mother', 'widow', 'live long', 'young', 'heir' and 'inheritance'.

The significant difference is the adoption of a free verse line. The free verse line does not necessarily break the speech up into a larger number of shorter units as when distinguishing between English prose and verse. Taking each unit as coming after every new punctuation mark, the prose translations of Tsubouchi and Fukuda comprise thirteen units each. Including the breaks that come at the end of each line as well, Odashima comprises twelve units and Matsuoka thirteen. Nor does the use of free verse necessarily affect the accentuation, even if it does resemble the versification of the source and is easier for actors and readers to read. In fact, it opens up an avenue of interpretation that is lacking in the older prose translations, offering a clearer indication as to how translators think words should be grouped and emphases made.

The Shakespearean iambic pentameter has an internal dynamic that suggests associations between its components in a way that differs from other forms. These associations may be elaborated through metaphor, paronamasia and other phonic effects but a more applicable tendency is for the movement of one line into the next to shift the centre of the line's gravity into the second half, usually on the fourth iamb. Although the pattern is often varied by Shakespeare, the word in which the line's momentum reaches its climax is often the key word of the line, the word that conveys the gist of

---

[102] Like Fukuda, they both elaborate on the last sentence in order to make a plausible rendition of that complex image.

the line. The lines of Odashima and Matsuoka can hardly be compared to the iambic pentameter in formal terms, since they always vary in length and in accent distribution, but the variation from line to line is not so great that a basic pattern of accumulating momentum and release cannot be observed. The mere organisation of the words into a succession of lines forces a movement between one line and the next. Applied to the two passages, the following series of words can be identified as key words in their lines:

ODASHIMA: 1. konrei ('wedding'); 2. yokka ('four days'); 3. modokashii ('irritating'); 4. nozomi ('desire'); 5. miboujin ('widow'); 6. zaisan ('inheritance')

MATSUOKA: 1. konrei; 2. yokka; 3. kakeru ('wane'); 4. matta ('waited'); 5. miboujin; 6. suriherasu ('wear away')

  The identification of key words in Shakespearean blank verse is of course made easier by the iambic structure whereas only two out of the twelve lines from the two translations are totally beyond question. Yet, they give a clearer outline than that indicated by accent as to how the speech might progress in translation: in Odashima's version, the subject moves from the wedding to money, and in Matsuoka from the wedding to a verb meaning 'deterioration'.
  The sense of movement is created by the break at the end of the line, which also contributes to the overall pace of the speech. The level of tension in that break depends, as in Shakespeare, on the relationship between consecutive lines. There are three types of relationship: the break may concur with the closing of a sentence, or with the closing of some clearly defined phrase, or there may be no break at all in the actual sentence (enjambement). In Odashima, the sixth line is of the first type, the second and third lines of the second type, and the remaining three lines are examples of enjambement. In Matsuoka, the fourth and sixth lines are of the first type, the second of the second type and the other three are enjambement.
  The types of break exercise a varied influence on the pace of the speech and may be categorised according to three kinds of influence. The first type of break tends to decelerate the speech, in other words to act against the line's rhythmic momentum. The extent to which the second type is capable of the same influence depends on the nature of the semantic and syntactic relationships between the lines. Where these relationships are strong, and the phrase that ends the line of only incidental significance, then the influence exerted by the second type may be the same as that of the third, which accelerates the pace and heightens the line's rhythmic climax. This is not to suggest that the break is ignored by enjambement. The break is fully apparent on the written page and often registered in performance as well and, when so registered, can introduce a slight emphasis on the beginning of the second line, an emphasis which may be supported or suggested by additional poetic and semantic elements.
  Both Odashima and Matsuoka develop meaningful relationships between the lines. In Odashima, the proximity of labial *m-* sounds in *mo* at the end of the first line

and *majika* at the beginning of the next introduces a hiatus that gives emphasis (and pace) to the succeeding phrase, *majika ni sematta*. The phrase literally means 'has rushed close', since Theseus is referring to the imminence of his wedding. A similar hiatus is felt in the proximity of glottal *k-* sounds in *nakanaka* and *kanaesasete* in the fourth and fifth lines. The effect of this hiatus is to bolster Odashima's rather free translation of 'lingers my desires', literally 'does not in any way grant me my desires'. His version loses the metaphorical content of 'lingers', no doubt so as to communicate the meaning more directly, but it does translate the subtext of delay and frustration into a phonic image combining alliteration and hiatus. The appearance of these two examples of rhythmic tension within the first six lines of Odashima's translation can be said to exemplify his style of translating Shakespeare as a whole but will not necessarily be sustained with such regularity for the rest of the translation. They risk making the drama too tense, even monotonous. Matsuoka avoids the technique altogether in her first six lines. Where Odashima seems to be rushing toward the critical moment, Matsuoka falls away. Her enjambement at the end of the first line fades into the softer, more succinct *chikazuita* ('approached') and then at the end of the second line into another pentasyllabic phrase, *shingetsu da* ('is the new moon'). However, the brevity of those phrases also introduces a stress (missing in Odashima) on the beginning of the next sentence: in the first case, *shiawasena* ('happy'), and in the second, *daga* ('however'). Movement and tension may be less obvious in her version but are actually just as palpable.

RHYTHM FOREGROUNDED: PUCK'S 'EVERY TURN'

The propensity of blank verse for variation and subordination to the flow of human speech means that when iambic rhythm is emphasised, it is all the more prominent. Such occasions provoke comparison with their Japanese translations, since where for subdued rhythms it is only the tension between meaning and rhythm that requires translation, foregrounded rhythm demands a stricter approach. Rhythms in their typical usage (neither foregrounded nor suppressed) may be translated into alternative forms; but if the contrast between background and foreground is to be more rigidly maintained in translation then straightforward metathesis is less easily justified. In the context of *A Midsummer Night's Dream*, the persistent foregrounding of rhythm is inappropriate to dialogue. In the following example, however, of incantatory speech by Puck in Act 3, it serves a special function (3.1.101-106):

> I'll follow you: I'll lead you about a round!
> Through bog, through bush, through brake, through briar;
> Sometime a horse I'll be, sometime a hound,
> A hog, a headless bear, sometime a fire;
> And neigh, and bark, and grunt, and roar, and burn,

Like horse, hound, hog, bear, fire, at every turn.

Puck's speech crystallises those acts of metamorphosis that distinguish the dramatic and thematic development of the play. If it is a speech that celebrates his capacity to take a variety of shapes and yet remain the same, it can also be read as a metaphor for the range of personae through which reality and imagination can lead the human characters of the play. Puck stands outside this process as the actual agent of metamorphosis, a position reflected in his poetic, which usually differs from the norm. The norm of the play is blank verse but he uses a range of rhyming couplets and short lines. His style is linguistically self-referential, persistently preempting the possibility of dramatic discovery or change. Puck does use metaphor but – unlike human beings – he is actually capable of becoming what they can only compare themselves to.

The rhythm is foregrounded by the repetitive listing of common nouns in the second, third, fourth and sixth lines and of verbs in the fifth. Only the second and fifth lines are fully iambic but the alliterative rhythm of the second line is enough to establish the rhythmic pace of the rest of the speech. Odashima's translation is equally rhythmic (64):[103]

```
     1     /    1    /       4               2
   Yoshi, aitsura ni tsuite yuki, tentekomai wo sasete yarou,
       2         3        3      /    /              4
   numachi mo shigemi mo toorinuke, ibara mo yabu mo kaikuguri,
    /       3           2    2     1 2      1
   ore wa migoto ni bakete yarou, uma demo ii inu demo ii,
    /     /   1    2         2          2        1
   buta demo kubi no nai kuma demo, aruiwa hi no tama demo ii na,
    2   2  /    2       2     /  3   5         2     /
   uma, inu, buta, kuma, hi no tama to, yukusakizaki de bakete yari,
    1    1      1         1      1       2
   hin hin, wan wan, buu buu buu, woo woo, boo boo, unatte yaru.
```

This translation can hardly be cited as an example of alternate leading into successive rhythm, since there is little evidence of either. Yet an analysis that embraces word as well as accent distribution and also syntax reveals a dynamic rhythmic structure similar to the source. The first line of the translation is dominated by successive rhythm and the final one by alternate; the tension between the two is figured in the intervening two lines.

The dominance of successive rhythm in spoken Japanese is often due to the location of main verbs at the end of sentences rather than in the middle or near the

---

[103] The rhythm is imposed mainly by the repetitive listing of nouns (*uma, inu* etc.) but does not seem to affect the accentual patterns.

beginning (as in English). Verb forms often contain long vowels (*yarou*) and double consonants (*yatta*) that can be accented, which with the rhythmic movement towards the end of the sentence creates a greater likelihood of successive rhythm. In the first line of the translation, two of the three pitch accents after *yoshi* are within verbs and also all in successive rhythm. The strongest of these (*-rou*) falls after six unaccented syllables but it is its place at the end of the line that asserts the dominance of successive rhythm in this line. The following four lines also contain both verbs and successive rhythms but the coordination of rhythm and line is less definitive.

A reverse technique in the final line accounts for its alternate nature. The onomatopoeia of this series of animal noises devolves on a regular repetition of sound. The association of animal noises with alternate rhythm might be understood as an association of the animal and sensuous with an alien rhythm but if the dialectic of rhythmic types is to be interpreted as such then its conclusion in this sixth line is ambiguous.[104] As a main verb the accent in *unatte yaru* would usually be the culmination of a successive rhythm but here, the possibility of elision between the preceding *-boo* and *u-* allows for either an alternate or successive rhythm.

Although there are three instances of a successive rhythm in the second and third lines, they are not sustained but serve rather to contrast with the disjointed, even syncopated rhythms that follow. The contrast is neither as obvious nor as organized as in the source but could certainly become so in performance. In particular, accentual variation within the series of disyllabic words for names of animals together with the accented word *ii* – repeated three times – generate a syncopation that leans phonologically and rhythmically into the final line, which resolves the tension as a kind of abstraction of sound and rhythm.

Tsubouchi's version of Puck's speech is a seemingly more literal translation than Odashima's of the source rhythms (236):[105]

```
  /       /       /
Okkake, bokkake, kisamara ni,
  /           /
guru guru odori wo sasete kuryo,
    2         2
numa demo, kawa demo, koyabu demo,
  /    5         2      1
ibarappara demo kamau koto nai,
   2       3       2    4
uma ni baketari, tokidoki wa,
```

---

[104] The alternation of successive and alternate rhythms to create a tension between the rhythms themselves as well as other features of the line.
[105] Here again, an imposed rhythm seems designed to support the accentuation.

      /   2   1 1   2
buta nimo, inu nimo, kubi nashi guma nimo, hidama nimo,

      3   1   1   1
baketarya hin hin, wan wan, guu guu,

  2   /   /   /
hoetari, moetari, tokkae, hikkae,

  /   /
okkake, bokkake,

  /   /
guru guru odori wo sasete kuryo.

Tsubouchi draws analogies of sound and rhythm in his response to the incantatory nature of the speech, whose difference is also marked by the adoption of a quasi-poetic lineation where elsewhere in his translation of blank verse he usually translates in prose. The lines are too short, however, to allow for that elasticity of rhythm characteristic of blank verse; instead, their function is to sustain the naïvety of the rhythms. As in the source, the rhythms are foregrounded by means of repetition and alliteration: the repetition of *demo* in the second and third lines and then of *nimo* in the fifth is particularly effective at generating the galloping rhythm of the speech. The sense of metamorphosis is figured in the change of phonic focus from one group of words to the next: from *-e* in the words linked by *demo*, to *-i* in the words linked by *nimo* and to *-o* in the series of words beginning in the seventh line with *h*<u>o</u>*etari*. Except for some syncopation at the end of the third line, the rhythms of the speech are rigorously successive and so there is no kind of dialectic rhythm as there is in Odashima. There may, however, be a rather Shakespearean resolution to be found in the dominance of short *-o* sounds in the last three lines: the sound occurs nine times in those lines, seven times in initial syllables. For Tsubouchi the frequency of the sound may foreground a connotation of the word *odori* in the final line. The word *odori* means 'dance' and its importance here is evidenced by its position in the final line, supplemented in meaning by the onomatopoeic *guruguru* ('round and round'), and the fact that the two previous occurrences of words containing more than one syllable (*koto* and *tokidoki*) are isolated instances that are subordinate to the later usage.[106]

    Odori has a special significance here. In the context of recreational dancing involving more than one person, *odori* very often refers to dances at Japanese religious festivals in which participants dance in a circle.[107] The circle signifies harmony so

---

[106] Like successive rhythm, the *o-* sound is developed cumulatively over the course of the speech.

[107] The best example is the Bon Odori, a circle dance which is still danced by millions of Japanese people each summer at the climax of the three-day Buddhist festival of the dead (*Obon*). On the first day, the spirits of dead ancestors are invited to return to earth by the lighting of bonfires; the dance at the end of the three days sends them back to the underworld and unites the living in their sense of loss.

that when carried on for long enough the dance can indeed lead to a merging of group identity, a mesmeric effect analogous to the magical power of Puck's verse and Tsubouchi's incantatory style. Brooks notes that Puck's 'round' can refer to ring-dancing but that in this context it is used ironically (Brookes 1979, 57). Unlike English 'round', Japanese *odori* refers only to dancing, although Tsubouchi's usage is presumably ironic as well. Yet the connotation with loss of identity already noted may suggest an interpretation that Puck's intervention in the mechanicals' rehearsal causes a temporary fissure in their actual identities, those identities which they seem unable to conceal when acting. The one mechanical who tries most desperately to step out of his professional role, who wants all parts for himself, is Bottom, and it is Bottom whom Puck leads on into the dance. Tsubouchi's translation turns out to be far from naïve literalism. Both he and Odashima produce highly interpretive versions. Odashima's Puck generates a dialectic of rhythm that can be compared with other stylistic and thematic tensions in the play in that he is a more readily identifiable character than one who is unwilling to admit debate (i.e. dialectic). Tsubouchi's Puck, however, is more of a magician, one who leads the dance but whose psychodynamic secrets remain concealed. Both approaches have been admitted within recent Western criticism, although discussion of Puck's characterisation within different Japanese translations requires a broader range of examples.[108] As for the matter of rhythm, the comparison suggests that direct substitutions of one rhythmic type for another are feasible and rarely inevitable but that the more successful substitutions are those that take account of their rhythmic and phonological contexts and which are justified within the interpretive context. There is no strict analogy of alternate with successive rhythm.

THE LONG AND THE SHORT OF IT: PUNCTUATION AND SENTENCE STRUCTURE

Features of punctuation and sentence structure can be seen to influence rhythm in a more defined and definable manner than accentual patterns. Punctuation marks beginnings and ends; it more closely describes the organisation of language than, for example, debatable patterns of accentuation; it is, in other words, one of the most basic tools of rhetoric (if not as immediately noticeable as prosody or metaphor).

The analysis of Shakespearean punctuation is conditioned by the likelihood that Shakespeare did not punctuate his scripts himself and that punctuation used in

---

[108] Bevington (1975) argued against Jan Kott's eroticised reading of the play in *Shakespeare Our Contemporary* (1964) with his view that the fairies 'do not govern themselves by the conventional sexual mores of the humans'. This argument does not necessarily imply that the fairies are asexual, since Oberon and Titania self-evidently have sexual impulses, but that their behaviour is not determined by traditional Christian morality. In Japanese culture, the most obvious comparison is with *kappa*, who are mischievous but not lascivious by nature.

modern editions is derived from that inserted by his (first) printers and (later) editors. If punctuation is understood as an interpretation of the original sense and meaning, then Japanese translators are for once equal to the source. The quotation from a speech by Oberon to Puck in Act 2, Scene 1, is an example of uncontroversial punctuation (2.1.148-54):

> *Obe.*   My gentle Puck, come hither. Thou rememb'rest
> Since once I sat upon a promontory,
> And heard a mermaid on a dolphin's back
> Uttering such dulcet and harmonious breath
> That the rude sea grew civil at her song
> And certain stars shot madly from their spheres
> To hear the sea-maid's music?
> *Puck.*   I remember.

The only questionable punctuation mark is the comma at the second line, which is necessary for actors to take a breath in a long speech of almost seven lines; the second line is the only one apart from the last without definite enjambement onto the next. This positioning of one rather long sentence between two much shorter ones not only typifies the tendency towards variation of sentence length in oral and written discourse but also says something of the various discourses at work in the play. The long sentence is necessary for the expansive, fantastical image it contains while much shorter sentences are appropriate for simple requests and acknowledgements ('come hither', 'I remember'). Similar contrasts of sentence length and style occur in the preceding scene between Oberon and Titania (ll. 60-145) and in the rest of this scene with Puck (up to l. 176); it is a contrast between the languages of pure imagination and pure action. In modern parlance, Oberon has the vision and Puck implements. That the two do not and will not necessarily concur is suggested by the exaggerated difference between Oberon's expansive question and Puck's curt dimeter. Whether translators choose to respond to this discrepancy is a matter of interpretation. The importance of punctuation, however, in setting the speeches' boundaries and containing sentence structures cannot be ignored.

The translations by Fukuda (36) and Matsuoka (42) provoke an immediate comparison between their respective prose and free verse forms:

FUKUDA

O: 　　1　　　/　1　　　 3　　 1 1　　　 2
　　Oo, Pakku, koko e koi ... Oboete iyou na, itsuka no koto wo.

　　/ 　/　　/1　　　/　　　　　　 2　 1　　　/
　　Sore, ore wa misaki no debana ni koshi wo oroshi, ningyo ga iruka no

　　/1　/　　　　/　　/　 3 /　　　　　　 4　 2
　　se de utatte iru no wo kiite ita. Sono uttori suru you na utsukushii kowane ni,

<pre>
            / 3   3   1   5   /   /
      sasuga no araumi mo odayaka ni nagishizumari, tenjou no hoshi mo,
            / 2
      sono uta no
          2   2   3   4   2
      shirabe wo kikou toshite, kuruoshiku sawagitatta mono da.
           1   3
P: Ee, oboete imasu tomo.

MATSUOKA
      / 1 /   /   /   1   3
O: Oi, ii ko da, Pakku, koko e koi. Oboete iru darou,
      /   /   2   /   1 2
      misaki no hashi ni suwatte ita toki no koto wo.
      /   1   1   1   3   2
      Ore wa ningyo ga iruka no se de utau no wo kiite ita.
             4   4   3
      Amayakana utsukushii utagoe ni
            3   3
      sashimono araumi mo nagishizumari
      /   1   2   2   2
      hoshiboshi mo umi no otome no uta wo kikou to
          2   1   1
      kurutta you ni ten kara futte kita.
           3
P: Oboetemasu.
</pre>

The conspicuous differences between the source and the two translations come in the second, lengthy sentence, and can be described as follows. The sentence ('Thou rememb'rest...') comprises sixty-one syllables in the source, one comma coming after the fourteenth. Fukuda's translation comprises 134 syllables distributed over three sentences as follows (starting at *Oboete*): a short sentence of fifteen syllables, a comma after the eighth; a rather longer sentence of forty-two syllables, commas after the second and eighteenth; and an even longer third sentence of seventy-seven syllables, punctuated by commas after the twentieth, fortieth, forty-eighth and sixty-third syllables. Matsuoka's version is closer in its abnormal structure to the source (from *Oboete*): a short sentence of twenty-eight syllables (a comma after the ninth) followed by a slightly shorter one of twenty-four syllables and a much longer one of sixty-five syllables, making a total 117, somewhat shorter than Fukuda.

Fukuda's apparent decision to ignore the punctuation may hinge on a cultural resistance to overt rhetoric. Eloquence of the kind that Oberon displays here is sometimes regarded as spurious by Japanese people, which is an impression that Fukuda may well wish to avoid in his translation of what is fundamentally a simple question.[109] Except for the opening *sore*, none of his sections are significantly longer or shorter than any other. His choice of punctuation may be in imitation of the line breaks in the source, although none of his breaks disturb the organisation of their sentences and so can hardly be compared to enjambement. The first explanation seems more likely.

Fukuda's punctuation serves to break the sentence down into more digestible chunks and so postpone the cumulative impact. These chunks can be rendered as follows: 'don't you remember'; 'that time'; 'that'; 'I looked down on a promontory'; 'I heard a mermaid singing on a dolphin's back'; 'at this ecstatically beautiful sound'; 'truly the rough sea was becalmed'; 'even the stars in the heavens'; 'trying to hear the sweet melody of that song'; 'they went into a mad uproar'. Fukuda's translation is close to both the semantic content of the source and its structure, and that for his audience was quite possibly enough. Most of these clauses constitute integrated images that are something akin to the pithy single images of traditional Japanese poetry, whose very brevity allows them to resonate, and which are not normally part of a longer narrative structure. Fukuda cannot escape the narrative structure of this particular context but he can use punctuation to contain the resonance of its component images. Matsuoka's translation includes an unbroken sentence of seventy-seven syllables, whose length exceeds the norms of all traditional forms of Japanese poetry and is unusual even in unstructured prose discourse. Yet when its four lines are examined apart from each other, they are seen to comprise four distinct units which do not have to be read in a single flow in order to be understood. The rhythm of each line leans towards an accent on the penultimate (or near penultimate) syllable that rounds off one line before moving on to the next. The choice between reading the four lines in an integrated flow or emphasising their distinctness is of course left to actors and directors, a strategy typical of a translator like Matsuoka.

Matsuoka's version may be less overtly rhetorical if a rhythmically subdued reading is adopted, since Fukuda inserts a moment of rhythmic variation in the dactylic pitch rises in *tenjou no hoshi mo* (although his rhythms are otherwise identical). The sheer complexity of Shakespeare's sentence leads both translators to isolate the subordinate clause ('That the rude sea grew civil ...') within a single sentence, with the sentence structure pushing the second verb ('shot') to the end. Fukuda responds to the stress on 'madly' and stresslessness of 'shot' by ignoring all ideas of 'falling'. *Sawagitatta* is the preterite intransitive form of a verb meaning 'make an uproar' used in conjunction with the adverb *kuruoshiku* ('madly').

Matsuoka's stresses give equal weight to the ideas of 'madness' and 'falling', this

---

[109] It is necessary to historicise Japanese attitudes to rhetoric in the context of the influence of English rhetoric on the development of the Japanese language in the late 19th and early 20th centuries, as well as to distinguish between situations where homogeneity can be assumed and those where it cannot. Moreover, Japanese speech cannot be taken seriously when the appropriate honorifics are inappropriately ignored.

latter word justifying the slight rhythmic cadences at the ends of the preceding three lines. It is in this final difference that the approaches of the two translators might be finally compared. Fukuda's attempt to protect his audience from a surfeit of rhetoric cannot in fact overcome the rhetoric, which simmers up from within Oberon in that final phrase. In Matsuoka's version, the rhetorical energy is released more gradually over the course of the speech, thus distancing Oberon from the memory. Fukuda's Oberon would seem to belong more emphatically to Theseus' category of 'lunatic' and definitely to be a player in the drama.

In order to make a more complete and reliable understanding of the role of pitch accentuation in these translations (and its interaction with syllabic metre), it would be necessary to record Japanese actors speaking excerpts from the verse in translation and then to subject the recordings to electronic analysis; this kind of analysis is attempted in Chapter Five. Yet even the findings presented in this chapter reveal significant correspondences of accent and meaning. It would be surprising indeed if the translators had ignored their native accentuation when rendering the raw material of the source into a Japanese literary context.

It would be equally surprising if the personal rhythms of the translators – as expressed in the accentual patterns of the words they select – were to reach the reader without any reference to the traditional prosody; the translator cannot afford to individuate his response to the complete neglect of the target culture. The next chapter, therefore, moves to the extrinsic prosody, those external features that connect more overtly with Japanese literary tradition, even if they are foreign as such to the source text or colloquial language. A dual perspective on the intrinsic and extrinsic offers valuable information as to how and where Shakespeare's play meets with the recipient, offering some kind of compensation for the unattainability of literal equivalence.

CHAPTER THREE   SYLLABIC METER

SYLLABICS AND FREE VERSE (1): DETACHMENT AND ENGAGEMENT

The linguistic developments of the post-war era rendered the archaic Tsubouchi style all but redundant by the 1960s; Shakespeare's role in the process of cultural modernisation had changed also. Yet these were changes that had already been in effect for some time. Contrasting attempts at innovation made by traditionalist and free verse and prose poets, Dennis Keene observed that (Keene 1980, 11)

> no amount of experimentation with fives and sevens could stand up to the flood of European modernism which entered the country in the 1920s, and the literary language itself gradually became something quite remote from everyday life.

Keene refers to a movement away from the early Meiji poets and translators who believed that the literary language dating back to the 7th century was most appropriate to poetic expression (including translations of Western poetry). The poets of late Meiji and Taishō asserted that lyricism was equally possible in the colloquial language, which was more accessible to a wider swathe of the population. The early Meiji poets sought to develop poetic style by experimenting with native forms while their Taishō successors rejected such experimentation as inconsequential and looked to European models instead.

Tsubouchi's choice of style established Shakespeare as a classical playwright who could be appropriated by modern Japanese, but the irony of his success was that the younger generations who first learnt their Shakespeare from the Tsubouchi translations and understood well enough that Shakespeare was their contemporary, were eventually to demand a contemporary style as well.[110] The 1920s is the decade when Tsubouchi

---

[110]   Most of the generation of Shakespeare scholars and translators born between 1930 and 1950, including Odashima and Takahashi Yasunari, would have first encountered Shakespeare through the Tsubouchi translations. The notion of Shakespeare's contemporaneity was considerably advanced ↗

completed his translation of the Complete Works. Although he was not affected by 'the flood of European modernism' in any obvious way, the history of Tsubouchi's translating style is itself one of steady experimentation that begins with his early adaptations in the 1880s and continues up to the revisions he was making just before his death on 28th February, 1935.[111]

It is insufficient to compare translators solely in terms of single styles when those styles have themselves showed development, which in Tsubouchi's case is a gradual move towards the colloquial and contemporary. The development can be demonstrated by a comparison of Tsubouchi's 1909 and 1933 translations of Hamlet's oft quoted line 'To be, or not to be: that is the question' (3.1.56). The difficulties posed by this line for translators have already been discussed but for Tsubouchi came the peculiar challenge of producing a rendition that would, as it were, confirm his position as the leading translator of Shakespeare: one that made sense within its context and the context of Tsubouchi's stylistic development but which also managed to sound memorable. The early translation from 1909 is a literal rendition in archaic style (Tsubouchi 1909, 110):

Nagaraeru ka [6] ... nagaraenu ka [6] ... sore ga gimon ja. [7]

This one is in a literary style and probably functions better as poetry than rhetoric. *Nagaraeru* is an archaic verb that does indeed mean 'to continue living' or 'live out one's life'. It is also related etymologically to *nagare*, literally 'flow' but used in classical poetry as a metaphor for existence (Rycroft 1999, 198). Yet even among an audience of Tsubouchi's day, it is unlikely that either of these meanings would have been understood without knowing that *nagaraeru* was written with a character meaning 'existence' or 'cognition' (*son*). The second translation is more easily understood (Tsubouchi 1933, 24-25):

Yo ni aru, [4] yo ni aranu, [5] sore ga gimon ja. [7]

Tsubouchi has replaced a single verb with a metaphor for existence – 'to be in the world' – that accommodates both the literal and existential meanings and does not cause the audience to think twice before comprehending its meaning. It is also rhythmical, a regular 5-5-7 in construction, if the missing fifth syllable in the first group is read as a caesura.[112]

↘ by the translation of Kott's *Shakespeare Our Contemporary* by Hachiya Akio and Kishi Tetsuo in 1968 (Hachiya and Kishi 2009).

[111] At the time of his death Tsubouchi had just completed his final revision of his *Othello* translation. This was the most radical revision he made of any of his translations, as he appreciated more fully on the second reading that Othello was the victim of prejudice as well as his own flaws.

[112] *Jitarazu* (shortage of final syllables) is a long accepted practice in *haiku* and *tanka* poetry, although there is a problem of comparing it with the caesura in that there is naturally assumed ↗

Tsubouchi's syntax and vocabulary may have altered since the 1910 version but his use of the seven-five syllabic is still conventional. In contrast to English poetry which has become increasingly fragmented over the last hundred years,[113] traditional syllabic forms such as *haiku* and *tanka* remain dominant, and adherence to the traditional syllabic is still an issue of debate.[114] The issue for *tanka* and *haiku* poets has been partly one of survival of their forms but, since they belong to the mainstream culture, more one of responding to a changing world. Shakespeare translation (like free verse and prose poetry) enters the culture from the outside and so has been more strictly conditioned by the demand for cultural accessibility. Shakespeare has only occasionally been at the core of Japanese culture and – with competition from native playwrights and dramatic genres – often at the periphery. A period of growing interest would be 1885 through to about 1915 when Shakespeare was being read and translated for the first time in Japan. A period of relatively low interest would be 1915 through to Fukuda's *Hamlet* in 1955 when Shakespeare was subordinated to other Western playwrights, and in the 1930s by a militarist regime that eventually prohibited the teaching of English literature in Japanese universities. Against this background of shifting interests, it is unsurprising that the repeated call of directors and translators has been to make the language of Shakespeare in Japanese accessible to as wide an audience as possible.[115]

The seven-five syllabic is not in itself inaccessible but has always, as a number of commentators have suggested (Kawachi 1995, 92-3; Kinoshita 1997, 23-6), been as available to the Japanese translator or poet as iambic rhythm was to its early modern exponents writing in English; both forms depend on a technically straightforward organisation of words and syllables. Yet when the metre is imposed upon the raw output of translation, the words are likely to become larded with the compressions, verbal inflexions and archaic conjunctions that are typical of the old literary style but whose function in translation will simply be self-serving: to support the metre.

A further reason for rejecting the traditional metre was its association with outdated ideologies. The modernist Hagiwara Sakutarō (1886-1942) developed a 'naturalist' poetic similar to *shingeki* realism that rejected the artifice and sentimentality of conventional poetry as it had become by the time of the Meiji Restoration. The syllabic itself was probably less of a concern than the stock imagery and subdued

---

↘ to be a pause between syllabic groups. In dramatic speech, however, it can be read like a caesura with contingent pauses being determined more by punctuation and interpretation than by syllabic boundaries. The reduced number of syllables also matches the pithiness of Hamlet's statement.

[113] Apart from the basic standard of stress accent, English poetry has traditionally embraced a broader range of poetic forms than has Japanese. Even the dominance of free verse in the present age is questionable when one can find numerous poets writing metrically.

[114] The brevity of these forms (seventeen and thirty-one syllables respectively) can make the slightest variation look like an innovation and therefore one that requires convincing explanation.

[115] In fact, since the linguistic preferences of audiences vary, it is probably truer to say that the main demand has been for actorly translations that can be quickly grasped and effectively interpreted by actors.

coloration which poets were expected to employ, although the belief persisted until well into the 20th century that the only genuine poetry was that written in the old syllabic. The problem was more one of the value attached to poetry and its constituent parts in the modern world. The *waka* poets of the Heian era had believed that their poems were as much a part of nature as the natural phenomena with which they were conventionally concerned (Ōoka 48-9),[116] and this too was a belief that survived through to Meiji. Yet it is natural that a modern such as Hagiwara should have felt alienated from such sentiments: to write in a naturalist style was the best he could hope for to regain that precious sense of a vanishing world, a style which would probably involve a liberal use of syllabics. Hagiwara was highly critical of the various insipid experiments in poetic form by his contemporaries, but hints that a productive perspective on traditional poetics can be found in the realisation that

> Why certain poems impress us as true poetry while some others do not is due to the delicate and complex relationship between meanings and sounds in language. Human reason is totally unable to calculate that relationship. (If this calculation were possible, men would be able to create immortal poems with only their intellect.)
> (Hagiwara 1998, 93)[117]

Tsubouchi himself was a realist rather than a naturalist but, as Sōseki's review of the 1911 *Hamlet* so poignantly suggested, his challenge was to make an effective blend of Shakespearean poetry and realism (Gallimore 2010a, 49-50):

> Dr Tsubouchi's *Hamlet*, even through simple intonation, does not reproduce the poetic beauty that Shakespeare achieves in compensation for his distance from reality, and so we cannot be seduced by its elegant mystique; nor does it enable us to be fascinated by the sight of ordinary human beings acting on a stage.

Neither Sōseki's review nor the production itself can be underestimated for their significance as a meeting of Shakespeare with mainstream Japanese culture. Natsume Sōseki (1867-1916) was the leading novelist of modern Japan and a man who knew Shakespeare well and admired his style although not his ideas (Kawachi 1995, 55-61).

---

[116] By tradition, this influential idea was first expounded by the Heian poet Ki no Tsurayuki (884-946).

[117] Hagiwara also contrasts the full-blooded, rhythmical romanticism of much Western poetry with the subtler lyricism of Japanese forms (ibid., 62), from which one might infer that one of the innate problems of Shakespeare translation is that it tries to cross the two. Yet against this pessimism, one may observe that there is a similar dichotomy of lyric and epic in Japanese literature, that Shakespeare translation has consistently served to stretch standards of literary acceptability, and that moments of lyrical beauty can often be attained in actual performance.

His critique was a critique of more than just the acting: the production seemed to offer poetry and false illusion when what was needed was a dose of reality. Yet it is only as acting standards have improved – Brecht and Stanislavski would be key models – that Shakespeare has come to seem more 'real' to Japanese audiences.[118]

It seems that at this transitional point in his career Tsubouchi's ambitions might have got the better of him, although the way forward was already evident from his earlier writings.[119] In particular, his long essay on historical drama (1893-94) and his essays comparing Shakespeare with Chikamatsu (1910) establish the generic identity of Shakespeare's play, distinct that is as drama from the naturalism of a Hagiwara or Sōseki.[120] The techniques of the novelist and poet were certainly relevant to shaping the line and organising the dramatic structures but they were subordinate to Tsubouchi's other important realisation, expressed in his writings on characterisation (e.g. 1885): that the function of dramatic speech was primarily rhetorical rather than poetic. Language was an open medium that could be used by characters in any way appropriate to express their feelings and affect each other in the way that dramatic characters do. In its new context, syllabic metre moved away from its lyrical function in traditional Japanese poetry and from its narrative function in traditional drama in order to acquire a newly rhetorical function in Shakespeare translation, in that syllabic metre can serve the rhetorical purpose of drawing attention to the speaker when it stands out against an ametrical context. The early translations often suffered from excess metricality but post-war translators have found a diversity of purposes in the ornate syllabic style. Four potential uses of syllabics (the first two less clear, admittedly, than the others) are illustrated as follows.

1. In Odashima's version of Hal's outburst to Francis in *Henry IV, Part 1* (4.4.68-

---

[118] Stanivlaski's 'method' was introduced to Japan by Osanai Kaoru in the 1910s, and Brecht became known in the 1950s through the pioneering work of Senda Koreya. Yet more than these models, it is likely that acting standards improved simply through the experience gained with the small companies set up by Osanai and others in the Taishō era, and then through the influence of Western and homemade films.

[119] One of Tsubouchi's most important contributions to Meiji literary criticism was his introduction of the idea of *botsu risō* (literally, 'theory of hidden ideals') in a series of essays published in the early 1890s, some of which referred directly to his Shakespeare studies. The term can be translated as 'realism' or 'anti-idealism' and in Shakespeare criticism implies a critical distance from Shakespeare's characters, ideas and so on, a reluctance to absorb them personally; roughly speaking, one might say that Tsubouchi was fascinated by Shakespeare but resolutely Japanese to the end in his refusal to 'become' Shakespeare. To develop Sōseki's argument, Tsubouchi's philosophy may have been incapable of a complete physical (i.e. theatrical) interpretation of what it means to be Hamlet but Hamlet's plight could at least be conceived in the mind of the translator (Gallimore 2005).

[120] 'Waga kuni no shigeki' ('The historical plays of Japan', 1893-94) (Inagaki 1969, 287-315); 'Chikamatsu to Shēkusupiya' ('Chikamatsu and Shakespeare') and 'Chikamatsu tai Shēkusupiya tai Ipusen' ('Chikamatsu as compared with Shakespeare and Ibsen', both 1909). The second of these is translated in Matsumoto (1960).

70) (Odashima 1983b, 70), there is an awkward syllabic lilt that suits Hal's comic hyperbole, and is defined by the rhetorical force of the individual phrase rather than conventional syllabics as such:

Wilt thou rob this leathern-jerkin, crystal-button, hot-pated, agate-ring, puke-stocking, caddis-garter, smooth-tongue Spanish pouch?

Omae, [3] ano yarō kara [7] zurakaru ki wa [6] nai no ka, [4] ano kawa chokki ni [8] garasu botan, [6] gobu gari no [5] atama ni [4] menō no yubiwa, [7] ke no nagagutsushita ni [9] keito no [4] kutsushita dome [6] Supeingawa no [7] sagebukuro ni [6] obenchara [5] jōzu no shitasaki [8]

2. Hamlet's speech on providence (5.2.215-18) prior to the dénouement of the play has a circular, manic rhythmicality. A consistent syllabic in Fukuda's version would have made the speech sound more rhetorical than it is; the one five-seven phrase is enough to capture the tone of the original, and so to dramatise the absurdity of his situation (Fukuda 1967, 70):

There is special providence in the fall of a sparrow. If it be now, 'tis not to come; if it be not to come, it will be now; if it be not now, yet it will come. The readiness is all.

Ippa no suzume ga [8] ochiru no mo [5] kami no setsuri. [6] Kurubeki mono wa, [7] ima konakutomo, [7] kanarazu kuru [6] – ima kureba, [5] ato niwa konai [7] – ato ni konakereba, [8] ima kuru dake no koto [9] – kanjin na no wa [7] kakugo da. [4]

3. Syllabics can be used to complement other rhetorical devices, as in this pre-war translation of Jaques' speech in *As You Like It* (2.7.139-43) by the poet Abe Tomoji (Abe 1939, 71-2), which combines syllabic metre with repetition and metrical variation.

All the world's a stage,
And all the men and women merely players.
They have their exits and their entrances,
And one man in his time plays many parts,
His acts being seven stages.

Sekai wa subete [7] oshibai da. [5]
Otoko to onna, [7] toridori ni, [5] subete yakusha ni [7] suginu no da. [5]
Tōjō shite mitari, [9] taijō shite mitari, [9]
otoko hitori no [7] isshō no, [5] sono samazama no [7] yaku dokoro, [5]

maku wa, [3] nanatsu no [4] jiki ni naru. [5]

4. Nakano Yoshio's version of the Prologue to *Romeo and Juliet* is quite self-consciously syllabic in a tragic mode (Nakano 1967, 319):

Two households both alike in dignity
(In fair Verona, where we lay our scene)
From ancient grudge break to new mutiny

Butai mo hana no [7] Berona nite, [5]
izure otoranu [7] meimon no [5]
ryōke ni karamu [7] shukuen wo [5]
ima mata arata ni [8] fushō sata. [5]

The shift of function from the poetic to the rhetorical is typical of a further phenomenon of modern Japanese literature, the prose poem.[121] If the purpose of traditional forms such as *waka* was detachment from a transient and unsettling world towards a tranquil and lyrical acceptance of disharmony, then the modernist prose poem aspires to something the opposite. The prose poem describes an actual engagement with evil and injustice in which the presence of syllabic rhythms hints at an underlying order that is actually made elusive by the rhetorical *esprit* (Keene 1980). Shakespearean drama, and therefore Shakespeare translation as well, lie somewhere between these two poles of detachment and engagement: being driven toward catharsis by the force of Shakespeare's dramatic narratives and yet distracted along the way by emotive, even polemical ideas.

SYLLABICS AND FREE VERSE (2): 'RIDING THE HORSE'

The poles of detachment and engagement plot the history of Shakespeare criticism in Japan. The Meiji fascination with 'depth' is an attempt to engage with the mind of Shakespeare, although it was an abyss of which Tsubouchi in particular was wary. The image of 'the bottomless lake' (*soko shirazu no mizuumi*) was central to Tsubouchi's theory of *botsu risō* (Moriya 1986, 24-25).[122] The lake was conceived as a cultural and spiritual black hole which admitted into its depths every kind of species but was

---

[121] This form was developed in Japan at the beginning of the 20th century, following the example of Ueda Bin's translations of Baudelaire and Mallarmé.
[122] Tsubouchi was typical among other Meiji writers in having inherited a vertical or hierarchical view of society from the Tokugawa era that would also include a notion of depth. That notion becomes politicized when one realizes the political perils attendant on interfering too deeply with the spiritual icons of Meiji society, in particular the person of the Meiji Emperor.

treacherous to any human being who dared to ventured in; Shakespeare and Goethe he compared to two great swamps similar in character to the lake (if not exactly the same phenomenon).[123] It is almost certain that Tsubouchi borrowed the image from Ernest Dowden's *Shakespere: A Critical Study of His Mind and Art* (1875) in which Dowden writes of Shakespeare that (Dowden 1875, 35)

> It is by virtue of his very knowledge that he comes face to face with the mystery of the unknown. Because he had sent down his plummet farther into the depths than other men, he knew better than others how fathomless for human thought those depths remain.

Dowden's description was open both to Tsubouchi's realist interpretation[124] and to Mori Ōgai's idealism; the antagonism of the two was to constitute one of the famous literary disputes (*ronsō*) of the Meiji era (Moriya 1986, 26-27). In the 1920s, a more idealistic school supersedes, inspired in part by Ōgai's poetic yet thoroughly colloquial translation of *Macbeth* (1913). Shakespeare criticism became idealistic at this time as the comparativism of Tsubouchi was neglected and interest shifted to textual and historical issues, as typified by the annotated Kenkyūsha editions begun by Ichikawa Sanki in 1917; in other words, Shakespeare becomes detached from the main point of reference, the recipient culture. One of the meanings of Ōgai's translation, which was completed in less than a month, was that in showing that good style and a passion for the play were enough to produce an effective translation, the authority of the polymath translator was challenged and more specialist pursuits permitted. The fact that Tsubouchi remained both productive and highly respected until his death in 1935 must be due partly to the fact that he was generally favourable towards innovations such as Ōgai's (Kawachi 1995, 50). Ōgai may be considered the first in a long line of memorable translators (e.g. Kinoshita, Mikami) who did not feel the need to translate all of the Complete Works.

In the 1950s, the myth of Shakespeare as philosopher is reasserted by Nakano Yoshio and others under the guise of liberal humanism. These scholars were part of a cultural revival in the 1950s that reacted against the intellectualism of pre-war scholars and sought to promote Shakespeare as a playwright of general human interest; their agenda was pedagogic (Nakada 1989, 43-84). In the late 1960s, scholars like Takahashi Yasunari realised 'the absurdity of existence' but insisted at least on Shakespeare's place in history.[125] Finally, the present climate of postmodernism can be said to allow for a

---

[123] Tsubouchi puns on Shakespeare's name, rendering it as 'shake sphere' (i.e. 'move the cosmos'), and on Goethe's name as *gyōten* (meaning 'amazement') (Tsubouchi 1978, 392).

[124] According to Brownstein (1997, 281), Dowden was a seminal influence behind 'the new criticism' (*shinki hihyō*) that Tsubouchi advocated among his students: the replacement of an aesthetics of taste with a more scientific and truly critical approach. Another influential text was Moulton's *Shakespeare as a Dramatic Artist* (1885).

[125] Takahashi is also responsible (as a translator and critic) for having introduced the plays ↗

broader spectrum of engagement than ever before. It goes without saying that the four translators are products of this heritage. Tsubouchi and Fukuda would seem to be based on the linguistic, mythopoeic concerns of Shakespeare the philosopher and Odashima on the historical and cultural.

Tsubouchi's Shakespeare was mythic by default; Shakespeare was always new territory for Tsubouchi, whatever his realism. Fukuda may still have believed in the myths, but for Odashima the mythic is a mutual experience created jointly with the audience. Matsuoka's culture is theatrical and so best identified with the postmodern. She acts out a space distinct from her numerous possible influences, writing that (Matsuoka 1998, 199):

> Translation is an uncouth business. Tied to every little word and phrase of the original, nothing ever seems quite right, but somehow in the end the translator finds a Japanese equivalent. When the original is Shakespeare, it's an even more daunting task: like an insect crawling along the ground, you first make out the veins of the leaves on the tree and it's only then that you get an idea of what the tree looks like as a whole – or you become a bookworm and surround yourself with piles of books.

The chancy nature of the postmodernist enterprise is determined partly by the sheer weight of recent tradition behind it.

All four translators possess a distinctive prosody in the sense that the differences between prose and verse are consistently registered and the lines clearly organised in phonic patterns around accented syllables. In the case of Tsubouchi, the spur comes from the 19th century poets and novelists who fed the earliest attempts at literary translation, writers that included Scott and Thackeray as well as Keats and Longfellow. Tsubouchi's main interests were in Shakespeare and Japanese drama, but in 1880, a few years before he undertook his first Shakespeare translation (*Julius Caesar*), he jointly translated with his friend Takata Sanae part of Scott's Romantic novel, *The Bride of Lammermoor* (1819), and later in his career also published essays on Wordsworth and Tennyson. This interest in narrative puts his other interest in Shakespearean prosody into a perspective.[126] The two combine to form the genre of the narrative or epic

---

↘ of Samuel Beckett to Japan in the 1960s, and in 1967 Odashima translated Martin Esslin's *Theatre of the Absurd* (1961). Beckett seldom denied the privilege of actors to occupy a stage (or, by implication, of Shakespeare to have filled that stage with characters of his own). What fascinated Takahashi and others within the Japanese theatre was Beckett's relentless philosophical questioning of linguistic and theatrical boundaries. The introduction of Beckett to the Japanese stage therefore belongs very much to this era of experimentation.

[126] In 'Waga kuni no shigeki' ('The historical plays of Japan', 1893-94) and 'Rekishi shōsetsu ni tsuite' ('Historical novels', 1906) (Inagaki 1969, 283-84), Tsubouchi argued that a problem with Japanese historical dramas and novels of the pre-modern period was that they lacked narrative consistency.

poem, themselves key genres in the translated literature of the Meiji era, which when transferred to traditional and later realist idioms becomes drama.[127] Tsubouchi's critical output shows a consistent and methodical grappling with unfamiliar literatures and genres that leads inevitably to his translation of the Complete Works.

Certainly as far as his criticism is concerned, he seems unaffected by the translations of French Symbolist poetry that started to enter Japan at the beginning of his career; he did not read French and never mentions Ueda's seminal *Kaichō on* (1905). As Corn explains, French is closer to Japanese in its accentual structure, more open to syllabic metre (Corn 1998, 115), and so not only was the prosody of French symbolism more literally translatable but also more easily imitated. Tsubouchi's style does have some of the musicality of the French Symbolists and indeed seems closer to this *fin-de-siècle* movement than to the modernism which began to replace symbolism in the 1920s. Tsubouchi's Shakespeare is a personal, oral experience but although his translations become the objects of mass production, the style itself is an age away from the colloquialisms of free verse modernists such as Hagiwara.

Although free verse translation starts as early as Mikami in the 1930s, Fukuda (for one) does not use it in the 1950s and might therefore be said to stand in the same relation to modernism as Tsubouchi to symbolism. In Fukuda's case the influence of Japanese modernism is ideological rather than poetic; but one influence that may be both ideological and poetic is D.H. Lawrence, whom Fukuda translated and whose prose style is often notably rhythmical.[128] The opening of *The Rainbow* (1915) demonstrates a version of pastoral that looks back to Shakespeare and beyond but which is also at the same time modernist, first in the candour of its language and then in the realisation that the scene can only make sense through its acute rhythmicality (Lawrence 1981, 42):

> The young corn waved and was silken, and the lustre slid along the limbs of the men who saw it. They took the udder of the cows, the cows yielded milk and pulse against the hands of the men, the pulse of the blood of the teats of the cows beat into the pulse of the hands of the men. They mounted their horses, and held life

---

[127] Milton's *Paradise Lost* (1667) was first translated in the 1880s. Yuasa Hangetsu's collection of epic poems based on the Old Testament Book of Joshua, *Jūni no ishizuka* ('The twelve cairns') (1886) was one of the most successful examples of *shintaishi* of its time. In *Shōsetsu shinzui*, Tsubouchi writes of Defoe that he 'made good use of the style of epic poetry in writing his social exposés; Scott and Bulwer-Lytton, among others, used it to impart a knowledge of history.' (Twine 1981, 10) There was never any attempt to make a Japanese drama out of *Paradise Lost*.

[128] In 1936 Fukuda wrote his graduation dissertation for the Faculty of English Literature at Tokyo University on Lawrence, who was then little known in Japan, but whose thought had a decisive impact on Fukuda's development. He had already published translations of *Apocalypse* and *Women in Love* by the time he started directing Shakespeare. Fukuda was drawn to Lawrence's anti-egoism which is readily associated with Fukuda's post-war stance against the Japanese 'I' novel and leftism in literature.

between the grip of their knees, they harnessed their horses at the wagon, and, with hand on the bridle-rings, drew the heaving of the horses after their will.

The influence of T.S. Eliot and the Arechi poets on the young Odashima Yūshi was discussed in the previous chapter. For Fukuda they probably came too late in his career to be called real influences but he certainly shared common concerns, in particular his belief that the colloquial language could be used to convey spiritual values. Fukuda regretted the decline of the literary language (*bungo*) due to *genbun icchi* but realised that the colloquial language facilitated the universalisation of Shakespeare's meanings on the modern stage. He wrote that (Fukuda 1961, 237),

The so-called literary language is more suited to the individual voice than the colloquial. To say that *bungo* lacks a voice just because it's different from everyday conversation is no more than an ignorant layman's point of view.

According to Kawachi (Kawachi 1995, 96), Fukuda 'stands in isolation as if he were an exile when he translates Shakespeare. He says that both languages elude him when he tries to find the precise word to fit the original'. Fukuda's theatricality, or rather preoccupation with theatre, inevitably sets him at a distance from the surrounding language and culture.

Odashima acquired from his reading of contemporary British playwrights such as Christopher Fry and John Osborne an emotive, rhetorical register that could be blended with the Arechi idiom to produce an updated illusion of poetic drama in Japanese. He is the only translator to have a background in poetry, which he wrote as a young man, having initially majored in engineering as an undergraduate: there is perhaps something of the engineer's eye for detail in his calculation that the actor can utter no more than about twenty-five syllables in a single breath and that this line therefore represents the best approximation of blank verse (Kadono 1989, 152). Yet just as Fukuda the dramatist discovers poetry as he translates Shakespeare so too might the same process be seen to make a playwright out of a poet. Odashima insists that poetic devices are subordinate to dramatic narrative in his translations (Odashima 1976, 48-49):

Just as Japanese poetry can suffer from being too strictly metrical, so too in the theatre must dramatic effects be considered first before one worries about the fluidity of the sounds.

In this aspect, Odashima would seem to be an heir of those modernist poets who were (Keene 1980, 1)[129]

---

[129] Keene is paraphrasing an important article by the prose poet Kitagawa Fuyuhiko, published in 1929, in which it was argued that 'the new prose poem was written in reaction against naturalist description, and also against the idea of the poet's singing spontaneously' (ibid.). Naturalism ↗

no longer recorders of the inner movements of the soul; nor were they concerned with exposing their emotions. They were technicians who selected from innumerable words those which could be built into one single and perfected construction. The words and phrases were to be fitted together like bricks and, although the cement used should hold, the pattern in which they were arranged was to imply the impossibility of other patterns, the perfect construct being an expression of the arbitrary nature of the material arranged.

Within the semiotic frameworks of traditional genres such as *kabuki*, metrical fluidity supports the actor in the totality of his performance, but what Odashima and the modernists are suggesting is that drama and poetry in the 20th century demand an arbitrary prosody that is capable of convincing audiences and readers of the authenticity of the experience conveyed.

As language changes, so too is the authenticity of translations challenged. In the 1990s, we can observe a subtle shift away from a strictly 'authentic' Shakespeare towards one that is more engaged with its cultural context, in particular in areas of significant Western influence such as feminism and post-colonialism. Odashima's translations reached their height of popularity during the late 1980s, just at the time the Japanese economy was reaching the peak of its global influence. The fact that the economic 'bubble' was to burst soon after is not meant to suggest that his translations have fallen out of use, since in fact they are still popular for both reading and in production, but it does hint at how the conditions of Shakespeare performance have changed since that time. Against the self-confidence or *jouissance* of Odashima's translations, Matsuoka is translating within a society that is arguably more aware of its limitations, more critical of its past and even more aware of the politics of human relationships. The experience of Japan's 'lost decade' (the 1990s) is mirrored in Matsuoka's experience of translating such politically engaged contemporary playwrights as Caryl Churchill and her deep knowledge of how Shakespeare is performed in the British theatre. While Fukuda and Odashima acquired an understanding of the techniques of stage translation from the British theatre, Matsuoka is the most theatrically aware of all four translators (Gallimore 2010 b). This is not to deny her debt to any of her predecessors, nor her reliance on traditional devices such as syllabic meter.

Syllabic and free verse translation happens in a dramatic context which, in correspondence with the dynamic interaction of poetry and drama in the original texts, cannot be ignored in translation. The interaction is best appreciated by looking at the translations themselves, although one clue as to the nature of the beast is given by Kinoshita Junji (1995). He used the figure of equestrianism (his personal hobby) to describe a subtle subordination of writer to text by which the play gets written and, by implication, the translation of a foreign play completed. In terms of prosody, the

---

↘ was largely redundant by the time of Odashima but his Shakespeare can be said to share the same urban, mechanistic background as the rapidly industrialising society in which Kitagawa came of age.

Sino-Japanese character for 'horse' happens to be both a semantic and graphological representation of 'the turn', for example, the turn (or *volta*) at the end of a line and the shift from short to long lines in free verse: 馬. If the intrinsic features of Japanese prosody are considered as the terrain over which the horse gallops, then the extrinsic features result from whatever the rider makes of that terrain as he or she moves from start to finish: to the end of the line, speech, scene, act, play. The rest of this chapter lists some of those devices.

IGNORING PITCH ACCENT: TITANIA'S LAMENT

Titania's elegy in Act 2, Scene 1 (2.1.81-117) on the disorder that has befallen the natural world as a result of her quarrel with Oberon is a speech that hovers between passive resignation and a clear rhetorical impulse directed at her husband; it is both lament and dramatic statement. The lament arouses a pity of which Titania is fully aware and which is voiced in occasional outbursts but mainly subordinated to the overall structure. The speech is organised as follows: line 81, an accusation; lines 82 to 86, a personal lament leading to another accusation in line 87 and to a general lament up to line 92. The lament is then exemplified in a series of nine emblematic figures up to line 102 which move once again from the specific to the general in lines 103 to 114 with personifications of the moon, seasons, and finally the world itself. In fact, a similar movement has been registered in the speech overall from the specific case of infidelity to Titania's admission of their shared responsibility for the disruption of natural harmony (ll. 115 to 117).

>These are the forgeries of jealousy:
>And never, since the middle summer's spring,
>Met we on hill, in dale, forest or mead,
>By paved fountain, or by rushy brook,
>Or in the beached margent of the sea, 85
>To dance our ringlets to the whistling wind,
>But with thy brawls thou has disturb'd our sport.
>Therefore the winds, piping to us in vain,
>As in revenge have suck'd up from the sea
>Contagious fogs; which, falling in the land, 90
>Hath every pelting river made so proud
>That they have overborne their continents.
>The ox hath therefore stretch'd his yoke in vain,
>The ploughman lost his sweat, and the green corn
>Hath rotted ere his youth attain'd a beard; 95
>The fold stands empty in the drowned field,

> And crows are fatted with the murrion flock;
> The nine-men's-morris is fill'd up with mud,
> And the quaint mazes in the wanton green
> For lack of tread are undistinguishable. 100
> The human mortals want their winter cheer:
> No night is now with hymn or carol blest.
> Therefore the moon, the governess of floods,
> Pale in her anger, washes all the air,
> That rheumatic diseases do abound. 105
> And thorough this distemperature we see
> The seasons alter: hoary-headed frosts
> Fall in the fresh lap of the crimson rose;
> And on old Hiems' thin and icy crown,
> An odorous chaplet of sweet summer buds 110
> Is, as in mockery, set; the spring, the summer,
> The childing autumn, angry winter, change
> Their wonted liveries; and the mazed world,
> By their increase, now knows not which is which.
> And this same progeny of evils comes 115
> From our debate, from our dissension;
> We are their parents and original.

Titania's argument is constructed along classical lines but its conclusion is far from predictable as she does not in the end blame Oberon directly but accepts dual responsibility.[130] Her admission is a rhetorical 'turn' that works on both the audience's sympathies and on Oberon's conscience. In the latter case it seems to have the desired effect as Oberon's response is no more than perfunctory; he has been rhetorically winded.

Over such a long speech of thirty-seven lines, the analysis of pitch accentuation becomes recondite within the context of the whole speech. It is preferable to analyse how translators have organised the syllabics and varied the lengths of the spoken line, and for this reason, Matsuoka's translation is given with only the syllabic structure indicated (38-40):[131]

---

[130] The argument is syllogistic, i.e. consisting of two propositions and a conclusion. The first proposition (ll. 81-7) describes the personal consequences of their disunion and the second (ll. 88-114) gives examples of disorder in the human and natural words. Titania concludes (ll. 115-7) that they have only themselves to blame.

[131] In performance, the prominent structure will shift from the syllabic group to the line or sentence, but this is not to suggest that the shorter group would be inaudible as a matter of individual interpretation. My groupings are determined by syntax and to a lesser extent by accent and surface meaning; a particle such as *mo* or *no* will always be grouped with the preceding phrase, and also a prominent accent will determine the shape of the group as a whole. For example, if we take ↗

Sonna no wa [5] minna shitto ga [7] koshiraeta [5] detarame da wa. [6]
Kono natsu no [5] hajime kara [5]
oka ya tani, [5] mori ya bokujō, [7]
koishijiki no [6] sunda izumi [7], igusa no [4] shigeru ogawa, [6]
umibe no sunahama, [8] doko de aō ga [7] misakai nashi, [6]
watakushitachi ga [7] wa ni natte [5] kaze no kuchibue de [8] odorō to suru to, [8]
sō yatte kenka wo [9] fukkakete, [5] watakushitachi no [7] tanoshimi wo [5]
dainashi ni [5] shite shimau. [5]
Dakara, [3] mudabue wo [5] fukasareta kaze wa, [8]
shikaeshi ni [5] umi kara doku no [7] kiri wo suiageta. [8] Sore ga [3] ame to natte [6] oka ni furu to [6]
chiisana kawa made [8] zōchō shi, [5] daichi wo [4] mizubitashi ni [6] shite shimatta. [6]
Sono sei de, [5] ushi ga kubiki wo [7] hiite mo [4]
nōfu ga ase shite [8] tagayashitemo [6] minori wa naku, [6] midori no mugi mo [7]
ho no deru mae ni [7] tachigusare. [5]
Mizu ni nomareta [7] denpata niwa, [6] hitsujigoya ga [5] kara no mama [5] torinokosare, [6]
byōshi shita [5] kachiku wo esa ni, [7] karasu bakari ga [7] koefutoru. [5]
Morisu asobi no [7] tame shibachi ni [6] kizanda mizo mo [7] doro ni umari [6]
meirogata ni [6] karikonda [5] ikegaki mo [5]
tōru hito mo naku [8] are hōdai de [7] miwake ga tsukanai. [8]
Natsu no sanaka ni [7] toki naranu fuyu, [7] demo [2] fuyu no tanoshimi no [8] yoru no sanbika mo [8] seika mo kikoenai. [9]
Shio no mankan wo [8] tsukasadoru [5] tsuki no omote wa [7]
ikari no tame ni [7] massao ni nari, [7] taiki wo shimerase [8]
riumachi yamai wo [8] hayaraseru. [5]
Kono tenkō [6] ihen no ageku, [7] kisetsu mo [4] kurutte shimatta. [8]
Shiraga atama no [7] oita shimo wa, [6] sakisometa [5] shinkū no bara ni [8] hizamakura.[5]
Fuyu shōgun no [7] kōri no hageatama wo [10] karakau yō ni [7]
natsu no tsubomi ga [7] kaguwashii hana [7] kanmuri wo [5] kaburaseru. [5]
Haru, [2] natsu, [2]

↘ a take a line from Odashima's translation of Theseus' opening speech studied in the previous chapter, *tanoshii hibi wo ato yokka sugoseba* ('four happy days'), where the pitch accents are underlined, we can see that the first phrase forms a distinct semantic unit of seven syllables ending with the object particle *wo* (*tanoshii hibi wo*, 'happy days'), whereas the second part contains two accented phrases, a temporal expression (*ato yokka*, 'four more days') qualifying a verb (*sugoseba*, 'will pass'); these two phrases would most naturally be read as a single unit of nine syllables but could also be read as a five and a four. In this chapter, however, I have generally avoided units of ten or more syllables.

hōjō no aki, [7] ikari no fuyu, [6] sorezore ga [5] kinareta fuku wo [7]
kigaete shimatta. [8] Ningentachi wa [7] sukkari tomadoi, [8]
sono yosōi wo [7] mita dake dewa, [6] ima ga [3] dono kisetsu yara [7] kentō mo
   tsukanai. [9]
Kō shita wazawai mo [9] moto wo tadoreba [7]
watakushitachi no [7] isakai, [4] watakushitachi no [7] kenka ga hottan, [8]
watakushitachi ga [7] umi no oya na no yo. [8]

It should be clear that Matsuoka has kept with the traditional metre and that she uses it to deliberate ends. The two longer units in the first line (the eight and six) turn on the two key lexical items, the words for 'jealousy' and 'forgeries'. The unambiguous tone is supported by rhythmic balance but is not enough to tell the story. This Matsuoka does by a shift of register to two short lines, the first comprising two fives and the second a five and a seven. As with the source, the list of natural features (four in line 3, 'hills', 'vallies', 'woods', 'farms') prepare the reader for the flood of natural imagery that ensues.

The following four lines are each longer than the previous one and are all part of the one sentence that begins with *kono natsu* ('this summer'). The summer season springs to mind before being utterly negated in that fourth line by the verb *dainashi ni suru* ('to annihilate') and the auxiliary verb *shimau* ('to finish doing'). The first character in *dainashi* is the same as that in *taifū* ('typhoon'). Both words suggest a physical force that comes down to earth from some height.[132] As in the recent past that Titania is describing, the glories of summer are something that can be experienced only in the imagination. Given the finality of Titania's statement, it is difficult to make another rhetorical turn that will sound anything other than what is to be expected; change is both expected and unavoidable. After four lines of seasonal syllabics, Matsuoka breaks in with a resounding *dakara* ('therefore') which is a three rather than a seven or five, and reasserts the logical framework of the speech. The syllabic metre returns, however, in the next unit with two fives leading into another three. The symmetry of the two threes at the beginning and end and the association of the second with a word for 'wind' (*kaze*) suggests that the logical argument can indeed be sustained in a native idiom.

The next two lines are only unevenly syllabic, neither consistently seven-five nor patterned. Titania is regaining her breath after that first outburst, trying to give some shape to her rather fragmented examples. The shape is only externalised at first, by the alternation of long with short lines, but by line 14 it has become internalised through the connection made at last between the foul weather and the suffering agriculture. Once again, a concrete – actually liquid – substantive *mizu* ('water') is enough to straighten out the syllabics, although there are a few metrical variations and the emphatic *bakari* after *karasu* ('only crows') expresses more than a hint of emotional tension. The process is repeated in the next four lines as the syllabic line

---

[132] Most of the possible meanings of the character denote raised position, e.g. 'stand', 'pedestal', 'mounting', 'platform'.

begins to fall apart again before being reasserted by the key word *natsu* at the start of line 19. Matsuoka seems to be realising the limitations of her metre. One can almost hear her drawing in the reins with an alliterative rhyme on *Morisu* ('morris') and *meirogata* ('maze') and the emphatic repetition of *nai* ('not') at the ends of lines 18 and 19. Her interpretation of Titania's rhetoric has been cautiously progressive: one which permits the queen to admit the vulnerability of her situation but is unswerving in its ultimate goal. Her rhetoric aspires to a reconciliation of opposites that cannot yet happen dramatically. Matsuoka, for example, keen to include foreign loan words such as *Morisu* and *riumachi* ('rheumatism') in line 22. The ideographic reading of the two characters in *hayaraseru* is *ryūkō*, which alliterates with the other loan word *riumachi* ('rheumatism').[133]

Lines 20 to 22 are conventionally syllabic. Here at last is Matsuoka's opportunity to use the metre to lyrical effect. The primacy of sound has been subtly signalled with the words for 'carol' and 'hymn' (*sanbika, seika*): that eery repeated *ryū-* sound in line 22 is distinctly musical. Titania has reached her element and the tone remains resolutely patterned to the end of the speech. The divisions made by punctuation and the syllabic breaks are more distinct and there are no more unexpected turns as she gallops to the finish. The two lines comprise four fives and a four in line 32 and a six and an eight in line 33. The strongest support for such a reading comes from Matsuoka's careful positioning of the words for the four seasons in lines 27 and 28. *Haru* ('spring') and *natsu* ('summer') stand alone in line 27, unattached to any adjective or conventional epithet. The words for 'autumn' (*aki*) and 'winter' (*fuyu*) belong not only to epithets but to a new line. Thus the seasons of youth are free, belonging only to themselves, which contrasts with the shackles imposed by the older seasons.

Matsuoka foregrounds a rhetorical undercurrent that has belied her version of this passage so far. This is nothing more than a tension between the abstract freedom of youth, a state that is free to ignore fixed measures and emotional undercurrents, and the confinements of middle and old age, which enforce the structure of the line. The abstraction of the seasonal content by those four words fixes the relationship between abstract and concrete in a way that when developed over a short passage is quite pointed. Each of the main and subordinate clauses in the last four lines contains either a demonstrative or personal pronoun.

A translation of Titania's lament that swings either to the theatrical or excessively poetic risks trivialising the lyric. Titania creates a poem of undeniable force that her husband can either accept, and so lose the argument, or reject and lose face. The poem needs no further dramatisation since the events it describes are quite dramatic enough. Nor does it need further poeticisation that might serve to detract from the rhetorical flow of the speech. Matsuoka's strategy is to translate the first line as literally as possible, even reproducing the rhythmical symmetry of the source.

---

[133] The characters used are 流行, which means 'fashion' or 'popularity' which is here a causative inversion of the intransitive 'do abound'.

Sonna no wa [5] minna shitto ga [7] koshiraeta [5] detarame da wa. [6]

This allows that smouldering metaphor – 'the forgeries of jealousy' – to govern the whole speech, working through a series of rhetorical modulations to the sustained accusatory tone of the last eight lines. In comparison with the other three translators, Matsuoka is the only one who does not turn the metaphor into an abstract (*koto* or *goto* meaning 'thing') but sustains the metaphorical thrust with the colloquial *detarame*. This word is understood to mean 'nonsense' but a more appropriate rendering might be 'codswallop' as *tara* is the codfish and the word literally means 'out of the eye of the cod'. Matsuoka renders the metaphor utterly comprehensible to a Japanese audience while at the same time retaining the figurative edge which can so easily be lost in translation.

The other three translators are also quite subtly figurative but to dramatic rather than self-referential effect (Tsubouchi, 212; Fukuda, 33; Odashima, 35):

TSUBOUCHI   Sorya minna [5] yakkami konjō ga [9] koshiraeta [5] nenashi goto yo. [6]

FUKUDA   Sore mo kore mo, [6] shitto ga [4] tsukuriageta [6] nenashi goto. [5]

ODASHIMA   Sonna no wa [5] minna shitto ga [7] koshiraeta [5] detarame da wa. [6]

Matsuoka's *sonna* is, admittedly, a deictic adjective but immediately subordinate to alliteration with *minna*. Tsubouchi and Fukuda also use an alliterative *n* in their *nenashi* ('without roots') but in that case Titania would seem to be saying to Oberon, 'You're a spirit not a tree. You have no roots.' In fact, all three of the men use variations on the deictic *sore* ('that') that can only refer to somewhere beyond the text. Tsubouchi creates an illusion of lyric with his bombastic conglomeration of six characters (two each in *minna yakkami konjō*) which can only signify if intended satirically. A satiric reading would suit the more dramatic interpretation.

Tsubouchi's series of three double consonants is quite unusual in Japanese and contrasts with Fukuda's more elastic rendering. Fukuda uses only single consonants and thus manages to avoid another source of phonological hiatus by repeating the same vowel sound consecutively only twice (*sore mo kore mo* and *tsukuri*). If phonological elasticity is to be associated with the freedom of movement enjoyed by the spirit world, then this difference between the two treatments might suggest an interesting difference in their understandings of what it means to be a spirit. Fukuda's Titania is quite happy to be labelled as such while Tsubouchi's is carefully defined as an actor on the stage by his assumption of a theatrical prosody that at least gives the illusion of human rootedness. Odashima's is the least opaque of the four translations in that he divides the image of 'forgeries' into two components, 'birth' (*unda*) and 'fabrication' (*koshirae*), which sustains the impetus of the metaphor but only at the semantic level.

The relegation of pitch accent has led the discussion beyond the dimension of pure rhythm into a prosody with clear metaphorical associations. For Matsuoka, her translation of these thirty-seven lines may be one of those few occasions when all three elements – semantic, metrical and metaphorical – do indeed come together in her translation but for now it is necessary to return to a more strictly metrical analysis of the translated language.

BACK TO BASICS: AN ANALYSIS OF THE SYLLABIC STRUCTURE OF ACT I, SCENE I (FUKUDA)

No Japanese translation is so strictly syllabic that it reads like a classical poem, a strict succession of fives and sevens. Such a translation would be as difficult as a strictly iambic one to write for the reason that the translator works with a language that is not his own, and would also be undermined by the major differences between the two prosodies. Iambic rhythm is based on the individual syllable and is therefore too weak to resist the unevenness and rhythmic tensions that typify Shakespeare's usage and indeed of all the great practitioners.[134] The rhythm of the seven-five syllabic is more structural; not only was unorthodox usage less appreciated within the classical tradition but more likely to be achieved by unusual treatment of other conventions, such as seasonal references.

Rather than being disappointed that a translation is not uniformly syllabic, it is more valuable to identify phrases that do conform to some kind of seven-five syllabic and to relate those phrases to a structural interpretation. An analysis of a single, moderately lengthy scene from just one of them might be considered representative of how the modern translator has used the traditional metre, comparable perhaps to how a modernist poet like W.H. Auden would make occasional use of older forms for purposes of historical perspective.[135] Developing the analogy with modernism, one can argue that Fukuda's period and ideology makes him the most quintessentially modernist of the four translators. He translates mainly in prose and yet is admired as a poetic translator who is not averse to syllabics. He benefits from the hindsight of some seventy years of stylistic experimentation by predecessors such as Tsubouchi but is still translating for a

---

[134] Hobsbaum writes that 'What is required is not an adherence to rule but the discovery of a pattern that makes sense to oneself and to other readers.' (Hobsbaum 1996, 13) Shakespearean blank verse is similarly characterised by a freedom of syntax and light rhythms suitable for dramatic speech.
[135] Auden's ingenious villanelle 'If I Could Tell You' creates a richly ironic tension between the experience of history (first line, 'Time will say nothing but I told you so') and the reality of the moment (final couplet, 'Will Time say nothing but I told you so? / If I could tell you I would let you know.') (Auden 1989, 201).

1950s audience who had been educated in the pre-war classical tradition.[136]

Syllabic analysis is problematic (although hardly as difficult as trying to scan free verse) and the analysis below of Fukuda's translation of Act I, Scene 1 is far from definitive (11-22). The syllabic breaks between phrases are often unclear, usually because of interference by accentual rhythms or by syntax: a short phrase of three or four syllables is sometimes strong enough to stand by itself but will at other times be absorbed by the longer syntactic or rhythmical unit. In the longer speeches (particularly Helena's soliloquy), there is a tendency for the phrasing to become more complex, and a few examples of this tendency are given in the footnotes. Compound verbs and auxiliaries (e.g. *shinde yukitō gozaimasu*) can also be problematic, as one is unsure whether or not to break the momentum initiated by the main verb. It is unlikely, however, that any actor or reader would observe these groupings strictly. The syllabic rhythms are more significant as undercurrents.

Given these limitations, the analysis does yield at least three features worthy of discussion. One is the occasional and unambiguous use of seven-five in various combinations. Other syllabic groupings may be rhythmically effective, as may broken rhythms or sudden changes in the rhythm of the line, but the analysis concentrates on the conventional syllabic for reasons already discussed in this chapter. The second feature is the grouping of phrases of consecutively more and more or fewer and fewer syllables so that the phrases rise or fall like rhythmic accidence and cadence. The third feature is very uneven syllabic groupings, such as a one preceding a ten, which may sometimes act as an equivalent of some kind of unevenness in the source.

The interest of this expository scene is that it is not one in which one would expect a lot of syllabics. Seven-five is thought appropriate to moments of dramatic tension: it articulates the boundaries between phrases, opening out the space between actor and audience. Although the dialogue between Theseus and Hermia – in which Hermia is threatened with possible death – is certainly dramatic, nothing is decided as yet; the play is only beginning to reveal itself. The numbers listed below indicate the number of syllables in consecutive phrases or syllabic groupings; new sentences indicated with oblique strokes and Fukuda's commas are also indicated.[137]

---

[136] My personal impression of Fukuda's style from seeing a production of his *Hamlet* by the Shiki theatre company in June 2010 is that, having modestly disclaimed any attempt to translate Shakespeare as poetry, what he produces instead is a single, integrated and sustained poem that is capable of exerting great dramatic force. This approach is quite different from that of contemporary directors like Ninagawa, who play more freely with the audience's responses and thereby create a series of dramatic effects that encourage one to see the plays from a variety of angles. Fukuda, however, was occupied with the more basic problem of making Shakespeare possible on the Japanese stage. See also Gallimore (2001).

[137] Groupings of less than four and more than eight syllables are understood as asyllabic or ametrical. Thus, Theseus' first speech is numbered as follows: *Sate*, [2] *utsukushii Hiporita*, [9] *warera no kongi mo* [8] *majika ni semata*. [8] / *Matsu mi no* [4] *tanoshisa mo* [5] *ato yokka*, [5] *sou sureba* [5] *shingetsu no* [5] *yoi ga kuru*. [5] / *Sore ni shitemo*, [6] *kakete yuku tsuki no* [8] *ayumi no,* ↗

Enter Theseus and Hippolyta.

Theseus
    2, 9, 8 - 8 / 4 - 5 - 5, 5 - 5 - 5 / 6, 8 - 4, 9 / 9 - 4 / (1) <u>5, 7, 5</u> - 5 - 6, 6 - 5 - 5 - 6 - 6

Hippolyta
    2, 6 - 4 - 6 - (2) <u>5, 7 - 4</u> - 5 - 5 / 3 - 5, (3) <u>4 - 7 - 5</u> - 4, 6 - 5 - 5

Theseus
    2, 7, (4) <u>5 - 7 - 4</u> - 5, 8 - 6 / 5 - 5 - 5 - 5 / 5 - 5 - 4, 8 - 5 - 5 / 4, 8 - 5 - 9 / 4, 4 - 5, 3 - 7 - 4 / 1, 7 - 7, 3, 5, 8 - 5 - 3

Enter Egeus, Hermia Lysander and Demetrius.

Egeus
    4 - 5 - 5, 10

Theseus
    2, 4 / 7

Egeus
    (5) <u>6, 7 - 5</u>, 2, 4, 4, 8, 4 - 7 - 10 / 2, 7, 6 / 4, 10 - 8 - 5 / 1, 3, 6 / 2, 4, 7 - 9 - 9 / 4, 4, 6, 7 - 8, 7 - 10 / 8, 8 - 5, 9 - 9 - 4 - 6 / 4, 9 - 8, 4, 6, 3, 7 - 7 - 8 - 9 - 9, 8 / 8 - 7 - 4 - 4 - 7, 6 - 6 - 7 - 4 - 5 / 7 - 3, 8 - 7, 7, 7, 4 - 6 - 4, 4 - 6 - 8 - 4 / 7, 4, 5, 4 - 8 - 5 - 9 - 4,[138] 4 - 6, 3 - 6 - 8 - 5 - 6 / 4 - 6 - 8, 6 - 4 - 5 / 3, 7 - 4, 5, 4, 8, 9, 3 - 6

Theseus
    4, 4 / 8 - 2 / 7, 5 - 9, 7 - 4 - 5 / 7 - 6, 3 - 7 - 8, 4 - 4 - 6 - 3 / 7 - 7 - 2

Hermia
    7 - 7 - 5

Theseus
    4, 6 / 1, 5, 5 - 5 - 5, 7 - 7 - 3 - 7

Hermia
    9 - 8 - 5

Theseus
    5, 6 - 3, 5 - 5 - 8 - 3

Hermia
    2, 4 - 6 / 7 - 7 - 5 - 7, 4 - 4, 4 - 7 - 7 - 7, 5 - 5 - 6 - 6, 6, 2 - 7 - 8, 5 - 9 - 5, 7 - 7

↘ [4] *ika ni osoi koto ka!* [9] / *Kono hayaru kokoro wo* [9] *jiraseru.* [4] / *Mamahaha ya,* [5] *yamome yoroshiku,* [7] *kuchihateta* [5] *oi no mi wo* [5] *ikinagarae,* [6] *wakai mono ni* [6] *zaisan wo* [5] *yuzuru no wo* [5] *jama shite iru* [6] *youna mono da.* [6].

[138] *Shouchi itashimasenu* [9] *to nareba* [4] (l. 40, 'Consent to marry ...').

Theseus
    4 - 6, 6 - 5 - 5 - 5 - 3 / 5, 4, 9 - 8, 6, 6 - 4, 9 - 9, 8 - 5, (6) 5 - 8 - 5 - (7) 5, 7 - 4, 7 - 7 - 7, 5 - 5 - 5 - 6,[139] 8 - 3 / 4, 5 - 3, 6 - (8) 5 - 7 - 6 - 4 / 3, 9 - 7, 6 - 6, (9) 4 - 7, 5 - 8 - 6, 5 - 7, 7, 5 - 4 - 6

Hermia
    3 - 7, 10 - 5,[140] 9 - 8, (10) 4 - 7 - 5 - 5 - 4 - 8

Theseus
    2, 9 - 5, (11) 5 - 7 / 4 - 5 - 9, 7 - 6 - 6 / 3, 7, 4 - 5 - 5 - 7 - 3, 4 - 9 - 7 - 7, 6, 6 - 5 - 9, 5 - 8 - 8, 6 - 8 - 6

Demetrius
    5, 4 / 7, 7 - 8 - 4, 8 - 3 - 7

Lysander
    6, 9 - 6 / 5 - 7 - 7, 6 - 9

Egeus
    9 / 5, 7 - 8 / 3, 6, 5 - 9 / 1, 4 - 5, 5, 8 - 7, 5 - 7 - 7

Lysander
    7, 6, 7, 4 - (12) 5 - 7 - 5 - 5 / 7 - 7, 7 - 8 / 5 - 9 - 4[141] / 7 - 7 - 4 - 5 / 2, 7 - 6 - 7 / 3, 9 - 8, 5 - (13) 5 - 8 - 5 - 3 - 6 / 4, 6, 6 - 7 - 3 - 7 / (14) 4, 7, 5 - 5 - 4 - 8, 6 - 6 - 5 / 5 - 3, 4 - 4 - 7 - 6, 7 - 6, 8 - 8 - 7 - 9 - 9

Theseus
    3, 5, 6 - 7 / 8 - 8 - 8 / 7 - 4, 6 - 4 / 3, 6, 5, 4 - 6 / (15) 6 - 7 - 5 / 1, 4, 8, 4 - 9 - 6 - 8 - 5 / 6, 5 - 8 - 5 - 4, 6, 7 - 4 - 6, 2, 5 - 4, (16) 4 - 7 - 5 - 4 / 1, 4, (17) 6 / 7 - 5, 1, 3 / (18) 5 - 7 - 5 - 5 - 6, 8 - 4, (19) 4 - 7 - 5

Egeus
    2, 5 - 8

Exeunt all but Lysander and Hermia.

Lysander
    6 - 4 / 6 - 7 - 3 / 6, 6 - 8

Hermia
    3, 3 - 6 / 5, (20) 5 - 7 - 6

Lysander
    2, 5 / 4 - 6 - 7 - 4 - 6 - 3, 7 - (21) 5 - 7 - 6 / 4, 4 - 8

Hermia
    3 / 4 - 5 - 6, 7 - 3

---

[139] *Okuraneba* [5] *naranu no da ga* [6] (l. 72, 'To live a barren sister ...').
[140] *Soshite shinde* [6] *yukitou gozaimasu* [9] (l. 79, 'So will I ... so die, my lord').
[141] *Shourai no* [5] *mikomi to iu koto ni* [9] *kakete wa* [4] (l. 102, 'If not with vantage ...').

Lysander
    6 - 5
Hermia
    7 - 3 / 8, 7 - 7
Lysander
    6 - 10 - 8
Hermia
    7 / 6 - 5 - 6
Lysander
    4, 7 - 7, 6, 3, 5, 6 - 6 / 4, 3 - 7 - 5, 6 - 4, 6 - 4 / 5, 8 / 6 - 7 - 4, (22) 4, 7 - 5 - 8 - 4, 4 - 6, 4 - 9 - 9, 7, 8, 8 - 3, 4 - 5
Hermia
    2, 5, 4 - 7 - 8 - 4 - 6, 4 - 5 - 8 / 4, 4 - 8 - 5 - 6, 6 - 7, 6 / 6 - 7, 7, 4 - 8 - 8 - 4, 6 - 8
Lysander
    4 - 6 - 6, 4, 4, 5 / 4 - 10 / 7, 8 - 5, 7 / 6, 2, (23) 6 - 7 - 5, 5, 6 - 7 - 9 / 4 - (24) 5 - 7 - 5 - 9 - 5 - 7 / 7 - 7 - 6, 5, 5 - 5 - 5 / 3, 7 - 7 - 3, 2, 3, 9, (25) 5 - 6 - 5, (26) 4 - 7, 5, 6 - 8
Hermia
    4, 6, 3, 5, 6 - 10 - 3, 10 - 6 - 5, 5 - 5 - 7 - 3, 4 - 4 - 6, 3 - 7 - 6, 4, 6 - (27) 5 - 6 - 5 - 6 - (28) 5, 7 - 5 - 4 - 6 - 7, 4 - 7 - 6 - 8 - 6 / 6 - 4 / 3 / 3 / 4 - 8
Lysander
    7 - 4 / 1 - 8

Enter Helena.

Hermia
    6, 8, 9
Helena
    9 / 8 - 6 - 7 / 7 - 4 - 6 - 7, 5 - 8 / 6 - (29) 5, 7 - 4, 6, 5 - 4 - 5, 5 - 6 - 4 - 4, 6 / 4 - 6, 4 - 4, 5, 4, 4 - 6 - 4 / 7 - 7, 4 - 6, 3 - 7, (30) 5 - 7 - 4 - 4 - 5 / 6 - 8, 9 - 6, 6 - 4 - 6 / 2, 4, 5 - 3, 9, (31) 5 - 8 - 5
Hermia
    6 - 5, 8 - 4 - 3
Helena
    2, 6 - 6, 8 - 4 - 8 - 4
Hermia
    4 - (32) 5 - 6 - 5, 4 - 6
Helena
    2, 8, 8 - 7 - 4
Hermia
    4 - 5, 6 - 5

Helena
    7, 8
Hermia
    2, 3, (33) 5 - 7 - 6 - 6
Helena
    2, 6 - 6 - 6 / 7, 7 - 7
Hermia
    8, 3, 3 - 6 - 8 / 7 - 4 - 8 / (34) 4, 7 - 5, (35) 5 - 7 - 5, 2, 9 - 7 - 6 - (36) 4, 7 - 5 - 4 - 10
Lysander
    3, 4 - 5 - 8 / 5, 7 - 7 - 4 - 9, (37) 5 - 7 - 5 / 6 - 3 - 7 - 4 - 5 / 5 - 5 - 5 - 8 - 7
Hermia
    3, 5, 6 - 4 - 6[142] - (38) 5 - 7 - 5, 5 - 7 - 8 - 4 - 5, 5, (39) 4 - 7 - 5, (40) 5 - 6 - 5 - 6 - 4 - 8 - 5[143] / 5 - 8 / 9 - 4 / 5 - 5 - 5, 4 - 7 - 8 / 4, 4, 6 / 5 - 8 - 6, 6 - 3

Exit Hermia.

Lysander
    6 - 4 / 2, 5, 3, 3 - 7 - 9, 7 - 7 - 5 - 7

Exit Lysander.

Helena
    5, 6, 7 - 7 / 7 - 5 - 4 - 6 - 5 - 5, 2, 7 - 6 / 7, 7 - 8 / 4 - 8, 7 - 7 - 8 / 2, (41) 5 - 7 - 4 - 4 - 7, 4 - 5 - 6 - 9 - 8 - (42) 6 / 7 - 5 - 4, 4 - 10 - 6, 7 - 7 - 8 - 6 / 5, 6 - 3, 7 / 3 - 7 - 6, 7 - 7 / 3, 5 - 6 - 4 - 7 / 7, 4, 6 - 5 - 5 - 5 - (43) 5 / 8 - 5 - 6 - 4, 3, 3, 8 - 6 - 4 - 4 / 9 - 5 - 8 - 8 - 5, 6 - 8, 4 - 7 - 3 / 7 - 6, 9 - 6, 4 - 9, 7 - 4 - 7, 3, 8 - 7, 5 - 6, 7 - 4 - 7 / 2, 9 - 8 - 7 / 5, 5, (44) 5 - 7 - 5 / (45) 5 - 7, 4 - 8, 7 - 7 - 4 / 2, (46) 5, 6 - 5 - 4 - 7, 8, 7 - 5 - 5

Exit Helena.

The groups underlined are either conventional 5-7-5, or (according to my arbitrary reading) 'imperfect' groups where two of the phrases are 5 or 7 and the symmetry of expansion and contraction is closely enough observed; thus, 4 - 7 - 5 and 5 - 8 - 5 are

---

[142] *Yoku anata to* [6] *issho ni* [4] *sakurasō no* [6] (ll. 214-5, 'where often you and I / Upon faint primrose beds ...').
[143] *Asenzu no* [5] *miyako wo se ni* [6] *atarashii* [5] *otomodachi wo* [6] *motomete* [4] *mishiranu sekai ni* [8] *tabidatsu no* [5] (ll. 218-9, 'And thence from Athens turn away our eyes, / To seek new friends, and stranger companies.').

acceptable, but not 4 - 7 - 6 or 5 - 9 - 5. By this measure, there are nine conventional groups and thirty-seven 'imperfect', which means that out of 960 possible tripartite combinations (in other words, excluding groups where only one or two phrases are possible), only 4.79% are in any way conventional. Yet fives and sevens are the two most popular syllabic phrases within the passage as a whole, in which the phrases may be categorised as follows: 7 of one syllable (0.66% out of a total 1,057 phrases); 30 of two syllables (2.84%); 63 of three (5.96%); 181 of four (17.12%); 241 of five (22.80%); 174 of six (16.46%); 196 of seven (18.54%); 104 of eight (9.84%); 50 of nine (4.73%); and, 11 of ten syllables (1.04%). The mean length is 5.04 syllables.

The examples of perfect and imperfect syllabics are numbered for later categorisation, with a brief commentary on each example as follows:

(1) *Mamahaha ya,* [5] *yamome yoroshiku,* [7] *kuchihateta* [5]
'Like to a step-dame or a dowager / Long withering out ...' (ll. 5-6, Theseus). The syllabic organises the unaccented, repeated vowels of the first two phrases into a unit that is shattered by the strong accent in *kuchihateta*.

(2) *tokehairi,* [5] *yondo no yoru mo* [7] *tachimachi* [4]
'steep themselves ... / Four nights will quickly ...' (ll. 7 and 8, Hippolyta). The first of several examples that connects separate sentences or clauses, the syllabic corresponds with the poetic devices used to connect the two lines in the source.

(3) *misora ni* [4] *hikishiborareta* [7] *gin no yumi* [5]
'a silver bow ... bent in heaven' (ll. 9-10, Hippolyta). The first example of enjambement, the rhythmic tension between the first and second phrases prefigures the phonic imitation of the bending bow in the second phrase.

(4) *Asenzu no* [5] *wakamonodomo no* [7] *kokoro wo* [4]
'Stir up the Athenian youth ...' (l. 12, Theseus). The uncomplicated rhythm and rhymes make this a highly regular syllabic suitable for clear instructions. In other words, the metaphor 'stir up' does not require elaboration.

(5) *koujihatete,* [6] *makaridemashite* [7] *gozaimasu* [5]
'Full of vexation come I, with complaint ...' (l. 22, Egeus). Shakespeare's word order, placing the verb after the qualifier, is the usual word order in Japanese. The syllabic corresponds with the pithiness of the source construction.

(6) *eikyuu ni* [5] *kurai shinden no* [8] *oku fukaku* [5]
'For aye to be in shady cloister ...' (l. 71, Theseus). The syllabic rhythm emphasises the haunting phrase *kurai shinden* ('dark temple'), with the tripping *k-* sounds in *oku fukaku* (literally 'deep at the back' of the shrine) sounding deliberatively perjorative.

(7) *tojikomori,* [5] *tsumetai tsuki ni* [7] *mukatte* [4]
'mew'd … [facing] the cold … moon' (ll. 71 and 73, Theseus). Phrasing and alliteration work together here to create a particularly strong example of syllabic rhythm, with *tsumetai* (meaning 'cold') the key word.

(8) *isshou wo* [5] *sugosu mono koso* [7] *shiawase tomo* [6]
'To live a barren sister all your life' (l. 72, Theseus). The syllabic is supported by repetitive alliteration on the soft *s-* sound (turning into *shi-* in the third part) and assonance on the bold *o-* sound. The patterning supports a portrayal here of Theseus as stern and yet gentle.

(9) *kono yo no* [4] *sachi to iu mono,* [7] *mi wo mamoru* [5]
'earthlier happier …' (l. 76, Theseus). The syllabic is lifted poetically from its context by the repetition of short *o* no less than nine times. The language sounds classical, suited to this conventional image.

(10) *kokoro ni* [4] *somanu otoko ni* [7] *shougai wo* [5]
'his lordship, whose unwished yoke' (l. 81, Hermia). The light rhythm and assonance of the first two parts leads naturally into the key word *shōgai* ('my life'). The slightly archaic negative form *somanu*, meaning that her heart is 'unstained' by this man's love, adds a native poetic tinge to her argument.

(11) *shingetsu no* [5] *yoi made matou* [7] – *aisuru* [4]
'by the next new moon … my love' (ll. 83 and 84, Theseus). The key word *matō* ('let us wait') harks back to Theseus' own complaint that he must wait until the next new moon before he can marry Hippolyta, who is brought back into the conversation with the epithet *aisuru* ('my love').

(12) *isasakamo* [5] *Demetoriasu ni* [7] *ototte wa* [5]
'As … as … Demetrius' (ll. 101-2, Lysander). The rhythmic first and third groupings, leading successively to the accent in *ot<u>o</u>tte wa*, contain the rhythmically awkward foreign name.

(13) *Haamia no* [5] *kokoro wo kachiete* [8] *iru to iu* [5]
'I am beloved of … Hermia' (l. 104, Lysander). The heavy alliteration in the second part and the stress given to the copula *iru* ('I <u>am</u> beloved') emphasise the keenness with which Lysander attempts to stake his claim.

(14) *ippou,* [4] *Demetoriasu wa,* [7] *tounin no* [5]
'Demetrius, I'll avouch it to his head' (l. 106, Lysander). The syllabic associates the name of Demetrius with a legalistic word for 'that person' (*tōnin*), which is appropriate to the setting and also open to a scornful manner of utterance.

(15) *futari dake ni* [6] *iikikasetai* [7] *koto ga aru* [5]
'I have some private schooling for you both.' (l. 116, Theseus). The syllabic structure places the emphasis on the verb of saying (*iikikasetai*) and is therefore complemented by the quadruple assonance on the vowel *i*.

(16) *omae wa* [4] *sono izureka wo* [7] *erabaneba* [5]
'To death, or to a vow of single life.' (l. 121, Theseus). Fukuda adds this phrase, meaning 'You must choose between the one or the other.', with the syllabic rhythm supporting his rhetorical intent.

(17) *doushita no da?* [6] *Demetoriasu mo* [7] *Ijiasu mo* [5]
'what cheer, my love? Demetrius and Egeus' (ll. 122-3, Theseus). The syllabic rhythm, supported by alliteration on the *d-* sounds, moves Theseus surely, if heavily from his private to his public affairs. The rise in the first part is equivalent to the accidence in 'what cheer, my love?'

(18) *futari niwa,* [5] *kongi ni tsuite* [7] *tetsudatte* [5]
'... employ you in some business / Against our nuptial' (ll. 124-5, Theseus). Unlike the previous example, which is also headed by *futari* ('you two'), the punctuation gives equal emphasis to the first and second groupings, perhaps ironically. *Kongi* means 'nuptial'.

(19) *iroiro* [4] *soudan shitai* [7] *koto ga aru* [5]
'confer with you' (l. 125, Theseus). A straightforward positioning of the accented *sōdan* at the beginning of the seven foregrounds this word, meaning 'consultation', as the keyword of the whole speech.

(20) *kono me kara* [5] *arashi no you ni* [7] *furasemashō.* [6]
'Beteem them from the tempest of my eyes' (l. 131, Hermia). The juxtaposition of vowels at the end of the first and beginning of the second groupings delays the momentum of the line to the third, imitating the effect of welling tears.

(21) *odayaka ni* [5] *jitsu wo musunda* [7] *tameshi wa nai* [6]
'... never did run smooth' (l. 134, Lysander). Perhaps in reflection of Lysander's distress, the syllabic is not very smoothly coordinated with the other rhythms. The accents fall on *jitsu* and *nai*.

(22) *isshun,* [4] *katto tenchi no* [7] *zenbou wo* [5]
'That, in a spleen, unfolds both heaven and earth' (l. 146, Lysander). The syllabic supports the hyperbolic drama of Lysander's image (*katto* meaning 'flashing' for 'spleen').

(23)   *kuri hanareta* [6] *inaka ni sunde* [7] *iru no da ga* [5]
'is her house remote seven leagues' (l. 159, Lysander). The emphasis that the rhythm places on the word *inaka* ('countryside') could be read comically or even with a touch of embarrassment.

(24)   *sokode nara* [5] *kekkon dekiru,* [7] *soko made wa* [5]
'There ... may I marry thee, / And to that place ...' (ll. 161-2, Lysander). The syllabic recreates the rhythmic spontaneity of Lysander's deixis by giving the deictic word (*soko*- meaning 'that') rhythmic symmetry.

(25)   *sanzashi no* [5] *hana wo tori ni* [6] *itta toki* [5]
'To do observance' (l. 167, Lysander). This phrase, literally meaning 'when we went to pick the hawthorn flowers', is a gloss on the May morning observance which the syllabic brings into its poetic context.

(26)   *Herena to* [4] *issho ni atta,* [7] *ano mori de* [5]
'Where I did meet thee ... with Helena' (l. 166, Lysander). An example of how Japanese word order can be manipulated in the Shakespearean way. Two accents on the verbal clause in the seven precede the phrase of place in the five.

(27)   *Toroijin* [5] *Iiniasu ga* [6] *fune ni ho wo* [5]
'When the false Troyan under sail' (l. 174, Hermia). Japanese word order puts this line the other way round from the source, with Fukuda adding the name of 'the false Troyan', Aeneas, for the benefit of his audience.

(28)   *itta toki,* [5] *sore wo nagamete* [7] *Karutago no* [5]
'And by that fire which burn'd the Carthage queen' (l. 173, Hermia). Another reversal of word order creates a vigorous rhythmic momentum from the verb (*nagamete*) on to the object, which is the Japanised form of Carthage.

(29)   *Hokutosei,* [5] *anata no shita wa* [7] *soyokaze* [4]
'lodestars, and your tongue's sweet air' (l. 183, Helena). With reference to Hermia's melodramatic speech about Aeneas fleeing Carthage by boat, this arrangement emphasises the nautical metaphor by translating 'air' as 'breeze' (*soyokaze*), and allows for a bitterly sarcastic stress on *Hokutosei* ('lodestars') and *soyokaze* ('air').

(30)   *sono shita no* [5] *torokeru you na* [7] *shirabe wo* [4]
'My tongue should catch your tongue's sweet melody.' (l. 189, Helena). The unbroken sequence of short vowel sounds up to the long vowel *yō* makes that latter word the turning point in the whole 5-7-5. Meaning 'like' or 'as if', the word's foregrounding also foregrounds the conventionally figurative mood of

Helena's speech.

(31) *ano hito no* [5] *kokoro no ugoki wo* [8] *ayatsuru no* [5]
'You sway the motion of Demetrius' heart.' (l. 193, Helena). The use of a syllabic structure is justified by the simple poetic image.

(32) *warukuchi wo* [5] *itte yaru no,* [6] *sore na no ni* [5]
'I give him curses; yet …' (l. 196, Hermia). The six is too slight a grouping for the syllabic to stand out from its context, perhaps in imitation of the conventionality of the stychomythia.

(33) *ano hito no* [5] *kichigai zata wa* [7] *atashi no sei* [5]
'His folly … is no fault of mine.' (l. 200, Hermia). The rhythm serves to stress the three key lexical items as in the source, namely *zata* ('folly'), *atashi* ('mine') and *sei* ('fault').

(34) *sou na no* [4] *Raisandaa ni* [7] *au mae wa* [5]
'Before the time I did Lysander see' (l. 204, Hermia). The syllabic phrasing serves to shape the flow of Hermia's thought, literally 'I remember now, before I met Lysander I …'

(35) *rakuen to* [5] *mieta Asenzu* [7] *datta no ni* [5]
'Seem'd Athens as a paradise to me.' (l. 205, Hermia). The syllabic is supported by the assonance on *en* that connects the two key words *rakuen* and *Asenzu*. Perhaps it is even a pun, with *en* being a word for Japanese currency (yen) and the capital a place which one would naturally associate with money.

(36) *iru no deshou* [6] *Raisandā wa* [7] *tengoku wo* [5]
'O then what … he hath turn'd a heaven …' (ll. 206-7, Hermia). An example of no particular interest.

(37) *kusa no ha ni* [5] *shinju no kiri wo* [7] *yadosu koro* [5]
'Decking with liquid pearl the bladed grass' (l. 211, Lysander). The image itself is so clear as to require no more than the syllabic structure; there are no other rhythmic features.

(38) *yawarakai* [5] *hana no shitone ni* [7] *nesobette* [5]
'Upon faint primrose beds were wont to lie' (l. 215, Hermia). As elsewhere, Fukuda develops Hermia's fond memory into a more fulsome expression of sisterly love than is necessarily present in the original; the word *nesobetto* ('to lie down and sleep') may also be looking forward to Act 2, Scene 2, when Lysander proposes to Hermia that they sleep together in the wood.

(39) *atashi wa* [4] *Raisandaa to* [7] *ochiatte* [5]
'There my Lysander and myself shall meet' (l. 217, Hermia). The focus of this one is definitely on Hermia's lover, Lysander.

(40) *Asenzu no* [5] *miyako wo se ni* [6] *atarashii* [5]
'And thence from Athens turn away our eyes' (l. 218, Hermia). The regular metre suits this classical image of passion turning its back (*sena*) on the seat of wisdom. The elision of an adjective *atarashii* with the succeeding phrase adds further impetus.

(41) *ano hito ga* [5] *Hāmia no me ni* [7] *hikarete* [4]
'doting on Hermia's eyes' (l. 230, Helena). The obvious feature is the alliteration on the light, open aspirate *h*. Helena knows all about Hermia's eyes and how open they are!

(42) *kamo shirenai ...* [6] *donna iyashii* [7] *yokoshimana* [5]
'Things base and vile' (l. 232, Helena). Fukuda puts Helena in full rhetorical mode here with the exclamatory *donna* ('however much ...').

(43) *iru no da wa.* [5] *koi no kamisama ga* [7] *kodomo da to* [5]
'And therefore is Love said to be a child' (l. 238, Helena). The syllabic structure supports the alliteration on *koi* ('love'), *kamisama* ('god') and *kodomo* ('child').

(44) *ano hito wa* [5] *mori made otte* [7] *yuku deshō* [5]
'Then to the wood will he' (l. 247, Helena). The rapid rhythm, with just a little chicanery in the second part and a slight hiatus in *otte*, supports the stealthy tone of Helena's plan.

(45) *sono koto wo* [5] *shirasete agete,* [7] *orei wo* [4]
'and for this intelligence / If I have thanks' (ll. 248-49, Helena). The key word becomes *orei*, or 'thanks from Demetrius', which is clearly what she desires most.

(46) *sou sureba* [5] *yukikaeri ni* [6] *ano hito no* [5]
'his [sight] thither and back again.' (l. 251, Helena). The slight syllabic shift emphasises Helena's desire both to go with him to the wood and to come back together with him.

The above syllabics are distributed evenly throughout the scene, but with a definite bias toward the stylised dialogues between Hermia, Lysander and Helena in the second half; twenty-seven of the forty-six structures come after line 126. Helena's soliloquy is also syllabically rich. To take the analysis a step further, the distribution of lines in the source and syllabics in translation with respect to speech length and among characters is as follows:

SPEECH LENGTH

Number of lines	1	2-10	more than 10
as % of scene	4	38	58
as % of syllabics	4	33	63

CHARACTERS

	as % of scene	as % of syllabics
Theseus	26	26
Hermia	22	26
Lysander	20	22
Helena	17	20
Egeus	12	2
Hippolyta	2	4
Demetrius	1	-

These figures show a general consistency between the organisation of the source and target texts, the most noticeable difference being that the two young women have 15-20% more syllabics than one would expect, whereas Egeus (who plays a stereotypical role in this scene) has very few.

For an even clearer understanding of the syllabics, it is useful to categorise the forty-six examples annotated above according to their rhetorical functions, in other words by comparison with the source. Does the phrase look inward, being a lyrical expression of feeling? Is it rhetorical, moving another character toward a defined action? Or would it seem to combine both the lyrical and rhetorical modes? Or finally, is it no more than a locutive act, even about language itself? Many of the examples are quite difficult to categorise. Example 25 is only part of a longer phrase detailing the place where Lysander plans to flee with Hermia but Fukuda's paraphrase gives it a seasonal reference that has a definite lyrical resonance. Example 27 is one of a series of oaths sworn by Hermia to assure Lysander that she will keep their tryste and can therefore be construed as rhetorical. Examples 2 and 3 could also be construed as rhetorical assurance but are not framed as such and so their functions are ambiguous.

The examples can be roughly categorised as follows:[144]

LYRICAL (13) : 1, 3, 10, 16, 20, 27, 28, 29, 30, 35, 36, 38 and 40

---

[144] In Jakobsonian terms, the first category would correspond with poetic and conative speech acts, the second with the emotive and denotative, the third with both the poetic and emotive, and the fourth with the purely lingual.

RHETORICAL (6) : 4, 13, 32, 33, 42 and 43
LYRICAL-RHETORICAL (11) : 2, 6, 7, 8, 9, 21, 22, 25, 28, 31 and 37
LOCUTIVE-FUNCTIONAL (18) : 5, 11, 12, 14, 15, 16, 17, 18, 19, 23, 24, 26, 34, 39, 41, 44, 45 and 46

These figures suggest first and foremost that the syllabic metre is open to all the main types of dramatic utterance. There is perhaps less need to use it with phrases where rhythms and imagery are already prominent, and one should not forget that all the phrases are syllabic if not metrical. In the case of functional language, the seven-five syllabic can be an equivalent to iambic metre, sustaining a rhythmic momentum that is otherwise absent.

Syllabic metre is just one of a range of poetic devices available to the translator. Chapter Two looked briefly at how punctuation can be varied and controlled to register rhetorical modulations in the source, and such modulations can also be observed over the narrower range of the syllabic phrase. The following analysis charts the syllabic movement in Fukuda's translation of Hermia's oath to Lysander against the source (ll. 168 to 178). The rising arrows mark an increase in the number of syllables in the succeeding phrase, the falling arrows vice-versa (18-19):

> My good Lysander,
> Ureshii, 4/ Raisandā, 6/

I swear to thee by Cupid's strongest bow,
atashi, ↗ / chikaimasu, ↗ / Kyūpiddo no ↗ / ichiban tsuyoi ↘ / yumi ni kakete, ↗ /

By his best arrow with the golden head,
kin no yajiri no → / tsuita ichiban → / ii ya ni kakete, ↘ /

By the simplicity of Venus' doves,
Bīnasu no → / otonashii ↗ / otsukaibato ↘ / ni kakete, ↗ /

By that which knitteth souls and prospers loves,
kokoro to kokoro wo ↘ / musubiawase, → / koi wo moeru ↘ / agaraseru ↗ /
kami ni kakete, ↘ /

And by that fire which burn'd the Carthage queen
sore kara, ↗ / ano fujitsuna ↘ / Toroijin ↗ / Īniasu ga ↘ / fune ni ho wo ↗ /
agete satte ↘ / itta toki, ↗ /

When the false Trojan under sail was seen;
sore wo nagamete ↘ / Karutago no ↗ / joō ga mi wo ↗ / tōjita honō ↘ / ni kakete, → /

By all the vows that ever men hath broke
ima made ↗ / ari to arayuru ↘ / otokotachi ga ↗ / yabutta chikai no ↘ / kazu ni kakete - ↗ /

(In number more than ever women spoke),
onna no chikai nado ↘ / oyobimotsukanu ↗ / sono kazu ni kakete - ↘ /

In that same place thou hast appointed me,
ee, ↗ / arayuru mono ↘ / ni kakete, ↗ / ima osshatta ↘ / basho de, → /

Tomorrow truly will I meet with thee.
ashita, → / kitto, ↗ / anata ni oai ↘ / itashimasu.

Out of forty-six phrases (excluding the first and last), twenty (43.5%) move on to longer phrases, nineteen (41.3%) to shorter ones, and seven (15.2%) stay the same. The syllabic movement is positive and expansive, a rhetorical equivalent of the source, as Hermia's speech is a brave and highly patterned oath of loyalty to Lysander, one sentence in eleven lines. Apart from the trisyllabic *kakete*, which serves a separate function in a figure of repetition, all but one of the twos, threes and fours come in the first three lines and the last two. Fukuda's Hermia needs the short phrases to gain Lysander's undivided attention and prepare herself for her rhetorical *tour de force* while the short phrases in the last two lines return the rhetoric once more to a softer register.

While the whole scene is too large a structure to identify any unifying factors, rhetorical patterns can be established within individual speeches and rhetorical functions identified. There is also a syllabic movement to be observed over the dramatic structure of the scene, which is outlined below by line numbers and speaking characters:

1. ll. 1-19 (19 lines) – Theseus and Hippolyta
2. ll. 20-127 (107 lines) – Theseus, Egeus, Hermia, Lysander and Demetrius
3. ll. 128-179 (51 lines) – Lysander and Hermia
4. ll. 180-225 (45 lines) – Lysander, Hermia and Helena
5. ll. 226-51 (25 lines) – Helena

The scene moves from dialogue to the group, back to dialogue, then to the small group and finally soliloquy. The movement is also one from reflective action (Theseus' decision to hold a party) to confrontation (Hermia's refusal to marry Demetrius) to reflective action (Lysander and Hermia's decision to flee the city) to confrontation (between Helena and Hermia) and finally reflective action (Helena's decision to follow Lysander and Hermia). The movement is similar in form at least to the five-seven-five movement of the Japanese syllabic and will be repeated in the patterns of detachment and attachment to be enacted by the lovers.

RIDING THE HORSE: THE LOVERS' FIGHT

The tendency in *A Midsummer Night's Dream* for symmetry as a stylistic and structural trait is intimately connected with Kinoshita's problem of 'riding the horse' in the rhetoric of dramaturgy and with Hazlitt's awareness of the subordination of poetry to dramatic purpose in this play: the difficulty of knowing when and where to turn the line. Fukuda's translation of Hermia's speech quoted above offers one example as to how Hermia may be made 'to ride the horse' in Japanese prose translation. The rhetorical turn becomes even clearer, graphologically at least, in free verse translation, as in Odashima's version (19):

> Maa, Raisandā!
> Atashi, chikau wa, Kyūpiddo no ichiban tsuyoi yumi ni kakete,
> sono kane no yajiri no tsuita ichiban rippana ya ni kakete,
> Bīnasu no kuruma wo hiku seijō mukuna hato ni kakete,
> tamashii to tamashii wo musubiawasete shiawasena koi wo umu kami ni kakete,
> fujitsuna Toroijin Īnīasu ga fune de saru no wo mite
> Karutago no joō Daidō ga mi wo tōjita honō ni kakete,
> ima made onna to iu onna ga chikatta kazu wo uchiyaburu hodo
> otoko to iu otoko ga kazu ōku yabutta arittake no chikai ni kakete,
> ima anata ga osshatta basho de, ashita no ban,
> machigai naku atashi wa anata ni au koto ni suru wa.

The obvious feature of this translation is the repetition of the idiom *ni kakete* at the end of the second, third, fourth, fifth, seventh and ninth lines. The verb *kakeru* means 'to hang' but has a number of idiomatic variations including the adverbial *ni kakete*, which literally means 'swearing by'. With a different Sino-Japanese character, the phonologically identical *kakeru* can mean 'to canter' or 'gallop', a quite plausible pun on its semantic meaning as it is used at the turn of each line. There is a danger of Hermia's ornate similes getting lost in the galloping prolixity of translation, especially in the long fifth line, but – like Hermia – Odashima keeps his hands on the reins. After four repetitions, the word is missed in the sixth line, reestablished in the seventh and an alternating pattern initiated with the repetition in the ninth. This slight manipulation of audience expectations is not only a literal equivalent of the source but it also encourages the audience to listen to Hermia's oaths. The overall sensation is heavy, but a convincing imitation of iambic, as the idiom relentlessly forces the rhythmic momentum to the end of the line. When Hermia finally does state her promise in the last two lines the key phrase *machigai naku* ('without fail') is placed quite emphatically at the beginning of the line. The speech has been 'turned', none too subtly perhaps, but effectively enough for both context and listener.

Lysander's plan is hardly as courageous as what we have just heard from Hermia, who puts her life on the line with a far more immediate gesture than her lover. It is Lysander, if anyone, who is moved to action by the courage of the other, and Hermia is unlikely to reject his plan. Within the confines of the court they are still behaving quite conventionally but having moved into the savage wood they start to lose their rationality. The grammar and vocabulary of their style stays the same but it seems that their rhetoric truly starts to have consequence. Of course, with all four running around in circles, the rhetoric is ultimately self-defeating and they do indeed exhaust themselves. The horse is released, as it were, from its fold and allowed to run free before finding home in the wild but harmless character of Puck, who puts the four lovers to bed.

The tone of the lovers' quarrel in Act 3, Scene 2 is not uniformly wild and includes such tender moments as Helena's memories of Hermia as a child (ll. 192-219). Yet tenderness cannot be sustained for long nor the madness suppressed. The following excerpt moves swiftly from rudeness (Lysander) to astonishment (Hermia) to rudeness and surprise again (Lysander/Hermia) to irritation (Helena) to indignation (Lysander) to scorn (Demetrius) and finally to indignation again (Lysander) (ll. 260-70):

Lys.	Hang off, thou cat, thou burr! Vile thing, let loose,
	Or I will shake thee from me like a serpent.
Her.	Why are you grown so rude? What change is this, Sweet love?
Lys.	Thy love? Out tawny Tartar, out!
	Out, loathed medicine! O hated potion, hence!
Her.	Do you not jest?
Hel.	Yes sooth, and so do you.
Lys.	Demetrius, I will keep my word with thee.
Dem.	I would I had your bond, for I perceive.
	A weak bond holds you; I'll not trust your word.
Lys.	What, should I hurt her, strike her, kill her dead?
	Although I hate her, I'll not harm her so.

The dialogue is driven by a blind passion that answers outburst with outburst, rebuttal with rebuttal, but never reaches a conclusion. The speeches are too short to achieve any kind of logical development and the longer speeches elsewhere are more often than not personal laments that are easily pushed aside. Although there are opportunities for spondaic interspersion (e.g. 'Vile thing', 'bond holds'), the iambic rhythm is surprisingly consistent.

The rhythm is important to the dialogue as the one stylistic feature that unifies the lovers that one has every right to expect a degree of consistency in Odashima's treatment (88):

L: Hanase, [3] kono neko, [4] ginyō! [4] Hanase to iu no ni. [8]

                Hanasanai to [6] hebi no yō ni [6] furitobasu zo, [6] ii ka! [3]

Hm: Dōshite kyū ni [7] sonna ni ranbō ni [9] natta no, [4] nē? [2] Atashi no [4] daijina anata ... [7]

L: Daijina anata! [7] Baka iu na, [4] dattanme! [5] Kiechimae, [5] kusuri no yō ni [7] iyana, [3] doku no yō ni [6] norowashii onna! [8]

Hm: Jōdan deshō, [7] anata? [3]

Hl: Mochiron yo, [5] anata datte. [6]

L: Dimītoriasu, [7] yakusoku wa [5] mamoru kara na. [6]

D: Omae no yakusoku wa [9] shinyō dekin na, [8] shōko ga hoshii yo, [8] shōkori naku [6] onna ni jiku wo [7] hippararete iru [8] yō jā. [4]

L: Nani, [2] kono onna wo naguri, [9] kizutsuke, [4] korose to iu no ka? [8] Ikura kiraina [7] onna demo, [5] kizu wo [4] owaseru ki wa [6] okoran. [4]

Looking at the outline of the printed text, Odashima's translation seems as broken and formless as its semantic meaning. Yet the line endings do reveal a pattern of some significance. Each of the lines spoken by a character who loves the person addressed (that is, Hermia to Lysander, Hermia to Helena, and Helena to Hermia) ends with a soft or neutral word (e.g. *nē*, *anata*) and each of the lines spoken by a character who hates the person addressed (Lysander to Hermia, Lysander to Demetrius, and Demetrius to Lysander) ends either with a hard-sounding, isolated particle (*yo*, *ka*) or with some equally abrupt label (e.g. *onna* meaning 'woman') and in the final line with the colloquial negative *okoran*. The pattern is therefore as follows: hard - hard - soft - hard - hard - soft - hard - hard - hard - hard - hard. The hard tone dominates in Odashima's version and continues in that way for the remainder of the scene. As in the source, the horse gets away; the lovers seem incapable of creating any kind of symmetrical pattern out of their dialogue. The resulting effect is of an absurd sameness, equivalent to the thunderous rhythm of the source and only saved from tedium by the licence of performance.

    Odashima's particles are not absent from the early modern Japanese of Tsubouchi but one would not expect the earlier translator to achieve the rapid pace of Odashima. In fact, it might even be possible by the use of syllabics and *kanji* compounds to slow the dialogue down so that the emotions become suppressed, delayed, all the more poisonous (255-56).

L: Ei, [2] hanase, [3] unu, [2] neko. [2] Gobō no togeme! [7] Iyana yatsume, [6] ei, [2] hanase. [3] Hanasanai to, [6] tataki otosu zo, [7] hebi no yō ni. [6]

Hm: Dōshite sonna ni [8] ranbō ni [5] onarinasutta no? [8] Ma, [1] dōshita to iu no? [8] Yō anata? [5]

L: Yō anata da? [6] Unu, [2] akatobiiro no [7] dattanjinme, [7] chikushō! [4] Unu, [2] tamaranai [5] kusagusurime, [6] iyana iyana [6] nigagusurime, [6] icchimae! [5]

Hm: Jōdan deshō? [7]

Hl: Sō tomo, [4] jōdan desu tomo. [8] Anata datte sō yo. [9]

L: Dimitoriasu, [6] yakusoku wo [5] kitto mamoru zo. [7]

D: Anmari [4] mamoraresō nimo [8] nai ne, [5] yowai [3] omamorihimo ga [7] tomete iru kara. [7] Kimi no iu koto wa [8] ate ni naran yo. [7]

L: Nan da to? [4] Kono onna wo bute, [8] korose to iu no ka? [7] Nikui to wa [5] omotte iru keredo, [9] masaka sonna ni [7] shiyō to wa [5] omowanai. [5]

Tsubouchi is no more prolix than Odashima and with a few exceptions, such as the arcane *akatobiiro* ('the colour of a red kite'), is surprisingly comprehensible to a modern audience. He does not use sentence-ending particles as Odashima does but it is noticeable that every sentence does end with a word or phrase that expresses either doubt (*Yō anata?*, 'What you?'), negativity (*omowanai*, 'I don't think') or aggression (*mamoru zo*, 'I will keep my promise'). The two translations are highly colloquial, with Odashima using a brusque imperative, *kiechimae* ('Get out of it!'), and the *-me* suffix meaning 'woman'. In their distracted condition, the lovers' language becomes more phatic and expletive in both the translations. The language of Lysander and Demetrius is rich with insults (*chikushō*, 'beast') and alliteration (*kizutsuke, korose ...*, 'injure, kill ...') while the language of the two women is characterised by brokenness and unanswered questions. In both cases and in both translations, the seven-five syllabic is entirely absent. The more passionately the lovers stake their claims over each other, the more separate they in fact become, and this is reflected also in the lack of metrical coordination from one phrase to the next. The one slight exception is the final exchange between Demetrius and Lysander where Demetrius sustains a string of eights and sevens in both translations.

Tsubouchi lacks the distinct boundaries of the free verse line with which to embroider some kind of pattern across the dialogue. The pattern, if such it is, comes from the negative verb endings and negative vocabulary (*norowashii*, 'damned', *nigagusuri*, 'bitter medicine') that predominate. The source text, as indeed the whole scene, is patterned in a way that demands translation. Yet unlike comic dialogue, where characters may have control over their linguistic games, the iambic metre and the structured dialogue seem beyond the control of the lovers. The challenge for the translator is to register these controlling factors without compromising the spontaneity of the dialogue. The examples above suggest that the first resource is the colloquial language itself with its particles that can be used with varying degrees of emphasis to mark the barriers between both sentences and people. The need to be heard becomes ever stronger as the habitual securities disintegrate.

THE RHYTHMS OF PROSE: BOTTOM'S DREAM

With all four translations being written in either prose or free verse, the presence of prose passages would seem to make special demands on the translator's ingenuity. Shakespeare's prose, certainly in *A Midsummer Night's Dream*, is usually confined to comic or socially inferior characters outside a courtly milieu, but the prose translator can (as Tsubouchi does) register the change by using dialect or an imitation of working class speech.[145] Tsubouchi writes that (Tsubouchi 1977, 187)

> in order to communicate the earnest naïvety of these characters with a natural good humour, I have deliberately mixed in a lot of rural dialect with their language.

The free verse translator too can make a straightforward enough shift into dialect or prose or both. Yet the extent to which these approaches achieve anything like pragmatic equivalence can only depend upon the extent to which the relationship between the blank verse and prose genres is interpreted in the translation process.

The fundamental difference between the two genres is that blank verse adds a rhythmic principle to the normal constraints of English grammar but that in prose it is only syntax that limits the possible range of morphologies. The pace of a dramatic performance depends among other things on the rhythmic momentum of dramatic speech utterances. In a play such as *A Midsummer Night's Dream* which is mainly blank

---

[145] Prose-speaking characters are not necessarily social inferiors but, as Hussey notes, prose 'is likely to be contrastive in intention' (Hussey 1992, 154), reflecting 'something other than the norm' (ibid., 153), and in all the comedies except *The Merry Wives of Windsor* the norm is aristocratic and blank verse.

verse, the world of prose is set apart from the main plot and the dramatic illusion of chronological movement. Although prose can be the vehicle of sub-plot and sometimes of main plot, the relaxation of generic constraints is often seen to afford characters a certain freedom with words and imagery.[146] Characters such as Launcelot Gobbo (*The Merchant of Venice*) and Parolles (*All's Well That Ends Well*) may be tragic or tragicomic in themselves but their use of language is inevitably comic when it is freed from the often tragic necessity of shaping human events.[147]

Bottom is too naïve a character to be called a clown or wordsmith in the tradition of Gobbo or Feste[148] but his soliloquy in Act 4, Scene 1, when he awakes from his unearthly experience with Titania, shows some of the characteristics of clowning discourse (4.1.199-217):

> When my cue comes, call me and I will answer. My next is 'Most fair Pyramus'. Heigh-ho! Peter Quince? Flute, the bellows-mender? Snout, the tinker? Starveling? God's my life! Stolen hence, and left me asleep! I have had a most rare vision. I have had a dream, past the wit of man to say what dream it was. Man is but an ass if he go about to expound this dream. Methought I was – there is no man can tell what. Methought I was – and me – thought I had – but man is but a patched fool if he will offer to say what methought I had. The eye of man hath not heard, the ear of man hath not seen, man's hand is not able to taste, his tongue to conceive, nor his heart to report, what my dream was. I will get Peter Quince to write a ballad of this dream: it shall be called 'Bottom's Dream', because it hath no bottom; and I will sing it in the latter end of a play, before the Duke. Peradventure, to make it the more gracious, I shall sing it at her death.

The speech is utterly arhythmical at first, the speech of someone who has just woken up. From that low point, it is gradually, if loosely, structured by the use of repetition and rhythm. The two most significant repeated items are 'methought' and 'dream', which are both variations on 'methinks', which commonly refers to dreaming or imagination in Shakespeare.[149] The phrases 'methought I was' and 'methought I had' are both iambic. Repetition is used again in the sentence beginning 'The eye of man ...', which is also metrical. The succession of iambs and anapaests is a comic complement to the

---

[146] It is the vehicle of one of the sub-plots of *A Midsummer Night's Dream* and of the main plot of *The Merry Wives of Windsor*.
[147] It is in the nature of Parolles' linguistic sophistry that he can never take meaning seriously so that he too is dismissed as unserious in the end. As the King says at the final unravelling, 'thou art too fine in thy evidence; therefore, stand aside.' (*All's Well That Ends Well*, 5.3.262-63).
[148] Bottom differs from Gobbo and Feste in that he is not a servant of a higher master and therefore not privy to the rhetorical sophistication of a higher class.
[149] 'Methinks' ('I think') typically carries the ratiocinative meaning in Shakespeare but four out of the nine usages in *A Midsummer Night's Dream* refer more to thought as imaginative supposition, e.g. Titania (3.2.191), 'The moon, methinks, looks with a watery eye'.

thunderously trochaic 'bottom' and mark Bottom's growing excitement as he envisages his new entertainment.

'The Ballad of Bottom's Dream' belongs to 'Pyramus and Thisbe' and therefore points, perhaps even belongs to the language of the court. It is natural then that Bottom's prose should aspire to poetic metre since at the very least he knows he is duty bound to provide them with something they will appreciate. The comic irony of the speech is that his audience already know of what Bottom's dream consists, but there is a seriousness in his comment that 'man is but a patched fool if he will offer to say what methought I had'. Bottom has been told often enough of his stupidity but he has no desire to be separated from his fellow mechanicals, as would happen in the lonely role of Theseus' 'patched fool'. The gist of the speech, therefore, is toward the reassertion of the hierarchy. The metrification of courtly language serves to define the relationship of their discourse to time. The behaviour of all four groups of characters is conditioned from the start by the decision of Theseus and Hippolyta to get married in three days' time: the lovers as the time which Hermia has to make up her mind about her future; the mechanicals as the time they have to rehearse their play; and, the fairy world (by implication) as the time which it has to sort out its affairs. The mechanicals are unique, however, in the sense that time is never an emblematic or poetic presence in their discourse: it does not frighten them; what scares them is the threat of punishment by Theseus for contravening his ducal timescale. Their language is motivated more by such fears rather than by any inner impulse.

The pragmatic translation will not only register the change from verse to prose but also something of the relationship between the differing forms. Tsubouchi's register of the shift from poetry to prose is immediately apparent (278-79):

Ore no kikkake ni [8] natta dara [5] yobatte kun na, [7] henji subei kara. [8] Ore no kikkakea [8] 'Ā, [2] utsukushiki [5] Piramasu dono' [6] da ze. [2] ... Oya oya! [4] Pītā Kuinsu san! [10] Fuigoya no [5] Furūto san! [6] Kajiya no [4] Sunauto san! [6] Sutāberingu san! [9] Oya oya, [4] sotto nigeta ne, [7] ore ni nekokashi wo [8] kuwasete, ore [6] meppōkai mo nē [9] fushigina yumē [7] mita da. [3] Ore ningen no [7] chie ja [3] nantomo iu to no [8] dekinē yōna [7] yumē mita da. [6] Konna yume no [6] setsumei shibei [7] omou yatsu ga [6] ariyā [4] ten roba dā. [6] Nandemo sono ore ga [9] ... totemo korya [5] dare ni datte, [6] dō iun da ka [7] ieru mon jā nē. [9] Nandemo sono, [6] ore ga omotta [7] nyā, nani wo, [5] sono nani shiteru [7] chu to [3] ... ga, [1] totemo ningen de [8] wakaru kon jā nē, [9] ore ga sono nani wo [8] nani shite ita ka, [7] sore iwau to [6] shiru yō dara, [6] Ōbaka da.[5] Ore no yumea [6] tsuizo mada [5] ningen no [5] manako de motte [7] kiita koto mo [6] nakereba, [4] mimi de motte [6] mita koto mo, [5] te de motte [5] ajiwatta koto mo, [8] shita de motte [6] kangaeta koto mo, [8] kokoro de motte [7] iitsutaeta koto mo [9] nē yume da ni. [6] Ore [2] Pītā Kuinsu san ni [11] tanonde, [4] kono yume wo [5] tsukutte moraubei. [9] Gedai wa [4] Botomu no yume to [7] tsukebei, [4] nazette, [4] marukkishi [5] Botomu ga [4] nuketeru dakara yo.

[8] Sōshite ore [6] sono uta wo, [5] shibai no [4] donjimai ni, [6] kōshaku san no [7] mae de utatte [7] kurebei. [4] Koto ni yoru to, [6] gutto omoshiroku [8] shiru tame ni, [5] shinde kara [5] utaubei ka na. [7]

The shift in register is apparent from the colloquial personal pronoun *ore* ('I') and plain form of the conditional, *natta dara* ('when ...').[150] The neutral verb forms are sustained throughout the translation and are liberally sprinkled with colloquial particles such as *ze* and *nē*. Many of the verbs, such as *subei* for *suru* ('to do'), are dialectal forms in modern Japanese but were in more general usage as colloquial forms before the homogenisation of the language by Tokyo dialect after World War II. The comparison, therefore, is with the language of Theseus' court who indeed quite frequently use the polite *subeshi*. *Dekinē* (*dekinai*, 'unable') is another form still heard in regional dialect.

The shock of prose becomes the shock of the colloquial in Tsubouchi's version. Shakespeare's Bottom uses no deliberate colloquialisms. The stylistic idiosyncracies come from Bottom himself, for example his malapropisms. Tsubouchi replicates the rhythmic antitheses made in the source to emphasise the comic clumsiness of the malapropisms (e.g. 'the <u>ear</u> of man hath not <u>seen</u>') by alliteration and assonance (e.g. <u>mi</u>mi de motte <u>mi</u>ta koto mo, *mimi* meaning 'ear' and *mita* 'seen'). The seven-five syllabic is absent from the translation as a controlling force but it is certainly possible to detect a more deliberate use of syllabic metre. The first four phrases average a length of seven, an unvaried syllabic which seems appropriate to someone still half asleep. As the speech becomes more rhetorical, the shift from high to low syllable count becomes quite marked, especially in the lengthy sentence with the malapropisms: 6 - 5 - 5 - 7 - 6 - 4 - 6 - 5 - 5 - 8 - 6 - 8 - 7 - 9 - 6.

The main rhetorical device in the translation is repetition. In the source, the repeated items 'methought' and 'dream' combine in the mind of the audience to become the statement 'I had a dream'. Tsubouchi translates the second word easily enough with its equivalent *yume* but for 'methought' there is no such lexical equivalent. Tsubouchi uses the interrogative pronoun *nani* ('what') and its compound *nandemo* ('whatever'). This translation seems to be aiming at something like the relationship between actor and audience in a pantomime version: Bottom's 'Methought' might be taken by the audience as a cue to shout out 'What did you think?', and in Tsubouchi's version Bottom's 'What?' begs the question 'Yes, what?'

The comparison with pantomime is not as trivial as might seem, since that kind of vocalised relationship between actor and audience is also found in *kabuki* where seasoned *kabuki*-watchers call out the names of their favourite actors at highpoints in the drama. Although *kabuki* was central to Tsubouchi's own theatrical experience, the theatrical environment with which Matsuoka is familiar is inevitably less vocal and more European, and in translating Bottom's speech, her main resource is standardised, homogenised Japanese (126-27):

---

[150] As opposed to *narimashitara* (polite) or *nattara* (plainer).

Kikkake ga kitara, [8] yonde kure. [5] Sugu ni serifu wo [7] iu kara na. [5] Tsugi no kikkake wa [8] 'Waga uruwashi no [7] Piramasu sama' da. [7] Ōi! [3] Pītā Kuinsu? [8] Fuigo naoshi no [7] Furūto? [4] Ikakeya no [5] Sunauto? [4] Sutāburingu? [7] Nante kotta! [6] Zurakariyagatta na, [9] nemutteru ore wo [8] oite kebari ni [7] shite! [2] Nantomo [4] kettaina yume wo [8] mita mon da. [5] Tashika ni yume da, [7] daga [2] donna yume ka wa [7] ningen no chie ja [8] ienai na. [5] Kono yume wo [5] setsumei shiyō [7] to suru yatsu wa, [6] tonmana roba da. [7] Dō yara ore wa – [7] ore ga nan datta ka, [9] ieru yatsu wa inai. [9] Demo, [2] dō yara ore wa – [7] de, [1] kokontoko ni [6] tsuiteta no wa – [6] nani ga tsuiteta ka [8] iō to suru yatsu wa [9] doaho da. [4] Ningen no me ga [7] kiita koto mo nai, [8] ningen no mimi ga [8] mita koto mo nai, [7] ningen no te ga [7] ajiwatta koto mo nai, [10] shita ga [3] kangaeta koto mo nai, [11] shinzō ga [5] iitsutaeta koto mo nai, [11] are wa zendai mimon no [11] tondemonai [6] yume datta. [5] Hitotsu [3] Pītā Kuinsu ni [9] tanonde, [4] ore no yume wo [6] uta ni shite moraō [9]. Dai wa [3] 'Botomu no yume' ga ii. [9] Potto munashii [7] yume dakara ne. [6] Soitsu wa [4] shibai no owari ni [8] kōshakusama no [7] mae de [3] utatte yarō. [7] Iya sore yori [6] Shisubī ga shinu toko de [10] utatta hō ga [7] motto gutto kuru na. [9]

As it happens, colloquial *hyōjungo* more than adequately meets Matsuoka's needs. The elision of the verb form with the auxiliary in *nemut<u>te</u>ru* is hardly dialectal, nor the abbreviation of *mono* in *mita mon da*. Other words and usages that are unlikely to be found in formal, written Japanese include *yatsu* (slang for 'person'), *kettai* ('strange') and *gutto* ('fast, firmly' but could mean 'good' here).[151] Bottom is no different from the other characters in using neutral verb endings but his emphatically alliterative style is certainly unique and is established in the first sentence, *Kikkake ga kitara, yonde kure*.

Matsuoka's response to the speech as a whole seems to go further than mere clumsiness and to achieve a wonderful vagueness. The more that Bottom tries to organise his thoughts, the more they elude him. She organises the speech into paragraphs, with each one ending with the open-mouthed *na* (meaning, 'Isn't it?'). This technique helps the actor playing Bottom to develop the speech according to the five sections and thus gives a motive for Bottom not to reveal his secret: he is rooted from the start in his role as an actor and, as such, loath to reveal his professional secrets;[152] he is acting a comic version of Macbeth's soliloquy on 'signifying nothing' (5.5.23-27). Matsuoka's paragraphs centre the speech on the malapropisms in the fourth paragraph. Her repetitive device here is the word *ningen* ('human being') which, as in English, can

---

[151] *Gairaigo* (words borrowed from foreign languages) are typically used in contemporary colloquial situations (and also in advertising slogans) to emphasise the strangeness of a situation. Bottom's use of the word *gutto* in this context could certainly seem comic.

[152] The first section is Bottom waking up, the second his recollection that he has woken from a dream, the third his statement of how marvellous a dream it was, the fourth his realisation that he cannot describe the dream, and the fifth his decision to put the dream to use in the mechanicals' play.

mean almost anything as a generic term. *Dō yara ore wa* is the rhetorical equivalent of 'methought' although it literally means 'Somehow or other I ...'. The dental *d* comes again in *demo* and *de* and then again in *doaho*, which does indeed mean 'a real fool' or 'really stupid'.

The comparison between the two versions suggests that the historical differences between their respective languages is insufficient to affect the dramatic relationship between formal and colloquial that is developed in the source. Both pick on key lexical items (e.g. *nani*, *ningen*) which are then exploited for all their ironical value. After all, Tsubouchi's *nani* could just as easily be in answer to mutterings from the audience, 'How about a shave!' Matsuoka's talk of human beings foregrounds the irony of Bottom's recent metamorphosis. Her version is slightly more syllabic than Tsubouchi's with an overtly theatrical use of five-seven in both the first and last sentences.

THE LIMITATIONS OF STYLISTIC MIXING: QUINCE'S PROLOGUE

Matsuoka's theatricality makes her an obvious starting point for an analysis of translations of Quince's Prologue to the play of Pyramus and Thisbe in the final act (5.1.108-17). The point of the speech is that as mispunctuated nonsense it contrasts absurdly with the dramatic fullness of the marriage setting and for its naïvety with the dramatic irony of Bottom's dream.

> *If we offend, it is with our good will.*
> *That you should think, we come not to offend,*
> *But with good will. To show our simple skill,*
> *That is the true beginning of our end.*
> *Consider then, we come but in despite.*
> *We do not come, as minding to content you,*
> *Our true intent is. All for your delight,*
> *We are not here. That you should here repent you,*
> *The actors are at hand; and by their show,*
> *You shall know all, that you are like to know.*

The comedy of the speech is twofold: Quince emasculates the theatrical experience by telling his audience how to react (in other words, what as actors is their intent) but more importantly, he makes a nonsense of his assurance that he has 'come not to offend' by suggesting exactly the opposite ('All for your delight, / We are not here.'). Moreover, except in lines 113 and 115, the speech is thunderously iambic, with a conventional rhyme scheme and punctuation insisting on heavy accents on the final beat of eight of the ten lines. The speech is a parody of stylistic mixing since while its intention is rhetorical – to persuade the audience to look kindly on their performance – the form and content are comically the reverse. The actual effect of this kind of mixing can only be to make the audience feel sorry for Quince.

Matsuoka's translation shows that the most obvious feature of the source, the eccentric punctuation, can be quite easily rendered in Japanese (139):

> Manichi [4] gofukyō wo [5] kau naraba, [5] sore koso [4] warera ga negai [7]
> to wa oboshimesu na. [8] Makari idemashitaru wa, [10] gofukyō wo kau tame [9]
> niwa arazu. [5] Warera ga [4] tsutanaki gi nite [7] onme wo yogosu koto [9]
> koso warera no [7] shin no mokuteki nari. [9]
> Warera ichidō, [7] akui mote [5] makaridetaru mono [8]
> niwa arazu. [5] Hitasura [4] gomanzoku [5] itadakitai to [8] no negai naku [5]
> shite wa, [3] oyorokobi [5] itadakeru [5] hazu mo naku [5]
> kakunaru ue wa, [7] goran ni natte [7] son wo suru [5]
> yōna shibai wa [7] ome ni kakenu shozon. [9]
> Yakusha no yōi mo [7] totonoimashitareba, [9] mazu wa mokugeki [7] nite
> shibai no [6] ichibu shijū, [6] goran kudasatte [8] kudasaimase. [6]

The speech is intended to make nonsense of the natural breaks within sentences and so is difficult to metrify with any accuracy, especially the first seven lines. It is likely, however, that an actor would register the enjambements as such since they are central to the speech's awkwardness. Enjambement draws the rhythmic momentum of the succeeding line towards its beginning but the words so emphasised above are all semantically unimportant words and phrases, like *shite* and *yōna*, whose syntactic function is confused as they are separated from whatever they are meant to qualify. Perhaps the most painful of these examples is *niwa arazu* which is used in enjambement in lines 3 and 6. The phrase is an arcane negative which is common in Tsubouchi but not in contemporary Japanese and is all the more dislocated, stuck as it is at the beginning of the new line.

Matsuoka's Prologue is written in a more formal Japanese (which might still be heard) than that of Tsubouchi's (which probably would not). One example is the almost meaningless *ome ni kakenu shozon*, whose only purpose seems to be a rather obvious alliteration with *shibai*.[153] Matsuoka gives Quince an exaggerated version of how he might imagine the court to speak.[154] It is clear that his confidence grows during the course of the speech. The phrase *Yakusha no yōi mo totonoimashitareba* (alliteration followed by a polite conditional) can be spoken with a flourish as can the *kabuki*-like *goran kudasatte kudasaimase* ('Please look at our show.') Quince's parting phrase, 'that you are like to know', is surely a case of *lèse-majesté* as he tells the court what they can

---

[153] *Ome ni kakenu* is the negative form of an honorific verb for 'show' and is nominalised by *shozon* meaning 'thought' or 'idea'. It is equivalent for 'We are not here' and comes after a ludicrously ornate rendition of 'All for your delight'.

[154] Typified by his liberal use of the honorific *go-* prefix before nouns.

and cannot know (although the punctuation makes the point ambiguous). Yet the final sentence as a whole can also be understood as nothing more than blunt: 'a spade is a spade' and 'what you see is what you get'. In translation as well, those last two lines are prosodically the only two sensible lines. In each of the first nine lines, the rhythmic momentum is either spoilt by unrhythmical enjambement or by a heavy, abstract noun (e.g. *mono*, 'thing') or functional verb form (*nari*, 'is'). Yet *dangeki* ('masque') connects rhythmically and semantically with *shibai* ('play').

The syllabic does become rather easier to identify in the last four lines, which would coincide with the speech's slight change of tone, and there is a rhythmical use of seven-five in the last two. For the last phrases, the Prologue even goes into eight and six which is what Quince had suggested at the rehearsal in 3.1.22-25 despite Bottom's protestations:

Quin.   Well, we will have such a prologue; and it shall be written in eight and six.
Bot.   No, make it two more; let it be written in eight and eight.

This slight though effective use of seven-five is typical of a translating strategy that recognises the differences of Shakespeare from the classical Japanese drama.

* * * * *

One of the conclusions to arise from Chapters Two and Three is that although most contemporary translations have used a free verse format, there is no clear development to be observed from a traditional translating style to a modern one. There are obvious historical differences between the languages of Tsubouchi and Odashima, and even Fukuda and Matsuoka, but they each achieve their poetic effects in quite similar ways. This is partly due to the lack of an integrated model in modern Japanese poetics for the translation of poetic drama. Rather than translating in the style of Chikamatsu, or Hagiwara, or Nishiwaki Junzaburō, the translators pick and mix their styles as much as possible.[155] There is no clear association to be made between *shichigo chō* and the older translations and free verse and rhetorical phrasing and the more recent ones. It would be strange indeed if any translation did adhere strictly to any single rhythmic style. It would sound strange in Japanese, as modern plays are mainly in prose and even Chikamatsu kept *shichigo chō* only for narrative sections, and it would also be a strange choice for a Shakespeare translator. Although blank verse is certainly the dominant form, it acts more as a template for considerable rhythmic variety, and the individuation of rhythm is one of the basic means for the individuation of character as well.

---

[155]   Pioneer of modernism and free verse writing in pre-war and post-war Japan; called 'the Eliot of Japan'.

A further conclusion to be drawn is that Tsubouchi and Odashima seem more resonant in their use of the phonic qualities of words, and Fukuda and Matsuoka to be more conscious of pace and phrasing. This comparison can be extended into the next chapter which discusses the treatment and use of rhyme and wordplay in the four translations. While rhythm is more of a matter for the individual poet (and translator) – more strictly a personal matter as it were – rhyme and wordplay belong more to the domain of shared discourse, and it is perhaps for this reason that rhyme and wordplay constitute a more integrated tradition for the translators, one by which the distinctly Japanese qualities of the translations can be more easily discerned.

CHAPTER FOUR   RHYME AND WORDPLAY

RHYME AND WORDPLAY: PROPERTIES AND POSSIBILITIES

The prosodic potential of accentual metre in Japanese translations of Shakespeare is phonologically restricted, but the same phonology allows for a huge variety of rhyme and wordplay; Japanese is a naturally rhyming language. The great majority of Japanese words end in one of five vowels, with a minority ending with the single consonant *n* (negative verb forms, for example) but the fact that a majority of initial and middle moras also end in vowels (e.g. six in *tabesaserareru*, 'to be made to eat') means that rhymes of all kinds are commonplace in Japanese. The narrower range of consonantal sounds in the syllabary also facilitates alliteration and assonance. Rhyme (*ōin*) can be categorised in both Japanese and English to include both end and internal rhyme. The latter includes head rhyme (alliteration) and assonance.

The commonplace nature of rhyme in Japanese means that end rhyme is so pervasive as to be meaningless while internal rhyme is also pervasive but allowed to function in a more discrete and therefore meaningful way. Rhyming verse is theoretically quite possible in Japanese but can only seldom be coordinated with pitch accent or syntax to produce the kind of rhymes found in English poetry. Moreover, the end rhymes in Japanese free verse are often insignificant words or parts of words with little semantic or figurative resonance, such as particles and inflexions. As Matsubayashi explains (Matsubayashi 1996, 223),

> The effect of end rhymes or simple rhymes comprising only vowels is a weak one. A degree of effect can be expected when rhythms overlap each other but when there is a limit to the range of possible words the diction will inevitably sound unnatural.

Internal rhyme, however, acts as an undercurrent of sound and meaning: phonemic patterns which are not rendered insignificant on account of isolation – as is usually the case with end rhyme – but support the semantic drift of the surface meanings. The contrast with English rhyme is a matter of proportion. English also has a large number of vowel sounds, if one counts short as well as long vowels, the semi-vowels *w* and *y*, and dipthongs. The challenge for poets writing in English has always been to coordinate their rhymes with other effects (e.g. surprise) but above all the stress-based rhythms of the language, which (as has already been argued) are largely absent from Japanese. Effective end rhymes have historically been admired in English poetry and, since medieval times, excessive alliteration avoided.

Traditional rhyme

In metrical English poetry, rhyme often works with stress accent to produce masculine end-rhymes, as in Pope's couplet from *The Rape of the Lock* (Tillotson 1941, 38-39):

Bright as the sun, her eyes the gazers strike,
And, like the sun, they shine in all alike.

The iambic rhythm produces the momentum on which the end-rhyme hinges but this rhyme is unsettled by the caesuras and assonances ('Bright', 'eyes', 'strike' etc.) that occur in both lines. This kind of effect depends almost inevitably on the possibility for disruption within the line, all the more so in the case of rhymed verse.

This example comprises a single sentence, but a passage of Shakespearean blank verse might embrace several sentences and half-sentences; the effect of flexibility, especially enjambement, on the movement of the line was discussed in Chapter 2. The seven-five metre of traditional Japanese verse allows for enjambement (*kumatagari*),[156] but the lines and poems are so short as to put the caesural pause between the lines or as some imagined interval that follows immediately upon the poem's utterance. The syllables at the end of each phrase might be supported by syllabic rhythm and pauses – the reader or hearer expects conclusion – but the sounds themselves are repeated so often in most contexts as to forestall effective patterning. The lack of strong end-rhyme is apparent in the following *haiku* by Buson (Blyth 1981, 241):[157]

inazuma ni	A flash of lightning!
koboruru oto ga	The sound of drops
take no tsuyu	Falling among the bamboos.

---

[156] The following poem by the *haiku* reformer Masaoka Shiki (1867-1902) is an example of *kumatagari* from the first five to the seven (Watson 1997, 94). The movement is syntactic and could therefore be considered equivalent to enjambement, whereas the seven ends on a verb and will therefore precede a slight pause.
ware kotoshi / botan ni yande / kiku ni okishi
This year / I took sick with the peonies, / got up with the chrysanthemums.
[157] Yosa Buson (1716-83) was well known for his pictorial style.

Yet even in this poem of seventeen syllables, rhyme can be said to play an essential role. Assonance on the short *o* in *koboruru oto* produces the onomatopoeic effect of dripping water which is echoed by the alliteration of *take* ('bamboo') with *tsuyu* ('rainy season').

The assonance and alliteration in Buson's *haiku* serve a clear function but the phonemic connections can be subtle to the point of obscurity. The obscurity of the rhyme in this *haiku* by Ringai is saved by the fluid rhythm which supports it (ibid., 250):

kumiageru	In the water I draw up,
mizu ni haru tatsu	Glitters the beginning
hikari kana	Of spring.

The assonance of *haru* with *hikari* is supported by a regular successive rhythm with pitch accents on the fourth mora of the first two phrases and on the second mora of the last.

Buson and Ringai were both poets of the 18th century, but a similar effect can be detected in a *tanka* by a poet of the early 20th century, Yosano Akiko (Ueda 1996, 40):[158]

mune no shimizu	a clear spring
afurete tsui ni	inside me overflowed
nigorikeri	and grew muddy
kimi mo tsumi no ko	you are a child of sin
ware mo tsumi no ko	and so am I

The key word that haunts this poem is *tsumi* ('sin'), and not simply because it is repeated twice in the phrase (*tsumi no ko*, 'child of sin') but because it has already been concealed in the assonance of *shimizu* with *tsui ni*. The word is split and then joined together.

Free verse rhyme

Moving a step closer to the style of Japanese translations of Shakespeare, the following poem by Tanikawa Shuntarō ('Kimi', 'You') makes use of end as well as internal rhymes (Tanikawa 1996, 9).[159] This is a poem about the lyricism of passivity, about how an inert and expressionless body can arouse strong feelings in the one who loves.

kimi wa boku no tonari de nemutte iru	You're asleep beside me.

---

[158] Yosano Akiko (1878-1942) was a pioneer of the New Romantic movement in *tanka* poetry.
[159] Tanikawa Shuntarō (b. 1931) is regarded as one of the most inventive stylists of post-war Japan The poem was first published in 1988.

shatsu ga mekurete oheso ga miete iru	I can see your belly button showing out of your messy shirt.
nemutteru no dewa nakute shinderu no dattara donna ni ureshii darō	I'd be so glad if you were dead instead of sleeping.
kimi wa mō jibun no koto shika kangaete inai me de jitto boku wo mitsumeru koto mo nai shi	You could no longer look at me with those self-centred eyes.
boku no kiraina Abe to issho ni kawa e oyogi ni iku koto mo nai no da	You'd no longer go swimming in the river with that damned Abe.
kimi ga soba e kuru to kimi no nioi ga shite boku wa mune ga dokidoki shite kuru	Near me like this, I smell your smell and my heart begins pounding.
yūbe yume no naka de boku to kimi wa futarikkiri de sensō ni itta	Last night in my dream we went to war, just the two of us.
okāsan no koto mo otōsan no koto mo gakkō no koto mo wasurete ita	I had forgotten about mother, father, school.
futari tomo mō shinu no da to omotta	We thought we'd die, both of us.
shinda kimi to itsumademo ikiyō to omotta	I thought I'd go on living with you who had died.
kimi to tomodachi ni nanka naritaku nai	I don't want to be just friends with you.
boku wa tada kimi ga sukina dake da	For I love you.

The word *kimi* ('you') resounds throughout the poem,[160] first as an object of desire and hatred and eventually as an active object as the speaker cannot hold back his love. It is written in a colloquial, non-figurative style that makes less of the sophisticated phonic effects achieved by a Buson or Yosano. Tanikawa's technique is less conventional: the 'feminine' end-rhyme[161] of the opening two lines – *nemutte iru* with *miete iru*[162] –

---

[160] *Kimi* is used between people of equal status and by a person of higher status addressing an inferior.

[161] The lack of stress accentuation in Japanese means that double end rhymes in Japanese sound equivalent to single rhymes in English. Single rhymes in Japanese seldom stand out except by unorthodox means.

[162] Rhymes of this kind that hinge on an auxiliary (in this case *iru*, literally 'to be') are parallelisms rather than end rhymes in the sense used in English poetics. Although a phonic association is made between the acts of sleeping and seeing, it is weakened somewhat by the functionality of the rhyme on *iru*. Moreover, the verb form of 'see' is the spontaneous *mieru* rather than the potential *mirareru*, adding to the nuance of chance in the rhyme. In fact, the line might be better translated by omitting ↗

which suggests that despite the passivity of the scene, it is still a scene of great potential happening; 'we are both doing something (you sleeping, me seeing).' The rhyme then softens and fades with the more colloquial (and unanswerable) *shinderu* (literally, 'being dead'). The third and fourth lines do not rhyme as such but *dattara* and *darō* belong to the same copula, while the combination of the long line against the short with the accent on *dattara* contrasting with the double vowel in *darō* produces a rhythm of rise and fall. *Dattara* is conditional, *darō* the more ambiguous suppositional form; these are the natural tenses of this poem. Physical reality (the sleeping body) suggests possibilities which must be imaginatively reflected on. Possibility leads to supposition: the tension is developed later in the poem, as in the half-rhyme on *itta* ('went') and *ita* ('was').

The impulse to destroy is conditioned by the reality of the family who would be left behind. The repetitive rhyme *to omotta* sounds childish[163] – this poem is one of a series of poems about childhood – and like the rhyme at the beginning of the poem it seems to collapse in the poem's resolution where *nai* ('not') is contrasted with *da* ('is'). The speaker has given up trying to live the other's life, and in simply recognising the other's otherness is finally able to say 'I love you'.

THE SONNET IN JAPANESE AND IN TRANSLATION

Nakamura Minoru's fourteen liners

While internal rhyme is a transparent and prevalent feature of traditional Japanese forms and of free verse poets such as Tanikawa, there is inevitably less evidence of either end or internal rhyme being used in the context of Western forms. These forms have been merely accidental to 'the content-derivative' approach of Shakespeare translators, and yet there are examples not only of Shakespeare's sonnets being translated into something resembling sonnet form but also of original poets experimenting with the form. The best known of these is probably Kambara Ariake (1876-1947), of whom Keene writes that 'he may have found it congenial to express his thoughts within a fixed form of relatively brief compass that imposed a discipline welcome to a poet of his essentially conceptual (rather than lyrical) bent', suggesting that Ariake's sonnets may have profited from a long line of seventeen syllables and judicious use of rhyme (Keene 1999, 231).

Another prolific sonneteer of more recent vintage is Nakamura Minoru (b.

↘ the verb altogether: 'Your belly button showing / out of your messy shirt.'
[163] The rhyme can be construed as childish in that it emphasises the act of thinking above the actual thoughts, thus creating an impression of insecurity, which is partly borne out by what the speaker does indeed 'think', since the speaker knows that his thoughts are fantasy but that they do contain some emotional truth.

1927),[164] whose sonnet 'Kirameku hikari no naka ni' (Into the glistening sunlight) is dated April 1988 (Nakamura 1996, 61):

lines 1 to 3

Yashiotsutsuji ga saki, midori wa fukaku
Nihon rettō ni, haruka tōku kara
shimerike wo obita taiki ga chikazuite iru.

The azaleas are in bloom and the greenery deepening.
A mass of air, charged with moisture, is approaching
the Japanese archipelago from a long way off.

lines 4 to 7

Cherunobuiri no sekkan ni tsuite kataru mo ii.
Kuchi wo tsugunde tachitsukusu nanmin ni tsuite,
horobiyuku Kushiro shitsugen ni tsuite,
ureigao ni kataru mo ii.

We can talk about that sarcophagus at Chernobyl,
and about the refugees standing exhausted, their mouths sealed shut,
and about the swamp at Kushiro running dry
we can pull long faces.

lines 8 to 11

Sono koe wa doremo utsuro ni hankyō shi,
hajike chitte sora no takami ni kiete iku.
Ureigao no kishi yo, kimi wa katari yamenai,
iyoiyo anzen to, shikashi kōzen to kao wo agete.

Our voices will all of them echo in the void,
they will burst open and be scattered, lost among the heights of the sky.
Oh doom-laden rider, you who cannot stop speaking,
your face is flushed with tears as it is with pretense.

---

[164] Nakamura's first volume, *Mugenka* (Songs without words), was published in 1950, and his volume *Hanemushi no tobu fūkei* (A prospect of flying springtails) won the Yomiuri Literature Prize. His professional career has been as a lawyer. The poem seems lightly humorous or satirical in the way that it posits contemporary environmental concerns against a traditional reverence for seasonal change, here represented by the blooming of azaleas in May.

lines 12 to 14

Gogatsu, jinrui no mirai yori mo, chikyū no mirai yori mo,
kirameku hikari no naka no isshun isshun ni, watashi wa
hisokana watashi no sei wo kakeru koto to shiyō.

As hopes for humanity and the earth recede,
I can at least risk my secret hopes
on the May sunlight glistening moment by moment.

Nakamura's poem departs from the conventional European forms in every point except the number of lines.[165] The poem contains fourteen lines, organised into a non-rhyming tercet (i.e. sequence of three lines) followed by two rhyming and one non-rhyming quatrain (four lines) and another non-rhyming tercet. Iambic rhythm is absent (as one would expect), and the lengths of lines vary considerably, and yet despite these departures the poem does use rhyme in a way that can be thought equivalent to the logical development of a conventional sonnet.[166] The poem does not stand still (as a more lyrical form such as *haiku* might) but describes a logical movement from the climactic (first tercet) to the human scale (the two central quatrains) and finally the individual, himself. The movement contains a sub-text of concealment: the moisture concealed by air, the nuclear power station entombed in concrete, the poet's guilt – perhaps – at living his life in the sun when humanity has lost hope in itself, and of course one can infer that the rain droplets (*shimerike*) in the air mass have been polluted by radiation.

Nor does the prosody stand still. It is striking how the symmetrical structure, which could have been such a static device, is developed by a clear but not exaggerated use of rhyme and repetition. The abba rhyme scheme of the first quatrain is one that would probably sound contrived if sustained throughout the whole poem but it here does serve two useful purposes. It foregrounds the mournful 'We can talk about [these terrible things]' (... *ni tsuite kataru mo ii*) and it prepares the reader for the contrast of *koe* and *kao* in the second quatrain. These are both small words, easily 'lost among the heights of the sky'; the poet does not want his words to be forgotten, and they are foregrounded by the prosody.

Parallelism is often a more accurate term than metaphor for the figuration that happens in traditional Japanese verse. Even in Nakamura's poem, there is a reluctance to make explicit the correspondence between the seasonal changes and the human

---

[165] Nakamura's early sonnets, as in *Ki* (Trees, 1954), are true to the traditional form, consisting of two quatrains followed by two tercets and with some kind of developed rhyme scheme.
[166] Notably in this context, the Shakespearean sonnet consisting of three quatrains, rhyming abab, cdcd, and efef, which rhyme the argument, theme and dialectic respectively, before a rhyming couplet gg at the end, completing the poem.

world; in the traditional way of thinking, the human world is so much a part of nature as to preempt further explication. At the same time, the sonnet form forces a degree of correspondence that is inherently more explicit than the short forms, and while the conclusion expresses relief that at least the azaleas will bloom this year, and thus might be said to resist forced correspondences, the very framing of these sentiments within such an artificial form as the sonnet suggests that humanity still has the power to destroy nature. Such amibiguities are, of course, essential to Shakespeare's technique as well.

Translating Shakespeare's Sonnet 12

Shakespeare in translation poses numerous challenges to traditional forms and genres. Nakamura's sonnet gives evidence of how the traditional poetic may be challenged from within: in other words, that Japanese poetry has changed not so much for change's sake but for various social and historical reasons as well, which is reassuring evidence if Shakespeare translation is to be considered to have any kind of relevance to the modern culture. Yet Shakespeare translators are still constrained first and foremost by the words on the page, and in Takamatsu Yūichi's version of Sonnet 12 we find a translation that addresses the formal, rhetorical problems of this poem before achieving a remarkable interpretation of its actual content (Takamatsu 1986, 21-22; Kerrigan 1986, 82):[167]

> Toki wo tsugeru tokei no oto wo hitotsu hitotsu kazoe,
> When I do count the clock that tells the time,
>
> kagayakashii taiyō ga minikui yoru no yami ni shizumu no wo miru toki,
> And see the brave day sunk in hideous night;
>
> sakari wo sugisatta sumire no hana wo nagame,
> When I behold the violet past prime,
>
> kuroi makige ga kotogotoku hakugin ni ōwareru no wo miru toki,
> And sable curls all silvered o'er with white;
>
> katsute wa kachiku no mure wo shonetsu kara saegitte yatta
> When lofty trees I see barren of leaves,
>
> taiboku ga, ha wo hagi torare, hadaka ni naru no wo miru toki,
> Which erst from heat did canopy the herd,

---

[167] For a comparison of Takamatsu's translation with other versions by Tsubouchi (1927), Nishiwaki (1966), Odashima (1994) and Shibata (2004), see Gallimore (2007 a).

natsu no midori no ōmugi ga tabanerare, himo de kukurare,
And summer's green, all girded up in sheaves,

shiroi kowai hige wo sarashite, teguruma de hakobareru no wo miru toki,
Borne on the bier with white and bristly beard;

sonna toki ni, watashi wa kimi no utsukushisa wo omoi, kō kangaeru.
Then of thy beauty do I question make,

Kimi mo, toki no kōhai kara nogareru wake ni wa ikanai,
That thou among the wastes of time must go,

yasashii mono mo, utsukushii mono mo, yagate wa suitai shite,
Since sweets and beauties do themselves forsake,

hoka no bi ga sodatsu no wo minagara, onaji hayasa de shinu no da, to.
And die as fast as they see others grow;

Toki no kami ga kimi wo kono yo kara hissaratte yuku toki ni,
And nothing 'gainst Time's scythe can make defence

kare no ōgama wo fusegi tachimukau no wa, shison shika inai to.
Save breed to brave him when he takes thee hence.

For Takamatsu the key word of Shakespeare's poem is 'time'. Shakespeare uses the word only three times, which is quite enough to secure its various emblematic and metaphorical figurations over the rest of the poem.[168] The main irony of the poem is that while the speaker lectures another on the transience of life, the speaker is equally subject to the movement of time; in the line 'And die as fast as they see others grow', it is surely the speaker who is closer to death and the beautiful other who still grows. The movement of time is figured most deeply in the movement of the iambic metre and logical progression of the poem. In addition to its insistent emblematisation, time is also connoted by the word 'prime' in line 3, which can refer to the first part of the monastic day and also has a possible sexual meaning.[169] In translation, such cultural

---

[168] The figure in line 8 ('Borne on the bier with bristly beard') is emblematic of the subjection of fecundity to time and is expressed metaphorically in line 10 ('the wastes of time'). 'Time's scythe' in line 13 is a familiar emblem.
[169] The male erection. This meaning is possible only if 'past prime' is understood to refer to the time of beholding rather than the violet's condition (although it is still present as a semantic association). The word *sakari* in Takamatsu's translation has the connotation of 'the prime of one's life'.

references, not to mention Shakespeare's prosody, are either absent or obscure but can be compensated by devices such as alliteration. The word *toki* occurs ten times in this translation, including in the compound word *tokei* meaning 'clock'. As a word meaning 'time', it is a less substantial word than the abstract 'time' in English for the reason that it usually means 'when'. *Toki* is used five times for the series of 'whens' in the source but the fact that the same word has these two meanings gives the translator liberty to exploit its alliterative potential, most strikingly in the first line.[170]

Toki is reduced to its basic alliterative element *to-* which is repeated five times in the first line to imitate the ticking of a clock. As in the source, the two *-k-* sounds precede the *to-* sounds in *hitotsu hitotsu kazoe* ('counting one by one'), so that alliteration is used not only for its own sake but to support a rhythm that is only apparent by its artificiality. What we see is an unstressed syllabic rhythm giving way to an accented syllable followed by two unaccented syllables (equivalent to a dactyl) in the second half of the line (... *no oto wo hitotsu hitotsu kazoe*). *Toki* meaning 'time' becomes a banality – a word that requires explanation – which is indeed just what Takamatsu makes of it. Just as Shakespeare's elegiac pastoral is extended over two whole quatrains, Takamatsu methodically concludes the second, fourth, sixth and eighth of his lines with this word and then registers the change in mood in the source by bringing the word back to the beginning of the line (in line 9) and again so in the next.

Takamatsu's sudden shift in register is if anything more 'dramatic' than in the source. In his final six lines, the word *toki* – so much a reassuring presence in the first two quatrains – is quite literally torn asunder to become a feeble *to* at the end of the twelfth and final lines. As with other of the Sonnets, the moral dialectic stated by Sonnet 12 suppresses an emotional ambiguity about the relationship between the 'I' and the 'thou' in that the subordination of Other to Time can be a metaphor for whatever emotional grip the other has over the speaker. The emotional tension is figured in a graphological tension in the translation. Except in lines 1 and 10 where the Sino-Japanese character is used, the word *toki* is always written in *hiragana*, and is a proto-Japanese word rather than one borrowed originally from Chinese. Written in this way, the word contrasts with the character for 'beauty'. The fact that it appears first in its native Japanese form (*utsukushii* in line 11 meaning 'beautiful') and in the next line in its Sino-Japanese form (*bi*, 'beauty') corresponds with the similar treatment of *toki* and underlines the dynamic relationship between the two concepts.

Next to the graphological tension an even more subtle tension occurs, one that provides perhaps the strongest evidence that this poem has been absorbed within its Japanese context. This involves a contrast between the words *mono* and *koto*. Both words are proto-Japanese that broadly mean 'thing', but whereas the English word 'thing' can refer both to concrete and to abstract entities, *mono* is representative of concrete objects and people, *koto* always of abstract quantities such as emotions and ideas. Like *hitotsu*

---

[170] As is conventional in modern Japanese, Takamatsu writes *toki* meaning 'time' with the Sino-Japanese character but with *hiragana* when he means 'when'.

hitotsu in line 1, *mono* is foregrounded by repetition and phonic echo in line 11: *yasashii mono mo* ('both a gentle person'); *utsukushii mono mo* ('and a fair one'). The sudden and unexpected association of the concrete with the abstract is rhetorical and compelling; the opposing *koto* is pushed outside of the poem, being implied in the word *to* at the end of the twelfth and fourteenth lines. *To* means 'that' in this context, as in 'I think that ...', and could therefore be linked with *kō kangaeru* ('thus to think') in line 9. Even as the translator is conscious of an abstract dimension, he manages to distance himself from it.

The inference of the verb in this way is typical of spoken Japanese and therefore in keeping with the colloquial style of the translation but still has the effect of pushing the verb of thinking or speaking into the mind of an imagined speaker. The prosodic effect is abrupt, final, even angry, but also (as I have suggested) concealing a hidden brokenness. The use of the verb *kangaeru* at the end of line 9 is also interesting since it is combined with another word for 'think', *omou*. *Kangaeru* means 'to think over a process of time' ('to consider'); *omou* is more spontaneous and can even mean 'feel' and in classical poetry 'to love'. This combination of two verbs is Takamatsu's rendering of Shakespeare's 'do I question make'. His interpretation suggests that six lines of rhetorical argument do not happen spontaneously: they have to be properly mulled over. Takamatsu could equally have used a verb like *utagau*, which means 'to doubt', but the fact that he gives such weight to the cerebral process reinforces this anxiety about the transience of youth and beauty.

Takamatsu reinterprets a profound poem about time in the language of a culture where time seems to move so quickly that the concept has become a cliché; to refer to Keir Elam on Shakespeare, Takamatsu brings 'directly into force the sense and meanings of words' (Elam 1984, 14).[171] His strategy is to seek out rhetorical as opposed to literal equivalents within his target language; rhetorical equivalence is not only a matter of flexibility within a single category of poetic devices (e.g. between accentual and syllabic) but also across categories. If there is little opportunity for accentual rhythm then one adequate alternative is that of phonemic patterning, i.e. rhyme and wordplay.

SHARE LIGHT AND SERIOUS

Suzuki Tōzō (1975) divides Japanese wordplay into three categories: *hayakuchi kotoba* ('tongue-twisters'), *share* ('paronamasia') and *nazo* ('riddles'). Riddles and tongue-twisters are basically naïve devices, which may still serve a supplementary function in translation,[172] but it is *share* that is most relevant: a category that describes

---

[171] Elam describes such 'verbal doings' as 'among the most potent modes of linguistic self-activity' in Shakespearean comedy.'
[172] The Japanese riddle is usually too specific (involving ideographic links, for example, between Sino-Japanese characters) to be of much use to the translator of a foreign text. The tongue-twister

phonemic patterns and connections within the translated phrase, whether serious or humorous, simple or ingenious. It is a comprehensive term, such that a writer in the Meiji era claimed that 'most poems are *share*' and that 'the rhyme of Western poetry is *share*'.[173] Yet the writer's terminological confusion is not so different in character from the creative license of Japanese translators. 'Rhyme' and *share* come at each other like two circles in a Venn diagram: *share* excludes end-rhyme, the most distinctive of rhymes in English, as impractical, but includes assonance and alliteration; 'rhyme' counts those two in as well but would exclude straightforward euphony – *goro* (also known as *goro awase*) – as too diffuse. The standard Japanese dictionary *Kōjien* defines the term as a turn of expression in which 'sounds overlap between words'.

The term *share* (or *dajare*)[174] embraces many stylistic characteristics of the classical literary language, described by Royall Tyler with regard to *nō* drama as follows (Tyler 1992, 9):

> The true poetry of *nō* can be extraordinarily dense and complex, even though its vocabulary is relatively restricted. The difference between the lyrical prose and the poetry of *nō* is roughly that between the poetry of Walt Whitman and that of Hart Crane, or between Charles Péguy and Stéphane Mallarmé. Cascades of images, telescoped into one another far beyond the limits of consecutive grammar, like double and triple exposures on film, and echoing each other in an inspired play of precise conventions, renders the very concept of literal translation meaningless.

Nō and *jōruri* dramatists such as Zeami and Chikamatsu not only exploit wordplay of their own making but also play on words and images borrowed from the tradition.[175] A famous example of the latter would be *matsu*, which homophonically can mean both 'pine tree' and 'wait'. This can be dramatically effective as not only is the pine a symbol of longing in Japanese poetry but also an artificial pine tree is a feature typical of both the *nō* and *kabuki* stage sets, a place where one character might wait for his or her lover. In his commentary on Chikamatsu's domestic tragedy *Shinjū ten no Amijima* (The love suicide at Amijima, 1721), Shively noted that puns with triple meanings are not uncommon and that onomatopoeia is also a significant stylistic feature (Shiveley 1953,

---

↘ might be useful for translating passages of an equivalently naïve tone (e.g. Puck's incantations).
[173] Remarks by the economist and amateur philosopher Tsuchiko Kinshirō (1864-1917) in his essay *Share tetsugaku* (The philosophy of witticisms). Quoted in Wells (Wells 1997, 56), source and date unidentified.
[174] *Share* has both a strictly linguistic and a more generally semiotic connotation, i.e. verbal acuity and chic. In contemporary Japan, *share* more usually refers to fashion sense. *Dajare*, however, is punning.
[175] Wordplay is related to the classical technique of *honkadori* whereby well-known *waka* poems were freely alluded to and sometimes rewritten by later poets. Some *honkadori* were regarded more highly than the poems they were based on and the technique was never regarded as plagiarism.

44-46).[176]

Share is usually recognised as witty but not necessarily funny, and perhaps because it is so basic a device there is less fuss made of *dajare* than there is in English. *Dajare* may simply be euphonious and therefore used to support dramatic dialogue; they are not expected to make a point. The *share* of Japanese tradition shares that which Mahood (1957) defined as the capacity of Shakespeare's wordplay to associate thematic material. That *A Midsummer Night's Dream* has less than thirty 'quibbles'[177] is of little consequence so long as other types of rhetorical patterning that Shakespeare uses in the play (e.g. antithesis) can be rendered as *share* in translation.

The Augustan reformers in the early 18th century sought to remove Elizabethan wordplay from literary language for the sake of stylistic lucidity, and it was not until the 20th century that editors started to admit the ingenuity of Shakespeare's puns. The Japanese literary language (*bungo*) did not undergo significant reform until the Meiji era when *share* and humour in general both became objects of intense debate. As in English literature, the debate centred on aesthetics and ethics but unlike the English model (which undoubtedly influenced Meiji thought) vulgarity has seldom been incriminated. According to Wells, the conclusion that 'humour is a mark of humanity' that should not be subject to controls has been the most pervasive in Japanese society (Wells 1997, 162). *Dajare*, therefore, is tolerated as harmless even if vulgar. Wells also notes that Japanese humour – around the dining table, for example – is 'a more formal game than it is in English' where 'the rules of aggression and offence' are deliberately 'suspended' (ibid., 160). This freedom favours both *share* and the translation of dramatic structures; Japanese audiences expect to hear some verbal chicanery in the theatre.

Share also offers a clue to the nature of wordplay in Japanese literature. In the Heian court plays, *kakeai* were performed as dialogues between the gods and human beings, figuring the exchange of divine and human wisdom by plays on words (Nishimura 1988, 894-96). The idea of exchange through dialogue is represented in a device that is even more fundamental to Japanese poetry, the seven-five syllabic, whereby the poem provides a context in which the shorter or 'lower' phrase (*shimo no ku*) responds to the longer or 'upper' phrase (*kami no ku*), exchanging poetic elements.[178]

In the 16th century, the idea was developed into the genre of *renga* or *renku*. Two or more poets would take it in turns to write short poems, each related to the previous by a theme, word, image or seasonal reference. A modern example of *share* is the following

---

[176] One example Shively notes of a double pun is *nori oete*, written to mean 'finish mounting [a horse]' but sounding like *nori wo ete*, 'attain the Buddhist Law'. Both classical and modern Japanese are rich with *giongo* (onomatopoeia) and *gitaigo* (mimetic words).

[177] Dr Johnson's influential term for a Shakespearian pun. *Romeo and Juliet* by contrast, which was probably written in the same year as *A Midsummer Night's Dream*, contains at least 175 quibbles. The difference between the two plays is that Romeo and Juliet are forced into a consciousness of what they say that is seldom apparent in the romantic comedy.

[178] In modern Japan, *kakeai* has an equivalent in the comic dialogue or 'cross talk' performed by *manzai* comedians.

tanka by Yosano Akiko (Yosano 1943, 131):

risshun no	even days in early spring
hi mo sabishikere	can be sad –
ochikochi no	that waxy gloss of snow
ko no moto no yuki	beneath the trees,
rō no iro shite	you can't get away with it

In this example, the play on *ko-* in *ochikochi* (a colloquialism) with *ko* meaning 'tree' humorously foregrounds the repetition of the short o vowels; the sadness is surely ironic.

Bottom eats his words

Despite the lack of quibbles, *A Midsummer Night's Dream* is also a play about exchange: dramatic exchange between the human and the supernatural and exchange in its thematic sense as a device for pleasure and of transformation. Above all, Titania must first be humiliated in her rapture for an ass before she can return her true allegiance to her husband. Bottom must be transformed beyond the wildest imaginings of his fellows and returned to them safe and sound before they realise how much they depend on him.

The exchanges between Bottom and Titania offer good material for *dajare* as the rustic and ethereal are juxtaposed to obvious comic effect (4.1.21-33):

> *Mus.* What's your will?
> *Bot.* Nothing, good mounsieur, but to help Cavalery Cobweb to scratch. I must to the barber's, mounsieur, for methinks I am marvellous hairy about the face; and I am such a tender ass, if my hair do but tickle me, I must scratch.
> *Tita.* What, wilt thou hear some music, my sweet love?
> *Bot.* I have a reasonable good ear in music. Let's have the tongs and the bones.
> *Tita.* Or say, sweet love, what thou desir'st to eat?
> *Bot.* Truly, a peck of provender; I could munch your good dry oats. Methinks I have a great desire to a bottle of hay: good hay, sweet hay, hath no fellow.

Bottom himself seems aware of the new context as he tempers his prose with a Frenchified version of court language ('mounsieur', 'Cavalery', 'marvellous') but when it comes to speaking his mind the language is bestial. The allusions to food and music (a potentially comic contrast in itself) are all typical components of Japanese *share*: taste, sound, high and low. Yet *share* is hardly a conspicuous feature of Odashima's translation (104-5):

M: Goyō wa?
B: Iya ne, Musshū, tada kumo no itokun wo tetsudatte atama wo kaite moraitai dake da. Sanpatsuya ni ikanai to dame kana, Musshū. Nandaka kaojū ossoroshiku kemukujara ni natta yō na ki ga surun da. Ore wa kō mietemo roba mitai ni baka ni binkan de ne, ke ni kusugurareru to kayukute shikata ga nain da.
T: Nē, itoshii kata, ongaku wo okiki ni naranai?
B: Ongaku ni kakete wa kekkō ii mimi wo motteru tsumori da. Hitotsu, janjan garagara yatte moraō ka.
T: Soretomo, anata, nanika meshiagaritai?
B: Sō da na, kaiba wo hitooke itadakō ka. Jōtō no karasumugi wo mushamusha yaritai na. Hoshigusa wo hitotaba itadakeru to arigatai, jōtō no hoshigusa, amai hoshigusa to kitara, saikō no gochisō da.

The typical components of *dajare* are already present as lexical items and so do not require further elaboration. The contrast between high and low is summed up in the translation 'hath no fellow', *saikō no gochisō da*. *Gochisō* is the standard polite expression of appreciation for food, *saikō* a colloquial word for 'best'. Titania uses wordplay in her prompts to Bottom. In the first, she takes his word *shikata* (in the phrase *shikata ga nai*, 'there's no way') and elongates it slightly into the more graceful *ito<u>shii</u> kata* ('sweet love'). She seems to be trying to draw him toward a more sophisticated style of speech and conduct; the play with sound would suit the subject of music which she then introduces. The next instance, however, is less clear. *Soretomo* certainly imitates the rhythm of *yatte moraō ka* but apart from that has no other function than as a new link to the subject of food. Titania's aim is to seduce Bottom and she tries out a variety of bait to tempt him. Bottom effectively deconstructs the first of these, music, when he rearranges her *ongaku wo okiki ni naranai* into *ongaku ni kakete wa kekkō ii*. A similar wordplay Bottom commits himself. The gallant *Musshū* ('Mounsieur') of Bottom's address to Mustardseed becomes an onomatopoeic word for munching in his last speech (*mushamusha*).

Titania and Oberon: twisted meanings

The potential for *share* seems to be conditioned by the nature of the dialogue: whether this is cooperative or antagonistic or mismatched to begin with. *Share* in a longer speech, not necessarily soliloquy, might suggest a mind at odds with itself. Antagonistic *share* would suit an equal relationship like that between Oberon and Titania, where neither has a lot to lose by taking linguistic advantage of each other. Their argument is conducted through an exchange of long speeches in 2.1.60-145 but there are opportunities for *share* in the one and two-line dialogues at the beginning and end of their scene together.

Obe.   Ill met by moonlight, proud Titania.

Tita.	What, jealous Oberon? Fairies, skip hence;
	I have foresworn his bed and company.
Obe.	Tarry, rash wanton; am not I thy lord?
Tita.	Then I must be thy lady; ...
	[...]
Obe.	Give me that boy, and I will go with thee.
Tita.	Not for thy fairy kingdom. Fairies, away!
	We shall chide downright if I longer stay.

The scene is patterned symmetrically around Titania's monologue on 'the forgeries of jealousy' (l. 81). Both sides wish to make their points known, the purpose of the initial exchange being to establish that Titania, as the lady, has the right to speak first. Oberon casts aspersions on Titania's virtues but she has the upper hand and leaves Oberon begging pathetically for the 'little changeling boy / To be my henchman' (ll. 120-21). In the source text, the dramatic tension between the two characters is brought out prosodically as well. Oberon opens iambically ('Ill <u>met</u> by <u>moon</u>-') which Titania counters with an indignant trochee ('<u>What</u>, jealous <u>Oberon</u>?'). Oberon then comes in with a trochee of his own which Titania repulses once more this time with iambs. The interplay foregrounds the following sequence of key words: 'proud', 'what', 'tarry', 'I', 'lord', 'I' and 'lady'. The closing exchange is both briefer and simpler: Titania contradicts Oberon's statement 'I will go with thee' with a cheeky 'not'.

Odashima does now use *share* (34; 39):

O:	Tsukiyo ni mazui deai da na, kōmanna Taitēnia.
T:	Ara, shittobukai Ōberon! Yōseitachi, iku wa yo,
	ano hito no beddo nimo soba nimo chikazukanai to chikatta no dakara.
O:	Mate, asahakana onna, ore wa omae no otto de wa nai ka.
T:	To sureba atashi wa anata no tsuma.
	[...]
O:	Ano ko wo kuretara issho ni ittemo ii.
T:	Iie, agemasen. Yōseitachi, iku wa,
	kore ijō koko ni iru to mata kenka ni naru wa.

The first *share* involves an elision of the last sound in Titania's name (as uttered by Oberon) with her opening exclamation, *ara*. *Ara* means nothing more than 'well, then' but the vowel a has positive connotations in Japanese speech, and is thus a fitting prelude to her accusation *shittobukai* ('full of jealousy'). The sound is heard at the end of her brief rebuff as well – *chik<u>att</u>a* no *d<u>akara</u>* – and although Oberon borrows the sound it is no more than pallid imitation. He also loses the force of his question, *otto de wa nai ka*, as Titania suborns it within a clause of her own (*to sureba*). Her closing shot is even more ingenious (and typical of *share*). Her pun on Oberon's *ii* ('OK', 'good') produces a completely opposite meaning, 'No' (*iie*).

Finding a voice

As for *share* in consensual dialogue, it is evidently more plausible in a humorous mode than in a tragic or sentimental one. There is, for example, no evidence or indeed need for *share* in the stychomythia between Lysander and Hermia and Helena and Hermia. There is, however, *share* in Odashima's translation of the mechanicals' scenes, particularly between Quince and Bottom where it can be used to define a relationship that is benign but competitive. Flute has just protested at being given a woman's part as he has 'a beard coming' (1.2.45-53; 27):

Quin.   That's all one: you shall play it in a mask; and you may speak as small as you will.
Bot.   And I may hide my face, let me play Thisbe too. I'll speak in a monstrous little voice: 'Thisne, Thisne!' – 'Ah, Pyramus, my lover dear! thy Thisbe dear, and lady dear!'
Quin.   No, no, you must play Pyramus; and Flute, you Thisbe.
Bot.   Well, proceed.
Quin.   Robin Starveling, the tailor?

Q: Onnaji koto sa. Kamen wo tsukete, dekiru dake ka hosoi koe wo daseba iin da.

B: Kao wo kakushite ii nara, Shisubī mo ore ni yaraseru yo. Monosugoku hosoi koe de shabette miseru ze. Hora, konna chōshi de na. 'Ā, Piramasu, atashi no itoshii hito! Anata no itoshii Shisubī yo, anata no koibito yo!'

Q: Iya iya, omae wa Piramasu wo yaranakereba naran no da. Furūto, omae ga Shisubī da.

B: Sō ka, dewa shinkō.

Q: Shitateya no Robin Sutāburingu.

The first example of *share* shows Bottom's tendency to change the subject in whichever way pleases him. *Kao* ('face') sounds like *koe* ('voice') and is also a part of the human body but from Quince's point of view, Bottom is jumping the gun. The *share* alliterates on a series of *k* sounds (*dekiru dake ka, koe, kao, kakushite*), regarded as 'a strong, clean' sound in Japanese (Takiguchi 1997, 102). Bottom's benevolence is firmly established in the second example. Perhaps he has an idea of whom Quince is about to address since he has just alliterated <u>shin</u>kō ('proceed') with <u>shi</u>tateya ('tailor') which might allude to the joke in the source: the tailor cannot proceed without the cloth provided by Nick Bottom the Weaver.

Unlike earlier comedies such as *The Two Gentlemen of Verona* (1593) or *Love's Labour's Lost* (1595), this play seldom indulges in wordplay for its own sake, and the humour is at least as visual as it is verbal. Yet in the mechanicals' play in Act 5, there is opportunity for Bottom (as Pyramus) to play with the sounds uttered by Duke Theseus. It should be remembered that Bottom is almost guilty of *lèse majesté* when he contradicts the Duke (5.1.180-82; 132):

> *The.*   The wall, methinks, being sensible, should curse again.
> *Pyr.*   No, in truth sir, he should not.
>
> T: Kono hei wa dō yara ningen no kanjō ga aru rashii kara, kitto noroi kaesu zo.
>
> P: Ie ne, kōshakusama, jitsu wa sō wa ikimasen no desu.

In Odashima's translation, Bottom's retort takes the *i* and *k* in *iwai kaesu* and transforms it into *ie ne, kōshakusama*. The *dajare* is so slight as to be barely noticeable but it leads an extra impetus to the exchange which, after all, interrupts a public performance.[179]

RHYMING VERSE: HELENA'S LAMENT

The examples of *share* examined in the previous section indicate a technique that is used to lend pace when pace is needed but which is not a particular feature of Odashima's translation, since *A Midsummer Night's Dream* is not essentially a play *about* language. This is not, however, to deny the role of poetry in the play, in particular the

---

[179] In a recent study of *dajare*, Odashima finds examples of *dajare* in the contemporary playwright Noda Hideki, who professes to dislike the device. He also finds examples in the plays of Inoue Hisashi, who was well known for his interest in language and dialect. Similar to Wells, Odashima argues that *dajare* is rooted in Japanese cultural tradition and contemporary discourse; it is one of the features that makes the Japanese language amenable to Shakespeare translation (Odashima 2000, 152-53).

force of lyric within dramatic narrative. Lyric serves not only to break the narrative, especially important with such an incredible plot as this one, but also to articulate sub-texts which may have been suppressed in preceding dialogue.[180] Rhyming verse (as an example of lyric) has an integrative function that alleviates the tragicomic undercurrents of the play.[181] The principal rhymester is Puck; his rhyming couplets underscore the archetypal comedy of his character, suggesting that nothing can come to serious harm in his hands.[182] Rhyming verse is also used by the lovers to conclude both scenes and speeches but inevitably separates its speaker from the continuity of blank verse. Finally, the rhyming couplet is, with alliterative iambic metre, one of the two poetic devices of the mechanicals' play.

Rhyme in Shakespeare can serve a range of purposes (Flint 2000), but principally as sound closure it serves to register the limits to the illusion of dramatic narrative, for example by closing a soliloquy or introducing a change of scene.[183] One example of a soliloquy that also closes a scene is Helena's speech at the end of Act 1, Scene 1, which brings the drama of that expository scene to an effective conclusion (1.1.226-51):

> How happy some o'er other some can be!
> Through Athens I am thought as fair as she.
> But what of that? Demetrius thinks not so;
> He will not know what all but he do know;
> And as he errs, doting on Hermia's eyes,
> So I, admiring of his qualities.
> Things base and vile, holding no quantity,
> Love can transpose to form and dignity:
> Love looks not with the eyes, but with the mind,
> And therefore is wing'd Cupid painted blind;
> Nor hath Love's mind of any judgement taste:
> Wings, and no eyes, figure unheedy haste.
> And therefore is Love said to be a child,
> Because in choice he is so oft beguil'd.
> As waggish boys, in game, themselves forswear,

---

[180] One example is Oberon's lyrical image of Cupid loosing 'his love-shaft' at 'the imperial votress' (2.1.155-74), which comes just after his remonstration with Titania. The speech lightens the mood of the drama, presents another side to Oberon's character from the adulterer and pederast, and inspires hope that the argument will be resolved. The sub-text is that if Oberon and Titania can argue with passion then they can also love with passion.

[181] Couplets are used to heighten the farce of the scene at the end of Act 3 when Lysander and Demetrius are being tricked into sleep by Puck (3.2.401-30).

[182] Although Puck's rhymes manifest his magical powers, their extended use is too self-conscious to be anything but comic. The most serious use of rhyme is as a closing device; the only time that Oberon speaks in couplets is at the end of the play (5.1.387-408).

[183] Aphoristic couplets can also have this summative function.

> So the boy Love is perjur'd everywhere;
> For, ere Demetrius look'd on Hermia's eyne,
> He hail'd down oaths that he was only mine;
> And when this hail some heat from Hermia felt,
> So he dissolv'd and show'rs of oaths did melt.
> I will go tell him of fair Hermia's flight:
> Then to the wood will he, tomorrow night,
> Pursue her; and for this intelligence
> If I have thanks, it is a dear expense.
> But herein mean I to enrich my pain,
> To have his sight thither and back again.

Rhyme has been used by Hermia just prior to Helena's entry at line 180. It is the style appropriate to the young lovers at this stage in the play, of those who desire a rapid solution to their troubles, and that includes Helena whose desire is for an instant, everlasting love. Yet Helena can only listen with envy as Hermia and Lysander trill their way through successive rhyming couplets. Helena speaks in couplets too, being in love with Demetrius, but her love is unrequited. Except for the rhyme in lines 248 and 249, all the rhymes in this speech are final rhymes that mark the ends of sentences and clauses. Rhyme suits Helena's condition, since as an unrequited lover, she imagines 'love' in a literary but formal representation.

The rhyme scheme changes slightly as Hermia and Lysander step out of the classical image in which they have figured themselves to become living beings with a plan of escape. As Helena realises her own potential role in the plan and her relationship with the other two, a single enjambement is admitted: 'and for this intelligence / If I have thanks, it is a dear expense.' The dual meaning of 'dear' reflects the ambiguity of her role, facing either continued, if picturesque, frustration or else uncertainty but possible fulfilment. The rhyme scheme seems to be stuck in the first of the two roles.

The two prose translations by Tsubouchi (201) and Fukuda (21-22) adopt a kind of rhyme scheme for the first two-and-a-half lines but after that, return to unstructured prose.

TSUBOUCHI

Dōshite mō hito ni yotte, konna ni shiawase ga chigau darō! Asensujū de watashi wa ano hito ni otoranai kiriyō da to omowarete ita mono wo. Datte, sore ga nan ni narō? Dimitoriyasusan wa sō omowanai no da mono. Hito wa minna shitte iru koto wo ano hito dake wa shirō tomo shite kurenai. Hāmiyasan no metsuki ni me ga kurande iru no da, chōdo watashi ga ano hito no kiryō ni oborete shimatte iru yō ni. Koi wa bunryō to iu koto wo shiranai kara, donna somatsuna mono wo mo hōgaina rippana mono ni shite shimau. [up to l. 233 in source]

FUKUDA

Shiawase ga, hito ni yotte, dōshite kō mo chigau no deshō! Asenzujū de ano hito ni otoranu kiryō yoshi to omowarete ita atashi, demo, sore ga nan da to iu no deshō? Demetoriasu wa, sō wa omotte kurenai no da mono. Dare demo shitte iru koto wo, ano hito dake wa shitte kureyō to shinai no da mono. Sō, ano hito ga Hāmia no me ni hikarete mayotte iru no to onaji, atashi wa ano hito no ii tokoro ni bakari akogarete iru no kamo shirenai ... [omitting ll. 232-46 in source] Sō sureba, asu no ban, ano hito wa mori made otte iku deshō. Sono koto wo shirasete agete, orei wo itte morattemo, kono atashi niwa ōkina itade da keredo. Demo, sō sureba, yukikaeri ni ano hito no sugata ga kaima mirareru, sō shite atashi wa, jibun wo motto kurushimete yaritai no.

The long vowels in Tsubouchi's rhyme of *darō* ('would be') with *narō* ('would become') are alternated with broken verbless sentences ending with the emphatic *mono*. The clauses and sentences that follow do not correspond exactly with the line breaks in the source, and although the rhyme scheme is discontinued it is striking how many of these clauses and sentences end in negatives or words containing double vowels that reproduce the depressed tone of the source, for example *shite shimau* (literally, 'finish doing something') and *nai to itte* ('saying no'). Most of these endings are not overtly negative but many of those which are not express either uncertainty (e.g. *kokoro ga toroke*, literally 'Demetrius' heart melted' for 'he dissolv'd') or an inflexible state of mind (e.g. *mottomo yo*, 'it's the principle'). A further parallel is drawn between the word *kiriyō* (meaning 'estimation' for 'I am thought as fair as she') and *kiryō* ('charms' for 'doting on Hermia's eyes').

Perhaps the reason why Tsubouchi does not make more of Shakespeare's prosody is that this kind of public statement of unrequited love would have itself been rare enough in traditional drama and in soliloquy nonexistent. By the time that Fukuda translated the play, soliloquy had become well established as a dramatic technique in *shingeki*. His version of Helena's lament is less of a melancholy lyric, more of a personal reflection that leads inexorably to the conclusion that Helena must join in the chase. He does this partly by the use of conjunctions such as *datte* and *demo*. Isolated by punctuation (as they are in eleven cases in the complete excerpt), conjunctions help to dramatise Helena's situation and could even be interpreted as caricature. *Demo, sō sureba* marks the turn in her speech. These are decisive conjunctions that come at the beginning of her final sentence. Tsubouchi's version, however, is more like prose narrative, the conjunctions embedded in a sequence of sentences rather than being speech acts in their own right. Fukuda's conjunctions give the speech a structured tone which is obliquely equivalent to the rhyme scheme of the source.

Unusual as Helena's speech may have seemed in the 1920s and even 1950s, Tsubouchi and Fukuoka can only be considered experimental against the translations by Odashima (23-24) and Matsuoka (24-25):

ODASHIMA

Hito ni yotte shiawase ga kō mo chigau to wa!
Atashi no utsukushisa datte makenai hazu da wa, ano hito ni wa.
Demo Dimītoriasu wa sō wa omotte kurenai,
minna shitteru koto wo ano hito dake wa shitte kurenai.
Ano hito wa Hāmia no me ni hikare, ayamari wo okashite iru,
atashi ga ano hito no biten ni hikareru no mo onaji ne, okashii koto.
Iyashii minikui tsuriai no torete inai mono wo
koi wa rippana utsukushii hin no aru mono ni kaeru mono.
Koi wa me de mono wo miru no dewa nai, kokoro de miru,
dakara tsubasa motsu Kyūpiddo wa mekura ni egakarete iru,
koi no kokoro ni wa doko wo sagashitemo funbetsu nado nai,
dakara mufunbetsu wo shimesu yō tsubasa wa aru kedo me wa nai.
Koi wa aite wo erabu toki shocchū damasareru,
dakara koi no kami Kyūpiddo wa kodomo da to iwareru.
Itazurana kodomo wa tawamure ni heiki de uso wo narabetateru,
dakara kodomo de aru koi no kami wa yatara ni uso no chikai wo tateru.
Dimītoriasu mo Hāmia no me ni fureru made wa,
atashi dake no mono da to arare no yō ni chikai wo furasete ita,
tokoro ga sono arare wa, Hāmia no netsu wo ukeru to,
arare mo nai, ano hito morotomo tokeru to wa.
Sō da, ano hito ni Hāmia no kakeochi wo shiraseyō,
kitto ano hito wa asu no yoru Hāmia wo tsukamaeru yō
ano mori ni oikakete iku darō. Kore wo oshieta tame,
ano hito ni kansha wa saretemo, atashi wa gisei wo harawanai to dame.
Demo ano hito no yukikaeri no sugata wo mirareru dake de,
koi ni kurushimu orokana atashi no kurō wa mukuirareru wake ne.

MATSUOKA

Dōshite hito ni yotte konna nimo shiawase ga chigau no kashira!
Atene dewa watashi mo ano hito to onaji kurai bijin da to omowarete iru.
Demo, sore ga nan ni naru no? Dimītoriasu wa sō wa omotte inai.
Minna ga shitte iru koto wo, ano hito dake wa shirō tomo shinai.
Hāmia no me ni mayotteru no yo.
Chōdo watashi ga ano hito no subete ga subarashii to omotte iru yō ni.
Koi wa hodo wo shiranai kara, iyashiku minikui mono mo
namihazureta rippana mono ni kaete shimau.
Me de miru no dewa naku kokoro ga mitai yō ni miru.
Dakara, e ni egakareta Kyūpiddo wa itsumo mekakushi wo shiterun da wa.
Koi no kamisama ni wa handanryoku mo nai.

Chapter Four Rhyme And Wordplay

Tsubasa ga atte me ga nai no wa, mufunbetsu de sekkachina shirushi.
Koi no kamisama ga kodomo da to iwareteru no mo muri wa nai.
Omoichigai ya kentōchigai de aite wo erabun da mono.
Itazurakko ga fuzakete uso wo tsuku yō ni
koi no bōya mo itaru tokoro de uso no chikai wo tateru.
Datte, Dimītoriasu mo Hāmia no me wo miru made wa
boku wa kimi dake no mono datte, chikai no kotoba wo ame arare to abisete kureta.
Tokoro ga Hāmia ni netsu wo ageta totan
ano hito wa torotoro ni natte chikai no kotoba mo tokete shimatta.
Hāmia no kakeochi no koto wo oshie ni ikō.
Sōshitara ashita no ban, ano hito mo ato wo otte
mori e iku darō. Kono koto wo shirasete
arigatō to iwaretemo wari ni wa awanai kedo,
ikikaeri ni ano hito no sugata ga mirareru dake demo
watashi no kurō wa mukuwareru.

Odashima reproduces the aa-bb rhyme scheme in a translation of the same number of lines as the source. Four of the rhymes are penultimate rather than strict end rhymes (e.g. *okashite iru* with *okashii koto*) but then even Shakespeare rhymes 'quantity' with 'dignity' (a 'feminine' rhyme). The main difference between the two rhyme schemes is already suggested in their relationship to the key semantic items. Helena's judgement is based on what she sees; three of her rhymed words ('eyes', 'blind', 'eyne') are words to do with seeing. Yet most of Odashima's rhymes are on key syntactic rather than semantic items. The same conclusive impact is achieved by the imagery, built up within rather than at the end of each line.

It could still be argued that the overall effect is equivalent to Shakespeare's, since both are parodies of a style of amateur poetry that trusts too much in the power of conventional forms and imagery and neglects the inward movement of the verse. It is, after all, the logical consequence of the image of blindness that draws Helena into her final decision and thus initiates the process whereby an externalised image of love fulfilled can become part of her internal experience.[184] Odashima registers the turn at the end in a way that is probably even more subtle than the source: he reverses

---

[184] Helena's portrayal of Cupid is academic compared to Oberon's depiction in 2.1.155-74. Puck plays Cupid to Demetrius and Lysander but the two women remain immune to his darts as they remain faithful to their loves. Helena is confused by her situation but remains true to herself. The externalised image of love is a projection of her own insecurity; she is the one who has been deceived into believing in Demetrius' fidelity. The escapade in the wood frees her from her natural possessiveness by teaching her to differentiate her impressions of Demetrius' feelings from his actual self. As she exclaims in wonderment on finally being united with Demetrius (4.1.188-89), 'And I have found Demetrius like a jewel, / Mine own, and not mine own.'

Shakespeare's word order so that the second part of the final sentence becomes (in back translation) 'So that's why my labours will be repaid, isn't it?' The colloquial particle *ne* is often used in Japanese conversation to mean 'isn't it?'; it is one means of securing the listener's attention. In Helena's speech, it is the first real indication that she is talking to anyone but herself.

Matsuoka's version looks very different from Odashima's on the printed page, being neither rhymed nor at all regular in length of line. She follows Fukuda's strategy of dramatising Helena's mood changes. These mood changes originate in the source as a tension between a reflective mood and the closed structure. The correspondence between line length and mood change can be described as follows: statement of self-pity (long), self-comparison (long), reference to Demetrius (long), conclusion of first part of soliloquoy (long), reference to Hermia (short), comparison with Hermia (long), first mention of love (short), 'love can transpose' (short), 'love looks not with the eyes' (short), Cupid's blindness (long), love has no judgement (short), 'love is indiscriminate' (average), 'therefore is love said to be a child' (average), 'so oft beguiled' (short), like 'waggish boys' (short), so he is 'perju'rd everywhere' (short), before Demetrius saw Hermia (long), he swore he was 'mine' (long), but now he is passionate for Hermia (short), 'melting oaths' (long), 'I will go tell him' (short), 'tomorrow night' (short), 'to the wood' (short), 'if I have thanks' (short), 'to have his sight back' (short), 'to enrich my pain' (short).[185] The last line is the shortest and simplest of them all, Matsuoka's way of turning the corner; despite the odds, Helena is determined that there will be something in it for her.

Following Odashima, Matsuoka keeps her version to the twenty-six lines of the source but the awkwardness of Helena's speech comes not from using the prescribed form but from an emotive if unbalanced mix of logical progression, exclamation and lyrical expression. There is, in particular, a striking contrast between the seven shorter lines containing words for love and seeing and the nine longer lines which contain words to do with thought, speech and knowing. Matsuoka's translation manifests an almost schizophrenic division of cerebral and emotional processes. The hope expressed in that final line is, as a statement of hope, the only instance of thought and feeling being conclusively aligned.

The examples given so far of rhyme and *share* suggest that the four translators are, if anything, spoilt for choice by the phonological opportunities that the Japanese language offers and that rhyme and wordplay are used conspicuously only when justified as such by the literary context. Rhyme is evident in the translations but is only one of a number of devices at the translators' disposal to deal with Shakespeare's use of rhyme.

---

[185] The longer lines contain reflective statements, the shorter ones dogmatic or decisive ones.

TREES AND SPIRITS: TRANSLATING THE PUN

The homophone ki

As in English, the pun differs from soundplay in that the basic unit is the word. The aural similarity of one word with another is enough to make the pun stand out from its context, but the literary interest of puns is that they can often suggest some association of meaning as well. *A Midsummer Night's Dream* is hardly riddled with puns, but this pun of Demetrius' (2.1.192) is one interesting exception. Pursued by Helena into the wood, he exclaims

And here am I, and wood within this wood.

The pun has three possible meanings: a group of trees; an archaic word meaning 'frantic with anger'; and an indication of Helena's attempts to woo him (although she claims the reverse). The wood is established in a single line as a place for love and passion. As usual, it is Odashima who makes the fullest attempt to translate the pun as it is (42):

Kono mori ni kita ga, ki ni kakomarete ki ga ki ja nai

Odashima's is quite a liberal version: 'I came to the forest and, surrounded by trees, am not what I was'. The pun is on *ki* meaning either 'tree' or 'spirit' depending on the character used, and the *k*'s in *kita* and *kakomarete* provide the right phonic environment in which the pun can be noticed.

Matsuoka's version is similar (45). She writes with hindsight of Odashima's and, as with the example of Helena's soliloquy, is clearer in her dramatisation of the emotion implied in the source. The use of *dakara* ('therefore') at the beginning of the line and greater fluidity of sound indicate a person trying to make sense of a confusing new environment:

dakara kōshite koko ni kita ga, mawari wa ki bakari de ki ga hen ni naru

The phonic environment is strong enough for Matsuoka to avoid repeating the pun. Fukuda also is sensitive to the dramatic context (38):

kōshite koko e kita monono, ki ga ki dewa nai no da, ki bakari shigette

This approach avoids the danger of obviousness by making the audience wonder briefly why Demetrius should be 'out of his mind' before supplying an answer that is equally puzzling ('only trees flourish here'). Finally, Tsubouchi's version compresses the ideas of 'being here' and 'being within this wood' and so is the most straightforward (216):

kitan dakeredo, ki ga ki jā nai, ki no naka ni itatte

Fukuda follows the word order of the source most closely, although Tsubouchi's succeeds as a rhythmical flourish.

Lysander gives the lie

Whether or not Demetrius' pun is intentional on his part is impossible to tell, but one pun that is definitely intended is that perpetrated by Lysander in speaking to Hermia as the two lovers make their separate beds for the night (2.2.50-54).[186] The pun is the final shot in Lysander's self-consciously constructed speech of arch metaphors and rhymes:

	Then by your side no bed-room me deny;
	For lying so, Hermia, I do not lie.
Her.	Lysander riddles very prettily.
	Now much beshrew my manners and my pride,
	If Hermia meant to say Lysander lied!

Hermia registers the meanness of her lover's pun with her rhyme on 'prettily' which allows her to pretend that the only meaning of 'lie' she has comprehended is 'to tell a falsehood'.

This example points to the particular difficulty of finding two homophones in the target language which are semantically related to the source. The four translators employ a range of strategies but none of them are more than figurations of the pun's original intent. Tsubouchi, as so often, is surprisingly ingenious (224):

Dakara, anata no soba de yoko ni narasete kudasai yo. Soba de yoko ni natta karatte, yokoshima na koto nanka shiyashimasen.

H: Umai koto wo ossharu wa nē. Watashi ga anata wo kari nimo yokoshima wo hataraku hito da to iwau[187] toshita no de attara, watashi no burei busahō wo donna nimo shikatte kudasai.

---

[186] The pun would have sounded effective among Elizabethan audiences as the adverbial ending '-ly' was pronounced long. The combination of a homophone with the change from rhyming couplet to a triplet would have been more striking.

[187] The verb *iwau* means 'praise' or 'celebrate' but written in this context in *hiragana* the meaning is obscure.

Tsubouchi's Lysander plays on two words – *soba* and *yoko* that both mean 'beside' or 'next to', except that *yoko* is used as an adverb with *naraseru* ('to lie down'). The wordplay is resolved in the final clause with the word *yokoshima* meaning 'dishonest', and the final effect is enhanced by a rhythmic share on *yokoshima* and *shiyashimasen*. Hermia's retort is probably weaker than in the source, although her first sentence could certainly be pronounced in a riling manner.

Fukuda uses the same pun as Tsubouchi but adapts it to his usual narrative style (46-47):

> Sore nara, soba ni neta karatte, nanimo iu koto wa nai darō,
> kōshite kimi no yoko ni netemo, kesshite yokoshimana yume wa minai kara.

H: Kekkō, umai koto wo ossharu. Iie, atashi koso,
fushidara de, iyashii onna to iu koto ni naru, moshi anata ga sonna yokoshimana yume wo idaite iru nado to ittara.

In making Lysander promise that he won't have any naughty dreams (*kesshite yokoshimana yume wa minai*), Fukuda might seem to be taking an unforgivable liberty with the source but is one that can be appreciated as an equivalent to the archness of Lysander's riddle, especially as it amounts to something more than a riddle, representing a genuine attempt to make love to Hermia. Likewise, Fukuda captures the sense that Hermia is caught off guard by Lysander's rhetoric. She alliterates *kekkō* with Lysander's *kesshite* but the punctuation makes the use of *kekkō* ambiguous. It could be read adverbially with *umai* ('very prettily') but a rather more subliminal rendering might be to adopt its basic meaning, 'That's enough!' The punctuation has a similar effect on *iie, atashi koso* which by itself can be understood as meaning 'Yes, that's how I feel as well but ...'

Odashima also replicates the pun but on a totally different word (51-52):

> Kimi no soba ni nekasete kure yo, Hāmia, tanomu kara,
> soba ni itatte, itatte shinshi da itazura shinai kara.

H: Itadakeru kudoki monku ne, Raisandā, raisan suru wa,
Raisandā ga itaranai shinshi da nado to ittara,
Hāmia koso reigi shirazu no fushidarame ni naru kara.

He puns remorselessly on *ita-*: *soba ni itatte* ('lie beside me'); *itatte shinshi da* ('I'm a real gentleman'); *itazura shinai kara* ('I won't do anything naughty'). Were it not for the dynamic rhythm,[188] this would be punning verging on mere goro. Hermia take up the

---

[188] This is *dajare*, all the more sarcastic.

jest quite 'prettily': *itadakeru kudoki monku* (which could be loosely translated as saying 'You could charm the pants off anyone!'). Odashima is the only translator to make something of Shakespeare's pun on Lysander's name: *raisan*, coming just after and before two *Raisandaas*, means 'praise' or 'admire'; Hermia teases him with false praise into hearing her more serious pun on *itatte*.

Matsuoka reverts to Tsubouchi's joke (54-55):

> Soba ni neru na, nante iwanaide.
> Soba de yoko ni natte mo yokoshimana koto wa shinai kara.

H: Raisandā, azayakana goroawase ne.
Moshimo Raisandā ga yokoshimana koto wo suru nante omotta nara sonna watashi koso fushidara de tsutsushimi ni kakeru no dakara, un to shikatte.
Demo, anata wa shinshi, watashi wo aishite reigi tadashiku atsukatte kureru nara
motto hanarete.

Matsuoka Japanises the pun by writing the word *yokoshima* in *hiragana*. She is also the only one of the four to allow Hermia to comment on the pun in specifically literary terms, since *goroawase* is one of the standard terms for wordplay (and less specific than Odashima's *kudoki monku*).[189] Her Hermia savours the pun like a dish of food (*azayaka* means 'fresh') and although she doesn't spit it back in her lover's face, she does refuse to admit its sexual possibilities.

Drawing swords

The context of the pun shared by Lysander and Hermia is a romantic one that verges on the sexual but the pun itself is not sexual at all. The play is generally short on the sexual bawdy that lards the discourse of the Sonnets. Peter Quince has his joke about 'French crowns' (1.2.90-91)[190] and, of course, much of the humour of their own play in Act 5 is derived from unintended innuendo about chinks in walls and so on (to be discussed later in this chapter). The lovers' quarrel in Act 3, Scene 2 is an erotically-charged scene,[191] but the lovers take their situation too seriously for any overt use of sexual language; it takes the one character Puck, who delights in the comedy of misrule,

---

[189] *Kudoki monku* means 'wooing expression'.
[190] 'Some of your French crowns have no hair at all, / and then you will play bare-faced.' The joke refers to syphilis, 'the French disease'.
[191] The sexuality is apparent in the obscenities that the lovers fling at each other. The more that the language discriminates in this way between male and female, the emptier it becomes, and so the physical energies are released.

to realise the sexual humour beneath the shrinking violets and shaking of fists (3.2.404-12).[192] Through impersonating the voices of the two men, Puck articulates the absurdity of their quarrel: that they have not yet learnt to distinguish the language of emotions from the language of thought. In such conditions, double meanings are all the funnier for being accidental, subconscious.[193]

Dem.   Lysander, speak again.
        Thou runaway, thou coward, art thou fled?
        Speak! In some bush? Where dost thou hide thy head?
Puck.   Thou coward, art thou bragging to the stars,
        Telling the bushes that thou look'st for wars,
        And wilt not come? Come, recreant, come thou child!
        I'll whip thee with a rod; he is defil'd
        That draws a sword on thee.
Dem.   Yea, art thou there?
Puck.   Follow my voice; we'll try no manhood here.

A sexual reading might run as follows Demetrius shakes his sword/phallus at Lysander by mocking its small size (the head hidden in its bush). Puck (in the voice of Lysander) retorts that Demetrius is all words and no action: he cannot even 'come';[194] sex is too good for him, sadism (rods) better. Puck dupes Demetrius into his control and explicitly states the theme of this brief exchange: 'We'll try no manhood here' (in other words, 'we won't compare sizes here').[195] The approaches taken by the translators to possible double meanings can be glimpsed from whatever happens in the linguistic environment to the words for 'sword', 'bush' and so on. Tsubouchi's approach is masculinist (263):

D: Yai, Raisandā! Henji wo shiro, nigeta na, okubyōmonome, nigeyagatta na? Mono wo ie! Doko no yabu no naka ni iru no ka? Doko e atama wo kakushitan da?

P: Yai, okubyōmono, kisama wa hoshi ni mukatte kōgen wo haiteru no ka? Kore kara ōikusa wo yarun da to yabu ni hanashi wo shite iru no ka? Sorede ite kienai no da na? Sā kite miro, yowamushi. Yai, akanbo.

---

[192] In fact, the play is hugely sexualized, beginning with Theseus' frustrated longing for Hippolyta expressed at the beginning of the play, and this aspect is often apparent in contemporary productions, even if not immediately apparent from the language.

[193] Freud argued that comic pleasure is derived 'from an economy in expenditure upon ideation' (Freud 1976, 302); totally within Puck's control, the two men are acting totally out of instinct.

[194] The sexual connotation of 'come' was used in Shakespeare's day.

[195] Puck's line concludes the reassertion of language ('voice') over body ('manhood').

>   Shitsukebō de naguritsukete yarō. Kisama no yōna yatsu ni tsurugi wo nuku no wa te no yogore da.
>
> D: Yoshi, unu, soko ni iru na?
>
> P: Ore no koe ni tsuite koi. Konna toko ja shōbu shitakunai.

Tsubouchi translates the difficult metaphor 'try no manhood' as *shōbu shitakunai*, *shōbu* meaning 'win-lose situation'. Otherwise, the translation is quite literal. Demetrius' 'Speak!' is given as *Mono wo ie* ('Say something'), and the semantics of the exchange remain concrete. For example, Puck's 'recreant' becomes *yowamushi* ('weak insect'). The potential onanism in Puck's insult 'he is defil'd / That draws a sword on thee' is made explicit: *te no kegare da* states that it is the hands which will get dirty when the sword is drawn. Demetrius' *soko ni iru* ('to be there') sounds innocent enough except that in modern Japanese *soko* (literally, 'that place') is one of the slang words for male and female genitalia.

Fukuda makes little of the innuendo, leaving it to the imagination of actors and audience (87):

> D: Raisandā! Nanika ie. Nigeashi no hayai yatsu da, hikyōmonome, nigeuseta ka? Kuchi wo kike! Shigemi no naka ni kakurete iru no ka? Doko e atama wo kakushita no da?
>
> P: Hikyōmono, hoshi ni mukatte taigensōgo, shigemi wo aite no kenka, ore niwa te ga dasenai no da na? Okubyōmono, kozōkko, kisama nara, muchi de takusan da, kittemo tsurugi no kegare ni naru dake sa.
>
> D: Un, soko ni iru na?
>
> P: Koe wo tayori ni, tsuite koi. Koko dewa, omou zonbun tatakaenai kara na.

One indication as to whether or not Fukuda's ignoring the innuendo is deliberate can be gauged from his phrase *omou zonbun* ('to your heart's content') to translate Puck's parting quip 'we'll try no manhood here'. The phrase combines two words denoting thought, a verb (*omou*) and an adverbial noun (*zonbun*), and it cannot be emphasised enough that in traditional, non-Cartesian Japanese thought 'mind' and 'heart' (and 'thinking with mind and heart') are often regarded as one. Fukuda's phrase seems to make an analogy with Shakespearean fancy. Although the phrase has no actual sexual connotation, its rhetorical function is equivalent to the source. Both phrases serve to break the illusion of the scene by articulating essential sub-texts, sexual in Shakespeare's case and epistemological in Fukuda's. The sexual connotation in Japanese is almost too obvious a one to be worth articulating; what is worthier of comment (and therefore more disruptive dramatically) is the manner of thought and action.

Odashima uses the free verse form to produce a translation that is crisper and nastier (98):

> D: Raisandā! Oi!
> Henji wo shiro, nigeashi hayai hikiyōmono, nigeta no ka?
> Dōshita! Yabu no naka ni demo atama wo kakushita no ka?
>
> P: Nani wo, hikiyōmono, hoshi wo aite ni ibariyagatte,
> yabu wo aite ni kettō shiyotte no ka, noboseyagatte.
> Ore wo aite ni dekin no ka? Yai, okubyōmono, aonisai,
> omae nanka niwa muchi ga tegoro da, sharakusai,
> tsurugi wo nukeba yogoreru dake da.
>
> D: Yoshi, soko ni irun da na?
>
> P: Ore no koe ni tsuite koi, koko dewa tatakaenai kara na.

The end rhymes in the lines at the beginning of Puck's speech (in *-yagatte*) lead into a neatly punctuated series of insults (*yai, okubyōmono, aonisai*) and then a cutting rhythmic afterthought, *sharakusai*. *Yai* is a colloquial appellative, something like 'Man' (*Mensch*), *okubyōmono* means 'coward', and *aonisai* literally means 'green two-year old', i.e. 'little squit'. *Sharakusai* means 'stinking of *share*' ('witty sophistication'), which is the translator's interpolation on Demetrius' character. So, sexual unpleasantness finds its verbal equivalents.

Matsuoka's is the shortest and syntactically least complex translation (106-7):

> D: Raisandā, nanika ittara dō da.
> Nigeashi no hayai yatsu da, hikyōmono, nigeta no ka?
> Henji wo shiro! Yabu no naka ka? Doko ni atama wo kakushita?
>
> P: Hikyōna no wa kisama da, hoshi ni mukatte ōguchi tataki
> yabu ni kenka wo fukkakete
> dōshita, konai ki ka? Kakatte koi, okubyōmono, dōshita, hanattare!
> Muchi de oshioki ga ii toko da. Kisama aite ja
> tsurugi ga kegareru.
>
> D: Yōshi, soko ni irun da na.
>
> P: Ore no koe ni tsuite koi. Koko ja shōbu ni naranai.

Demetrius' questions *Shigemi no naka ka? Doko ni atama wo kakushita?* could be questions in a children's game or riddle;[196] likewise the alliteration in *konai ki ka? Kakatte koi*. Matsuoka follows Tsubouchi in her use of *shōbu* for fight at the end but whether the two are fighting with swords, or playing 'cavaliers and roundheads', or both, is left to the reader's imagination.

JUMBLED SOUNDS: ALLITERATION 'COOKED' AND 'UNCOOKED'

Soundplay has been one of the recurring themes of this and the preceding two chapters but has so far been discussed only in terms of pragmatic equivalence or as part of some greater effect (e.g. a pun). The Japanese words for alliteration, *tōin* ('head rhyme'), and assonance, *boinin* ('vowel rhyme'), are no more than technical terms for these most flexible of devices in Japanese prosody. Rather than marvelling at individual examples, it is more useful to refer to that cumulative and integrated euphony known as *goro*.

Goro occurs when a specific range of sounds combine within a literary text to support or subvert whatever is happening semantically; they are the phonological equivalent of rhythm, rhythm being the other essential dimension to euphony. Of course, euphony is hardly unknown to the English poetic tradition, as in the following lines from Dylan Thomas:[197]

> Though they go mad they shall be sane,
> Though they sink through the sea they shall rise again;
> Though lovers be lost love shall not;
> And death shall have no dominion.

These lines are all the more musical for the way that Thomas counterpoints alliteration, rhyme and repetition with an unmetrical rhythm. Thomas' modernist expression of beauty in contradiction is also a feature of many modern Japanese *tanka*. These are also lyrical poems but in the modern idiom became more open to the ugliness of experience and the possibilities of meaning in ugliness.[198] The following *tanka* by Miyazawa Kenji was composed in May 1918 (Ueda, 131):[199]

atama nomi a head

---

[196] This is unadorned language: 'Are you in the bush? Have you hidden your head?'
[197] 'And Death Shall Have No Dominion' (1933), ll. 6-9 (Thomas 1977, 62). 'They' refers to 'dead men' in line 2 of the poem.
[198] The universalism of Japanese modernism implies an openness to diverse subject matter.
[199] Miyazawa Kenji (1896-1933) is known as a free verse poet and writer of children's stories. His modernism combined devout Buddhism with his work as a teacher of agricultural methods.

> *ware wo hanarete* severed from the body
> *hagishiri no* grits its teeth
> *shiroki nagare wo* as it floats away
> *yogiri yuku nari* across the white stream

Miyazawa's *tanka* does not use rhyme or repetition as Thomas does but it is alliterative in quite the same way. The alliterated sound changes with each line and (except for the third line) the vowels are carefully varied. The conventional syllabic metre provides the framework in which the unconventional image can resonate. The *tanka* seems to make the same simple point as Thomas' poem but in more concrete terms: death can never overcome the power of human perception and imagination to refigure even lifeless objects.

It is simple enough to relate euphony to meaning within the structure of a brief lyric, but the matter becomes complicated when considered in the context of a long speech or whole play. With Japanese translators of Shakespeare, there is the danger of *goro* being used simply for effect and also of the natural euphonies of the Japanese language interfering with the semantics. It may therefore be worth returning to the distinction made earlier between intrinsic and extrinsic (or 'cooked' and 'uncooked'). Intrinsic ('uncooked') euphony is accidental to semantics and other poetic devices; it may enhance the overall effect or it may diminish it. The function of extrinsic ('cooked') euphony is more easily comprehended, although it may of course be equally redundant, and as the structuralist terminology of Lévi-Strauss is intended to suggest here the extrinsic features may function in a dynamic relationship with the intrinsic (Leach 1974, 30).[200]

Goro *harmonies: 'Following darkness like a dream'*

For examples of both types of *goro* in translation, it is natural to look first at extended lyrical passages. These passages open out the dark spaces vacated by dramatic dialogue and are structured ('cooked') and yet indeterminate ('uncooked'): 'like a dream'. When Puck enters for the first time at the end of Act 5, his lyric is heralded by Theseus' rather 'palpable-gross' mixture of lyrical evocation and brusque order to the lovers 'to bed', made all the more ironic by his warning that ''tis almost fairy time' (5.1.250). Depending on interpretation, Theseus has trouble getting his guests off to bed whereas Puck speaks his lines (5.1.357-76) with the utter conviction of his role; there can be no dramatic interruption of what is about to happen, if only because it belongs to a more

---

[200] Lévi-Strauss constructed 'a culinary triangle' out of the tension between a horizontal opposition of 'culture' and 'nature' and a vertical opposition of 'normal' and 'transformed': 'cooked', 'raw' and 'rotten'. The term 'uncooked' therefore embraces both 'raw' and 'rotten'; redundant euphony would be 'rotten' and functional but naturalised euphony 'raw'.

harmonious fairy world.

> Now the hungry lion roars,
> And the wolf behowls the moon;
> Whilst the heavy ploughman snores,
> All with weary task fordone.
> Now the wasted brands do glow,
> Whilst the screech-owl, screeching loud,
> Puts the wretch that lies in woe
> In remembrance of a shroud.
> Now it is the time of night
> That the graves, all gaping wide,
> Every one lets forth his sprite
> In the church-way paths to glide.
> And we fairies, that do run
> By the triple Hecate's team
> From the presence of the sun,
> Following darkness like a dream,
> Now are frolic; not a mouse
> Shall disturb this hallow'd house.
> I am sent with broom before
> To sweep the dust behind the door.

Puck's soliloquy is a prologue to the entrance of Oberon and Titania, functionally similar in other words to Quince's Prologue to the mechanicals' play. Yet the latter is a hotchpotch of lyric and rhetoric, while Puck speaks in rhyming trochaic catalectic tetrameters, the metre of lyrical incantation.[201] The irony of the contrast is that because his prosody is flawless and consistent, we take his words more seriously than we do the nonsense of a mortal.

Puck's incantation is static in its preference for metonyms over metaphors and its heavy prosody; that much is typical of a character who is allowed barely more than a representative role in the play. Puck represents Oberon and – disruptively – the lovers. The only extent to which he represents himself is in his self-introduction to the Fairy in Act 2 (2.1.42-57), and within fifteen lines we know all that there is to know about him. Yet the register is comic, and its simplicity is sufficient to present a series of vivid images, first of the night and then of the frolicking fairies, in other words to set the scene. It is also a musical speech. There is alliteration both within the lines (e.g. 'graves', 'gaping') and across lines (e.g. 'weary', 'wasted') and most of the images involve sound (e.g. 'roars', 'screeching loud'). The most abstract of the images is that describing the fairies, who

---

[201] Cf. the Three Witches in *Macbeth*, 4.1.10-11: 'Double, double toil and trouble: / Fire, burn; and, cauldron, bubble.' Only the last of Puck's lines is iambic.

could indeed be mysteriously soundless, quieter than a mouse.

The speech's musicality throws up a dilemma for the translator: whether to make it inherently musical, whether to impose some kind of musical pattern or whether to attempt both. Fukuda we have observed to be the most discreet of the translators, at least on the printed page, and so one would expect him to be inherently musical (127):

> Iyoiyo mayonaka, shishi mo uete unari, ōkami wa tsuki ni hoeru. Hiruma no shigoto ni tsukareta hyakushōdomo wa, guttari nedoko de takaibiki. Danro no nokoribi, chirachira moete, fukitsuna fukurō no surudoi koe ni, hinshi no toko no byōnin wa kyōkatabira wo omoidasu. Sā, iyoiyo yoru no sekai da zo. Haka wa anguri kuchi wo ake, mōja no mure ga uyouyo to, jiin no komichi tsudai ni sotto dearuku. Oira wa yōsei, nukari wa nai zo, tsuki no megami no basha wo kakonde, otentosama no me wo nusumi, yume no yō ni kurai sekai wo sematte yuku, sā, oira no sekai da, sawagimawaru zo. Nezumi ippiki, dete wa naranu, koyoi, kono ie wa omedetada ... oira no yakume wa, kono hōki, mazu sakibure ni, tobira no ushiro no chiriharai.

Fukuda uses no end rhymes at all and the nearest that he comes to Shakespeare's prosody is to divide the speech into short phrases which (in imitation of Shakespeare's enjambements) are occasionally doubled in length. Nor does he seem to use much internal rhyme. He does, however, draw on the resources of his language in two other ways. First, the abundance of vowels in Japanese means that even short phrases are likely to contain all five vowels, either with a consonant (*ka*) or as a long vowel (*saa*) or double vowel (*hou*).

Diversification of vowel sounds enhances the musicality of the translation. This effect is hardly conspicuous in itself but can be supplemented by other devices. A good example is *fukitsuna fukurō no surudoi koe ni* ('Whilst the screech-owl, screeching loud'), which contains all five vowels with alliteration on *fu-* and assonance on *–doi* and *koe*. The wordplay obliquely imitates the cry of an owl in Japanese[202] and gives phonic support to a figuration of the midnight hour that without such support would risk overstretching the audience's imagination. Another example is the word *iyoiyo*, meaning 'more and more', but often used in anticipation of some imminent event.[203] It is more precise than Shakespeare's 'Now', suggesting that the night does not arrive until Oberon does, that the tolling of the midnight bell is not sufficient in itself. It is an elastic, vowelly word, appropriate to the preparatory function of the speech.

Iyoiyo is not onomatopoeia (*giongo*) or one of those warm, mimetic words (*gitaigo*) so typical of colloquial Japanese, of which there are three examples in the speech: *guttari* (for 'weary'), *chirachira* (softening *moete*, 'burning', to become 'flicker'), *sotto* (qualifying

---

[202] The owl's hoot in Japanese is *hoohoo* (like long 'oh').
[203] *Iyoiyo toshi wo mukaemashō* ('Have a Happy New Year!') is a formal version of the standard greeting exchanged on the days leading up to New Year.

dearuku for 'glide'). The main function of these words is semantic but, as colloquialisms, add fuel to the fire of Puck's magnanimity.[204] Finally, one should mention the stock phrase *anguri kuchi wo ake* ('all gaping wide'). There is possibly a pun intended with the English word 'angry', since in both Japanese and Western tradition ghosts are regarded as restless, frustrated creatures.[205]

In line with the source, the register of Puck's speech changes slightly and the sounds become more interconnected. The phrase *yume no yō ni kurai sekai wo sematte yuku* ('Following darkness like a dream') involves alliteration on *ku* and *yu* that give it a crisp yet closed quality. That example may be accidental but the conglomeration of 'r' sounds in the final phrase – *tobira no ushiro no chiriharai* ('sweep the dust behind the door') – is surely not unintentional. The closed feeling is appropriate to a group of characters whose only ever interaction with the human world is by design.

There is little in Fukuda's translation that can clearly be identified as 'cooked'; the music arises quite naturally from within the poetry but not to such an obvious extent as the source even. Odashima's version is similar (143-44):

> Ima ya raiondomo wa ue,
> ōkamidomo wa tsuki ni hoe,
> tsurai shigoto ni tsukarehate
> hyakushōdomo wa yume no hate.
> Ima ya danro mo moetsukite,
> surudoku fukurōdomo naite,
> hinshi no toko ni fusu hito mo
> omoidasu no wa shi no koromo.
> Ima ya kusaki mo nemuru toki
> haka wa ōkiku kuchi hiraki,
> bōreidomo wa yami ni michi,
> samayoi aruku hakabamichi.
> Warera yōseisora wo kake,
> otentosama no kao wo sake,
> tsuki no megami no otomo shite,
> yami wo oiyuku, yume ni nite.
> Ima ya odoran tanoshige ni,

---

[204] Even *giongo* and *gotaigo* are not as exclusively colloquial in Japanese as they would be in English. Mimetic words such as *guttari* and *shikkari* ('firmly') function as adverbs and are commonly found in non-literary written texts as well. In the above context their function is poetic.

[205] In Buddhist teaching the ghost (*yūrei*) is a kind of lost spirit torn between heaven and hell as it seeks vengeance for a crime committed against it while alive. Consummated revenge or the intercession of a priest or monk might enable the ghost to pass into heaven. The *kaidanmono* ('ghost play') is one of the sub-genres of *kabuki*, of which the most famous is *Tōkaidō Yotsuya kaidan* (Yotsuya ghost stories, 1825) by Tsuruya Namboku. The ghost in Western tradition is in an equivalent state of purgatory.

nezumi yo deru na, kono ie ni,
ore wa sakibure, arakajime
haraiki yomeru no ga yakume.

This translation has a pithiness comparable (as the source is) with Feste's song at the end of *Twelfth Night*.[206] Odashima sustains the rocking rhythm for longer than Fukuda, but without increasing the number of lines, and he supports it with a simple rhyme scheme over the first ten lines. The rhymes in particular give the lines a degree of formality that makes them sound almost like orthodox syllabics, which is important as it encourages readers and actors to give equal stress to the syllables and so respond to the childlike simplicity of Puck's speech: one piece after another of the jigsaw until the speech shifts register in the second half.

There is some kind of *goro* in every line, which seems to support the main rhyme scheme – e.g. *ya*<u>mi</u> *ni* <u>mi</u>*chi* rhyming with *hakaba*<u>mi</u>*chi* – although that example apart, it is difficult to tell how much these euphonies are intended. The most conspicuous example is the line *Haka wa ōkiku kuchi hiraki* ('the graves, all gaping wide'), which is obviously intended and serves to define this 'Gothic' image of graves 'gaping wide'. It also marks the transition from images drawn from nature into the supernatural; *bōreidomo* ('ghosts') opens the succeeding line.

An even more dramatic register of the shift in style comes in the phrase *tsuki no megami no otomo* ('companions of the moon goddess'). Puck finally declares the fairies' alliegance to Diana (or Hecate), the moon goddess, an alliegance which is not always clear over the course of the play as Oberon and Titania meddle in human affairs. The fairies can function only at night, of which Diana is mistress. The poetic significance of the phrase is in the word *otomo*, 'companion'. *Tomo* has the same etymological root as a word used for pluralising, *-domo*, which has been used in that sense five times during the preceding fourteen lines: *raiondomo* ('lions'), *ōkamidomo* ('wolves'), *hyakushōdomo* ('peasants'), *fukurōdomo* ('screech-owls') and *bōreidomo* ('ghosts'). Shakespeare uses the singular in each case but Odashima interprets the image generically, connecting the five species with that of 'fairy'. His interpretation belongs to the festive grouping and coupling that is the comic culmination of the play: happiness generally, not just marriage, is about belonging to others. Finally, it can be observed that *domo* is a deep, round-sounding word, not unlike a tolling bell. Puck says it only six times and it is echoed in *shi no koromo* ('shroud') and the common particle *mo*. Odashima's famous *goro* is definitely cooked in this case, the repetition is so blatant.

---

[206] Puck's trochees have a manic quality whereas Feste's falling dactyls (*Twelfth Night*, 5.1.388-407) sound depressed with that stoical refrain, '*For the rain it raineth every day.*'. Puck's incantation is the clearest exposition in the whole play of the underworld.

Comic goro: *fierce alliteration*

The other side of the coin is represented by verse that is a parody of lyric, the lines spoken by Pyramus in the mechanicals' play (5.1.261-76). These lines exaggerate two features typical of lyric – internal rhyme and the shorter line length – in a way that is immediately absurd. The rhythms and musicality of the lyric are exaggerated to the point that they become melodramatic.[207]

> *Sweet Moon, I thank thee for thy sunny beams;*
> *thank thee, Moon, for shining now so bright;*
> *For by thy gracious, golden, glittering gleams;*
> *I trust to take of truest Thisbe sight.*
>   *But stay! O spite!*
>   *But mark, poor knight,*
>   *What dreadful dole is here?*
>   *Eyes, do you see?*
>   *How can it be?*
> *O dainty duck! O dear!*
>   *Thy mantle good,*
>   *What! Stain'd with blood?*
> *Approach, ye Furies fell!*
>   *O Fates, come come!*
>   *Cut thread and thrum:*
> *Quail, crush, conclude, and quell.*

Unlike Puck's speech, which is fluid and clearly structured, the fierce alliteration and short sentences of Pyramus impede the flow of speech and frustrate the dramatic illusion. This function is relevant to Odashima's translation (137-38) since alliteration is such a natural feature of the Japanese language, even more so of his style, that it would seem technically difficult for him to come up with a style that is even more heavily alliterative, and yet he does so, and in a way that can even be thought a parody of his 'normal' style.

> Natsukashii tsuki, arigatō, hiru to mimagō sono hikari,
> arigatō, tsuki, sono yō ni yoku zo terashite kudasatta.
> Kirakira kirameku kiniro no kichōna omae no hikari nite,
> makoto ni makoto no magokoro wo motsu Shisubī wo mīdasō.
> Daga mate, kore wa, ō, kanashi!
> Mate, kore wo miyo, awarena kishi,

---

[207] The word 'melodrama' is derived from the Greek meaning 'song drama'.

nanto kanashii koto zokashi!
Omae ni miyuru ya, ryō no me yo,
kore ga yume nara sugu sameyo,
kawaii kamo yo, waga kamo yo!
Omae no manto ga hikisakare,
sono ue makkana chi ni yogore,
fukushūgami yo, iza kitare!
Ō, unmei yo, kuru ga ii,
inochi no ito wo kiru ga ii,
chakichaki kecchaku tsukeru ga ii!

As with the source, the main alliterative effects occur in the third and fourth lines, for example *Makoto ni makoto no magokoro wo motsu Shisubī wo mīdasō* ('I trust to take of Thisbe truest sight.') Translating Shakespeare's iambic pentameters, Odashima's use of alliteration and assonance is generally much slighter than elsewhere, not so ruthless with those initial syllables. Indeed, the alternation of alliteration among differently-placed syllables of successive words is part of the illusion of naturalness. Likewise the use of rhyme. Odashima's rhymes are usually aa-bb but lines 5 to 15 of this excerpt are aaa-bbb.[208] None of these rhymes has anything to do with each other but the rhyming triplet on *ii* is the most absurd; *ii* means 'good' and yet there is nothing at all 'good' about Pyramus' situation. Odashima's translation ends up being quite a literal equivalent of the source, even literalist since *kamo* is the ordinary word that denotes 'duck' in Japanese.[209]

One wonders to what extent Matsuoka can repeat the joke in her version (150-51):

Yasashii tsuki yo, taiyō no yōna hikari wo arigatō.
Arigatō, tsuki yo, konna ni akaraku terashite kurete.
Kirakira to kirabiyaka ni kirameku kane no hikari nite
kanarazu ya kawaii Shisubī to no katarai ga kanau darō.
Daga, mate! Ō, nantaru koto!
Miru ga ii, awarena kishi yo
nantaru osoroshisa, nantaru kanashimi!
Me yo, mita ka?
Naze da, naze da?
Ō, kawaii ahiru! Ō, itoshi!
Natsukashii sonata no manto.
Kore wa, nanto! Chi ga nanto!
Kitare, fukushū no megamitachi!
Ō, unmei no kami, kitare, kitare!

---

[208] These rhymes could stand out like single rhymes in English prosody.
[209] The humour of the phrase *kawaii kamo* could be taken literally in Japanese also, especially as *kawaii* is a less dated word than 'dainty' and can mean 'cute', especially in the speech of Japanese girls.

Inochi no ito wo kiru ga ii.
Korose, kowase, kobose, kozuke!

Matsuoka does use alliteration, even the same alliterations as Odashima (e.g. *kirakira*), but in those third and fourth lines not only does she manage to sustain it over the whole two lines on the same *k* sound (which seems to be the favourite alliterative sound among all four translators, a cliché in itself) but also she keeps it going for the whole of each line. She does not use a rhyme scheme but chooses instead to make what she can of those short phrases. If anything, she goes the other way from Odashima by abstracting all she can of the poetry of the source and generating a series of dysfunctional phrases. For example, the short line *Me yo, mita ka?* ('Eyes, do you see?') foregrounds the absurdity of that question and is echoed not with a rhyme but with another short line. That said, Matsuoka's version swings more radically from overcooked alliteration to nothing at all, which is a more meaningful representation of Pyramus' melodramatic mood change from excitement to despair – Matsuoka once acted Bottom at university – than Odashima's more consistent treatment. It is not enough just 'to sound good'. Euphony can be related to meaning and – when it is not – is either accidental or even comically inappropriate. The next section takes *goro* one step higher up the formal hierarchy to the context of a whole dialogue.

BAYING HOUNDS: MUSICALITY IN ACT 4, SCENE 1

Act 4 is a transitional act, easily ignored, that fulfils the promise made by Puck that 'all shall be well' (3.2.463) and knits the couples together for the sacred and carnal unions that take place outside the confines of the play. The most dramatic confrontation is between Theseus and the lovers, although with the fairies on their side it is hard to believe that any harm will come of them; Theseus shows no hesitation in forgiving them. Yet, the dream-like mood is sustained throughout – even in Scene 2 when the mechanicals long for Bottom's return – and depends for its credibility on the lovers keeping silent with regard to their strange experiences, a silence which is partly filled by music. Music is referred to three times in the act, and is established right at the beginning when Titania asks Bottom if he will 'hear some music' (l. 27). Bottom interprets the question not as a signal for sensual pleasure but as a comment on his sensibilities: 'I have a reasonable good ear in music. Let's have the tongs and the bones.' (ll. 28-29).[210] The subject is taken no further. The exchange epitomises two very different concepts of music, the cultural and the natural. Music as culture is a human phenomenon, the coordination of body and instrument to express feelings beyond

---

[210] 'The tongs and the bones' were rustic musical instruments: the tongs similar to the orchestral triangle, and the bones to castanets.

words (or, in the case of song, to accompany words). The music of nature can be equally expressive but, because of its lack of artificial patterning, its existence beyond human control, can also provoke verbal description.

It is music of the first type that Titania summons to celebrate her reunion with Oberon, unearthly music 'such as charmeth sleep', yet still their own: music that may enter the human soul when asleep is music with the power to haunt a whole play. The music of the next movement of the scene, with Theseus and Hippolyta, is not song or instrumental music but the music of the Duke's hounds (4.1.102-25):

> *The.* Go one of you, find out the forester;
> For now our observation is perform'd,
> And since we have the vaward of the day,
> My love shall hear the music of my hounds.
> Uncouple in the western valley; let them go;
> Dispatch I say, and find the forester.
> We will, fair queen, up to the mountain's top,
> And mark the musical confusion
> Of hounds and echo in conjunction.
>
> *Hip.* I was with Hercules and Cadmus once,
> When in a wood of Crete they bay'd the bear
> With hounds of Sparta; never did I hear
> Such gallant chiding; for, besides the groves,
> The skies, the fountains, every region near
> Seem'd all one mutual cry; I never heard
> So musical a discord, such sweet thunder.
>
> *The.* My hounds are bred out of the Spartan kind,
> So flew'd, so sanded; and their heads are hung
> With ears that sweep away the morning dew;
> Crook-knee'd and dewlapp'd like Thessalian bulls;
> Slow in pursuit, but match'd in mouth like bells,
> Each under each: a cry more tuneable
> Was never holla'd to, nor cheer'd with horn,
> In Crete, in Sparta, nor in Thessaly.

Theseus and Hippolyta do more than give a name to what they hear (or are about to hear); they recreate the baying of the hounds in both the prosody and structure of their tripartite exchange. Theseus boasts of his hounds, promising Hippolyta an operatic performance to be viewed from 'the mountain's top'. Hippolyta echoes his boast with a memory of her own involving two other men of legend – Hercules and Cadmus – that might well prick the envy of her master. This indication of difference is also present in her use of the word 'discord' since although the sounds dissolve into 'one mutual cry' they are of themselves discordant. If 'confusion' is read in the Elizabethan way as four syllables, then this exchange is regularly iambic, like hounds pounding through the valley.

Theseus goes one better when he claims that his hounds have been selected according to sound as well as size: 'match'd in mouth like bells, / Each under each'. The resulting effect reaches toward the well-formed prosody of the two characters. The music of their exchange comes, as always, partly from alliteration (e.g. 'match'd in mouth') and repetition of lexical ('so', 'nor') and metonymic items ('the groves, / The skies, the fountains') but even more so through the variation of vowel sounds. The phrase 'their heads are hung / With ears that sweep away the morning dew' contains twelve different dipthongs and single vowels of which only two are repeated. An even more dramatic effect can be observed in her claim that 'they bay'd the bear / With hounds of Sparta'. These effects more than anything else recreate the music of the hounds, especially as hounds usually bay in vowels! A further important device is the use of enjambement and punctuation in the line. The punctuation marks do not have to be read as caesuras but when preceding a stressed syllable can lend extra stress.

Tsubouchi was the first to navigate a scene which may have been imaginable to Meiji audiences but still strange. The hunting of wild animals has been practised in Japan since ancient times, mainly in uncultivated, mountainous areas, but the custom of keeping packs of hounds is largely unfamiliar (273-74).[211]

T: Yai, dareka itte rinryōgakari no mono wo sagashite koi, gogatsu matsuri no shiki wa mō sunda kara. Saiwai hi mo nobori kakete iru kara, Hiporitadono ni washi no ryōkendomo no myōongaku wo kikaseru koto ni shiyō. Nishi no tanima de inudomo wo hanase. Sa, isoide rinryōgakari wo sagashite koi. ... Kisaki yo, sā kore kara yama no teppen e nobotte, inu no koe to sono hankyō to ga goccha ni natta ongaku to iu yatsu wo kiku koto ni shiyō.

H: Watashi wa, Hākyurīzudono ya Kadomasudono to tsukiatte imashita jibun ni, ano hitotachi ga, Kurīto no mori de, Suparuta no ryōken wo tsukatte inoshishi wo shichi e oitsumeta no wo mimashitakke ga, anna isamashii sakebigoe wa tsuizo kiita koto ga arimasen deshita. Mori mo yama mo sora mo, kinpen no dokomo kashikomo ga, minna isshokuta ni natte hankyō shimashita. Watashi ya anna ongaku no yōna sōon wo, anna kokoromochi no ii kaminari wo tsuizo kiita koto wa arimasen deshita.

T: Washi no ryōken wa, ano sunairo wo shita, agito no ōkii Suparuta tane wo sodateta no da. Yatsura no atama niwa asatsuyu wo harau hodo ni

---

[211] The opening scene of Kurosawa Akira's 1985 film *Ran* (based on *King Lear*) is of a spectacular wild boar hunt. *Inuōmono*, or hunting with hounds on horseback, was practised by *samurai* in feudal times for the purpose of military training.

nagai mimi ga tarete ite, hizamagari de, sōshite Sessarī no noushi no yō ni nodoniku ga tarunde iru. Oiashi wa noroi ga, nakigoe wa marude kakushu no rin no yō ni, shidai ni secchō wo nashite iru. Sō iu ongaku wo sō suru ryōken no mure wo, seko ya karibue de shieki shita rei wa, Kurīto nimo Suparuta nimo Sessarī nimo nakatta koto da.

The word 'hound' is itself a musical word, more so than Japanese *inu* ('dog'), which Tsubouchi aggrandises as *ryōkendomo*. *Ryōken* is a word for hunting dog but – as so often with his style – Tsubouchi adds plural *-domo* for literary effect. *Kanji* compounds often contain pitch accents or dipthongs that culminate the successive rhythms; it is one way of registering the poetic tone of the speech. *Rinryō* ('hunting in the forest') sounds even grander. The phonic similarity of *domo* for the hounds and *dono* as an honorific suffix for Hippolyta creates an association with 'hound' and 'mistress' that is probably unintended but does typify the masculinist discourse. *Mo* and *no* are particles meaning 'more' and genitive 'of' respectively and although not occurring more than usual in the exchange they do signify ideas of accumulation and property that dominate both speeches. The imagery of both characters is expansive and domineering. Tsubouchi rhymes *ryō-* in *ryōken* with *myō-* in *myōongaku*, the closest he gets to Theseus' evocative 'music of my hounds'. The language of both characters is quite uncomplicated, since dense metaphors and imagery would only detract from the vigorous canine imagery, and Tsubouchi is correspondingly easy to understand. Theseus' line beginning *Kisaki yo, sā kore kara ...* ('We will, fair queen ...') is childish in its simplicity, little more than a string of conjunctions and particles. He is also able to follow Shakespeare's word order that places the image of climbing the mountain before 'the musical confusion' (*goccha ni natta ongaku*). Tsubouchi's phrase is clumsier than in Shakespeare but there is an accent on *goccha* which recreates the sound they will hear as they reach 'the mountain's top'.

The first part of Hippolyta's speech (up to *arimasen deshita*, 'never did I hear') is more fluid than Theseus' speech as she recounts her happy memories. The long phrase beginning *Hākyurīzu* would be easy for an actress to say and trips pleasingly onto a Shakespearean inversion, *jibun ni* (reflexive 'I', 'myself'). The alliteration on 'bay'd the bear' is recreated in a neat paraphrase, *inoshishi wo shichi e oitsumeta. Anna isamashii sakebi goe* ('such gallant chiding') is an ebullient phrase, if not as condensed as Theseus'. The second half becomes denser as she boasts of all the places where the baying could be heard, but the list of places makes a good break before the resounding rhythms of *minna is<u>h</u>okuta ni <u>n</u>atte <u>h</u>ankyō shimashita* ('seem'd all one mutual cry'). The word order separates the idea of oneness (*isshokuta*) from that of echo (*hankyō*). The concentration of *ya*, *yō* and *n* sounds in the first phrase of the next sentence makes it musical as well as rhythmic: *Watashi ya anna ongaku no yōna sōon wo* ('so musical a discord').

In Tsubouchi, the echo itself is to be heard again in this excerpt. In Theseus' second speech, the exotic beauty of the Spartan hounds is partly recreated by the mass of compound nouns which the translator selects to describe their qualities. The most extravagant example is *seko ya karibue de shieki shita rei wa* ('holla'd to, nor cheer'd with horn'), where the regular stresses up to *de* contrast with an irregular rhythm in the second half in a way that could be likened to a burst of the hunter's horn.

Fukuda's version (83) is like Tsubouchi's but with most of the arcane and literary touches taken out (so proving the translator's own statement that ninety-percent of Shakespeare's poetry is lost in translation). In this case, he may have felt that a lot of poetry would have detracted from the momentum and excitement of the exchange, even obfuscating the clarity of the descriptions. Odashima does little better (110-11). His translation seems more self-indulgent in the way that most of his lines are headed by words with a strong semantic content and even picturesque quality, e.g. *asatsuyu* ('morning dew'), *oiashi* ('chasing feet').

Matsuoka rivals Tsubouchi for rigour and diversity of expression, a feeling that even Theseus and Hippolyta have their own 'brave new world', albeit one based on experience rather than expectation (119-21):[212]

> T: Dareka itte, ryōkengakari wo sagashidase.
> Gogatsu matsuri no gyōji mo koshikidōri okonatta.
> Kyō no kono hi mo akesometa bakari
> itoshii Hiporita ni ryōken no ongaku wo kikasetai.
> Nishi no tanima ni ryōken wo tokihanatsu no da.
> Sā, isoge, ryōkengakari ni meijite koi.
> Utsukushii Hiporita, ano yama no itadaki made nobori,
> ryōkendomo no hoetateru koe ga kodama suru
> nigiyakana ongaku wo kiku koto ni shiyō.

> H: Watashi mo mukashi Herakuresu ya Kadomasu to tomo ni
> Kuretajima no mori de Suparuta no ryōken wo tokihanachi
> kumagari wo shita koto ga arimasu.
> Are hodo isamashii hoegoe wa kiita koto ga nai. Mori dake de naku
> sora mo izumi mo, ari to arayuru basho ga
> koe wo hitotsu ni shite iru yō deshita.
> Are hodo fukyōwana ongaku mo, are hodo uttori suru raimei mo hajimete
> deshita.

> T: Watashi no ryōken mo Suparuta tane da.
> Ōkina ago, sunairo no kenami. Asatsuyu wo harawan bakari ni ōkiku tareta
> mimi.
> Hiza wa magari, nodo moto no tareguai wa Tessaria no osuushi sokkuri da.
> Emono wo ou ashi wa osoi ga, koe wa marude daishō samazamana kane no
> yō ni

---

[212] Matsuoka's word for 'hunting', *ryōkengari*, defamiliarises the idea as it sounds as if it is the dogs who are being hunted.

> hibikiau. Kakegoe ya tsunobue ni awase
> kore hodo chōwa shita koe wo hassuru ryōken no mure wa
> Kureta nimo Suparuta nimo Tessaria nimo inai darō.
> Kikeba wakaru hazu da.

Theseus' speech is brisk and businesslike but her rendition of Hippolyta's speech fluid and elegant. The placing of *mori dake dewa naku* ('not only the forests') at the end of the line after *kiita koto ga nai* ('I never heard') affirms the crisp *k* alliteration, and the subsequent enjambement gives added emphasis to the quasi-inversion *ari to arayuru basho ga*. The one exception to this melodious speech is, of course, the rather awkward compound adjective *fukyōwana* ('discordant'). Matsuoka's Theseus distances himself from Hippolyta's long and languid sentences with three short ones that return the topic of conversation to the present. Each of them ends either in a noun or the copula *da*. Yet having set the hounds back firmly on their feet, the tone is once again expansive. The line beginning *Kureta nimo* could even be an echo of Hippolyta's style because of its fluidity and reference to place. The phrase *Kakegoe ya kadobue ni awase* ('holla'd to' etc.) is more delicate than Tsubouchi's version, suggesting that this is a translation more about memory and response than dramatisation. Matsuoka's Theseus and Hippolyta are recreating images rather than sounds. The music of the speeches, in particular the contrasts between subtlety and finesse, expresses the resonance of the past and the present, not just barking dogs.

* * * * *

The translator Jeremy Sams writes of opera translation that (Sams 1996, 178)

> if you get music and words together in the same shape and contours those two things can cut through an audience; thought and music together can really change the world.

Shakespeare in Japanese is not opera, and yet there are moments in these translations when meaning, sound and image come together with a clarity that can be little enhanced by stage professionals. These are rhythmic, resonant moments that recreate 'the latent theatrical experience' implicit in the text,[213] recreate the same kind of rhetorical relationship between Japanese audiences of today and contemporary translations as (we may presume) existed between Elizabethan audiences and the original text.

To characterise these moments from the evidence of the examples discussed

---

[213] 'The text of a play is no mere verbal artifact complete in itself. Instead, it stands for the dramatic or theatrical experience embodied in it. The experience is the thing. What we have to aim at in translating a dramatic text is therefore not to translate its literal meaning but to re-create this latent theatrical experience.' (Anzai 1998, 124-25)

above, one can see that a couple of them (e.g. the baying hounds) enhance or harmonise a mood while the others (e.g. Hermia and Lysander 'lieing prettily') express embarrassment or tension. Of course, the effect on a live audience might be quite the opposite, as a little innuendo might relax rather than embarrass an audience and an excessively lyrical scene might indeed embarrass them. At both extremes, however, *goro* and *share* serve to break down barriers on page and stage, whereas the rhythms discussed in Chapters Two and Three are the property of individual poetic voices and tend more to erect barriers. This blend of rhythm and *share* is one of the key devices by which the poetic drama is reproduced in Japanese translation.

Another feature of the examples is that they are almost all somehow concerned with physical activities: eating (Bottom), cleaning (Puck with his broom), chasing (Helena and Demetrius), or the sexual. They play with a tension between drama and reality by a typically Shakespearean exploitation of poetic resources, and it is to the credit of the translators that they find equivalent resources in Japanese. Rhythm and *share* (like those tongue-twisters to which *share* is related) stretch the physicality of language to its limits so that the merely theatrical is almost realised. The comic exception, of course, was Pyramus' exaggerated lament over Thisbe's body, and even then the energy of his speech makes Bottom (who plays Pyramus) all the more credible.

It is difficult to discern any historical differences in the use of *share*, since it evidently belongs as much to the classical as to the modern traditions, and it is a device that emerges quite naturally from the sounds of the language itself. Yet just as the Augustan reformers sought to contain the pun within the constraints of stylistic civility, one might argue that *share* matters more to translators working in periods of linguistic uncertainty. Of the four, Tsubouchi can be said to live in the period of greatest flux, since not only did the language develop radically during his lifetime, but he himself experienced the uncertainty of pioneering a style of Shakespeare translation, and since pre-war society was still essentially hierarchical, the social divides that *share* transcends – between male and female, master and servant, and so on – become all the more dramatic. Fukuda, on the other hand, is translating during a period of democratisation and linguistic standardisation, as the writing system is simplified and literacy extended; although, as we have seen, Fukuda can not help using *share*, he must also be wary of anything that gets in the way of making Shakespeare too difficult. In fact, for reasons of his own, Fukuda is eventually accused of élitism, and his successor Odashima goes out of his way to open up the Japanese audience to Shakespeare's language. Yet at the same time, Odashima is translating during the period of high economic growth, when linguistic aptitude (not only for Japanese but also for English) was a prerequisite to social mobility, and so *share* is a mark of a potentially divisive cleverness. Finally Matsuoka, translating in a period of economic stasis and greater cultural awareness, obviously uses *share* but – in the context of a more experimental and technologically sophisticated theatre – it has become just one of several semiotic devices.

CHAPTER FIVE   SPEAKING SHAKESPEARE IN JAPANESE

HEIGHT AND DEPTH: THE SHAKESPEARE RECITALS OF ARAI YOSHIO

On 17th April, 1987, the Shakespeare scholar Arai Yoshio gave a public reading in Tokyo of Kinoshita Junji's translation of *The Merchant of Venice*.[214] It was the first in a series of readings of the plays and poems of Shakespeare he gave to raise money for the construction of the Globe Theatre in London, which concluded on 23rd March, 1992, with 'The Rape of Lucrece'. Arai's achievement was an unusual one in Japan, and yet typical of two basic means of Shakespeare's transmission within Japanese culture: as individual narrative and as texts that can be familiarised through the techniques of traditional drama. This matrix returns us to Shakespeare's initial reception in the Meiji era, when actors had no choice but to adopt the styles of *kabuki* and *jōruri* chanting, and when readers were more likely to encounter Shakespeare through the Japanese translations of the twenty *Tales from Shakespeare* by Charles and Mary Lamb (1807) than in the theatre.[215]

Apart from a handful of adaptations and translations, most Japanese readers at that time would have first encountered the plays as stories.[216] The *Tales from Shakespeare*

---

[214] Arai's account of the readings explains what each of the works has meant to him and how he approached them as texts for recital; critical reviews are also included (Arai 1993). Arai has been professor at Gakushūin and Komazawa Universities, and from 1968 to 1972 was familiar as a teacher on the daily NHK English programme. He has also directed and acted in numerous Shakespeare productions at both university and amateur level.

[215] The first tale to be translated was *As You Like It*, by Fujita Meikaku in 1883, but by 1907 translations of all twenty tales had been published, including one of *A Midsummer Night's Dream* by Shima Kasui in 1899. Until Tozawa Koya and Asano Hyokyō produced their translation of ten of the plays between 1905 and 1909, only five of the plays had been fully translated, and most of those were adaptations.

[216] A comparison can be drawn between the Lamb translations and the role of the *benshi*, or 'film interpreters', in the era of silent films in the Japanese cinema; both provided access to a textuality that was otherwise elusive.

were intended for private reading but for the actual style of his delivery, Arai mentions a debt to *jōruri* chanting. Unlike Arai's recitals, *jōruri* chanters chant from a seated position and avoid histrionic facial gestures, but their chanting is a stylised form of the pitch-based undulations of Japanese speech (known as *kōtei*, 'high and low'), which is a style that Arai does imitate. *Kōtei* is typical of *kabuki* speech as well, and even of *shingeki* actors. According to Arai, even *shingeki* actors, who have no experience of *kabuki*, use the set speeches from the *kabuki jūhachi ban* (*uirō uri*) as warm-up exercises. These are the eighteen plays selected by Ichikawa Danjurō VII in the mid-19th century for 'their excellence as performance texts' (Ortolani 1990, 201). Although 'the criteria for the choice reflect the Ichikawa family's preference for *aragoto* [rough] style' (ibid.), it should be assumed that the style is toned down somewhat in private practice outside the theatre, but that Arai is still to some extent influenced by the Tokyo-based *aragoto*. Arai himself acted for a *shingeki* group in the 1960s, the Kindai Gekijō, and also used *uirō uri* (by which name the *jūhachi ban* are known as single plays) in preparing himself for the Shakespeare recitals.[217]

Arai has also admitted a debt to the *kyōgen* speech style in which the pitch undulations tend to move in the opposite way to *jōruri*, similar to the comic effect created by trochaic rhythm in Shakespearean verse. *Kōtei* is based on Tokyo pitch accent, which rises to the high tone somewhere around the middle of the phrase, whereas in *kyōgen* delivery, the tendency is to place the accent as early as possible in the phrase. Likewise, the stress in iambic rhythm falls on the second beat (di-dum) but in trochaic rhythm on the first (dum-di). Arai himself is arguably more conscious of these accentual differences as he was brought up in Kyoto (with its different accentual system) before moving to university in Tokyo.[218]

The *kyōgen* style is appropriate for comic characters such as Falstaff, and for these characters a further parallel may be drawn with *rakugo*, which shares with the Odashima translations that Arai mainly used a strong undercurrent of word and sound play.[219] The *ochi* (or 'drop') in *rakugo*, the punning punchline, is a narrative device that is relevant to the way in which a Shakespeare speech or scene might be delivered. The comic repartie enjoyed by *rakugoka* has an equivalent in those stock comic characters found in all of Shakespeare's plays but which is mainly absent from the traditional theatre (except

---

[217] Arai attributes the flexibility of *shingeki* actors such as Nakadai Tatsuya and Emori Tōru to this practice. These are actors who have crossed the traditional divide not only in the Japanese theatre, appearing in *kabuki* as well as *shingeki*, but also in Shakespeare. Both actors have played Hamlet and Falstaff, an unusual achievement in the Western theatre, and this is partly due to their vocal flexibility.

[218] Kyoto dialect is related to other dialects in the Kansai region, but is renowned for its softness and politeness.

[219] There have been a number of successful adaptations of Shakespearean comedy in *kyōgen* style (e.g. Taki 1992 and Takahashi 1998 and 2003) but these have been mainly based on the plots and characters rather than the actual source texts (respectively, *Twelfth Night*, *The Merry Wives of Windsor* and *The Comedy of Errors*) or their various translations.

kyōgen).[220] This separation of a genre (*rakugo*), which is all speech and facial expression, from genres such as *kabuki* that combine all the theatrical arts at once hints at one way in which Arai's recitals were a significant departure from tradition. Arai was attempting a much broader range of characterisations than in *rakugo* and even *kabuki*: from drunken knights (Falstaff), to mad kings (Lear) to paragons of female virtue (Portia), and a bevy of monarchs and their minions in between. To do so, he depended entirely on the range of his voice.

In the 1960s, Arai was awarded a scholarship by the Japanese government to visit England to study the English theatre, and on a later visit received a lesson in speaking Shakespearean verse from Sir John Gielgud. The lesson is significant in that Gielgud was famous for his use of voice, indeed for subordinating the rest of his body to the power and influence of that voice. In the 1930s, Gielgud and Laurence Olivier developed a style of doing Shakespeare which remained influential until the end of the 1950s: Gielgud lyrical and cerebral, Olivier physical and realistic. Gielgud's voice was naturally at a disadvantage among non-English speaking audiences, especially in Japan where Olivier became popular with the release of his Shakespeare films in the late 1940s. The voice could be a disadvantage on the English stage as well: Gielgud 'could fall into a mannered delivery, a kind of 'singing' style which appeared to place sound above sense' (Warren 1986, 259).

When Gielgud's career faltered in the late 1950s, one of the ways in which he rebuilt it was by a Shakespeare recital entitled *Ages of Man* with which he toured the world between 1957 and 1967. Arai was highly influenced by *Ages of Man* and Gielgud's approach to public recital, which Gielgud described as follows (Gielgud 1997, 35):

> When I devised the solo recital *Ages of Man*, I discovered that, in doing speeches out of their proper context, I had to remember that in every speech there was a rise, a climax and a fall, having in my mind where I was going to and where I was coming from, and then I could put any amount of variations in between (as musicians often do in playing Chopin, for instance) while keeping the essential architecture of each speech intact.

The significance of voice is suggested in a recent work by Charles H. Frey, *Making Sense of Shakespeare* (Frey 1999), where Frey advocates the rediscovery of how Shakespeare (both on the page and in performance) becomes part of our sensory – as opposed to cerebral – experience (ibid., 10):

> The concreteness of Shakespeare's language, its sensuous, synaesthetic quality, impels readers and audiences away from ordinary consciousness, grounds rational sense in physical sense, reshapes sexual identity, destabilises gender, and freshens

---

[220] Although comic elements abound in *kabuki*, *kabuki* comedy does not exist as a separate genre as it does in Shakespeare.

the material world for reinterpretation.

He argues that reinterpreting Shakespeare as a physical phenomenon can be equally as effective as the reinterpretations advocated by traditional and postmodern 'abstract' criticism. Frey is referring to Shakespeare in English, and his argument should already be apparent from the previous three chapters, where I have I tried to show how the physical phenomenon of Shakespearean phonology has affected the phonology of the four translations. Translators are readers like anyone else, susceptible to the sensory impact of Shakespeare's language. How reading and seeing Shakespeare, whether in English or Japanese, has affected them as individuals is not my main concern, although helpful for understanding their approaches to translating Shakespeare. This chapter, therefore, deals not with the impasse between Shakespeare and modern Japanese culture but in how the sounds of *A Midsummer Night's Dream* have been reproduced in the Japanese theatre.

The formative influence on *shingeki* (and therefore Shakespeare) production in Japan has been Constantin Stanislavski (1863-1938), whose ideas were introduced by Osanai Kaoru in the 1920s (Fischer-Lichte 1996, 30-31).[221] Just as the Stanislavski 'method' is still considered relevant to Western theatre, the following advice from *An Actor Prepares* (1936) is relevant to understanding the contemporary theatre of Japan (Stanislavski 1980, 91):

> An actor should be observant not only on the stage, but also in real life. He should concentrate with all his being on whatever attracts his attention. He should look at an object, not as any absent-minded passer-by, but with penetration. Otherwise his whole creative method will prove lopsided and bear no relation to life.

Stanislavski himself was originally a director of contemporary realist playwrights like Chekhov and Ibsen, in which case the notion of the real was already inherent within the texts he was directing. The problem for Japanese actors has been twofold: first, that acting and speaking methods in the traditional theatre are stylised and inherently unrealistic, and secondly, that although the language of realist playwrights like Ibsen has always been accessible in Japanese translation, Shakespeare with his mixture of styles has been made less so. It may be quite possible to project a drawing room conversation to the back of a large auditorium but less so the metaphorically rich and complex language of Shakespeare.

Stanislavski's answer is for actors to abstract the meanings and imagery of Shakespeare from their context and to look for them in their environment. The text can itself be objectified such that it yields up not only its meanings but also some directions

---

[221] Osanai's pioneering production of *A Midsummer Night's Dream* for the Tsukiji Shōgekijō in July 1928 was strikingly modern, with a revolving avant-garde set designed by Yoshida Kenkichi and Osanai's expressed desire that he wanted his audience to come away from the theatre feeling that 'nothing is impossible' and that 'tonight I saw a dream' (Osanai 1928).

as to how the lines should be spoken. What those directions may constitute has been analysed at some length in the preceding chapters, and yet how they are interpreted on stage will of course differ from actor to actor and from director to director. The rest of this chapter analyses recordings of four Japanese theatre companies together with a recording of Arai Yoshio reciting lines from *A Midsummer Night's Dream* in Tsubouchi's translation.

A Midsummer Night's Dream has a particular significance for Arai as being the first Shakespeare play he encountered, while a student at Gakushūin University in 1955 (Arai 1993, 82-85); Arai and some fellow students formed a *rindoku kai* ('reading circle') which read the play over the course of a year. Further experiences accrued, including Peter Brook's production in Tokyo in 1973 (*odoroki de ari keiji de atta*, 'both a surprise and a revelation'), but it is nevertheless apparent that what is for Arai 'a comedy with which I enjoy a deep intimacy' (*najimi no fukai kigeki*) was experienced initially by way of the voice. He writes, for example, that again in his university days, he bought long playing records of the Old Vic production of the play, directed by Michael Benthall, and with Mendelssohn's incidental music performed by the BBC Symphony Orchestra. The reading took place at the Iwanami Cine Salon in Tokyo on 17th May, 1991, although in 1986, he had given a trial reading in front of the founder of the London Globe, Sam Wanamaker, Izumi Motohide of the Izumi *kyōgen* school, and the Shakespeare translator Kinoshita Junji (himself an expert on Japanese speech). He dispensed with ingenious props and lighting and concentrated instead on speaking the lines to maximum effect.

Arai describes his approach to this reading as *rōdoku sutairu no kansei*, 'a complete recital style'. In addition to honouring the personal associations which the play holds for him, Arai's purism also seems appropriate to registering those dualities which he lists in his basic understanding of the comedy as being a play about the transition from love to marriage, one of 'illusion and reality, truth and falsehood' (ibid., 86). If the medium is public recital, then there must be minimal distractions from how these dualities are expressed in the language.

Arai's recording of Tsubouchi's translation of the opening dialogue of the play between Theseus and Hippolyta (Tsubouchi 1977, 191-92) brings us back to my analysis in Chapter Two and to Tsubouchi's *rōdoku kai* of the 1890s. This is a dedicated recording in which Arai's skills as a reader of Shakespeare and interpreter of Tsubouchi are apparent; the reading is thoroughly textual with little extraneous interpretation. It is evident from the recording alone, and confirmed by computer analysis, that Arai's intonation corresponds to the sound values inherent in the translation. The graphs show how peaks in pitch accentuation correspond with dictionary accentuation and source meaning, being derived from a printout of an analysis conducted at the University of Oxford Phonetics Laboratory of pitch traces. The vertical axis shows levels of pitch frequency (marked at levels of 150 and 300 hertz) and the horizontal axis shows time in seconds.

Underlined syllables are accented, and the meanings of words containing accented syllables are also given. It will be noticed that dictionary accents are most likely to be ignored where they are preceded in the phrase by a strong accent, for example on *atarashii* in *atarashii tsuki ga kuru* where there would normally be an accent on the second mora of *tsuki*. Arai is perhaps more fastidious than everyday usage, since he adds a slight accent on *tsuki*, although slighter accents that come just before or after peaks are usually not marked. In all cases, accented syllables correspond with the peaks in the graph.

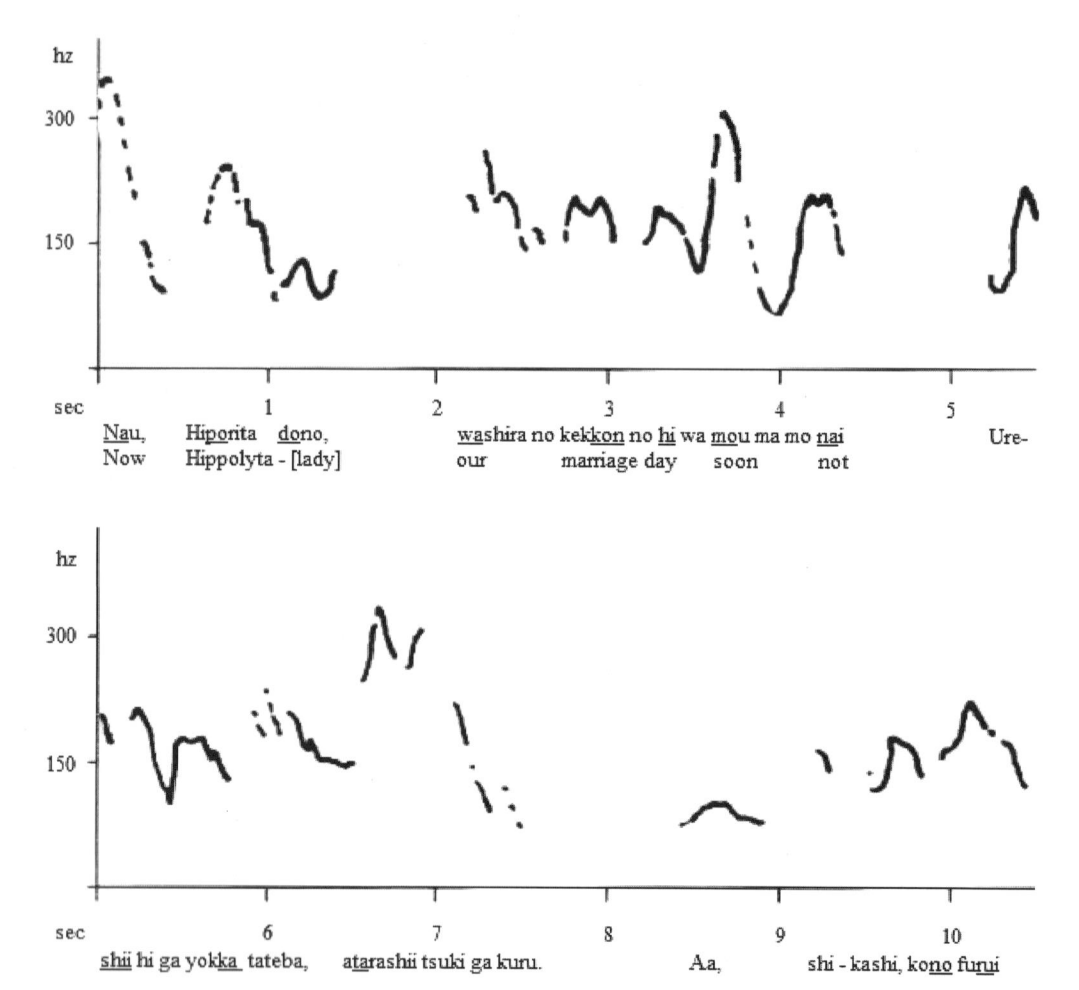

sec	1	2	3	4	5
Nau,	Hiporita dono,		washira no kekkon no hi wa mou ma mo nai		Ure-
Now	Hippolyta - [lady]		our marriage day soon not		

sec	6	7	8	9	10
shii hi ga yokka tateba,	atarashii tsuki ga kuru.		Aa,	shi - kashi, kono furui	

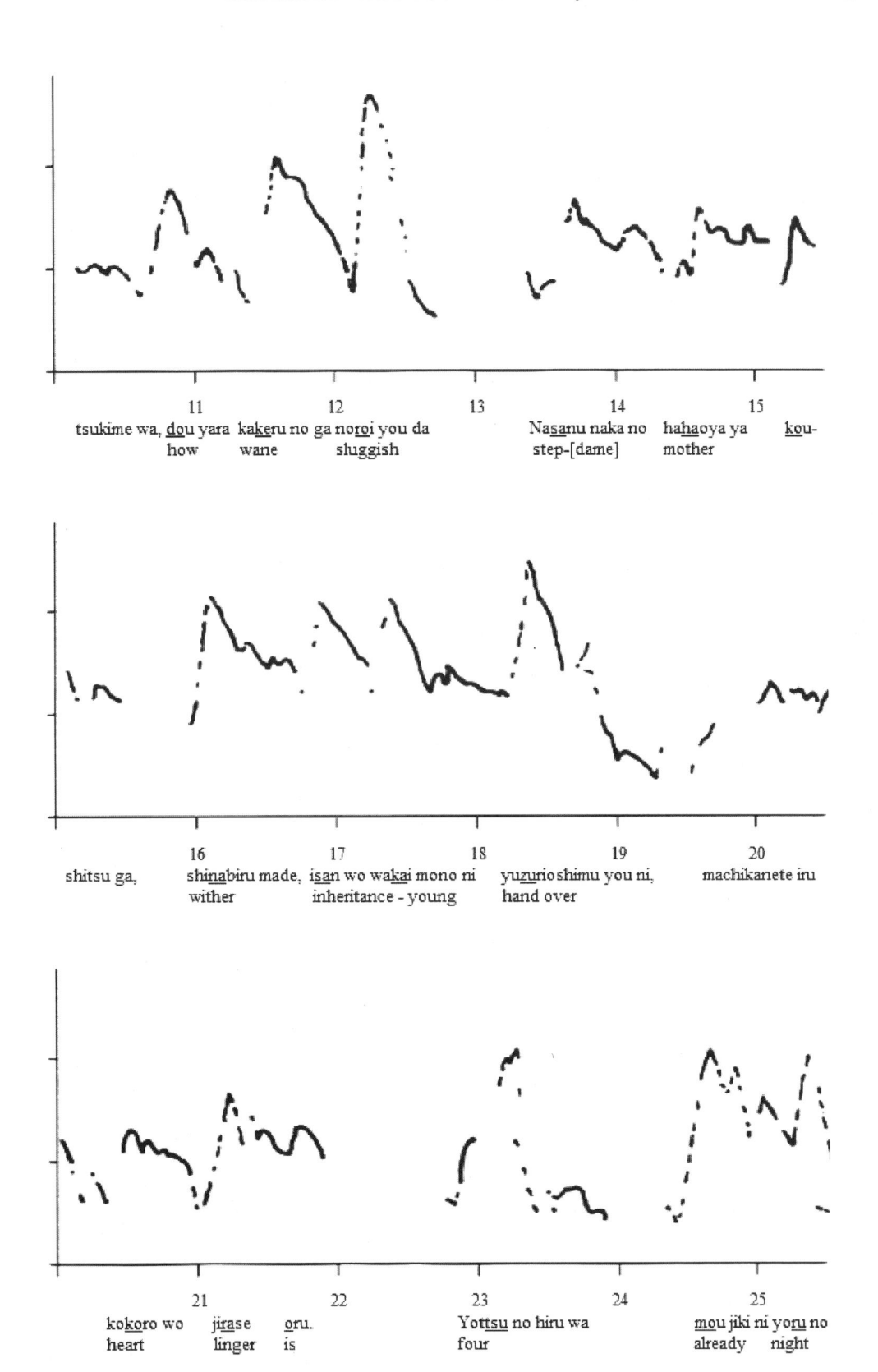

CHAPTER FIVE   SPEAKING SHAKESPEARE IN JAPANESE   163

11	12	13	14	15
tsukime wa, dou yara	kakeru no ga noroi you da		Nasanu naka no	hahaoya ya kou-
how	wane sluggish		step-[dame]	mother

	16	17	18	19	20
shitsu ga,	shinabiru made,	isan wo wakai mono ni		yuzurioshimu you ni,	machikanete iru
	wither	inheritance - young		hand over	

	21	22	23	24	25
kokoro wo	jirase oru.		Yottsu no hiru wa		mou jiki ni yoru no
heart	linger is		four		already night

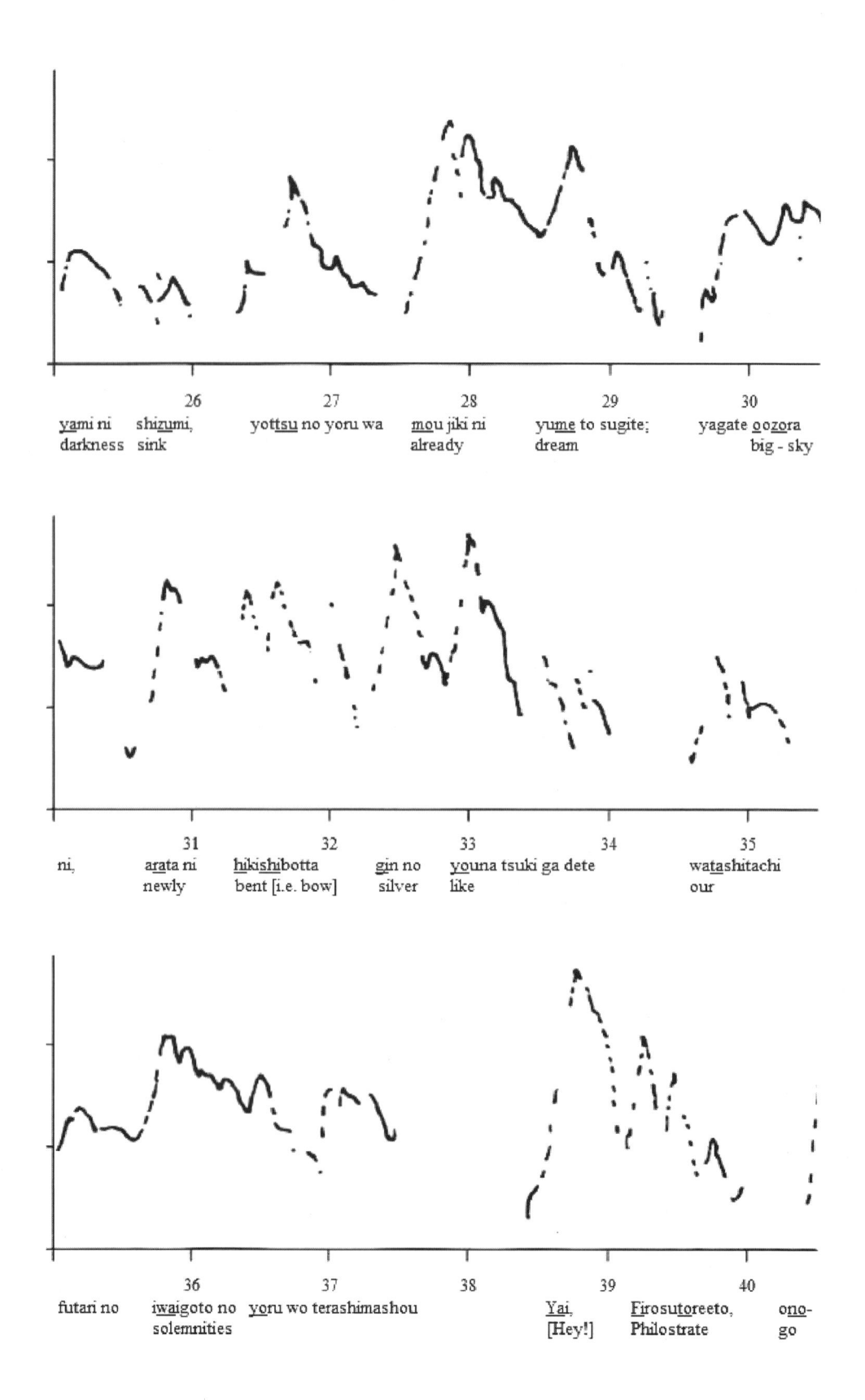

26	27	28	29	30
yami ni shizumi,	yottsu no yoru wa	mou jiki ni	yume to sugite;	yagate oozora
darkness sink		already	dream	big - sky

	31	32	33	34	35
ni,	arata ni	hikishibotta	gin no	youna tsuki ga dete	watashitachi
	newly	bent [i.e. bow]	silver	like	our

	36	37	38	39	40
futari no	iwaigoto no	yoru wo terashimashou		Yai,	Firosutoreeto, ono-
	solemnities			[Hey!]	Philostrate go

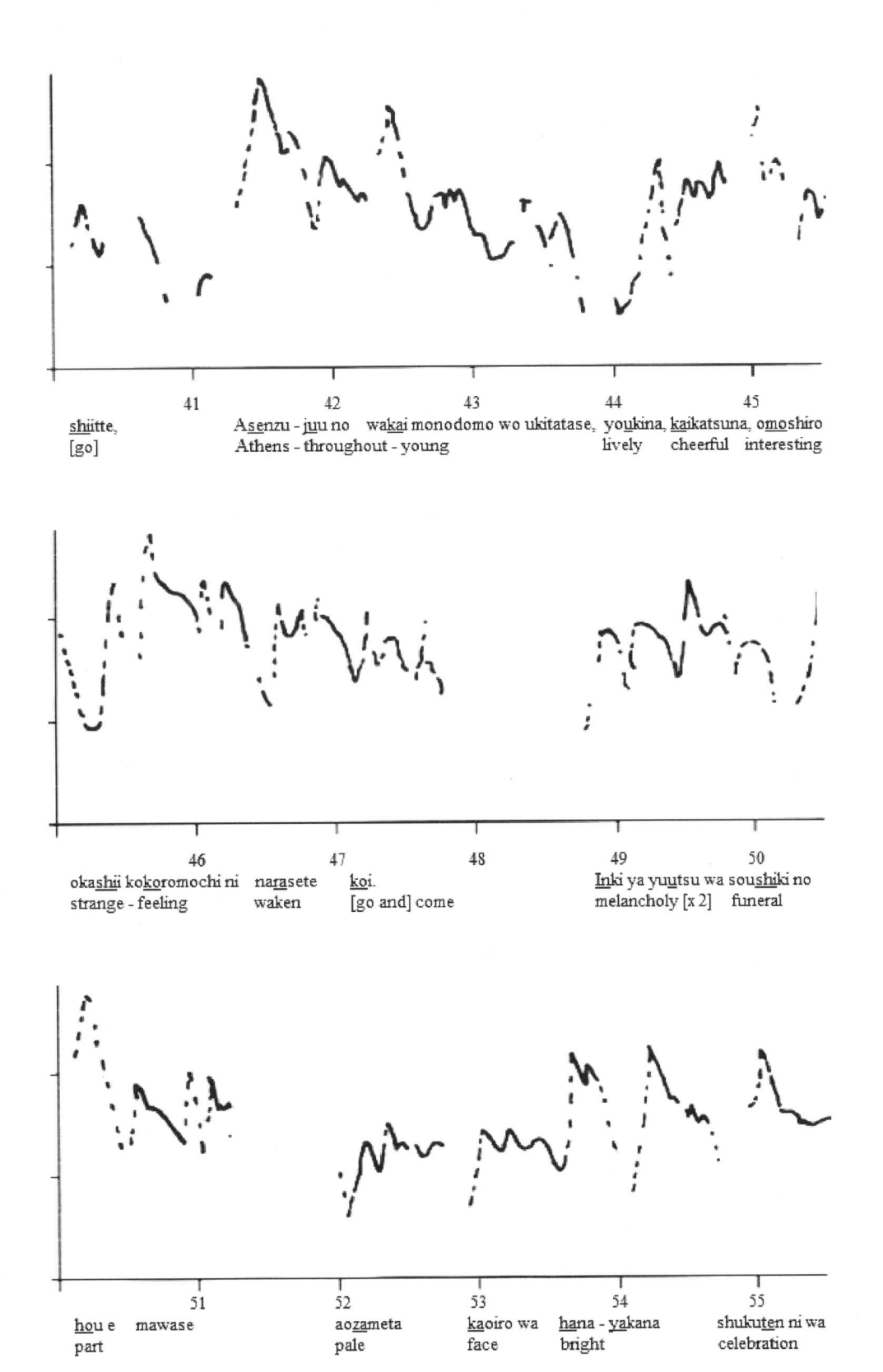

CHAPTER FIVE SPEAKING SHAKESPEARE IN JAPANESE   165

41	42	43	44	45
shiitte,	Asenzu - juu no wakai monodomo wo ukitatase,		youkina,	kaikatsuna, omoshiro
[go]	Athens - throughout - young		lively	cheerful interesting

46	47	48	49	50
okashii kokoromochi ni	narasete	koi.	Inki ya yuutsu wa	soushiki no
strange - feeling	waken	[go and] come	melancholy [x 2]	funeral

51	52	53	54	55
hou e mawase	aozameta	kaoiro wa	hana - yakana	shukuten ni wa
part	pale	face	bright	celebration

56	57	58	59	60
fusawashuu nai mono da.	Hiporita dono,		washi wa kono ken de omaesan wo	
suited not	Hippolyta		this - sword - you	

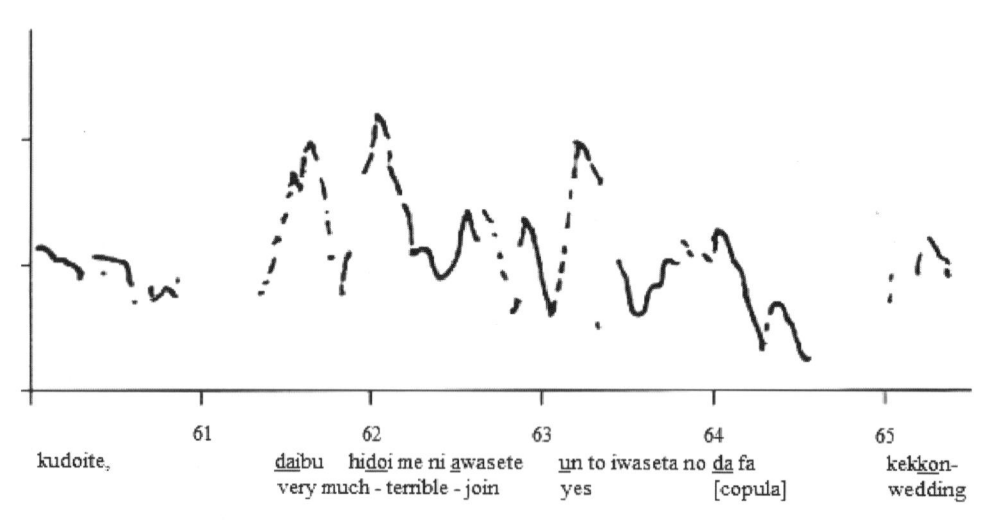

	61	62	63	64	65
kudoite,		daibu hidoi me ni awasete	un to iwaseta no da fa		kekkon-
		very much - terrible - join	yes [copula]		wedding

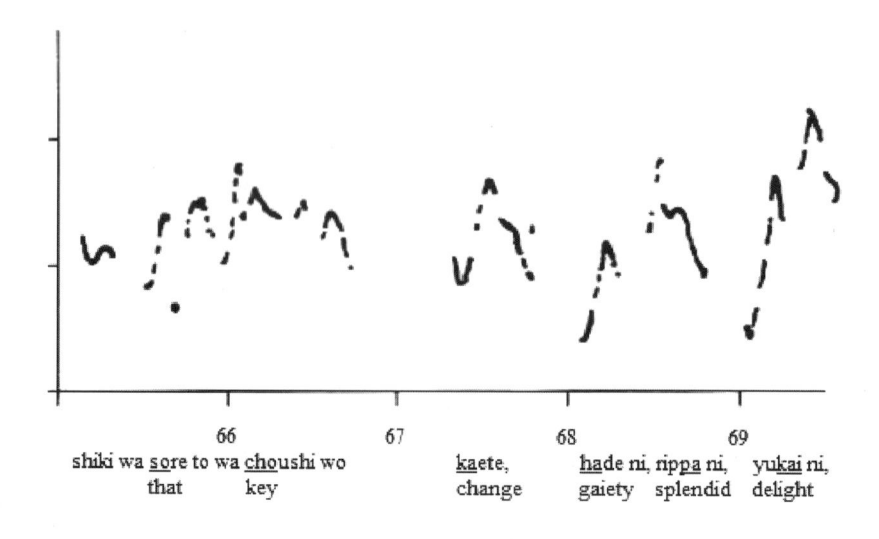

	66	67	68	69
shiki wa sore to wa choushi wo		kaete,	hade ni, rippa ni,	yukai ni,
that key		change	gaiety splendid	delight

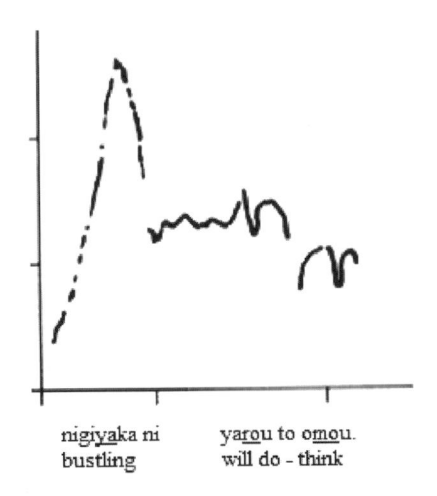

nigiyaka ni   yarou to omou.
bustling   will do - think

The reading is clipped and fluid, the boundaries between each phrase carefully marked. This approach brings out Tsubouchi's cadences and could well become monotonous were it not for the other tonal qualities that Arai introduces, of which the most obvious is the scale of height and depth. Accented words, such as *mō* ('already'), set the upper end of the register. These are words in which pitch rather than timbre dominate and, as discussed in Chapter Two, are mainly words to do with time. A contrastive set of words, that includes *Yai* ('Go!') and *noroi* ('sluggish'), are also accented but precede swoops in pitch frequency to deep growls of below 50 hertz; these are words in which the timbre dominates. The thematic contrast is between the coordination of human aspiration with the movement of time and its sublunary opposite (entropy), in which the establishment of a chain of command (represented here by Philostrate) is necessary for the festivity to be facilitated.

'NEITHER NOISY NOR DECLAMATORY': FUKUDA'S SUBARU

The recording from Subaru is also a dedicated one but is a dialogue, recorded by actors who are more used to acting the lines than reciting them. The company, which was founded by Fukuda Tsuneari in 1963, is one of the few groups that have continued to perform Shakespeare in the Fukuda translation (about once a year).[222] The language of the recording seems much closer to contemporary Japanese than does Tsubouchi, neither awkward nor particularly old-fashioned. The scene with Helena and Lysander (2.2.93-113; Fukuda 1971, 49-50) is not one analysed in any of the previous chapters

---

[222] Gekidan Shiki, a commercial company much larger than Subaru, have made their production of Fukuda's *Hamlet* one of their regular repertoire. Having seen the production in 2009, my impression of the language was that it inevitably sounded more rigid than a contemporary translation but contained considerable dramatic energy.

but is relevant to this discussion as one in which moods are challenged and altered over a short space of time by unexpected changes in circumstance; it is a passage in which one would expect a greater range of intonational flux. Helena is chased on stage by the man who had previously loved Hermia. When Demetrius wakes from his sleep to declare his passion for her, Helena pitifully assumes that both men are out to spite her.

	No, no; I am as ugly as a bear,
	For beasts that meet me run away for fear:
	Therefore no marvel though Demetrius
	Do, as a monster, fly my presence thus.
	What wicked and dissembling glass of mine
	Made me compare with Hermia's sphery eyne?
	But who is here? Lysander, on the ground?
	Dead, or asleep? I see no blood, no wound.
	Lysander, if you live, good sir, awake!
Lys.	And run through fire I will for thy sweet sake!
[*Waking.*]	Transparent Helena! Nature shows art,
	That through thy bosom makes me see thy heart.
	Where is Demetrius? O how fit a word
	Is that vile name to perish on my sword!
Hel.	Do not say so, Lysander, say not so.
	What though he love your Hermia? Lord, what though?
	Yet Hermia still loves you; then be content.
Lys.	Content with Hermia? No. I do repent
	The tedious minutes I with her have spent.
	Not Hermia, but Helena I love:
	Who will not change a raven for a dove?
H:	Iie, chigau wa, atashi wa kuma no yō ni minikui no da, kemonotachi mo atashi ni au to, kowasō ni nigete shimau. Dakara, chittomo fushigi wa nai, Demetoriasu ga atashi no sugata wo miru to, ā shite, marude bakemono ni demo deatta yō ni nigedashitatte. Nante ijiwaru de usotsuki na no, atashi no kagami wa? Hāmia no hoshi no yōna me to kurabesasetari suru no da mono. A, dare deshō, asoko ni iru no wa? Raisandā da wa! Jibeta no ue ni! Shinde shimatta no kashira? Soretomo nemutte iru no kashira? Chi wa nagarete inai, kizu mo nai. Raisandā, ikite iru nara, onegai, okite, me wo samashite.
L: [Tobiokite]	Uso wa iwanai, hi no naka ni datte, tobikonde miseru, kawaii kimi no tame nara, sukitōru yō ni utsukushii Herena! Masa ni shizen no genzuru maka fushigi, sono mune wo tōshite, kimi no kokoro ga mieru, te ni toru yō ni mazamaza to. Demetoriasu wa doko e itta

no da? Ā, kuchi ni suru no mo imawashii, kono yaiba ni kakatte kutabatte shimau ga ii!

H: Ikenai wa, Raisandā, sonna koto iu mono dewa arimasen. Ano hito ga Hāmia wo omotte iru kara to itte, sore ga dō na no? Nan no koto mo ari wa shinai! Dō naru to iu no? Hāmia ga aishite iru no wa, yahari anata dake, chittomo fusoku wa nai hazu yo!

L: Hāmia ni fusoku wa naitte? Ōari da. Boku wa kōkai shite iru, are to sugoshita taikutsuna jikan, mō torikaeshi ga tsukanai. Hāmia dewa nai, Herena na no da boku ga ai shite iru no wa – dare ga karasu wo hato to torikaezu ni irareyō?

One clue as to how these actors sound in Japanese is given by a review in the Tokyo Shinbun newspaper (23rd June, 1999) of a Subaru production of *Much Ado About Nothing*: 'Mimi ni shizenna serifu mawashi ni kōkan', meaning 'Favourable impression of a natural-sounding style of delivery' (Ehara 1999). *Serifu mawashi* is a rather old-fashioned word meaning 'elocution', which Tsubouchi used with regard to his *rōdoku kai*, and has a possible educative sub-text which the critic expounds as follows:

> This production is a model example of Shakespeare that is neither noisy and declamatory nor delivered at the speed of a machine gun, but which, instead, sounds natural to the ears and is clearly shaped.

The critic goes on to praise the way in which artificial elements of the plot are suppressed (*fushizensa wo kanjisasenai tame*, 'so that we are not made to feel their unnaturalness') and the marriages made real. He suggests that this success is due not only to a contemporary stage design but also to the way that each of the actors manages to characterise their roles through their different styles of delivery. Although the critic does not comment on the Fukuda translation in particular, two further deductions might be made. One is that the translation itself individuates the characters. The other is that Fukuda's rather old-fashioned language acts as a template, that, because it is difficult to enunciate, actually restrains the actors from running away with the lines (like a machine gun) and merging imperceptibly with each other, while at the same time encouraging them to look within the language for the meanings of their parts. This interpretation would seem to tally with what is known of the unique role which the Fukuda tradition has played in Shakespeare production in Japan since the 1950s (Namba 1989). As a university teacher, Fukuda was always interested in understanding Shakespeare through the educative process of stage production rather than through commercial success or a narrowly political agenda. Both Kumo and Subaru have been dedicated training grounds for student actors for almost half a century. Recently, Subaru has been instrumental in hosting the 'RADA in Tokyo' Summer School, and it is also noted for its performance of translated drama. The relevance to production of an anti-rhetorical, unconfrontational translating style is surely fundamental to the field of higher education (academic and vocational) with its goals of individuating and developing character for participation in adult life.

The scene from Act 2 is itself a model of individuation, as Helena retains her integrity against the successive frenzies of the two men; she never betrays her love for Demetrius. For much of these first two acts, she is depicted as a fated soliloquist, for whom no one has much time except the audience, and in this depiction there can be observed a striking parallel with two landmarks of modernism: the Stanislavski 'method' mentioned above and the *shishōsetsu* (or 'I' novel) genre that dominated modern Japanese fiction through to the early post-war era. In a comparison of two stories by Shiga Naoya and Tolstoy, Starrs characterises the genre as follows (Starrs 1998, 54):

> the *shishōsetsu* is deeply subjective but, at the same time, almost completely impersonal; the Western story, on the other hand, despite its pose of objectivity, is far more 'personal' in the sense that it presents individual human personalities and, as we have seen, even tends to 'personify' natural objects such as trees.

An impersonal style of delivery can be heard in the Helena of the Subaru recording, which is exploratory rather than declamatory, quieter and more reflective than the outbursts of Demetrius and Lysander. This quality could be true of the source text as well, where Helena's emotions are contained and controlled within the blank verse format, and of course one important factor behind both the source and the translation is that she is 'out of breath in this fond chase' (l. 87). The lack of breath shortens her utterances and could even account for her deprecatory thoughts:

> No, no; I am as ugly as a bear,
> For beasts that meet me run away for fear

Although there is undoubtedly pathos in Helena's situation, the speech remains impersonal in the absence of any attempt to transcend that situation by figurative means, typical in fact of *shishōsetsu*. She remains in the grip of her subjective feelings, and the fact that her resolution in Act 4 is a comic one is surely the reward for her integrity. As Starrs observes of Shiga's style, this kind of lyrical and integrated idiom is often achieved in *shishōsetsu* by means of loosely poetic prose structures bound together by the repetition of key words and phrases, to which one could add the rhythmic variation of phrase and sentence lengths.

In translation, the opportunity to repeat words and phrases is constrained by the lexis of the source text, but the repetition of those foreign names (*Hāmia* etc.) and the personal pronoun *atashi* (female 'I') is rare enough in colloquial Japanese to function as a discursive device. The foregrounding of these descriptive personality markers (names, pronouns) actually serves to deconstruct the idea of personality, while the rhythmically uneven line deconstructs the idea of progression (including that of character); the lyrical impersonality of Helena's character is confirmed. Stanislavski's 'method' is intended to apply to the whole range of Shakespearean characters but seems particularly apt with regard to 'the naturalness' of the Subaru Helena, especially in comparison to the unnatural behaviour of the two men. In *shishōsetsu*, truth to one's subjective nature and to the natural world protects the vulnerable individual from deceit and delusion. Stanislavski's agenda is similar, albeit one tinged with Old Testament morality (Stanislavski 1980, 313):

> Nature's laws are binding on all, without exception, and woe to those who break them.

'POWER UP': ODASHIMA YŪSHI AND SHAKESPEARE THEATRE

In 1965, the young Odashima Yūshi reviewed a revival of the 1962 Kumo production of Fukuda's translation for the periodical, *Teatoro* (Odashima 1965). He commented that it was more 'relaxed' (*motto yutori no aru*) and less 'a matter of life and death' (*inochigake no*) than the first time round, and that one of the effects of this sweeter atmosphere had been to make the lovers' chase more 'tedious' (*taikutsuna*) and therefore 'absurd' (*bakabakashii*). Indeed for Odashima, 'the lovers' world' became credible when laughter erupted spontaneously from the audience at Helena's tearful protestation to Lysander (which comes some twenty lines after the scene discussed above) (2.2.132-33) (Fukuda 1971, 51):

> Ā nan to iu kanashii onna deshō, hitori no otoko kara kirawarete, sore wo tane ni, mata betsu no otoko ni naburareru!
> O that a lady, of one man refus'd,
> Should of another therefore be abus'd!

What in itself was experimental and small-scale in Fukuda's theatre becomes more fully professional by the time that Odashima came to translate the play ten years later. Odashima developed a phonically ingenious style that sought not only to make imaginary bridges between the actors and audience (as Fukuda had done) but even to speak the same language as the contemporary audience. In contrast to Fukuda, the danger of Odashima's approach is that individuality and perspective are lost as audiences are brought too close to the drama. This would not necessarily have been unwelcome among the younger audiences of the 1970s who would otherwise have felt alienated by Shakespeare, nor among the small theatres who wished to make an event out of Shakespeare in the competitive Tokyo theatrical scene. Yet nor did it prevent Deguchi Norio, the director who staged most of those début productions for with his company

Shakespeare Theatre, from developing a controlled style of delivery which counters the more rhetorical aspects of the production.

This style has been compared to 'stroking the cat', the actors' equivalent to Kinoshita Junji's dramaturgy discussed in Chapter Three of 'riding the horse'. The lines are neither squeezed dry nor thrown away, but are treated with a mindful respect, half open and half closed. The impression given by a Shakespeare Theatre performance is that of a classical balance of text and performance that allows the drama to progress at an unforced pace, with the rhetorical elements expected of production provided by the design and sound plot (and, as suggested, Odashima's translations). Even in the rehearsal studio, the delivery of these actors is immediately arresting; the impression is one of the utmost seriousness, despite or perhaps because of the iconoclastic reputation which this group had in the 1970s.[223]

The premise for the Deguchi style is that Shakespeare's plays contain an unusual power or energy that requires careful treatment, more like a lion than a domestic cat. The extent to which the premise is fulfilled is partly borne out by audience responses to the company's production of *A Midsummer Night's Dream* (printed on the programme of a later revival):[224]

> This production made me feel powerful, and I felt that it was a power I had wanted!
>
> I was surprised by the fast pace of the production but impressed at the way all the actors spoke their lines. This was no wasted dream, not the kind of dream you would want to wake from.
>
> Shakespeare that is truly fresh and individual!
>
> This was the first time for me to see a Shakespeare production that was so easy to follow. The smooth delivery of the lines was excellent, and I was drawn along not just by the words but by the way the actors moved themselves.

---

[223] My first experience of their style was of a one-off performance they gave of *A Midsummer Night's Dream* for a group of a thousand high school students at a public hall in Shizuoka in October 2000. I was struck at how this rather controlled style kept the students' attention for two hours. A few days later, I visited the Shakespeare Theatre rehearsal studio in Kōenji, Tokyo, where I interviewed Deguchi Norio and recorded his actors speaking lines from all four of the translations. Although Deguchi himself participated in the *angura* theatre movement in the 1960s, Shakespeare Theatre was not inaugurated until 1975 with a memorable production of *Twelfth Night*. As a break from the full-dress productions that had been common up to then on the Tokyo stage, the actors appeared in jeans and T-shirts with a soundtrack that included songs by Elton John.

[224] The programme is not dated but lists previous productions up to 1993 and so is probably from 1994.

The Arai and Subaru styles, for all their performative passion, conceal an energy that remains trapped within the performance, although that is not necessarily a fault if the energy is to be released later. With Shakespeare Theatre, one feels that the energy is released as immediately as possible; the obvious danger of this technique is that it can discourage critical perspective. Enthusiastic spectators may become addicted to the theatrical sensation and fail to develop anything more than a vague and highly subjective understanding of Shakespeare's meanings.

It has to be admitted that Shakespeare Theatre has never harboured critical pretensions; they have never, for example, gone outside the small theatre or taken their productions abroad.[225] Moreover, the deepening of subjective awareness is a worthy enough goal in itself in a culture in which Shakespeare is still regarded as a foreign playwright. It is wholly aligned with the subjectivist tradition in Japanese fiction and at the same time capable of transformation toward the bigger scene, where Deguchi's contemporary, Ninagawa Yukio, would be the most obvious example of a director capable of producing a powerful immediate response.[226]

FILM OR OPERA? NINAGAWA'S 'DREAM'

Ninagawa has been accused of commercialism: of producing theatrical effects that pander to popular taste and undermine the integrity of both Shakespeare and the Japanese theatre. One of the more subtle critiques comes from Kishi Tetsuo:[227]

> Shakespearean theatre or rather Elizabethan theatre had virtually no scenery, while Ninagawa's productions of Shakespeare usually make use of a very prominent scenery which more or less dominates and clearly defines the nature of the whole space, as the Noh stage in his production of *The Tempest* does.
> (Kishi 1998, 111)

> The conventions of traditional Japanese theatre are used very loosely [in Ninagawa's Shakespeare productions] and sometimes quite whimsically, and their central purpose seems to be to evoke various emotional associations from the audience. In other words their use is rhapsodic rather than logical.
> (ibid., 113)

---

[225] Shakespeare Theatre's most innovative achievement to date is their *A Midsummer Night's Dream: Three Versions*, produced at the Tokyo Globe in September 1994. The play was performed three times in succession, each time in a different setting: in a school, wearing masks, and in a bar.
[226] Ninagawa was born in 1935, Deguchi in 1940.
[227] Kishi is professor emeritus at Kyoto University and a former president of the Shakespeare Society of Japan.

> To erect a kind of visually impressive edifice that dominates the stage makes the whole production totally un-Shakespearean, because – one cannot emphasise this point too much – Shakespeare wrote for an open stage with virtually no scenery. Impressive scenery can make language redundant.
> (ibid., 117)

This subordination of language may be typical of an era of production in which directors have succeeded translators in importance and has inevitable implications for the way that actors deliver their lines. The problem of shouting and 'machine gun' delivery has already been mentioned with regard to Subaru; it is an inevitable tendency in an environment where actors compete against considerable physical forces to make themselves heard, and is present at least in Ninagawa's 1994 production of *A Midsummer Night's Dream*.[228]

Ninagawa's interpretation of Act 2, Scene 1 of the play (Odashima 1983, 30-47) – which introduces the fairy world and their quarrel – is one in which one sometimes wonders whether it is drama at all but where the peculiar combination of speech, acting, music and other effects is eventually justified by the play itself. The scene lasts twenty minutes, and yet the first three minutes are taken up with an acrobatic demonstration by the Chinese actor Ninagawa hired from the Peking Opera to play Puck, Lin Yong Biao. This section is accompanied by a syncopated and (one assumes) Orientalised soundtrack of drums and woodblocks. These disjointed percussive sounds are meant to represent the character of Puck, and there is a simultaneous soundtrack audible, a grand, more Occidental sound of synthesised organ music, which will be heard for much of the rest of the scene and which represents Oberon and Titania. It is this sound (not the woodblocks) which is faintly audible throughout Puck's exchange with the Fairy and which dramatically increases in volume when the King and Queen rise through trapdoors from beneath the stage.

Ninagawa's use of programmatic music differs from contemporary RSC productions, where the music is often live, amplified to a minimum, and limited to the beginnings and ends of scenes. In the case of *A Midsummer Night's Dream*, there is an important precedent in Mendelssohn's orchestral accompaniment that was a regular feature of productions from the mid-19th century through to the 1960s, but even Mendelssohn's music has been quietly discarded by directors who found it outmoded and distracting.

---

[228] An example of a production where monumental scenery was seen to engage effectively with the play itself was Noda Higeki's production of *Twelfth Night* in 1986. Noda adapted the Odashima translation in an ornate style, adding a scene at the end, with the actors' delivery paced by the presence of a row of lifesize models of the Easter Island statues (Sugiki 1999, 138-39). The actors spoke exaggeratedly fast; their speed seemed a valid response to the psychological power which those icons of supernatural power had over them. See also Gallimore (2009) for a comparison of Ninagawa's *Dream* with a contemporary Korean production by the Yohangza company.

Ninagawa's score is certainly programmatic, illustrating and underlying the dramatic action. A good example of this is when after the initial, highly ritualised greeting of Oberon and Titania (ll. 60-2, 'Ill met by moonlight ...'), the music is suddenly cut as Oberon shouts out *Mate, asahakana onna, ore wa omae no otto dewa nai ka* (l. 63, 'Tarry, rash wanton; am I not thy lord?') (ibid., 34).[229] This sudden cut suggests not only that the ethereal music is representative of a deeper harmony, of a potential unity between the two, but also that moments and stretches without music are intended to challenge the ritualised concords and discords that dominate the play, and so advance the drama. There is accompaniment throughout this scene between Oberon and Titania but the one moment when it fades almost to nothing is also the least ritualised moment, the most overt expression of human weakness (2.1.135; ibid., 39):

But she, being mortal, of that boy did die

Demo shosen wa ningen, ano ko no osan de shinimashita

Music has a programmatic purpose in this interpretation but it is used so insistently and at such high volume that the total effect can seem like film or even opera. It can act not only as an illustrating device but also an essential integrative factor so that audiences listen not to what the actors are saying or even to how they say it but to what the music is saying. We hear the organ getting louder and assume, as one would watching a film, that either Oberon and Titania are about to do something significant.

The extent to which the text is undermined or trivialised by the loud music can be gauged from how the lines are spoken. On the whole, they are spoken more rapidly than in the two recordings analysed so far, especially the more functional sections, such as Oberon's instruction to Puck to fetch the love juice (ll. 148-76). Although the urgency and excitement of the exchange is effectively communicated, Oberon speaks too fast for any of the resonance of those images to be felt, or of Odashima's plosive, consonantal language (2.1.161-62; ibid., 40):

But I might see young Cupid's fiery shaft
Quench'd in the chaste beams of the watery moon;
And the imperial votress passed on,
In maiden meditation, fancy-free.

Sasuga no Kyūpiddo no hi to moeru ya mo,
mizu wo yobu tsuki no kiyorakana hikari ni uchikesare, sono mama
dokushin wo chikatta joō wa tachisatta no da, tsutsumashii

---

[229] The ritualised exchange of *mie*-like grimaces is highly choreographed, accompanied as the couple are by servants. Unless one knew the play, one would think that this exchange was only a passing one and that the two would soon exit.

otome no omoi ni tsutsumarete, itamashii koi suru kokoro mo dakazu ni.

There is a tendency in all the exchanges for the actors to become fixed in stylised poses that frame their speeches in a series of rapid, unmodified releases; in other words, the mood changes only as the frame does. One possible exception would be Shiraishi Kayoko, who plays Titania. Somewhat like the veteran British actress Judi Dench in both voice and demeanour, her voice is well-suited to the part, and indeed she is the only one that manages to slow the pace down and make something of her lines, in particular that tragic undertone, 'But she, being mortal ...'.[230] Yet, such moments apart, it must be difficult even for Shiraishi to find a depth of character in her voice when so much of the interpretation is supplied by music and other effects.

A further example of the subordination of voice comes in the section with Demetrius and Helena (ll. 188 to 268). Ninagawa echoes the previous exchange between Oberon and Titania in that Helena and Demetrius face each other, and yet the parallel is no more than an echo. His Helena has a plaintive voice that does little justice to the rhetorical changes of mood evident in the source, and the imbalance with Demetrius' louder voice succeeds in creating the effect of pathos but also masks the opportunity for a more nuanced delivery. This is not, however, to suggest that either this scene or indeed the production in itself lack artistic integrity but rather that in this kind of commercial production, especially as practised by Ninagawa, the role of voice is marginalised.[231] In a commercial environment, the potential for actors to play with time in their delivery is suppressed.

WHERE ACCENT MATTERS: SHIMODATE KASUMI AND SHAKESPEARE IN DIALECT

Critics of Ninagawa also note that his activities are biassed towards the Tokyo and foreign markets, and yet Ninagawa seems content with his work being labelled 'Japanese

---

[230] Shiraishi Kayoko (b. 1941) has played numerous Shakespearean roles, including a male Lear for Ryūtopia's production of *King Lear*, directed by Kurita Yoshihiro in 2005. She is a good example of an actor from outside the traditional theatre who has acquired the physical discipline associated with *nō* and *kabuki* actors. This is mainly because of her training under the director Suzuki Tadashi, whose footwork especially is based on *nō* technique.

[231] This is Allain's criticism of the Suzuki method, the most representative of acting techniques to have emerged in Japan since the 1960s: 'The voice is [...] considered primarily in terms of energy. There is no technical exploration of the voice as an organ of speech or the body as a site of resonators. [...] Rather than using the voice in a state of relaxation that is familiar to Western approaches, it is drawn out in positions of tension. The voice is added as you fight for balance when one leg is raised or when the stomach muscles are struggling to hold the upper torso off the floor.' (Allain 2002, 113-14)

Shakespeare'.²³² In fact, the Ninagawa Company regularly tours to venues outside Tokyo, but in such a heavily commercial market as the contemporary Japanese theatre, with most financial sponsors themselves based in Tokyo, there is the obvious danger that his success will hold back competing voices.²³³ That is certainly the concern of Shimodate Kasumi, founder and director of the Sendai-based Shakespeare Company of Japan.²³⁴ Shimodate has adapted several of Shakespeare's plays into the local Tōhoku dialect for annual productions by his group of amateurs. In 2000, they performed their version of *Macbeth* at the Edinburgh Fringe Festival. Shimodate is also raising funds towards the construction of a Globe replica in Sendai.

Shimodate has developed a production style he calls 'North Japanism', which combines both the use of dialect and references to Tōhoku culture in a deliberate reflection of equivalent dramatic movements in 20th century Europe and of the more contemporary ideology of regionalism.²³⁵ The relevance of this style to my thesis is that the use of dialect makes the productions sound different not only from Shakespeare in English but also from mainstream production in Japanese. As in the following exchange between Bottom and Titania, the different sounds of the dialect are celebrated, even exaggerated. They carry resonances that are strong enough to create dramatic connections in themselves. Where Ninagawa's facades may be a conscious representation of the Tokyo cityscape – dramatising a daily struggle for dignity – on the Shimodate set it is the soundscape that dominates. Vocabulary and inflexions that differ from standard Japanese are underlined.

> T: Aree, uttori suru wa, dare no koe kashira?
>   ah – I am enchanted – P [particle] – who – P – voice – I wonder

---

[232] Ninagawa, for his part, has insisted that one of his main roles is to make Shakespeare's obscure rhetoric and range of cultural references accessible to mainstream Japanese audiences (Ninagawa and Hasebe 2002, 328). One technique is his remarkable variety of metatheatrical devices that encourage audiences to observe more closely what they are seeing, but Ninagawa programmes also come complete with detailed background notes, historical maps, and essays by Japanese scholars. Moreover, his recent productions, such as his successful *kabuki* adaptation of *Twelfth Night* (2005) have shown a greater willingness to tackle the impasse between Shakespeare and *kabuki* drama.

[233] Japanese theatre companies receive very little funding from either central or local government.

[234] Shimodate is professor at Tōhoku Gakuin University in Sendai.

[235] In the programme for the Edinburgh Fringe production of *Macbeth*, Shimodate notes that one of the reasons he formed the company was to promote a new 'Tōhoku Dramatic Movement', 'intentionally echoing 'the Irish Dramatic Movement''. An obvious point of comparison would be the interest of the Irish playwright J.M. Synge in the language of the Aran islanders at the turn of the 20th century. Another comparison would be with Kurosawa's celebrated film version of the play, *Kumonosujō* ('Throne of blood') (1957), which set the play in the Warring States period of 16th century Japan. Yet, as Shimodate suggests, his production tried to go even further than Kurosawa by replacing a homogeneous view of Japanese feudal history, centred on the *samurai* with their code of honour and gruff manner of address, with a localised approach through which antagonisms are focussed more specifically on communal rather than national loyalties (Shimodate 2001, 71).

B: Enyādotto, enyādotto ...
          heave ho – heave ho

T: Onegai, tsuzukete!
          I beg you – sing – carry on

B: Enyādotto.
          Heave ho

T: Ā [glottal stop], kanjirū. Shibireru koe. Watashi no koko ira hen wo
              yusaburu wā. Guin, guin.
          ah – I feel it – paralysing voice – my – [place here] – P – shake – P
          emphatic – meow, meow

          Dotto, enyā.

B: Dotto. Okusan, hoya ni demo adattan ja nē no?
          good woman – me – even – did you mean? – P emphatic

T: Dotto, enyādotto. Nnn, ii wā.
          mmm – good – P emphatic

B: Daibu maitteru yō da ne ya. Koi wa, koko to nakanaka
          much – she's shaking – looks like – P emphatic – love – P – with me –
              rather

          oriai ga tsukanai mon da kedo, darega ki no kiita
          acquaintance – P – does not have – the thing is – but – who – P – smart

          otoko ga naka ni haitte mame ni ittari kitari shite kurereba,
          man P – inside – enter – vigorously – coming and going – if he gives you

          naka yogu natte, iin de nai.
          inside – good – become – nice – isn't it

T: Enyā.

B: Nani, ore ga sono otoko datte?
          what – I – P – that man – am?

T: Koe mo kao mo ii to omottara, atama mo ii

voice – also – face – also – good – that – if I think – intelligence – also good

no nē.
P emphatic

B: Ureshii goto itte kureru na. Mā, atama no hō wa māmā
happy – things – say for me – P – well – as for your intelligence – P – not bad

dakedo nantoka kono shima gara nugedashite egara, sonokkurai no chie
but – somehow – this island – from – escape – plan – about that – P – wisdom

wa hoshii na.
P – want – P emphatic

T: Kono shima kara nukedasu! Dame, sonna koto shicha, iya.
this island – from – escape – bad – that kind of thing – if you do – I hate it

Watashi wa, umi no sei no joō yo, anata ga hoshii mono nara nandemo
I – P – sea – P – due to – queen – P – you – P – want – think – if – everything

te ni ireru kara koko ni ite, zūtto, watashi no soba ni ite.
– obtain – from – here – am – [emphatic adverb] – me – P – beside – be

Unidon datte tabehōdai,
sea urchin on rice [name of food] – even – eat all you want

rairaiken no rāmen datte, tabetai toki ni
[type of noodle soup from Tokyo area] – even – want to eat – when

sugu demae wo shite kureru shi, sore kara, awabi datte
straightaway – you – P – make – give – and – then – abalone – even

sashimi de tabetai dake tabete ii shi,
sliced raw fish – is – want to eat – only – you can eat – and

osake datte abiru hodo nomeru ... sore kara, watashi mo ...
Japanese rice wine – shower – to the extent of – can drink – then – me too –

>   otabe tabetabe yō.
>   eat – eat, eat – P emphatic

B: Enyādotto.

T: Enyādotto.

The above is a very free adaptation of the following excerpt (3.1.124-49, 158-60), which should be apparent even from comparing how the adaptation looks against the source. Bottom's song is omitted but represented by a comic yodling word *Enyādotto*. Titania's first speech is telescoped into a series of one-line comments, e.g. *Koe mo kao mo ii to omottara, atama mo ii no nē* (literally, 'You sound good and you look good, and you aren't stupid either', i.e. l. 142, 'Thou art as wise as thou art beautiful.') The first part of Titania's second long speech is translated in sense, but lines 150 to 158 are omitted and the names of fruits replaced with the names of typical Japanese dishes (e.g. *rāmen* noodle soup) and *sake* rice wine. In this adaptation, Titania becomes Taita and Bottom Bon. Bon speaks in prose, Taita in iambic pentameters:

Tita.   What angel wakes me from my flowery bed?
Bot.   *The finch, the sparrow, and the lark,*
[Sings.]   *The plain-song cuckoo gray,*
               Whose note full many a man doth mark,
               And dares not answer nay –
          for indeed, who would set his wit to so foolish a bird? Who would give a bird the lie, though he cry 'cuckoo' never so?
Tita.   I pray thee, gentle mortal, sing again:
          Mine ear is much enamour'd of thy note;
          So is mine eye enthrall'd to thy shape;
          And thy fair virtue's force perforce doth move me
          On the first view to say, to swear, I love thee.
Bot.   Methinks, mistress, you should have little reason for that. And yet, to say the truth, reason and love keep little company together nowadays. The more the pity that some honest neighbours will not make them friends. Nay, I can gleek upon occasion.
Tita.   Thou art as wise as thou art beautiful.
Bot.   Not so neither; but if I had wit enough to get out of this wood, I have enough to serve mine own turn.
Tita.   Out of this wood do not desire to go:
          Thou shalt remain here, whether thou wilt or no.
          I am a spirit of no common rate;
          The summer still doth tend upon my state;
          And I do love thee: therefore go with me.

[…]

> Feed him with apricocks and dewberries,
> With purple grapes, green figs, and mulberries

The adaptation is not so different from standard Japanese, although the language and phrasing are more natural than a straight translation would usually allow. There are a few obvious variations such as the softening of *k* to *g* in the common words *koto* (abstract 'thing') and *yoku* ('well').[236] The rhythmic quality of the dialogue comes as much from the license of adaptation as the dialect itself, although the dialect does contribute to the festive mood and sexual overtones of the adaptation. It is interesting that Taita has lost all form of her civilised status in her rapture for Bon but that the rapture is primarily for the sounds he makes.

> Ā [glottal stop], kanjirū. Shibireru koe.
> Watashi no kokoira hen wo yusaburu wā. Guin, guin.

> Yes, I feel it. That voice paralyses me.
> I am shaken to the depth of my being (if you know what I mean). More, more!

The sexual undercurrent is brought out even more blatantly by Bon:

> dare ga ki no kiita otoko ga naka ni haitte mame
> ni ittari kitari shite kurereba, naka yoku natte, iin de nai.

> If only some smart guy could get inside and give it the old one-two, you'd feel alright in no time, I warrant you!

The motif of the dialogue is the word *Enyādotto*, the title and refrain of a traditional fishermen's song from the Sendai area. (Shimodate set his production in the Bay of Matsushima, a little to the east of Sendai). This word is foregrounded and repeated by both Bon and Taita so as to break down the hierarchical boundaries between them. The two revel in the sound, and without any need for musical accompaniment; they do not even sing. Although this is adaptation, it still suggests potential for a reassertion of voice and text through the use of dialect.

One of the major differentiating factors between Japanese dialects is accent (as it is between English dialects), and so it goes without saying that any dialect translation of Shakespeare will be conditioned by its accentual features. Standard Tokyo dialect

---

[236] Due to its mountainous nature, there is considerable variety even within the region, and taken as a whole Tōhoku dialect differs markedly from standard Japanese. The unvoicing of voiced consonants is the most telling feature in the excerpt.

is heavily accented so that accent can even have a rhythmic function, whereas Tōhoku dialect is hardly accented at all.

As the copy of the computer analysis of the first part shows on the next pages,[237] there is a tendency instead for speech to rise and fall more gradually and for accents to be made only for the purpose of emphasis or to register a change in mood. Thus, speakers are able to get away with a more blatant vain of eroticism than they would in Tokyo dialect, where it is accentuation that engenders the erotic rather than the semantics. The problem of rhetorical equivalence is not confined to the relationship between the source text and its Tokyo-based translators but is also a matter of how Shakespeare is translated and understood within and between the different localities of Japan.

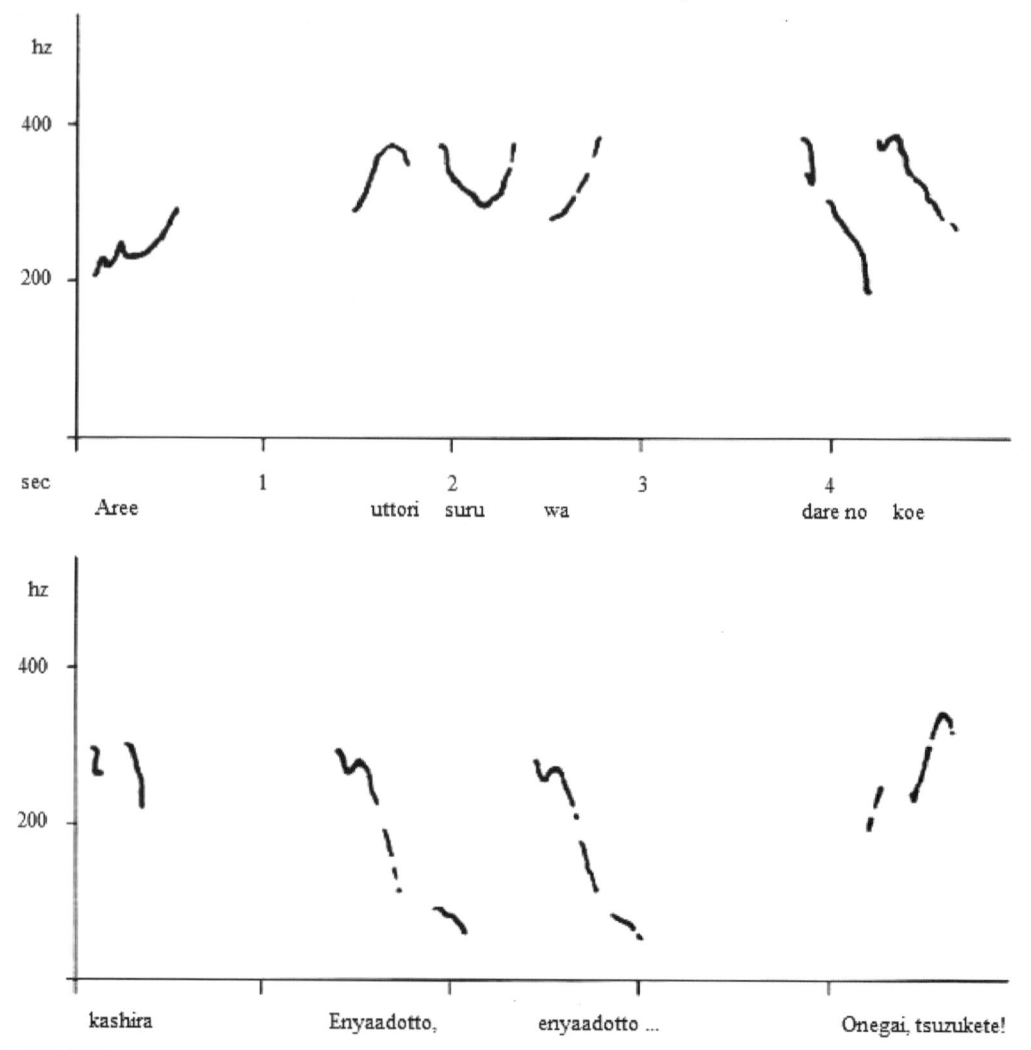

[237] The upper line on the graph represents Taita (around 400 hz), and the lower line Bon (around 200 hz). As with the previous analysis of Arai's reading, it should be observed that the graphs are only an approximation of the original computer printouts, and that the traces correspond with phrasal modulations.

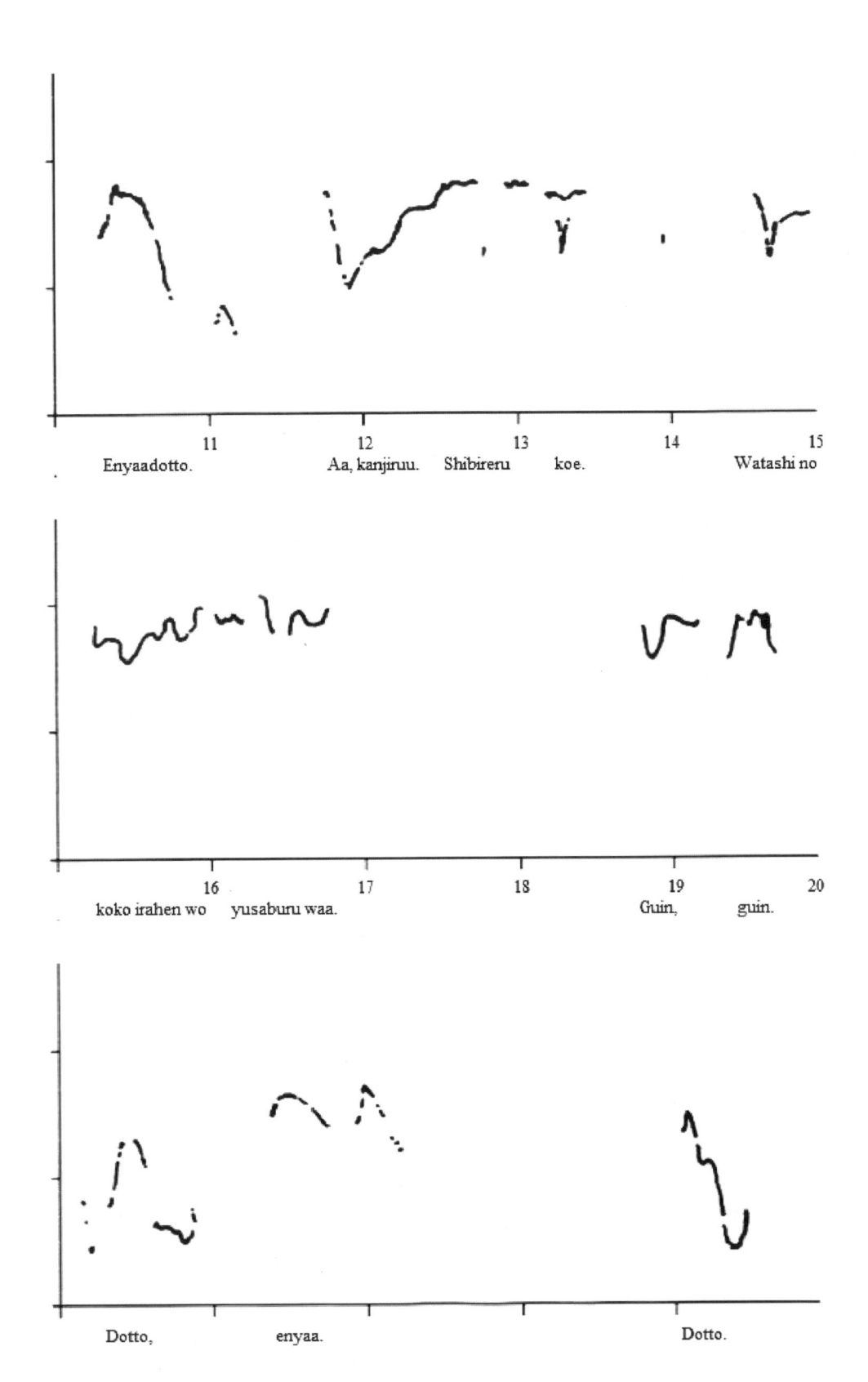

CHAPTER FIVE SPEAKING SHAKESPEARE IN JAPANESE

```
   11            12           13         14        15
Enyaadotto.   Aa, kanjiruu.  Shibireru   koe.    Watashi no

   16            17           18         19        20
koko irahen wo  yusaburu waa.                   Guin,    guin.


   Dotto,       enyaa.                           Dotto.
```

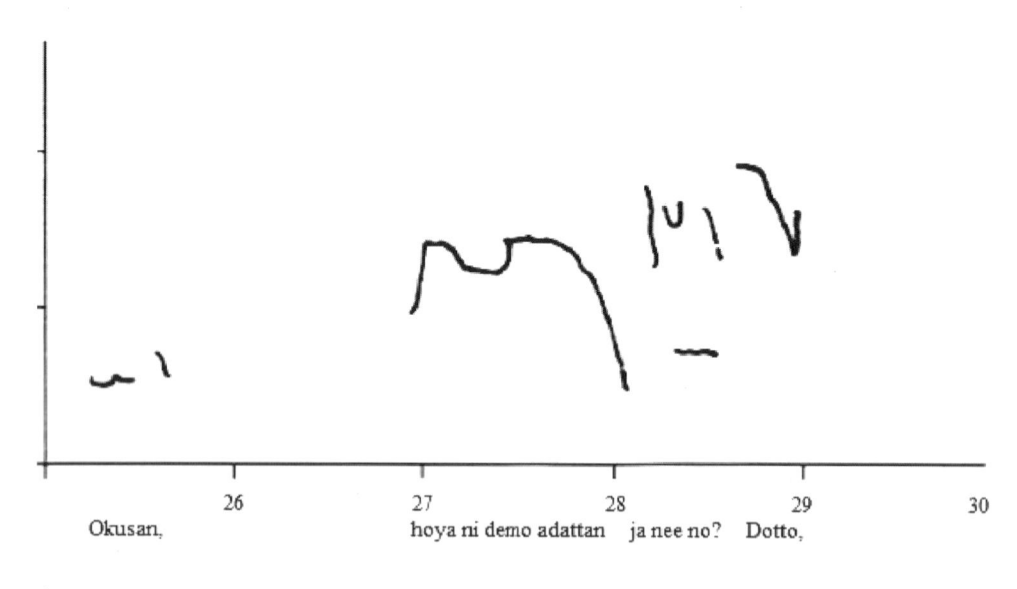

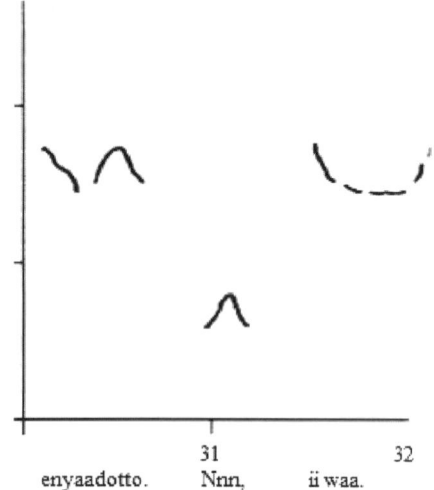

| 26   27   28   29   30
   Okusan,   hoya ni demo adattan ja nee no? Dotto,

| 31   32
   enyaadotto.   Nnn,   ii waa.

The requirement to speak in the local dialect is less straightforward than it seems, especially as about a third of the actors do not originate from the Tōhoku region. Even those who do must first overcome the natural embarrassment of acting in their dialect and then adapt it to their given role.[238] In facilitating this process, which takes about nine months of weekly rehearsals, Shimodate has drawn on the work of Cicely Berry, former Voice Director of the Royal Shakespeare Company (Shimodate 1996, 30-31), who insists (Berry 1993, 9):

whatever the style of the writing, the actor has to find the right energy for that

---

[238] The actor playing Bon (Izumori Isamu) was originally from Aomori, whose accentuation is much closer to Tokyo than Tōhoku, so that for him there is the additional challenge of adapting his voice to something other than the expected *hyōjungo*.

particular text; if his energy becomes too inward and controlled the words become dull; if he presses too much energy out the words will be unfocussed and the thought will be generalised. Either way the result is that the speaking of text or dialogue is too often not as alive or remarkable as the imagination that is feeding it.

Berry gives various exercises to develop that balance of energy, some of which Shimodate uses with his actors. In particular, these actors spoke with their diaphragms. There was nothing unnatural about the way they spoke. Where they did admit difficulty was in finding an authentic voice; the only fully authentic voice I heard among them was Ryōgoku Kōichi's performance as Macbeth in Edinburgh.

For all the virtues of Shimodate's adaptation, one of the dangers of moving even further away from the source text is the disintegration of clearly individuated characters (as Shakespeare created them), and this process may be enhanced by the creation of new communities based on dialect and accent. One of the features of Ryōgoku's Macbeth was how quickly he stood apart from that communality of colloquial discourse that belongs to any local speech community.[239] What this company needs perhaps is an acting as well as a voice method, something like the Suzuki method even, which will enable actors to discover more fully how their own personalities relate to the characters they have been assigned. Suzuki urges his actors to act before they speak whereas Shimodate's actors are clearly bound from the start by the text. In English Shakespeare, of the kind that Cicely Berry supervises, the text is the original Shakespeare, which is a factor that lends an authority to production that is not necessarily the case with Shakespeare in Japanese.[240]

* * * * *

[239] For example, when Duncan comes to stay with Macbeth in Act 1, Scene 7, Macbeth's speech contemplating murder ('If it were done, when 'tis done, then 'twere well / It were done quickly' ...) was quite rhythmically contrasted with the sound of laughter from inside the dining hall. He was already excluded from the security of an unchallenged hierarchy.

[240] Berry's work is of course greatly admired but she is nevertheless, rightly or wrongly, a part of the Leavisite establishment that has served to produce British Shakespeare over the last sixty years. In a critique of Berry's *The Actor and the Text* (1993), Knowles concludes that 'Ultimately, she constructs a series of binaries – depth vs. surface, nature vs. civilization or artifice, emotion vs. reason, even vowels vs. consonants or open vs. closed vowel sounds [...] – in which the first terms are linked and privileged through an association with truth and honesty, while the second are related to the corruptions of an essentially dishonest intellectual and cultural conditioning. And of course these binaries are constitutive of the individualist/universalist vs. social/historical polarities that function effectively to inhibit politicized readings and political dissent.' (Knowles 1996, 99) One of the meanings, therefore, of Shakespeare performance in Japan and other Asian countries is to reconstruct those binaries within different cultural frameworks, or indeed to deconstruct them altogether.

It should be clear that voice is taken seriously in Shakespeare production in Japan but whether this seriousness amounts to anything like a tradition of speaking the language seems far less certain. Actors have distinctive voices, but it seems from the examples given that these voices are marginalised, either since Shakespeare in Japanese is so specialised a pursuit or as subordinate to other production values. For a more substantial analysis, it would be necessary to research how styles of speaking have been passed down within the *shingeki* tradition from the Taishō era to the present day: whether certain styles are associated with certain companies, and the extent to which the voice is developed through the processes of professional acting. It would be surprising if either of these were not the case, but then there is the more ambiguous question of whether a predetermined style exists for speaking Shakespeare in the Japanese theatre.

The extent to which the translators translate with the actor's voice in mind is also ambiguous but can be partly understood in terms of the dichotomy of rhythm and *share* mentioned at the end of Chapter Four. Odashima famously argued that no actor can speak more than twenty-five lines in a single breath and his idea is connected with devices of rhythm and phrasing (Kadono 1989, 152). If the translator gives actors rhythmic structures that are coherent and support their given roles, then the speaking of the lines will follow naturally. Likewise, if the use of *share* and *goro* is coherent and justified, then it gives actors moments of heightened language on which to ground their speech (if not their actual interpretation). The actors are speaking not Shakespeare but Tsubouchi, Fukuda, Odashima and Matsuoka.

EPILOGUE

In Chapter One, two models of translation were proposed as approaches to understanding the four translations. The Schleiermacher model insisted on the subjectivity of the translation process; translators are writers as well as readers.[241] This model has been applicable to all four translators, as they have all forged distinctive styles, but perhaps especially so for Tsubouchi and Fukuda who inevitably lacked the depth of Shakespeare scholarship which has informed the two later translators. The pragmatic Holmes model, on the other hand, has been useful in understanding how the stylistic features of each of the translations can be construed as integrated responses to the source text. One overt example was the use of phonemic patterning as an equivalent to Shakespearean rhythm.

Holmes' pragmatism is representative of the gradual replacement over the last fifty years of a narrowly prescriptive focus on the product (the target text) with a scientific approach to translation as a process.[242] This approach, in turn, has been criticised for failing to provide grounds for assessing translation, which is a limitation that recent theorists such as Ernst-August Gutt have sought to redress by considering translation as just one of many types of communication, applying to translation the claims of contemporary relevance theory (Gutt 2000).[243] Gutt argues that the effective translation

---

[241] This may be something of a truism, but, as Bassnett and Bush argue (Bassnett and Bush 2007), one that demands continual assertion against the hegemony of translation theory. As one of their contributors, Ros Schwartz, who has translated mainly contemporary Francophone literature, comments, 'I call the translation process 'finding a voice' – there's a point in the translation where I suddenly feel very confident and I know what the mood should be, I know what the characters should say and I know what the register of language should be.' (Schwartz and de Lange 2007, 9)

[242] Bell writes that 'Translation theory finds itself today seriously out of step with the mainstream of intellectual endeavour in the human sciences and in particular in the study of human communication; to our mutual impoverishment. The fundamental cause of this state of affairs is, we firmly believe, the normative approach – the setting up of a series of maxims consisting of do's and don'ts', which he ascribes to the influence of the Scottish judge Lord Woodhouselee's *Essay on the Principles of Translation* (1791) (Bell 1991, 10).

[243] Gutt does not deny descriptivism but suggests instead that it should be considered apart from interpretation. According to relevance theory, the translator applies the same cognitive processes as were applied to processing the source text to reformulating it in the target language, so that ↗

is one that renders as complete an account as possible of the context in which the source text was produced and so makes what is read and understood in the act of translation as relevant to the target culture as it was to the source (realising, of course, that source and target relevance are different phenomena).

The difficulty of reconciling prescriptivism with the descriptive approach espoused within this monograph is related to the difficulty, indeed impossibility of establishing equivalence between the source and target texts; it goes without saying that a translation that is equivalent to its source is not a translation. Translators establish norms that may correspond effectively to the linguistic and cultural norms of their target audience, but it is impossible to refer those norms in any timeless or universal sense back to the source from which the translation is derived.

Prescriptivism, therefore, is a characteristic of early modern cultures in which, for example, it was considered important to distinguish 'good' from 'bad' translations of holy scripture. Moreover, if prescriptivism is very often a critique of the uses to which traditional forms and texts have been put in modern times, then we can argue that the trend in translation studies to reconcile ancient and modern is merely another example of the postmodern imperative to admit the constructedness of human experience. While Shakespeare's poetics and the poetics of his Japanese translators may occur within different historical frameworks, they are both derived from ancient models, Shakespeare from medieval and classical poetics and Japanese poetics from the syllabic forms that were introduced from China in the 7th century. Just as Shakespeare's plays became absorbed within the rising trajectory of British imperialism, we have glimpsed at how Shakespeare's Japanese translations became part of the trajectory of Japan's emergence as a modern state from the promulgation of the Meiji Constitution in 1889 through to the collapse of the economic bubble in the early 1990s; Odashima's translations are, in that sense, the summative expression of that trajectory.

In understanding the present and future states, therefore, of Shakespeare translation in Japan, it is useful to regard them as occurring in a climate that is more self-consciously postmodern than what has come before: aware that the ideals which inspired translators like Tsubouchi and Fukuda are largely defunct. This is not to suggest that what came before was not postmodern, since in a Buddhist, circular view of history, that is continuously deconstructing itself, differing perspectives can be accommodated alongside each other more easily than in a strictly linear trajectory, as for example in the technique of *mitate* (or 'collage') in traditional Japanese poetics, whereby the poet assembles a range of allusions within an integrated whole. In Shakespeare translation, Tsubouchi at least had no hesitation in drawing on a range of traditional and modern styles in order to do justice to the variety of Shakespeare's different voices. Feeling that

---

↘ (depending on effort and knowledge) the source text will translate itself. This theory can be usefully applied to drama translation, which (as has been noted) is difficult to theorise due to the range of external variables, but at the least it can be assumed that the translator will process hidden dramatic markers as well as the overt features of the source text.

the contemporary language of Taishō and early Shōwa had been impoverished due to linguistic standardisation following the *genbun icchi* movement, Tsubouchi called for a freely colloquial approach that was less bound by current convention and could therefore do justice to the creativity of Shakespeare's language (Tsubouchi 1978 a, 263-64; Gallimore 2010 a, 54-55):

> in Shakespeare translation one must first consider vocabulary and usage, and for this reason contemporary Japanese is just inadequate. To rely on the languages of the Yamanote, Tokyo suburbs and Ginza nightlife is terribly limiting; one must create a style that is liberally mixed with local dialect and includes slang words from Tokyo and its environs, such as *subarashii* ('wonderful'), *suteki* ('nice') and *hitokko* ('single child'). It should be a colloquial style that makes sense not only to the translator himself but also to the people who know him. Just as Shakespeare uses archaisms, foreign words, slang and dialect as the situation demands, the translator should do likewise: the refined and vulgar language of the ancients, the language of Confucianism and the Chinese classics, of the Tōhoku and Kyushu, the language of Akinari, Bakin, Saikaku and Chikamatsu, these should all be exploited in an approximation of the refined and vulgar language. If one does not, then one cannot hope to capture even one ten-thousandth of Shakespeare's original spirit.[244]

Fukuda is arguably the most 'modern' of the translators, the one best placed to criticise Japanese modernity, although his dichotomy is also the starting point for a post-war quest for national identities that is inseparable from postmodernity.[245] Finally,

---

[244] Tsubouchi's apologia itself requires some explanation. The Yamanote is the higher ground in present-day Bunkyō and Shinjuku wards that in Tsubouchi's day stood on the edge of the city of Tokyo. This was already developing into a suburb for the new middle class, who would have been educated to speak in the uniform way of which Tsubouchi disapproved; Tsubouchi would have had more time for the dialect of the *shitamachi*, or downtown locality of Asakusa on the low-lying land. The words *subarashii*, *suteki* and *hitokko* have long since passed into everyday usage, but would have sounded new to Tsubouchi. Knowledge of Confucianism was transmitted through the education system in support of the national ideology of *kokutai* ('national polity'), although the ability to read the Chinese classics or write Chinese poetry without *kana* (*kanshi*) would have been rarer; Tsubouchi's contemporary Natsume Sōseki wrote and published a number of *kanshi*. The dialects of Tōhoku in north-east Japan and the island of Kyushu in the south-west are markedly different from the standard Japanese of the Tokyo dialect. Ueda Akinari was a poet and scholar of the 18th century, and Takizawa Bakin and Ihara Saikaku writers of popular *gesaku* fiction of the 19th and 17th centuries respectively. Along with Chikamatsu, these were all writers whom Tsubouchi tended to admire for their style but less for what they said.

[245] Fukuda is sympathetic towards Tsubouchi's quest to capture the emotions that drive Shakespeare's language but is inevitably more realistic with regard to his contemporary language, which was standardized even further after 1945 (Fukuda 1988). Whereas Tsubouchi seeks to create a new language, Fukuda is concerned with understanding the language as it is, and thereby ↗

Odashima's playful, humorous approach creates 'a world of words' that detaches the translated texts from their immediate contexts.[246]

In the current Heisei era (starting in 1989), Shakespeare studies and production of all kinds have continued unabated in Japan, and this must be partly due to the efforts of predecessors such as Tsubouchi, Fukuda and Odashima in making the plays and poems accessible to Japanese readers. Even if Shakespeare's works do not necessarily reflect current Japanese realities, they have been thoroughly absorbed within the theatrical culture, so that in a heterogeneous society like Japan's it is appropriate to consider them in terms of that culture.[247] In determining, therefore, the future of Shakespeare translation in Japan, it would be as well to set it against the so-called 'cultural turn', or rise in culture studies, that has accompanied the realignment of the world order following the end of the Cold War, in particular the heightened tension between global and local ideologies. It is in this climate that Venuti calls for translations with 'a discursive heterogeneity which is defamiliarising, but intelligible to different constituencies in the translating culture' (Venuti 2000, 341).

While the cultural complicity of translators and interpreters has become all too apparent in their increased involvement in political negotiation in Iraq and Afghanistan (Apter 2005), Gutt offers a cognitive approach to how cultural referents are automatically, and sometimes quite unconsciously absorbed within the translation process, when he writes that (Gutt 2000, 164)

> poetic effects arise essentially when the audience is induced and given freedom to open up and consider a wide range of implicatures, none of which are very strongly implicated, but which taken together create an 'impression' rather than

---

↘ exploiting it for the purposes of stage performance. Fukuda would have no doubt hesitated to have called himself 'postmodern' with its various philosophical connotations, but if pre-war modernity had only been possible within the framework of *kokutai*, then the collapse of that ideology in 1945 and its replacement with the 1947 Consitution and the post-war culture in which Fukuda played a dominant role may all amount to a postmodern critique of Meiji, Taishō and early Shōwa Japan (and one that is not necessarily unsympathetic).

[246] It seems unjust to label Odashima's translations 'escapist', but Pinnington notices a transparency in his style that could be said to negate differences within an audience by reducing the language to its lowest denominator (Pinnington 1995), and in that sense to deny differences within the outside world as well. Odashima himself has suggested that Shakespeare is primarily 'the poet of love' (Gallimore 2009 a), in which case it is the capacity of individuals to triumph over social forces that is celebrated, or tragically denied, in the plays.

[247] Shakespeare has not been absorbed within mainstream Japanese culture in the way that they have provided recognizable titles, plot lines and even people's names in British culture, although there have been numerous references made along the way. The most remarkable of these must be Dazai Osamu's free *Hamlet* adaptation, *Shin Hamuretto* (1941), which rewrote the play as a novel about the disaffected of youth of Dazai's own generation, and despite its anti-authoritarian stance managed to escape censorship in the few months leading up to outbreak of war with the United States.

communicate a 'message'.

This is to say that effective translations invite readers to participate, subconsciously or otherwise, in 'an act of knowing', albeit one that is unlikely to result in any definitive conclusions. This avoidance of definitive conclusions is also reflected in the work of Susan Bassnett in her resistance to the notion of 'a gestic subtext' that determines exactly how Shakespeare's lines should be read and performed. She asserts that while such a notion may be relevant to the Western models of psychological realism it has had no place in 'post-modernist theatre, or a non-European theatre or indeed any form of theatre that is not based in [such] realism' (Bassnett 1998, 207). Bassnett does not deny the existence of subtexts, but rather insists on the necessity of translators, theatre historians and directors to collaborate in the discovery of their own subtexts, in other words to advance a culture of translated drama.

The main contribution to the field in English in recent years has been the collection of essays edited by Ton Hoenselaars entitled *Shakespeare and the Language of Translation* (Hoenselaars 2005). These essays argue strongly for the notion of textual continuity, or rather that translation merely fulfils a completeness that is inherent in the source texts, and which can be developed further through continued translations and adaptions; translations posit answers to questions that have been left unsolved by traditional Shakespeare studies, as well as posing new questions. In particular, it is the basic question of 'What does Shakespeare actually mean?' that is reflected in the efforts of translators. Shakespeare translators are also, arguably, in a position to convey the strangeness and elusiveness of Shakespeare's texts through the reality that basic cultural referents to do with early modern Christian theology, Elizabethan folklore and so on must be more carefully elucidated among their readers than would be necessary among the native culture.

In the Hoenselaars collection, Kishi Tetsuo advocates a sociolinguistic approach, suggesting that the abnormal abundance of personal pronouns in Shakespeare translation creates new kinds of dramatic relationships that are largely absent from everyday colloquial Japanese. The French translator Jean-Michel Déprats makes a related point as he argues that (Déprats 2005, 66)

> A translation for the theatre must be as oral and gestural as possible, but its function is not to reduce the Shakespearean flow or adapt it to more everyday modes of expression.

These views can be further subsumed into a postcolonial perspective on the inalienable inequalities that exist between cultures. While it is no longer possible to argue that 'Shakespeare has conquered the world' or that 'the Japanese have conquered Shakespeare', postcolonial theory does at least posit the desirability of a world of mutual respect and equality between different cultures. It is above all this 'consummation devoutly to be wished' that motivates Shakespeare translation and performance in contemporary Japan, and which owes much to the idealism of a Fukuda Tsuneari.

Matsuoka Kazuko is surely a participant in 'this brave new world' in her culturalism and her scepticism toward universal solutions. Her account of her Shakespeare watching during the 1980s, in particular her encounters with such luminaries as the veteran Peter Brook and the young Sam Mendes, addresses the theatricality of Shakespeare, and as such proves an apt prologue to her theatrical translations for Ninagawa later in the decade (Matsuoka 1993). Subtitled in English 'Shakespeare for all seasons', Matsuoka' book suggests that directors such as Brook and Mendes are sometimes able to align text and subtext in a way that detaches the theatrical experience from other realities. This experience is not of course universal, but a particular one that has to be worked at. As Matsuoka repeatedly notes, Shakespeare directors working in another language such as Japanese have an advantage in being able to adapt whatever translation they use with greater freedom than is possible with the original texts. Anglophone directors may well envy that freedom, but the lesson of Matsuoka's book is surely that if and when a production in English does succeed it is because the freedom to succeed has been found within Shakespeare's language, and so does not have to be sought elsewhere.

Matsuoka evinces a respect for British directors' understanding of how a Shakespeare play hangs together, as in one anecdote she told me (Matsuoka 2011, 187-92). In May 2007, her translation of *A Midsummer Night's Dream* was used in a production at the New National Theatre directed by John Caird, who has worked extensively in Japan. In the translation used in this monograph, Matsuoka had translated Titania's lament in Act 3, Scene 1, as follows (3.1.190-94) (Matsuoka 1997, 75-76):

> Come, wait upon him; lead him to my bower.
> The moon, methinks, looks with a watery eye,
> And when she weeps, weeps every little flower,
> <u>Lamenting some enforced chastity</u>.

> Sā, minna, osoba ni hikae, watashi no azumaya ni goannai shite.
> Nandaka tsuki ga namida gunde iru yō ne.
> Tsuki ga nakeba, chiisana hana mo kozotte naku.
> <u>Okasareta otome no misao wo nageite iru no</u>.

> violated – maiden – P – chastity – P – lamenting – P emphatic

As the back-translation indicates, Matsuoka's version of the fourth line is a literal rendition of the original, but as Caird suggested to her in rehearsal, Titania is referring specifically to Hermia and to the choice imposed on her at the beginning of the play: that she must either consent to marriage with Demetrius or face execution or the nunnery. It is not so much that she will be forced to remain a virgin for the rest of her life but that she will have to sleep alone in a narrow convent cell; Matsuoka tried to reflect this subtle difference in her revised version for Caird:[248]

Shiirareta hitorine wo arawende iru no.

強いられた独り寝を憐れんでいるの。

forced – sleep alone – P – lamenting – P

The surface meaning alone is unsufficient, since a translation that exposes Shakespeare's hidden meanings is also one that conveys the otherness of Shakespeare: that arrests audiences with its strangeness. A further example that I myself encountered in the theatre was from Matsuoka's translation of *Much Ado About Nothing*, published in 2008, for Ninagawa's production of the play at the Saitama Sai no Kuni Arts Theatre. Towards the end of the play, Hero protests her innocence to Claudio with the following striking phrase (5.4.64):

And surely as I live, I am a maid.

Hero is of course protesting her chastity and fidelity to her betrothed, with the word 'maid' carrying an arcane connotation of chastity. In a contemporary production, therefore, the word could well be emphasised to signify the harsh demands that Claudio has imposed on her, and for which she now forgives him; it is an unusual word reflecting an unusual experience. Matsuoka translates it in similarly oblique language (Matsuoka 2008, 182):

Watashi ga tashika ni ikite iru you ni, watashi wa otoko wo shirimasen!

私が確かに生きているように、私は男を知りません。

I – P – surely – am living – as – I – P – man – do not know

In Matsuoka's somewhat Biblical resonance, Hero 'does not know man'.

This foregrounding of otherness is central to the cultural turn in Shakespeare translation, in other words the assertion of cultural differences, which is a point developed by Kawai Shōichirō in a comment he makes about Dogberry's malapropisms in a discussion with Matsuoka reprinted in the programme for the Ninagawa production (Matsuoka and Kawai 2008, 40):

Jokes about gormless policemen are still popular in Britain today. He may look

---

[248] Caird's suggestion is noted in recent editions, although Matsuoka's original version remains unchanged.

strong, but actually he's as thick as two short planks. The way we make fun of the policeman's so-called power is fundamental to Shakespearean humour as well. Laughter breaks with the nomos, or established order, and (in my view) it's this smashing of systems and standards that is at the root of Shakespearean humour.

Kawai's point is related to an argument that the breaking of taboos is represented by linguistic fissures that are difficult to translate: in Dogberry's case the linguistic device of malapropism that humorously, but also painfully, exposes the hypocrisy of a social class that looks down on the uneducated.

Anzai Tetsuo regarded translation as the recreation of 'the dramatic or theatrical experience that lies hidden within the text' (Anzai 2004, 153); this experience may just as well be whatever Shakespeare intended it to be as the accumulated history of the play in performance, but is nevertheless dynamic and transformative. One might extend the point further by arguing that the task of the translator is to release the tragedy within the comedy and the comedy within the tragedy, since at the other extreme from Dogberry are characters such as Lear who achieve remarkable composure in the face of tragedies that they are largely responsible for creating. Scenes such as Lear's final speech are scenes of heightened otherness (5.3.304-9):

> And my poor fool is hanged. No, no, no life!
> Why should a dog, a horse, a rat have life
> And thou no breath at all? O thou'lt come no more,
> Never, never, never, never, never,
> [*to Edgar*] Pray you undo this button. Thank you, sir.
> O, o, o, o.
> Do you see this? Look on her: look, her lips,
> Look there, look there! *He dies.*

Matsuoka's translation is contemporary and colloquial, and theatrical in its use of the deictic *kono* and *kore* ('this') and its euphony, encapsulated in the phrase *Mō modotte wa konai* ('O thou'lt come no more', but literally 'it will never come back again') (Matsuoka 1997, 246):

> Kawaisō ni, ore no ahō ga shimekorosareta! Mō, mō, inochi wa nai!
> Inu ni mo, uma ni mo, nezumi ni mo inochi ga aru, sore na no ni
> naze omae wa iki wo shinai? Mō modotte wa konai,
> nido to, nido to, nido to, nido to, nido to!
> Tanomu, kono botan wo hazushite kure, arigatō.
> Kore ga mieru ka? Miro, kono kao, miro, kono kuchibiru,
> miro, dō da, sora, dō da!

As is evident, Matsuoka omits Lear's howling 'O, o, o, o', since she followed the Folio edition, but the undercurrent of grief can be felt in similar-sounding words like *mō* ('already'), which expresses the sense that it is too late to reverse the tragedy. The particle *mo*, meaning 'too' or 'also' but also by implication the presence of the consoling other (Lear's Cordelia), has been elongated into an adverb of despair. Moreover, the phrase *Mō modotte wa konai* that holds these tragic sounds is rendered peculiarly ambiguous by the lack of a subject word in Japanese grammar, since it could refer not only to the life that will not return but also to Cordelia herself as the one daughter who does finally return to her father in this play. Finally, the dull *do* and *dō* sounds can be said to prefigure Lear's imminent death, the figure of Lear's lifeless corpse on the stage.

The above example is a compelling illustration of how a translator may create a structure of text and subtext that serves not only to voice the otherness of a hidden theatrical experience but also to make it stand by itself, as Lear does at the end of this play, 'every inch a king'. Theatre is always a temporary illusion, but one that is made more credible by such structures. The dominant translators have always sought to integrate Shakespeare within Japanese culture, whether through nativisation or foreignisation, and such integration is necessary in a culture of niches (Gallimore 2009 a). The demand is not so much that Shakespeare become Japanese but simply that his translations are strong enough to stand out against a range of alternative realities. It is through the continuous interpretation of Shakespeare by the act of translation, above all the prosody of translation, that a culture of Shakespeare in Japan is born and continually regenerated.

GLOSSARY

angura	radical ('underground') theatre movement of 1960s Japan
Bungei Kyōkai	Literary Arts Association (1905-13), founded by Tsubouchi Shōyō to promote performance of modern drama of Japan
Chikamatsu Monzaemon	master *jōruri* and *kabuki* playwright (1653-1724), sometimes known as 'the Shakespeare of Japan'
bungo	literary or written Japan that remained distinct from colloquial Japanese until at least early 20th century
chōshi	tone or style of literary work, even rhythm
dajare	pun (often in bad taste)
gairaigo	foreign loan word
genbun icchi	late 19th century movement to integrate written and colloquial Japanese
giongo	onomatopoeia
gitaigo	mimetic words
goro awase	assonance
haiku	lyric poem comprising three groups of five, seven and five syllables respectively (popularised in 17th century Japan)
Heisei era	current reign of Emperor Akihito (since 1989)
hōgen	dialect
hyōjungo	standard modern Japanese based on Tokyo dialect
inritsu	prosody (rhythm and rhyme)
jōruri	traditional form of storytelling with musical accompaniment, typically associated with Japanese puppet theatre (*bunraku*)
kabuki	classical dance-drama genre developed in 17th century Japan
kana	syllabic Japanese scripts, including *hiragana* for Japanese words and syllables and *katakana* for foreign borrowings
kanji	Chinese writing system introduced into Japan in around 6th century, most characters having both Sino-Japanese and native Japanese readings
kōgo	colloquial Japanese
kotoba asobi	wordplay
kumatagari	technique of enjambement in *haiku* poetry
kyōgen	traditional comic theatre, that developed alongside *nō* drama in 14th century

kyōjaku gohōkaku	iambic pentameter
Meiji era	reign of Emperor Mutsuhito (1868-1912)
merihari	bright, lively style of speech, for example in performance
mie	classical pose struck by *kabuki* actors at significant moments of performance
mora	linguistic term that includes long syllables (e.g. dipthongs) as well as short single syllables
Natsu no yo no yume	*A Midsummer Night's Dream*
nō	classical musical drama originating in 14th century Japan, known for its refined aesthetic effects and use of masks
ōin	rhyme
pitch accent	characteristic of Japanese phonology for syllables to be accented by elevated pitch, varying according to dialect
rakugo	traditional one-man comic storytelling, known for its clever punchlines (*ochi*)
rōdoku	public reading, recitation
sanbun	prose
serifu mawashi	speech delivery
share	generic term for wordplay or playful style in spoken and literary Japanese, nowadays referring to fashion sense etc.
Sheikusupia	Shakespeare
shichigo chō	seven-five syllabic meter, most common of syllabic meters in traditional Japanese poetics and drama
shingeki	literally 'new drama', modern Japanese drama based on Western realist theatre which originated in early 20th century
shinpa	melodramatic 'new wave' of drama (and later cinema) that emerged in late 19th century Japan
Shōwa era	reign of Emperor Hirohito (1926-89)
Taishō era	reign of Emperor Yoshihito (1912-26)
tanka	major Japanese literary genre, meaning 'short poem' (as opposed to *chōka*, 'long poem'), dating back to 7th century, and comprising five groups of five, seven, five, seven and seven syllables (totalling thirty-one), often on themes of love
tōin	alliteration

WORKS CITED

Quotations from *A Midsummer Night's Dream* are from the 2nd Arden edition, and to other Shakespeare plays are from the 2nd and 3rd Arden editions.

Abe Tomoji, tr. (1939) *Oki ni mesu mama* (As You Like It), Tokyo: Iwanami Shoten
Akutagawa Ryūnosuke (1970) *Kappa*, tr. Geoffrey Bownas, London: Peter Owen, 1st pub. 1927
Allain, Paul (2002) *The Art of Stillness: The Theatre Practice of Tadashi Suzuki*, London: Methuen
Allen, Louis (1988) 'Playing with mirrors: contemporary Japanese poetry in translation', in *Stand* 29: 3, 26-33
Anzai Tetsuo, ed. (1989) *Nihon no Sheikusupia hyaku nen* (A hundred years of Shakespeare in Japan), Tokyo: Aratake Shuppan
——— (1989 a) 'Yottsu no jidai kubun' (The four periods of Shakespeare in Japan), in Anzai, 3-15
——— (1998) 'Directing *King Lear* in Japanese translation', in Sasayama et al., 124-37
——— (1999) 'A century of Shakespeare in Japan: a brief historical survey', in Anzai et al., 3-12
——— (2004) *Kanata kara no koe – engeki · saishi · uchū* (Voices from afar – drama, ritual, and the cosmos), Tokyo: Kawade Shobō
Anzai Tetsuo, Iwasaki Sōji, Holger Klein and Peter Milward, ed. (1999) *Shakespeare in Japan*, Lewiston, NY: Edwin Mellen Press
Apter, Emily (2005) *The Translation Zone: A New Comparative Literature*, Princeton, NJ: Princeton University Press
Apter, Ronnie (1984) *Digging for the Treasure: Translation After Pound*, New York: Peter Lang
Arai Yoshio (1993) *Rōdoku Sheikusupia zenshū no sekai* (Reciting Shakespeare in Japanese), Tokyo: Shinjusha
Arai Yoshio, Ōba Kenji, and Kawasaki Junnosuke, ed. (2002) *Sheikusupia daijiten* (Globe Shakespeare encyclopedia), Tokyo: Nihon Tosho Centre
Auden, W.H. (1969) *Collected Shorter Poems 1927-1957*, London: Faber & Faber
Auerbach, Erich (1968) *Mimesis: The Representation of Reality in Western Literature*, tr. Willard R. Trask, Princeton, NJ: Princeton University Press, 1st ed. 1953
Backhouse, A.E. (1993) *The Japanese Language: An Introduction*, Oxford: Oxford University Press
Baker, Mona, ed. (1998) *Routledge Encyclopedia of Translation Studies*, London: Routledge
Barnstone, Wallis (1993) *The Poetics of Translation: History, Theory, Practice*, London: Yale University Press
Bassnett, Susan (1993) *Comparative Literature: A Critical Introduction*, London: Routledge
——— (1998) 'Still trapped in the labyrinth: further reflections on translation and theatre', in Bassnett and Lefevere, 90-108
Bassnett, Susan, and Peter Bush, ed. (2007) *The Translator as Writer*, London: Continuum
Bassnett, Susan, and André Lefevere, ed. (1998) *Constructing Cultures: Essays on Literary Translation*, Clevedon, Avon: Multilingual Matters
Bell, Roger T. (1991) *Translation and Translating: Theory and Practice*, London: Longman
Berry, Cicely (1993) *The Actor and the Text*, London: Virgin Publishing
Bevington, David (1975) "But we are spirits of another sort': the dark side of love and magic in *A Midsummer Night's Dream*', *Medieval and Renaissance Studies* 13, 80-92
Blake, N.F. (1989) *The Language of Shakespeare*, London: Macmillan
Bloom, Harold (1997) *The Anxiety of Influence: A Theory of Poetry*, Oxford: Oxford University

Press, 1st ed. 1973
Blyth, R.H. (1981) *Haiku, Vol. One: Eastern Culture*, Tokyo: Hokuseidō, 1st ed. 1949
Brook, Peter (1990) *The Empty Space*, London: Penguin, 1st ed. 1968
Brooks, Harold F., ed. (1979) *The Arden Shakespeare: 'A Midsummer Night's Dream'*, London: Methuen, 2nd ed.
Brownstein, Michael C. (1997) 'Tsubouchi Shōyō on Chikamatsu and Drama', in Amy Vladeck, ed. *Currents in Japanese Culture: Translations and Transformations*, New York: Columbia University Press, 279-89
Connolly, David (1998) 'Poetry translation', in Baker, 170-76
Corn, Alfred (1998) *The Poem's Heartbeat: A Manual of Prosody*, Brownsville, OR: Story Line Press
Dazai Osamu (1974) *Shin Hamuretto*, Tokyo: Shinchōsha, 1st ed. 1941
Delabastita, Dirk (1993) *There's a Double Tongue*, Amsterdam: Rodopi
——— (1998) 'Shakespeare translation', in Baker, 222-26
Déprats, Jean-Michel (2004) 'Translating Shakespeare's stagecraft', in Hoenselaars, 133-47
Doi Kōchi, tr. (1940) *Natsu no yo no yume* (*A Midsummer Night's Dream*), Tokyo: Iwanami Shoten
Donner, H.W. (1974) 'Some problems of Shakespearian translation', *Shakespeare Translation* 1, 1-14
Dowden, Edward (1883) *Shakspere: A Critical Study of His Mind and Art*, London: Kegan Paul, Trench & Co.
Ehara Yoshihiro (1999) 'Mimi ni shizenna serifu mawashi ni kōkan' (Shakespeare that is pleasing to the ears', review, Gekidan Subaru, *Much Ado About Nothing*, *Tokyo Shinbun* newspaper (23rd June, 1999)
Elam, Keir (1984) *Shakespeare's Universe of Discourse: Language-Games in the Comedies*, Cambridge: Cambridge University Press
Eliot, T.S. (1936) 'The need for poetic drama', *The Listener* XVI, 994-96
Elliott, William J., and Kawamura Kazuo, tr./ed. (1996) *Naked: Poems by Shuntarō Tanikawa*, Berkeley, CA: Stone Bridge Press
Ernst, Earle (1974) *The Kabuki Theatre*, Honolulu, HI: University of Hawaii Press, 1st ed. 1956
Ewbank, Inga-Stina (1986) 'Shakespeare and the arts of language', in Wells, 49-66
Fischer-Lichte, Erika (1996) 'Interculturalism in contemporary theatre', in Patrice Pavis, ed., *The Intercultural Performance Reader*, London: Routledge, 27-40
Flint, Lorna (2000) *Shakespeare's Third Keyboard: The Significance of Rime in Shakespeare's Plays*, London: Associated University Presses
Freud, Sigmund (1976) *Jokes and their Relation to the Unconscious*, tr. James Strachey, Harmondsworth, Middlesex: Penguin, 1st pub. 1905
Frey, Charles H. (1999) *Making Sense of Shakespeare*, London: Associated University Presses
Fukuda Tsuneari (1961) *Watashi no engeki kyōshitsu* (Lessons in drama) Tokyo: Shinchōsha
——— tr. (1967) *Hamuretto* (Hamlet), in Fukuda et al., 1st ed. 1955
——— tr. (1971) *Natsu no yo no yume / Arashi* (A Midsummer Night's Dream / The Tempest), Tokyo: Shinchōsha, 1st ed. 1957
——— (1988) 'Sheikusupia no serifu' (1977) (Shakespeare's rhetoric), in Fukuda Tsuneari, *Fukuda Tsuneari zenshū dai gokan* (Complete works of Fukuda Tsuneari, vol. 5), Tokyo: Bungei Shunjū, 337-65
Fukuda Tsuneari, Mikami Isao and Nakano Yoshio, tr. (1967) *Sekai bungaku zenshū 4: 'Hamuretto' hoka* (Collected world literature, vol. 4: *Hamlet* etc.), Tokyo: Kawade Shobō
Fujita Minoru and Leonard J. Pronko, ed. (1996) *Shakespeare East and West*, Richmond, Surrey: Japan Library
Fussell, Paul (1979) *Poetic Meter and Poetic Form*, London: McGraw-Hill

Gallimore, Daniel (1999) 'Yukio Ninagawa', in J.E. Hoare, ed., *Britain & Japan: Biographical Portraits, Vol. III*, Richmond, Surrey: Japan Library, 324-37
—— (2001) "'Dreams come true': Fukuda Tsuneari and the Shakespearean sub-text', in Rebecca Copeland et al., ed., *Acts of Writing*, Vol. 2, West Lafayette, IN: Association for Japanese Literary Studies, 138-52
—— (2005) 'Measuring distance: Tsubouchi Shōyō and the myth of Shakespeare translation' (2005), in Theo Hermans, ed., *Translating Others*, Vol. 2, Manchester: St Jerome, 483-92
—— (2006) 'Private visions and public spaces – Shakespeare's *A Midsummer Night's Dream* in 1920s Japan', Japan Women's University Faculty of Humanities *Journal* 55, 13-25
—— (2006 a) 'Strength in weakness: a note on accentual rhythm in Japanese translations of *A Midsummer Night's Dream*', in Tom Bishop et al., ed., *The Shakespearean International Yearbook 2006*, New York: Ashgate, 331-48
—— (2007) review, Tetsuo Kishi and Graham Bradshaw, *Shakespeare in Japan* (Continuum, London, 2005), *Asian Theatre Journal* 24:1, 293-97
—— (2007 a) 'Sheikusupia honyakugaku – sonetto jūniban no mittsu no Nihongo honyaku' (Shakespeare translation studies: three Japanese versions of Sonnet 12), Japan Women's University Faculty of Humanities *Journal* 57, 77-87
—— (2009) 'Inside out: dreaming the *Dream* in contemporary Japan and Korea', in Hyon-u Lee, ed., *Glocalising Shakespeare in Korea and Beyond*, Seoul: Dongin Publishing, 225-41
—— (2009 a) 'Shakespeare in contemporary Japan' (2009), in Ross and Huang, 105-16
—— (2010) 'Speaking Shakespeare in Japanese: some contemporary exponents', in Dennis Kennedy and Yong Li Lan, ed., *Foreign Shakespeare: Contemporary Performance in the New Asias*, Cambridge: Cambridge University Press, 42-56
—— (2010 a) 'Shōyō, Sōseki, and Shakespeare: translations of three key texts', Japan Women's University Faculty of Humanities *Journal* 59, 41-61
—— (2010 b) 'Gendai Nihon ni okeru Sheikusupia honyaku – atarashii paradaimu ni mukete' (Shakespeare translation in contemporary Japan – towards a new paradigm), in Kobayashi Kaori, ed., *Nihon no Sheikusupia jōen · jōen kenkyū no ima* (Shakespeare performance and performance studies in contemporary Japan), Nagoya: Fūbaisha, 64-78
Gerstle, Andrew (1996) 'Shakespeare and Japanese theatre: artists' and scholars' use of the 'exotic'', in Fujita and Pronko, 61-76
Gielgud, Sir John (1997) *Acting Shakespeare*, London: Pan Books
Goodman, David G., tr./ed. (1988) *Japanese Drama and Culture in the 1960s: The Return of the Gods*, New York: M.E. Sharpe Inc.
Granville Barker, Harley (1993) *Granville Barker's Prefaces to Shakespeare*, London: Nick Hern Books
Gutt, Ernst-August (2000) *Translation and Relevance: Cognition and Context*, Manchester: St Jerome Publishing
Habicht, Werner (1976) 'International Shakespeare Association Congress 1976, seminar 'Shakespeare in translation': chairman's report', *Shakespeare Translation* 3, xi-xiv
Hachiya Akio and Kishi Tetsuo, tr. (2009) *Sheikusupia wa warera no dōjidaijin* (Jan Kott, 'Shakespeare Our Contemporary'), Tokyo: Hakusuisha, 1st ed. 1968
Hackett, Helen (1997) *A Midsummer Night's Dream*, Plymouth, Devon: Northcote House
Hagiwara Sakutarō (1998) *Principles of Poetry* (Shi no genri), tr. Chester C.I. Wang and Isamu P. Fukuchi, Ithaca, NY: Cornell University East Asia Program
Hara Takuya and Nishinaga Yoshinari, ed. (2000) *Honyaku hyakunen – gaikoku bungaku to Nihon no kindai* (A hundred years of translation in Japan: foreign literature and Japanese modernity),

Tokyo: Taishūkan Shoten
Hart, F. Elizabeth (2000) 'Charles H. Frey: *Making Sense of Shakespeare*', review, *Shakespeare Quarterly* 51: 4, 504-6
Hasegawa Kōhei, tr. (1947) *Manatsu no yo no yume* (A Midsummer Night's Dream), Tokyo: Keibunkan
Higurashi Yoshiko (1983) *The Accent of Extended Word Structure in Tokyo Standard Japanese*, Tokyo: Educa Inc.
Hirai Masao, tr. (1975) *Natsu no yo no yume* (A Midsummer Night's Dream), in Nakano Yoshio, ed., *Chikuma sekai bungaku taikei* 17 (World literature anthology, vol. 17), Tokyo: Chikuma Shobō, 77-115, 1ˢᵗ ed. 1964
Hobsbaum, Philip (1996) *Metre, Rhythm and Verse Form*, London: Routledge
Hoenselaars, Ton, ed. (2004) *Shakespeare and the Language of Translation*, London: Thomson Learning
Hokiyama Shigeru, tr. (1927) *Manatsu no yo no yume* (A Midsummer Night's Dream), Tokyo: Kindaisha
Holmes, James S. (1994) *Translated! Papers on Literary Translation and Translation Studies*, Amsterdam: Rodopi
Hussey, S.S. (1992) *The Literary Language of Shakespeare*, London: Longman
Inagaki Tatsurō, ed. (1969) *Tsubouchi Shōyō shū* (Works of Tsubouchi Shōyō), Tokyo: Chikuma Shobō
Ishihara Kōsai (1998) 'Shakespeare as Japanese Culture', unpublished paper, Komazawa University Shakespeare Institute
Joseph, Miriam (1947) *Shakespeare's Use of the Arts of Language*, New York: Columbia University Press
Kadono Izumi (1989) 'Odashima yaku to Sheikusupia juyō (Odashima and the reception of Shakespeare in Japan), in Anzai, 133-66
Katō Shūichi (1997) *A History of Japanese Literature*, tr. Don Sanderson, Richmond, Surrey: Japan Library
Kawachi Yoshiko (1981) 'Translating Shakespeare for the Japanese stage: an interview with Mr Tsuneari Fukuda', *Shakespeare Translation* 8, 79-93
―――― (1995) *Shakespeare and Cultural Exchange*, Tokyo: Seibidō
―――― ed. (1998) *Japanese Studies in Shakespeare and His Contemporaries*, London: Associated University Presses
―――― (1998 a) '*The Merchant of Venice* and Japanese Culture', in Kawachi, 46-69
Kawai Shōichirō (1997) 'Mikazuki to sanshikisumire to sankaku kankei' (Triple coincidences in *A Midsummer Night's Dream*), in Matsuoka, 301-7
Kawai Shōichirō, Noda Manabu, and Takada Yasunari, ed. (1998) *Sheikusupia e no kakehashi* (A way into Shakespeare), Tokyo: Tokyo University Press
Kawasaki Junnosuke (2010) 'Nichijōgo ni yoru shigeki no kanōsei' (The potential of poetic drama in everyday language', *Quattro Canti* 4, 5-20
Kawatake Toshio (1972) *Nihon no Hamuretto* (*Hamlet* in Japan), Tokyo: Nansōsha
Kawato Michiaki (2004) *Meiji no Sheikusupia* (The reception of Shakespeare in Meiji Japan), Tokyo: Ōzorasha
Keene, Dennis, tr./ed. (1980) *The Modern Japanese Prose Poem: An Anthology of Six Poets*, Princeton, NJ: Princeton University Press
Keene, Donald (1984) *Dawn to the West – A History of Japanese Literature, Vol. 3, Japanese Literature of the Modern Era: Fiction*, New York: Holt, Rinehart & Winston

────── (1999) *Dawn to the West – A History of Japanese Literature, Vol. 4, Japanese Literature of the Modern Era: Poetry, Drama, Criticism*, New York: Columbia University Press, 1st ed. 1984
Kerrigan, John, ed. (1999) *New Penguin Shakespeare: 'The Sonnets' and 'A Lover's Complaint'*, Harmondsworth, Middlesex: Penguin
Kino Hana (1996) 'Sheikusupia wa osoroshikunai' (Shakespeare isn't scary), in Mikami, 142-46
Kinoshita Junji, tr./ed. (1997) *Bara sensō* ('The Wars of the Roses' plays), Tokyo: Kōdansha
Kishi Tetsuo (1998) 'Japanese Shakespeare and English reviewers', in Sasayama et al., 110-23
────── (2004) "Our language of love': Shakespeare in Japanese translation', in Hoenselaars, 68-81
Kishi Tetsuo and Graham Bradshaw (2005) *Shakespeare in Japan*, London: Continuum
Knowles, Richard Paul (1996) 'Shakespeare, voice, and ideology', in James C. Bulman, ed., *Shakespeare, Theory, and Performance*, London: Routledge, 92-112
Kobayashi Kaori (2006) 'Shakespeare and national identity: Tsubouchi Shōyō and his 'authentic' Shakespeare productions in Japan', British Shakespeare Association: *Shakespeare* 2: 1, 59-76
Kott, Jan (1967) *Shakespeare Our Contemporary*, tr. Boleslaw Taborski, London: Methuen, 1st pub. 1964
Kubo Sakae (1928) '*Manatsu no yo yume* no rinkaku' (Outline of 'A Midsummer Night's Dream'), *Tsukiji Shōgekijō* 5: 4
Kubozono Haruo (1993) *The Organization of Japanese Prosody*, Tokyo: Kurosio Publishers
Kuramochi Saburō (1997) *Igirisu no shi – Nihon no shi* (English and Japanese poetry: a comparative study), Tokyo: Doyō Bijutsu Shuppan
Lamb, Charles and Mary (1993) *Tales from Shakespeare*, ed. Julia Briggs, London: J.M. Dent, 1st pub. 1807
Lawrence, D.H. (1981) *The Rainbow*, ed. John Worthen, Harmondsworth, Middlesex: Penguin Books, 1st pub. 1915
Leach, Edmund (1974) *Lévi-Strauss*, London: Fontana
Lee Yeounsuk (2010) *The Ideology of Kokugo: Nationalizing Language in Modern Japan*, tr. Maki Hirano Hubbard, Honolulu, HI: University of Hawai'i Press
Lefevere, André, and Susan Bassnett (1998) 'Introduction: where are we in translation studies', in Bassnett and Lefevere, 1-11
Mahood, M.M. (1957) *Shakespeare's Wordplay*, London: Methuen
Maruyama Masao and Katō Shūichi (1998) *Honyaku to Nihon no kindai* (Translation and Japanese modernity), Tokyo: Iwanami Shoten
Matsubayashi Shōji (1996) *Nihon no inritsu: goon to shichion no shigaku* (Rhythm in Japanese poetry: the poetics of fives and sevens), Tokyo: Kashinsha
Matsumoto Ryōzō, tr./ed. (1960) *'History and Characteristics of Kabuki: The Japanese Classical Drama' by Shōyō Tsubouchi and Jirō Yamamoto*, Yokohama: Heiji Yamagata
Matsuoka Kazuko (1993) *Subete no kisetsu no Sheikusupia* (Shakespeare for all seasons), Tokyo: Chikuma Shobō
────── tr. (1997) *Manatsu no yo no yume · Machigai no kigeki* (A Midsummer Night's Dream / The Comedy of Errors), Tokyo: Chikuma Shobō, 7th imprint 2009
────── tr. (1997 a) *Ria ō* (King Lear), Tokyo: Chikuma Shobō
────── (1998) 'Honyaku kara mita Sheikusupia' (Shakespeare from a translator's perspective), in Kawai et al., 199-223
────── tr. (2008) *Kara sawagi* (Much Ado About Nothing), Tokyo: Chikuma Shobō
────── (2011) *Fukayomi Sheikusupia* (Reading Shakespeare deeply), Tokyo: Shinchōsha
Matsuoka Kazuko and Kawai Shōichirō (2008) 'Discussion: humour in Shakespeare's comedies', programme, *Much Ado About Nothing*, dir. Ninagawa Yukio, Sai no Kuni Saitama Arts Theatre,

40-43

Matthews, Jackson (1966), 'Third thoughts on translating poetry', in Reuben A. Brower, ed., *On Translation*, Oxford: Oxford University Press, 67-77

Mikami Isao, tr. (1996) *Manatsu no yo no yume* (A Midsummer Night's Dream), Tokyo: Kadokawa Shoten, 1st ed. 1954

Milward, Peter (1997) *Sheikusupia to Nihonjin* (Shakespeare and the Japanese), tr. Nakayama Osamu, Tokyo: Kōdansha

───── (1999) 'Memories of forty years' teaching Shakespeare in Japan', in Anzai et al., 227-43

Minami Ryūta (1998) 'Chronological table of Shakespeare productions in Japan, 1866-1994', in Sasayama et al., 257-331

Minami Ryūta, Ian Carruthers, and John Gillies, ed. (2001) *Performing Shakespeare in Japan*, Cambridge: Cambridge University Press

Miner, Earl (1990) *Comparative Poetics: An Intercultural Essay on Theories of Literature*, Princeton, NJ: Princeton University Press

Miyoshi Hiroshi (1983) *Sheikusupia to Nihonjin no kokoro* (Shakespeare and the Japanese soul), Tokyo: Kōronsha

Mizusaki Noriko (2003) *Nihon kindai bungaku to Sheikusupia* (Shakespeare and modern Japanese literature), Tokyo: Nihon Tosho Centre

Mori Ōgai, tr. (1999) *Makubesu* (Macbeth), facsimile reprint, ed. Kobori Keiichirō, Tokyo: Yūshōdō, 1st ed. 1913

Moriya Sasaburō (1986) *Nihon ni okeru Sheikusupia* (Shakespeare in Japan), Tokyo: Yashio Shuppan

Morton, Leith (2009) *The Alien Within: Representations of the Exotic in Twentieth-Century Japanese Literature*, Honolulu, HI: University of Hawai'i Press

Moulton, Richard G. (1893) *Shakespeare as a Dramatic Artist*, Oxford: Clarendon Press

Nakada Yoshiaki (1986) 'Fukuhara Rintarō to Nakano Yoshio – kyōyō toshite no Sheikusupia' (Shakespeare in education – Fukuhara Rintarō and Nakano Yoshio), in Anzai, 43-84

Nakamura Minoru (1996) *Zoku · Nakamura Minoru shishū* (Selected poems of Nakamura Minoru, vol. 2), Tokyo: Shichōsha

Nakano Yoshio (1967) *Romio to Jurietto* (Romeo and Juliet), in Fukuda et al., 317-83

Nakano Yoshio and Mikami Isao, tr. (1953) *Manatsu no yo yume* (A Midsummer Night's Dream), Tokyo: Kawade Shobō

Namba Takio (1989) 'Fukuda Tsuneari to Sheikusupia – serifu geki wo tōshite no kindai no kakuritsu to chōkoku' (Fukuda Tsuneari and Shakespeare – creating and overcoming the modern through dramatic dialogue), in Anzai, 85-132

Niki Hisae (1984) *Shakespeare Translation in Japanese Culture*, Tokyo: Kenseisha

Ninagawa Yukio and Hasebe Hiroshi (2002) *Enshutsujutsu* (Stage directing), Tokyo: Kinokuniya Shoten

Nishimura Tōru, ed. (1988) 'Bungei to kotoba asobi' (Wordplay in Japanese literature), in Kindaichi Haruhiko, Hayashi Ōki, and Shibata Takeshi, ed., *Nihongo hyakka daijiten* (Encyclopaedia of the Japanese language), Tokyo: Taishūkan, 855-910

Nogami Toyoichirō, tr. (1951) *Natsu no yo no yume* (A Midsummer Night's Dream), Tokyo: Iwanami Shoten

Ōba Kenji (2009) *Sheikusupia no honyaku* (Shakespeare translation), Tokyo: Kenkyūsha

Odashima Yūshi (1965) 'Butai ni hāmonī ga atta' (Harmony on stage), *A Midsummer Night's Dream*, review, Gekidan Kumo, *Teatoro* 263, 39-41

───── (1976) *Sheikusupia yori ai wo komete* (From Shakespeare with love), Tokyo: Shōbunsha

───── tr. (1983) *Natsu no yo no yume* (A Midsummer Night's Dream), Tokyo: Hakusuisha, 1st ed.

1976
—— (1983 a) *Hamuretto* (Hamlet), Tokyo: Hakusuisha
—— (1983 b) *Henrī yonsei daiichibu* (King Henry IV, Part 1), Tokyo: Hakusuisha
—— (1990) *Dōke no me* (The eyes of the fool), Tokyo: Hakusuisha
—— (1991) *Odashima Yūshi no Sheikusupia yūgaku* (Diverting Shakespeare), Tokyo: Hakusuisha
—— (1995) *Shi to yūmoa* (Poetry and humour), Tokyo: Hakusuisha
—— (2000) *Dajare no ryūgi* (Punning and style), Tokyo: Kōdansha
Ōoka Makoto (1997) *The Poetry and Poetics of Ancient Japan*, tr. Thomas Fitzsimmons, Santa Fe, NM: Katydid Books
Ortolani Benito (1990) *The Japanese Theatre: From Shamanistic Ritual to Contemporary Pluralism*, Princeton, NJ: Princeton University Press
Osanai Kaoru (1928) '*Manatsu no yo no yume* ni tsuite' (About 'A Midsummer Night's Dream'), *Tsukiji Shōgekijō* 5: 4
Ōyama Toshikazu (1975) 'On translating Shakespeare into Japanese', *Shakespeare Translation* 2, 30-37
Ōyama Toshiko, tr. (1970) *Manatsu no yo no yume* (A Midsummer Night's Dream), Tokyo: Ōbunsha
—— (1975) *Shakespeare's World of Words*, Tokyo: Shinozaki Shorin
Ōzasa Yoshio (1993) *Gendai engeki no mori* (Collected reviews of contemporary Japanese theatre), Tokyo: Kōdansha
Pinnington, Adrian James (1995) 'Hamlet in Japanese dress: two contemporary Japanese versions of *Hamlet*', in Ueno Yoshiko, ed., *Hamlet and Japan*, New York: AMS Press, 155-68
Powell, Brian (1998) 'One man's *Hamlet* in 1911 Japan: the Bungei Kyokai production in the Imperial Theatre', in Sasayama et al., 38-52
Price, Antony W., ed. (1983) *'A Midsummer Night's Dream': A Selection of Critical Essays*, London: Macmillan
Pulvers, Roger (1984) 'Moving others: the translation of drama', in Ortrun Zuber-Skerritt, ed., *Page to Stage: Theatre as Translation*, Amsterdam: Rodopi, 23-28
Raffel, Burton (1989) 'Translating medieval European poetry', in Schulte and Biguenet, 28-53
Raleigh, Sir Walter, ed. (1925) *Johnson on Shakespeare*, London: Oxford University Press
Reiss, Katherina (2000) *Translation Criticism – The Potentials and Limitations*, tr. Erroll F. Rhodes, Manchester: St Jerome Publications
Ross, Charles, and Alex Huang, ed. (2009) *Shakespeare in Hollywood, Asia, and Cyberspace*, West Lafayette, IN: Purdue University Press
Rycroft, David (1999) 'Tsubouchi Shōyō's translation of *Hamlet*', in Anzai et al., 187-226
Saintsbury, George (1906) *A History of English Prosody*, London: Macmillan
Sakuma Kanae (1968) *Hyōjun Nihongo no hatsuon – akusento* (Pronunciation and accent in standard Japanese), Tokyo: Kōseikaku
Sams, Jeremy (1996) 'Interview: words and music', in David Johnston, ed., *Stages of Translation: Essays and Interviews on Translating for the Stage*, Bath, Avon: Absolute Classics, 171-78
Sasaki Takashi (1990) *Nihon Sheikusupia sōran* (Bibliography of Shakespeare in Japan), Tokyo: Elpis
—— ed. (1991-2000) *Shakespeare News from Japan, Vols. I to X*, Tokyo: Komazawa University Shakespeare Institute
Sasayama Takashi (1998) 'Tragedy and emotion: Shakespeare and Chikamatsu', in Sasayama et al., 145-58
Sasayama Takashi, J.R. Mulryne and Margaret Shewring, ed. (1998) *Shakespeare and the Japanese Stage*, Cambridge: Cambridge University Press
Satō Hiroshi, tr. (1929) *Manatsu no yo no yume* (A Midsummer Night's Dream), Tokyo: Sekai

Gikyoku Zenshū Kankō Kai

Sawamura Torajirō, tr. (1937) *Manatsu no yo no yume* (A Midsummer Night's Dream), Tokyo: Kenkyūsha

Schleiermacher, Friedrich (1992) 'On the different methods of translating' (1813), tr. Waltraud Bartscht, in Schulte and Biguenet, 36-54

Schulte, Rainer, and John Biguenet, ed. (1992) *Theories of Translation: An Anthology of Essays from Dryden to Derrida*, London: University of Chicago Press

Schwartz, Ros, and Nicholas de Lange (2007) 'A dialogue: on a translator's interventions', in Bassnett and Bush, 9-19

Senda Akihiko (1997) *The Voyage of Contemporary Japanese Theatre*, tr. J. Thomas Rimer, Honolulu, HI: University of Hawai'i Press

Shakespeare Company Japan home page <http://www.age.ne.jp/x/umi/e-welcom.htm> Accessed 9th December, 2010

Shiffert, Edith Marcombe, and Sawa Yūki, tr./ed. (1972) *Anthology of Modern Japanese Poetry*, Tokyo: Charles E. Tuttle

Shimodate Kasumi (1996) 'Nihon ni okeru atarashii Sheikusupia e no kokoromi – *Natsu no yo no yume* (Innovation in Shakespeare production in Japan: *A Midsummer Night's Dream*), *Hōsō Geijutsu Gaku* 12, 29-37

——— (2001) 'Owari ni' (Final note), programme, Shakespeare Company Japan, *Osorezan no Makubesu* (Tōhoku dialect 'Macbeth'), 69-72

Shively, Donald, tr./ed. (1953) *'The Love Suicide at Amijima' (Shinjū ten no Amijima): A Study of a Japanese Domestic Tragedy by Chikamatsu Monzaemon*, Cambridge, MA: Harvard University Press

Shōyō Kyōkai, ed. (1986) *Tsubouchi Shōyō jiten* (Tsubouchi Shōyō encyclopedia), Tokyo: Heibonsha

Stanislavski, Constantin (1980) *An Actor Prepares*, tr. Elizabeth Reynolds Hapgood, London: Methuen, 1st ed. 1937

Starrs, Roy (1998) *An Artless Art: The Zen Aesthetic of Shiga Naoya*, Richmond, Surrey: Japan Library

Suematsu Michiko (2009) 'The Tokyo Globe years, 1988-2002', in Ross and Huang, 121-28

Sugiki Yoshiaki (1999) 'Shakespeare and Hideki Noda', in Anzai et al., 132-47

Suzuki Gorō (1999) 'The Japanese character as mirrored in Shakespeare's great tragedies', in Anzai et al., 35-50

Suzuki Tadashi (1986) *The Way of Acting: The Theatre Writings of Tadashi Suzuki*, tr. J. Thomas Rimer, New York: Theatre Communications Group

Suzuki Tōzō (1975) *Kotoba asobi* (Wordplay in Japanese), Tokyo: Chūō Kōron

Takahashi Yasunari, tr. (1991) *Natsu no yo no yume* (A Midsummer Night's Dream), in Sōgōsha, ed., *Shūeisha gyararī – sekai no bungaku 2: Igirisu I* (World literature 2: Britain I), Tokyo: Shūeisha, 193-253, 1st ed. 1981

——— (1995) '*Hamlet* and the anxiety of modern Japan', in Stanley Wells, ed. *Shakespeare Survey* 48, Cambridge: Cambridge University Press, 99-111

——— (1998) 'Kyogenising Shakespeare / Shakespeareanising Kyogen: some notes on *The Braggart Samurai*', in Sasayama et al., 214-25

——— (2003) *Machigai no kyōgen* (The *kyōgen* of errors), Tokyo: Hakusuisha

Takahashi Yasunari and Kishi Tetsuo, tr. (1971) *Nanimo nai kūkan* (Peter Brook, 'The Empty Space'), Tokyo: Shōbunsha

Takamatsu Yūichi, tr. (1986) *Sonetto shū* (The Sonnets), Tokyo: Iwanami Shoten

Taki Seiju, ed. (1992) *Sheikusupia to kyōgen: tōzai kigeki hikaku kenkyū* (Shakespeare and *kyōgen*: a comparative study of Eastern and Western comedy), Tokyo: Shinjusha

Takiguchi Susumu (1997) *Kyoshi: A Haiku Master*, Rowsham, Oxfordshire: Ami-Net International

Tanaka Yasuo, tr., (1993) *Manatsu no yo no yume* (A Midsummer Night's Dream), Tokyo: Yamaguchi Shoten

Thomas, Dylan (1977) *Collected Poems: 1934-1952*, London: J.M. Dent

Tillotson, Geoffrey, ed. (1941) *Alexander Pope: 'The Rape of the Lock'* (1714), London: Methuen

Tomasi, Massimiliano (1999) 'Quest for a new written language: Western rhetoric and the *genbun icchi* Movement', *Monumenta Nipponica* 54:3, 333-60

Toyama Masakazu, Yatabe Ryōkichi and Inoue Tetsujirō, tr./ed. (1951) *Shintai shishō* (1872) (New poetic forms), in Yamamiya Makoto et al., ed., *Nihon gendaishi taikei dai ikkan* (Compendium of contemporary Japanese poetry, vol. 1), Tokyo: Kawade Shobō, 23-50

Toyoda Minoru (1940) *Shakespeare in Japan: An Historical Survey*, Tokyo: Iwanami Shoten

Tozawa Koya and Asano Hyokyō, tr. (1905) *Hamuretto* (Hamlet), Tokyo: Dai Nihon Tosho

Tsubouchi Shōyō, tr. (1909) *Hamuretto* (Hamlet), Tokyo: Waseda University Press

——— tr. (1933) *Hamuretto* (Hamlet), Tokyo: Chūō Kōron

——— (1960) 'Chikamatsu as compared with Shakespeare and Ibsen' ('Chikamatsu tai Shēkusupiya tai Ipusen') (1909), in Matsumoto, 207-39

——— tr. (1977) *Manatsu no yo no yume* (A Midsummer Night's Dream) (1915), in Shōyō Kyōkai, ed., *Shōyō senshū dai yon* (Selected works of Tsubouchi Shōyō, vol. 4), Tokyo: Daiichi Shobō, 171-304

——— (1977 a) "Makubesu hyōshaku' no shogen' (Preface to a commentary on *Macbeth*) (1892), in Shōyō Kyōkai, ed., *Shōyō senshū bessatsu dai san* (Selected works of Tsubouchi Shōyō, app. 3), Tokyo: Daiichi Shobō, 161-69

——— (1978) 'Soko shirazu no mizuumi' (The bottomless lake) (1909), in Shōyō Kyōkai, ed., *Shōyō senshū bessatsu dai yon* (Selected works of Tsubouchi Shōyō, app. 4), Tokyo: Daiichi Shobō, 385-92

——— (1978 a) *Shēkusupiya kenkyū shiori* (An introduction to Shakespeare studies) (1928), in Shōyō Kyōkai, ed., *Shōyō senshū bessatsu dai go* (Selected works of Tsubouchi Shōyō, app. 5), Tokyo: Daiichi Shobō, 1-277

——— (1981) *The Essence of the Novel* (*Shōsetsu shinzui*) (1885), tr. Nanette Twine, *Occasional Papers* 11, Department of Japanese, University of Queensland

——— (1998) *Kaki momiji* (Waka and haiku of Tsubouchi Shōyō), ed. Shōyō Kyōkai, Tokyo: Daiichi Shobō

——— tr. (1999) *Za Sheikusupia* (Complete works of Shakespeare), Tokyo: Daisan Shokan

Tsujimura Natsuko, ed. (1999) *The Handbook of Japanese Linguistics*, Oxford: Basil Blackwell

Tsutsumi Harue (1997) *Kanadehon Hamlet* (Kanadehon Hamuretto), tr. Faubion Bowers, David W. Griffith and Hori Mariko, *Asian Theatre Journal* 15: 2, 181-229, 1st ed. 1993

Tyler, Royall, tr./ed. (1992) *Japanese Nō Dramas*, London: Penguin

Ueda Makoto, tr./ed. (1996) *Modern Japanese Tanka: An Anthology*, New York: Columbia University Press

Vance, T.J. (1987) *An Introduction to Japanese Phonology*, Albany, NY: State University of New York Press

Venuti, Lawrence (1995) *The Translator's Invisibility: A History of Translation*, London: Routledge

——— ed. (2000) *The Translation Studies Reader*, London: Routledge

Warren, Roger (1986) 'Shakespeare on the twentieth-century stage', in Wells, 257-72

Watanabe Tamotsu (2004) *Kabuki no kotoba* (Kabuki words), Tokyo: Taishūkan Shoten

Wells, Marguerite (1997) *Japanese Humour*, London: Macmillan

Wells, Stanley, ed. (1986) *The Cambridge Companion to Shakespeare Studies*, Cambridge: Cambridge University Press
Yamanouchi Toshio and Yano Hōjin, ed. (1962) *Ueda Bin zenyaku shishū* (Complete translated poems of Ueda Bin), Tokyo: Iwanami Shoten
Yuyama Kiyoshi (1954) *Kokugo rizumu no kenkyū* (The rhythms of the Japanese language), Tokyo: Kokugo Bunka Kenkyūsho
Watson, Burton, tr./ed. (1997) *Masaoka Shiki: Selected Poems*, New York: Columbia University Press
Willcock, Gladys (1954) 'Shakespeare and Elizabethan English', in Allardyce Nicoll, ed. *Shakespeare Survey* 7, Cambridge: Cambridge University Press, 15-25
Yamamiya Makoto, ed. (1951) *Nihon gendaishi taikei daiichi maki* (Compendium of contemporary Japanese poetry, vol. 1), Tokyo: Kawade Shobō
Yosano Akiko (1943) *Yosano Akiko kashū* (Selected poetry of Yosano Akiko), Tokyo: Iwanami Shoten
Yoshiwara Yukari (1998) 'Money and sexuality in *Measure for Measure*', in Kawachi, 70-85

著者略歴

ダニエル・ガリモア

1966年ロンドン生まれ、1987年オックスフォード大学英語英文学部卒業。同年初来日、2年間佐賀県、1年間東京在住。1992年シェフィールド大学日本学修士号、2001年オックスフォード大学東洋学部博士号。2000年オックスフォード・ブルックス大学日本語学科非常勤講師、2003年日本女子大学英文学科専任講師、2008年同大学准教授、2011年関西学院大学文学部教授、現在に至る。'Measuring distance: Tsubouchi Shōyō and the myth of Shakespeare translation' (2005) (Theo Hermans, ed., *Translating Others*, Vol. 2, Manchester: St Jerome Press) など、「日本におけるシェイクスピア」という専門領域に関して、公刊されている論文多数。日本シェイクスピア協会会員。

Daniel Gallimore has been professor of English at Kwansei Gakuin University since April 2011, having previously worked as Sasakawa Lecturer in Japanese at Oxford Brookes University (2000-3) and as Lecturer and Associate Professor in the Department of English at Japan Women's University (2003-11). Since completing his doctorate at Linacre College, Oxford, in 2001, he has published a number of articles in both English and Japanese in the field of Shakespeare translation and reception in Japan, as well as translations of modern Japanese plays and Japanese Shakespeare adaptations.

SOUNDING LIKE SHAKESPEARE
A Study of Prosody in Four Japanese Translations of
A Midsummer Night's Dream

2012年3月20日初版第一刷発行

著　者　ダニエル・ガリモア

発行者　田中きく代
発行所　関西学院大学出版会
所在地　〒662-0891
　　　　兵庫県西宮市上ケ原一番町1-155
電　話　0798-53-7002

印　刷　協和印刷株式会社

©2012 Daniel Gallimore
Printed in Japan by Kwansei Gakuin University Press
ISBN 978-4-86283-103-3
乱丁・落丁本はお取り替えいたします。
本書の全部または一部を無断で複写・複製することを禁じます。
http://www.kwansei.ac.jp/press